TELL ME YOU LOVE ME

LOVE & WAR

EMILIA FINN

beelieve

PUBLISHING, Pty Ltd.

info@beelievepublishing.com

ISBN: 978 1 922623 97 3 (paperback)

ISBN: 978 1 922623 98 0 (hard cover)

Any references to historical events, real people, or real places are used fictitiously. Names, characters, and places are products of the author's imagination.

eBook and Paperback cover design: Amy Queue @ Q Design

Cover Photography: Katie Cadwallader

Cover Model: Jordyn

Hardcover design: Emilia Finn

Editing: Brit @ Bookish B Editing

Proofreading: Lindsi Labar

First printing edition 2025.

Beelieve Publishing, Pty Ltd

PO Box 407,

Woy Woy, NSW, 2256

Australia

www.emiliafinn.com

EMILIA FINN, the ROLLERS logo, the CHECKMATE SECURITY logo, STACKED DECK logo, and INAMORATA are all trade marks of Beelieve Publishing, Pty Ltd

FOREWORD

Tell Me You Love Me contains discussion of (but does not show on page) rape. Please take care of your mental health while reading.

AUTHOR'S NOTE

No roosters were harmed in the making of this story. All pyrotechnics were placed safely out of reach after the first incident.

TELL ME YOU LOVE ME

LOVE AND WAR BOOK 1

ROUND ONE

ALANA

All the greatest stories start with a question, no? A thought-provoking premise where the narrator asks the reader to consider a hypothetical situation its protagonist faces. A, '*How would you handle this?*' or '*Would you do it differently?*'

Often, the reader will have their own theories because of the lenses of their history, the glasses through which they see life, filtered through their personal experiences. Sometimes, the reader will know exactly how they would handle the hypothetical because they've already faced one exactly like it. Or, and possibly more likely, maybe they have absolutely no experience at all, and thus, their ideas are flawless... in their minds, anyway.

That's the beauty of ignorance. The gift of innocence.

Not knowing is a blessing. And I... well, I'm not sure I was in the correct line when God was handing those out.

"How long until we get there, Mom?"

I glance in my rear-view mirror, the New York City skyline slowly shrinking in the distance, but then I peel my eyes downwards and stop on my son and his dark, moppy hair.

He doesn't like it long. But he likes having it cut even less.

"It'll be a while, honey." I scan the traffic spread out in front of us, changing lanes and angling toward a life I've already escaped once, almost ten years ago to the day.

Ironic, really.

"You said it would take twenty-four hours."

"Twenty-four *driving* hours." I merge toward our exit and swallow the lump of nerves nestled in the base of my throat, then I pull sunglasses down to cover my eyes and the itching redness that fills them, because leaving New York is not just leaving a city. It's leaving our home, the only one Franky has ever known.

It's leaving my husband.

My best friend in the whole world.

My agent.

My contacts.

It's leaving my dreams. And dammit, I'm not ready to let go of those.

"We'll stop tonight and stay in a motel," I explain carefully, knowing with sickening certainty that if I allow my voice to break from emotion, my son will ask questions I'm not sure I can answer. He doesn't know how not to. "I booked us in at this nice place that overlooks a lake. We have a ground-floor room with a door that leads out to the grassy area, and I saw on the website they have a grill on the patio, so maybe we can stop by a grocery store and buy something to cook instead of hitting a fast-food place." I thumb the volume controls on my steering wheel and turn the music just a little higher. "We could sit outside and watch the sun go down. Doesn't that sound nice?"

"No." He stares straight into my mirror, his glasses reflecting the morning sun so I only see a portion of his perfect hazel gaze. Flattening his lips, he deadpans, "Sounds like we're gonna get bit by mosquitos and itch all the way to Grandma's tomorrow."

I breathe out a soft laugh, shaking my head as the traffic surrounding us thins. At this hour, most people are heading *in* to the city. Not *out* of it. "Are you excited to see Grandma Bitsy?" My stomach quivers with nerves. With dread. With the aching knowledge that, once we arrive in the small, six-thousand-person town aptly named Plainview, I'll no longer have the luxury of ignoring the ghosts I fled from a decade ago, nor the woman who hounded my youth with her constant onslaught of '*you're not good enough*' and '*you'll achieve nothing to be proud of*'.

The woman is a peach.

"She's been calling almost every hour since I told her we were coming, honey. She's busting out of her skin, waiting for you."

"I don't hardly know her." He folds his arms and looks out the side window. "And she's loud. *All* the time. Is she like that in real life?"

Yup. She sure is, kiddo.

"We can tell her you like things to be a little quieter." A text pops up on my dash, drawing my eyes to my best friend's name flashing for attention, though I don't read it yet. "Remember how we talked about speaking up for ourselves?"

"People think I'm rude when I do that."

"Some people get uncomfortable when a child advocates for themselves. We come from a world where kids are expected to be seen but not heard. It's that way in places like Plainview, especially." I search the mirror, catching just the side of his sweet face. "It's not rude to speak up, honey, even if they're uncomfortable. As long as you're being respectful, I'll back you up every single time."

"Do you think Grandma will try to hug me and stuff?" He's as nervous as me. As wary and worried and, simply put, not all that excited about this move. But life doesn't always go the way we want it. When your mother is sick and your husband and his assistant fall in love, it's time to pack a few things and consider a new plan.

"I don't want anyone to hug me."

"I think Grandma Bitsy will *want* to hug you. It's important to remember that, sometimes, people do the things they're accustomed to doing without thinking. She might even—" *definitely will* "—forget to ask, but you're allowed to tell her no. It's not wrong of you to expect personal space."

"What if she gets mad at me?" He drags his eyes away from the view and meets mine in the mirror. "It's rude to say no."

"No. It's rude to touch someone who doesn't want to be touched." I reach back and place my hand on the seat beside his leg, palm side up, and wait... wait... wait. Until finally, his little hand rests on top of mine. "This is going to be a learning experience for everyone, honey. You and Grandma are from different worlds, but you come from the same blood, so I think if we're all patient with each other and communicate clearly, everything will be fine."

He falls silent for a long moment, exhaling a long sigh and brushing his fingers along my wrist. My shoulder rejects the stretch and twist of my arm. My bicep aches after a minute. Two. Three. But I don't dare take my hand back.

"People in New York don't pick on me, Mom. We're all kind of weird there. But Plainview isn't like that. Plainview won't like me."

"I'll stand in front of you." My heart twists with the fears I've already considered. The worries that keep me awake at night. The paralyzing knowledge that he might be right. Plainview *is* a small town where most of its residents are already retired or close to it, and just like I did, their kids ran just as soon as they could.

That town is not ready for a special little boy like my son. But we don't have much of a choice in the matter, and I'll be damned if I let them make him feel anything less than the incredible human he is.

"We'll take it one day at a time." I nibble on the inside of my cheek and ignore the second text from my best friend. Then the third. "And you're not weird, honey. You're the most intuitive, smartest, kindest human I've ever met in my entire life."

"You're my mom." His cheeks warm in the mirror's reflection. And his lips quiver. Though he's careful not to let them curl too high. "You *have* to say that."

"No, I don't. There's no rule that says that. It's not the law."

He looks out the window again, his smile twitching to be freed.

"You're going to change the world, Franky. And I'll be right there with you, cheering so loud that you'll want to ban me from every ceremony they invite you to. F," I sing. "R. A. N. K. L. I. N. What's that spell?"

"Mommmm..." he groans.

I stroke the side of his wrist and snicker when he drags his lips inside his mouth rather than admit he's amused. "You're gonna invent something amazing. Or discover something. Or cure something. Or write something."

"Kinda like you. But you write loooove stories," he teases. "The boy and the girl who fell in love and..." he trails off on what I swear sounds like *blah blah blah*. "I'll write a thesis on negatively charged subatomic particles and an object's permanence."

I shake my head and search the rearview mirror. *He gets that brain from the paternal side of his family.* "You're nine, Franky. I'm twenty-eight. I don't even know what subat—"

"Doesn't speak highly of the school you're about to enroll me in." He casts his eyes back out to the road, his fingers gently stroking my wrist. "You're two decades older than me, but my education already outstripped yours."

"Yikes." I drive one-handed, fumbling to reach my turn signals and dismissing Fox's next text as it pops up on my screen. "I should probably have hurt feelings, huh? That was a burn if I ever heard one."

He laughs, though he does it so quietly, the sound barely travels to my ears.

"I made you with my body. So the fact is, your intelligence is a reflection of mine. I can't be burned by you because I created you. It's in the rules."

"That's not true." He kicks his shoes off and drags his feet onto the seat, folding them for comfort. *We'll be here for a while. May as well settle in.* "You don't get to keep my Nobel Prize just because we share DNA."

"Mmhm." I enjoy the way he so easily replaces the dread in my stomach with something so much better. Something sweeter and calmer and a hell of a lot more hopeful. "At the very least, I expect a mention in your acceptance speech. Something about how smart and wonderful I am, as a mother, a human being, a writer, a friend..."

"Can't celebrate you as a writer if you never publish."

Ouch! "Dude..."

"At this rate, I'll be on shelves before you. When you catch up, we can compare and see who receives industry recognition first."

"You're mean." I decline my best friend's incoming call and settle in, knowing my shoulder will fall asleep soon and, with it, the pain of twisting my arm in the wrong direction. "I'll publish. Eventually. I'm just waiting for the right time."

"You have an offer," he counters dryly. "You're just a chicken. Will we do half the driving today and half again tomorrow?"

Change of subject, just like that.

"Which means we'll arrive at Grandma's at dinnertime?"

"That's the plan. We could probably go slower, if you want. Break it up into three days. But I figure—"

"Drive faster," he grumbles. "I hate sitting in the car. I'm gonna read now, okay?" He releases my hand and snags his book from the back of my seat, digging his hand into the pocket a second time in search of his pen. "I don't want to talk anymore."

"What are you read—"

"Murdles. Shhh." He clicks his pen and pokes his tongue forward. It helps him think... allegedly. "I'll let you know when I need to pee. And can you tell me when you're planning to stop for food? Maybe twenty-five minutes before."

"Uh—"

"Actually, fifteen minutes is enough. Twenty-five is unnecessary."

"Right." I look out at the road spreading ahead of us, knowing I won't get another word from him from now until lunchtime. And because I know it, I snag my earbuds and press one into my ear, waiting for Bluetooth to connect and the soft music playing through the speakers to transfer to my ear instead.

All so I can listen to the music I like without bothering the little boy set on solving a murder mystery.

But of course, with the change in technology comes a robotic voice.

Text received by Fox:

Bitch, stop ignoring me!

Alana fucking Page! I'm watching your GPS dot move further and further away. I want it known I am NOT pleased!

Colin called. I was busy, so I couldn't accept, and he didn't leave a message. Did you chat with him today?

Callllll meeeeeeee! I promise not to talk you out of this stupid move. I'm having withdrawals, and I saw you, like, twenty-three minutes ago. If you won't come back, then the least you can do is call me so we can hang out.

I know your mom is sick, and I know Colin is with Tasha now. But you're punishing me for things outside my control! Divorce him and stayyyyyy.

You can live with me. Colin will probably even give you the apartment during settlement, and then you can sell it for oodles of money and bank that for Franky's future as a tech gazillionaire.

And did I mention staying with me? I won't charge you rent so long as you bake your brownies at least twice a month.

Helen called, too. She said, and I quote, 'I'm worried about Alana. What do you think we should do?'

Tommy's gonna be in Plainview, too, right? Have you considered what the F you're gonna say to the guy whose heart you broke before your ass busted outta town without a backward glance? Do you think he's still pissed?

Oh, God. Have you considered that he might have married a beautiful model and made thirty-seven beautiful kids? You won't cope, Alana! Come back to New York so we can talk this out and come up with a better plan.

7

> Because if you have a sudden psychotic break and kill the model wife of the guy you never got over, then you'll go to prison.

> If you go to prison, I'll be forced to co-parent with Colin for access to Franky! I don't want to co-parent with Colin.

And *that's* why I'm not calling her. Not yet, anyway. Fox Tatum has a tendency toward wildly unhinged and over-the-top dramatics, and her fanciful obsession with a story I told her once, eight years ago, about a guy I used to know in high school, is why I refuse to hit the green icon on my screen when her name flashes for attention once more.

No way.

No chance.

Not happening.

If I'm driving back to Plainview after all these years, willfully heading toward the life I already escaped and the trauma I'd rather not revisit, then I'd prefer to do it with my sanity intact, my heart beating a normal tune, and without my best friend screaming *but Tommy Watkins!* in my ear.

My high school boyfriend—*the love of my friggin' life*—may or may not be married to a model these days, and who knows, he may or may not have beautiful children with dark brown hair and perfect hazel eyes. But one thing is for certain: he's *not* sitting around thinking about me anymore.

ROUND TWO

TOMMY

"That's the lot, Miss Bitsy." I carry the aging woman's groceries inside her house and plop the bags on her dining room table. Gallons of milk already with chilled condensation on the side because of the heat of the midday sun. Tubs of yogurt toppled over, and bags of salad that, if it were for anyone else, wouldn't make me lift a brow. But *this* woman... the one who would rather churn her own butter and raise chickens so she can have the freshest eggs in a fifty-mile radius... a bagged salad may as well be tornado sirens screaming across town.

She's unwell, but she'd rather die in silence than admit weakness.

Stubborn old mule.

"I'm gonna head out back and clean up that felled tree, too. Last week's storm made a mess, and Chris just got the chainsaw serviced. I've been busting to take it for a spin, so..." I smile playfully, only to earn a look of exasperation from the woman who has been shooting them my way since I was old enough to notice folks didn't much like me. "If you hear someone scream, don't panic. I'm still learning how to use sharp things without supervision."

Frail, though she wouldn't like to know I know it, she sits at her dining table and looks me up and down. She has a way of staring that arrows straight for my gut. Eyes that see all, and a lifetime of knowing me and my brother *almost* better than we know ourselves.

"You're fussing, Thomas Watkins." She dips a hand into her grocery bags and pulls out a bag of tomatoes—another red flag, considering Beatrice 'Bitsy' Page has grown her own for as long as I can remember. "I don't need you to hassle me any more than I need your brother to pump my gas or check my tire pressure. It pisses me off."

Scoffing, I turn on my heels and grab the door. "It's a tree, and I'm not letting you use the chainsaw. If anyone gets to cut their hand off today, it's me. I've been nagging Chris for a week now to let me have a go."

"You get that call yet?" In my peripheral, she sets her tomatoes down and goes back to drag sticks of celery from the bag. "From Vegas."

"Yeah, I got the call. The fight is on." It's gotta be at least a hundred degrees outside today, which means sweat drips from my brow despite how cool it is inside Bitsy's house. I peel the hem of my tank up and wipe my face. "The date's been set, and Chris is already on me about scheduling. Christmas Eve." I drop my shirt and meet her beautiful eyes. They're almost exact replicas of a different pair I used to know. A pair I spent my entire youth looking into. *But that was a long, long time ago.* "Henry set it up so we get the Christmas Eve crowd and ratings. You could come, ya know? Watch me live instead of on the television."

"See you get your face rearranged in real life?" She sets the celery down. "No thanks. I'd rather watch it on my screen and avoid all the noise and blood." She reaches into the bag for strawberries. "You could have gotten a job down at the metal factory. A nice, normal, weekly wage kind of job instead of..." But she has no words for what it is I do. So she gestures my way, waving her hand listlessly up and down. "There are better ways to make money. People die fighting."

"First of all, Carlton Tanner worked down at the factory for the last thirty years. He died last year because of a machine malfunction that should never have happened. Now his wife is lonely, and his kids are barely scraping by because life insurance wasn't something he thought to organize, and the factory won't take responsibility for the death they caused. Second, I don't remember the last time someone died in the octagon. It's a sport, Bitsy. Not Sparta."

"It's punching someone in the face for a paycheck."

"Yep." I click my tongue and pull her door open. She won't change my mind any more than I'll change hers. "And that paycheck means my kids'll never be broke."

"What kids?! You have none, and no one is walking around town with a swollen belly because of you. Which," she adds with a downturn of her lips, mumbling almost as though talking to herself. "Is not how I expected things to be. I was sure you'd have them all over. You and your brother always stressed the hell out of me."

"You think you know me." I grab my hat from my back pocket and unfold the abused bill so it's not too curled. But I'm still inside, and around here, you don't wear a hat until you're out the door. "I should take offense to the assumptions you made about me in my youth, Miss Bitsy. Judging me because of where I came from isn't very nice."

"My judgment had hardly anything to do with your folks, and everything to do with how wild you were all across town. Worse, you hauled my daughter along for the ride, slapping her with a *guilty-by-association* reputation, no matter how hard I tried to keep her away. She wanted nothing to do with you, until she did, then those teenage hormones hit, and suddenly, the local cops had her prints on file."

"Because of me." I fake a laugh and ignore the spasm in my stomach, put there by a mere mention of the woman who took my heart and tossed it under a fuckin' train.

Alana Page was the town's good girl—or at least, that's what her innocent face would have people believe. And I... well, I was the town's good-for-nothin' son-of-a-nobody, and one half of a trouble-making duo with a future so bleak, the girl who claimed to love me still went cold after prom and left town the second she had her high school diploma in hand.

Forever, my ass.

"Your daughter knew her way around trouble, Miss Bitsy. But back then, her reputation was still reasonably shiny, and mine could shoulder more smudge. There was no need to blast her for her crimes when I could serve the sentence in her place."

Her eyes glitter with a deviousness I would recognize anywhere. Anytime. Any world where the Page family exists. Fuck, I fell in love with that tormenting stare when I was just nine years old and a girl who hated me admitted she was kinda curious, too.

"You always kept her strapped to your hip, didn't you?" Bitsy firms thin lips. "You *say* you'd take the blame for anything she did, but from where I stood, I reckon you'd have burned this town down and handed her the matches. If you were going to prison, you wanted to make sure she was coming, too. It's kind of wholesome, I suppose, in a totally nonsensical way."

"We were kids. Nonsense was the game we played. Anyway—" I cross the threshold and drag my hat on, knowing my day is already committed to clearing out a forty-foot spruce and, later, a shower of ice to take away the itch that'll crawl under my skin. "I'm heading out back to take care of that tree. I'll try to keep the noise to a minimum."

"I appreciate you helping." She sets her hand on the table, the other on the back of her chair, and with a grunt of exertion that makes me frown, she pushes to her feet and walks her produce to the sink. "And even though you didn't ask, since you know it's rude to do so, you can stop worrying so much. I have a carer coming to stay at the house."

"Really?" A breath of relief rushes through my system, emptying my lungs and replacing my frown with a giddy smile. "That's such good news, Miss Bitsy. I know you don't like the idea of having a stranger around, but it'll be so much better for you to—"

"Yeah, yeah." She flips the faucet on to wash her vegetables. "I want you to stay away for the next few days while we get settled. I'd hate for her to be scared off by those hooligan Watkins boys turning up at stupid o'clock like you do."

"It's not stupid o'clock. Chris and I run at sun-up. It's how we start our day."

"It's how I start my day, too," she grumbles. "I don't like it. I want no visitors until I say differently, so don't even try it. Run the other way. Because if you scare her and she quits, I'm gonna rain hell down on your heads."

"I'll leave you be." I straighten my hat and back up onto the wrap-around porch that could do with new boards. New nails. New lacquer.

Hell, it could do with a whole new porch.

"This carer will be here to help you inside? Like cooking and cleaning and stuff?"

"Mm. Something like that."

"So I'll keep up with the outside. But," I add when she glares over her shoulder. "Not for a few days till you settle in. When does she arrive?"

"This afternoon." She washes each tomato with shaking fingers, rubbing the skin until it shines bright red. "Dinnertime."

"I'll get started with that tree and make sure I clear out before your new friend arrives." Releasing the door and allowing it to swing shut, I turn on my heels and jog down the porch steps. "I'll come back on the weekend to mow. I can't leave it any longer than that," I call back, *knowing* she's apt to argue. "It'll get too long, and then you'll have to deal with critters. Chris." I lift my chin and wait for my twin brother to swing my way. He leans against the front of my truck, one foot on the ground and the other on the grille, while a hat not all that different from mine shades his eyes, and his lips, too often folded into a scowl, move into flat lines. "We're on the clock. She's got guests coming over tonight." I stride straight past him and reach into the bed of my truck to free the chainsaw. Then turning again, I start toward the tree at the rear of Bitsy's property, about thirty yards from her back door. "You ready to sweat?"

His two hundred and thirty pounds catch up to mine easily. His broad frame and long legs eat up the ground much like mine do. We're essentially carbon copies of each other, but where I typically default to a smile and smartass comeback, he's more of a quiet observer. A thinker.

And God help you if you fuck with his schedule.

"Class is at six," he rumbles, tugging his hat lower to shield himself from the glaring sun. "Means I gotta be done here by five-thirty so I can shower. Eliza's training the kids at four."

"Bitsy's got a carer coming in to take care of her. Starting today." I glance across and wait for his eyes, knowing so few others get to see the hazel coloring within them. The fact is, Chris prefers his own company—or mine—and once upon a time, he liked Alana Page's, too. But that was a lifetime ago, and she left him just as easily and permanently as she left me. "She doesn't like that she needs a carer. And she hasn't said the words out loud."

"About her cancer?" He drops his hands into his pockets and swallows, the bob of his Adam's apple as obvious to me as the llamas that bound away as we approach their little grazing area.

Llamas. Plural.

As in, a whole ass herd. Because Bitsy has always been a little ridiculous.

"I heard it got into her blood."

"Yeah." I stop in front of the massive spruce that took a bolt of lightning a week ago. It's a damn miracle a brush fire didn't erupt from the sparks, considering our too-dry summer heat. "Everyone is spouting off about doctor-patient confidentiality, but small-town livin' and all that..."

"She's dying."

"Well..." I set the chainsaw on the ground by my feet and study the long tree. *Where do I start?* "I don't know what it all means. Hugh Greenway had cancer in his blood when he was a kid, remember? And he's doing okay."

"Greenways were rich, then and now, and Hugh was young and strong. Bitsy's getting old, and you know she ain't following the doctor's advice. She'd rather spend her money on chicken feed than treatment."

"You think she's not even trying to fight it?" My stomach turns heavy, an anvil sitting where my breakfast should be. "She's just giving up?"

He only shrugs. "She's still got her hair. And I haven't seen her puke once. Hugh got real sick, swollen, and bald for the better part of a year because of the treatment he had." He drags a pair of gloves from his back pocket and slides them onto his hands. "I don't know what she's planning, but I don't think we're gonna like the outcome."

So she's dying... and she's allowing it?

"Fuck's sake." I bend and grab the chainsaw, yanking on the pull cord and powering the machine to life. "Wanna spar later? Get some anger out on the mats?"

He scoffs, then nods before backing up and giving me space.

Yeah. We fight to work through our emotions. So fucking what?

It got me through losing Alana Page a decade ago. It'll get me through losing Beatrice Page, too. The woman is prickly and mean, judgmental and hardly good for a man's self-esteem. But she's the only decent maternal figure I've ever known. The woman who would scowl at my existence in one breath, but pick me up off the street and put a meal in my belly on the other. She saved me and my brother from death too many times to count, and kept us out of the foster care system every time child services swung by town to check on us.

Our real parents preferred heroin, using us as target practice for their fists and feet, and had no interest in properly parenting a couple of kids they claimed ate too much and never appreciated a damn thing anyway. And though, as an adult, I can admit we probably *should* have been swept into the system and shipped off to a family that would treat us better, I know for a damn fact we wouldn't have gone even if they tried.

Forcing us apart would've ended with the world burning down.

And separating me and Alana would've led to blood on my hands. There was nothing I wouldn't have done to come back to her.

So Bitsy kept us around. Even when she didn't like us. Even when the hatred Alana and I shared turned to curiosity. Which turned to fire. Sneaking. A passion so hot, it burned us both up and left us charred when it was all over.

Or at least, it left *me* charred.

Alana, on the other hand, seemed fine, living it up in New York, marrying a banker looking motherfucker and having a baby quicker than it took me to catch my breath.

Such is life, I suppose.

"Focus," Chris rumbles, tapping my shoulder and sling-shotting me back to here. To now. To a tree Alana and I climbed a thousand times before we turned eighteen and a hard life got worse.

The fact I place the chainsaw teeth right above a carved *L&T Forever* is hardly relevant. Because just like the tree is dead and never coming back, the words we dug into it back when we believed love was possible and our circumstances wouldn't define us, well... that shit is dead, too.

I know exactly the date we fell in love. It's carved into my skin.

And I know exactly the date she left. That one is carved into my brain.

"Cut your hand off, and I'll kick your ass." Chris' shadow fills my peripherals, warning me of retribution if I don't calm the temper singing in my veins. "I know when you're about to do something stupid. It's a twin thing. You're pissy about Bitsy's cancer."

Am I?

Is that why Alana's on my mind so cruelly, callously, today, when usually, her ghost is easily tucked away like a box of treasures?

"You're doing that thing with your jaw," he continues. "You're angry. But you kinda need those limbs for your fight in December, so cool the fuck off and get yourself under control."

Lana & Tommy Forever.

With a gentle, barely there shake of my head, I rev the chainsaw and send steel teeth racing around the track, chewing through the wood until soft chunks spit backward and hit my legs.

Lana & Tommy Forever.

What a joke.

It's me. I'm the joke.

ROUND THREE

ALANA

"That's a cow." Franky's eyes widen behind his glasses, his jaw dropping open when we do, in fact, pass a cow. "It's a whole cow, Mom!"

"Yep." Giddiness and anxiety wreak havoc on my nervous system. Both thrilling adrenaline as nostalgia bustles through my veins, but dread, too, because I'm absolutely not ready to drive the final three miles and arrive at my old driveway.

I want so badly to get out of the car and stretch my limbs, and yet, there's a very real, dangerously vocal portion of my brain that insists I turn around and hightail it back to New York.

Where it's safe. Where anonymity is comfort, and my past isn't likely to jump up and bite me in the ass.

"Mom!" Franky rotates in his seat, staring out the opposite window. "It's three cows! There are *three* cows, and they're just... they're..." His lips open and close, guppy fish style. "They're wandering wherever they want. Is that normal?"

"They're not actually free." I point toward a large sign leading toward a much, much larger house. "All of this land belongs to Dave Dingus. He has fences that keep his animals where he needs them, so even though they kinda look free, they're not."

"Dingus?" He scrunches his nose, pushing his glasses back up to sit properly. "His name is Dingus?"

"Yeah, and no, you don't get to say anything if you meet him. It's an unfortunate name, but teasing isn't very nice."

Do I tell my son I rode Dingus' name when I was a kid, the way a bull rider clings on for their eight seconds and takes the trophy home at the end of the night?

No.

"Dave is an extremely wealthy man. He owns at least half of Plainview and a fair bit of the next town over, too." Which means he *could* have gone down to the courthouse and changed his name. But alas... "He was always pretty nice to me," I admit. "Despite how cranky Grandma Bitsy made him."

"Horses!" Franky smacks his hand on the side window, hissing from the pain and hurriedly tapping the button to move the glass out of the way. "There are horses, Mom!"

"There are." I set my elbow on my doorframe and my chin in my hand. "Those are Dave's, too. And before you panic, you should know he has pigs as well. And bulls."

His eyes widen. "Bulls?"

"Yeah." *To mount an unwilling cow and make babies.* "It's a farm. That's what farmers do."

"Fun fact." He goes back to glancing out the side window, awe playing across his features while Dave's horses race us as far as their fences allow. "Did you know you can breed sheep by making a red sheep and a blue sheep kiss?"

"Uh..." My son said breed. He said *breed*! "What?"

"When they stop kissing, there's a purple sheep. That's how you do it."

"Well..."

"But that's in Minecraft. Not real life. Everyone knows that's not how you breed animals in real life."

What the everloving fuck? "Okay..."

"To breed animals in real life, you need to make them marry first. Do you think Farmer Dingus marries his animals so they can make new animals?"

"Yep. Absolutely. They *have* to be married first. It's the law." My phone trills through the speakers, my agent's name flashing on the screen. And though I've declined a half dozen of her calls in the last week, I frantically accept this one. Anything to change the subject. "Hi, Helen. You're on speaker in the car."

"Oh, hey. Hi Franky. You in there, too?"

Sour, he folds his arms and flops back into his seat, wrinkling his lips and nose.

"He can hear you," I answer for him. "But he doesn't want to talk right now. We're almost at my mom's, so we're both a little tired. What's up?"

"Okay, so I was talking to the editor over at Elyte Publishing; she's willing to accept your manuscript as is. They've made an offer above that which we'd last discussed, so I emailed that to you, too. I told her you were traveling this week, so you probably wouldn't be able to take a look for a few days. So she's expecting a reply next week sometime."

"She wants to accept it as is?" My heart whips painfully against my diaphragm, knocking the wind from my lungs and leaving me anxiously searching for more. In my haste to escape *breeding*, I've run face-first into books. "She didn't like the main male lead. She wanted to change him."

"She didn't say she didn't like him. She said he was harsh and tossed around the idea of softening him a little, that's all."

"But I didn't..." I drag my bottom lip between my teeth. "I refused, so I expected them to rescind their offer."

"Well, now they're proposing more money, and Marianne is happy to take him as he is. That's great news!"

"That's..." I noisily exhale, slowing the car as we round a bend. God help me; a bull is doing the blue sheep-red sheep thing right there in broad daylight. "Hey, Franky?" I point to the other side of the road. "See that windmill? It harnesses the power of the wind to turn, and then it uses the friction it creates to pump water out of the ground. Isn't that cool?"

To him? To his brain? Hell yeah, it's cool.

"That's a lot of money, Helen. Why would they offer more and accept a manuscript they didn't like before?"

"They never *not* liked it! In fact, they *loved* it. They just worried the hero was too critical, especially in the third act. His anger makes for amazing tension, but that doesn't negate Marianne's concerns with how he'd be received. She was worried he wouldn't earn every reader's forgiveness."

"Why would she offer more money when I refused to change him? Her concerns remain unresolved." *Why am I such a self-sabotaging asshole?* "He's still harsh. He's still unlikable. And ya know what? Oh, Franky, look!" I point toward the lake as we pass, and the massive, picturesque home Edwin Sanderson built for his wife eons ago. *God, I always looked at that home and wondered what it would be like to live that life.* "My hero is still unlikable, Helen. He's mean and flawed. He probably won't convince all readers he's the right choice for the heroine." I pause, lifting my shoulder in a shrug, though she's not here to see it. "I'm not sure Elyte realizes the risk they're taking."

"This is Marianne's job, Alana. This is not her first day in the office, and you're not the first writer she's dealt with. If she's making an offer and allowing you to slide through with no major edits, it means she believes in the story. You should take the deal."

No. I don't think I should.

"Kinda makes me wonder if she's even good at her job." Pettiness seeps into my veins, kicking out the remaining dregs of being-in-Plainview anxiety. I only have room for one. "She *should* want to change stuff. There's no way the story is flawless. That she wants it *as is* makes me think she's phoning this in and doesn't believe in the story at all. Like she has a quota to fill and books to buy before her boss gets mad at her."

"Literally not how the industry works," she drawls. "And you're talking yourself in circles. You worked your butt off for this, Alana. You put in the hours, sweating and bleeding for it, but now that someone on the outside wants the book, you're tying yourself in knots trying to get out of making a deal. If I didn't know better, I'd wonder if you even want to be published at all."

Franky's scoff reverberates all the way to the front seat.

"Of course I want to publish. I just don't want to give my book to the wrong team and risk it being fumbled. I want an editor who truly understands what I wrote. A house that believes in the story and intends to have it read by the masses. Marianne allowing me to keep a hero she hardly likes is a red flag."

"You're being intentionally difficult."

"More cows, Mom!" Franky pokes his head between the two front seats. "Do you see them?"

"I see them." *I saw them every single day of my childhood. I was raised in this hellhole.* "We're about a minute out, Helen, so I'm gonna let you go."

"Read the offer!" She taps at her computer keyboard, the *click-clack* ricocheting through the line. "Read it, consider it. Then think about what that money could do for you now that you've moved. You could buy a shoe box in New York, sure, but you could buy an entire house out there in the sticks. Mortgage free. And your mom isn't doing so well, so having a little extra cash in the bank can only be a good thing."

"Oh, good. Business discussions, with a side of emotional manipulation. I love it when that happens."

She clicks her tongue, unimpressed. "You're obtuse on purpose."

"No, I'm just not interested in talking deals with an editor who lacks any semblance of a spine."

"Alana—"

"I'll call you sometime next week to go over the offer. But I doubt I'll accept it. Marianne was adamant that the hero change, and now she's just letting it go. She was wrong in both instances, and that's two strikes too many in my eyes."

"Is that a..." Franky's voice trembles. "Mom! Is that a llama?"

Oh god. Here we go. "I'll talk to you later, Helen." I end our call and swallow the lump of nerves nestled in the base of my throat, then I slow the car as a million memories sprint forward and smack me in the face. This is the road I've walked too many times to count. The mailbox shaped like a— God help me—sheep, perched out front.

Our fence isn't like Dave Dingus', where that rich old coot has money for days and a vested interest in keeping his animals inside his property. Our fences are more of a gentle suggestion. Rotting, white timber with missing sections, a llama thoroughfare, and animal droppings on the road.

My breathing grows thicker as we approach, and horrifyingly, tears itch the backs of my eyes.

I was so sure I would never come back here. Certain that New York would be where I live out my days, raising a son and writing books between his appointments.

It broke my heart to leave Plainview. But I was convinced I'd never return.

And yet...

"Is that..." Franky stretches his seatbelt and leans forward, setting his forearms on the front seats as I turn off the road and onto a potholed dirt driveway. "Mom, is that a *rooster*?"

"Mmhm." I clamp my lips shut and blink-blink-blink to clear my eyes. "The fact Grandma has a rooster isn't even a surprise to me, honey. But that it looks like Whacky II is just..." I release a long breath, shaking my head from side to side. "He has to be nearly twelve years old, at least."

"His name is Whacky?"

"Whacky II, actually. Whacky the First had an unfortunate ending that involved fireworks and bad choices."

He sputters. "What?"

"We didn't hurt him on purpose. I swear. It's not as psychotic as it sounds. But me and..." Don't say *that* name. Don't even think it. "A friend of mine. We were playing with fireworks one summer, though we knew we shouldn't. We had a whole crate of them, and believe it or not, we were being pretty careful. But one of my friends had a habit of playing with a magnifying glass back then. He enjoyed studying the bugs and stuff on the ground. Grandma Bitsy called us inside for lunch because it was blistering hot that day, and I figure she felt bad for us. My friend set his magnifying glass down in the sun, which kind of started a tiny fire, which, I guess, spread to the crate. The fuses had been lit and..." I grit my teeth, maneuvering our car around the potholes that've grown exponentially deeper in the ten years I've been away. "Well, we saw Whacky go up. We never saw him come down again."

"That's horrible!" And yet, my sweet baby boy giggles. "You blew up a rooster!"

"Unintentionally, and I'm definitely not proud of it. It's not a fun story to tell, honey. It's a cautionary tale. Don't play with fireworks, fire, or gallus gallus domesticus."

"Gallus gallus domesticus?"

The fact I know those words, even after all this time, is both comforting and a kick to the stomach. A reason to smile while simultaneously, a reason to fight the panic clawing at my throat. "Being here is a bit like time travel," I murmur. "Details I thought I'd forgotten, memories I'd long ago set aside, just jump right back to the front of my brain like no time has passed at all. My friend had a habit of calling things by their scientific name." I peek into the rear-view mirror, finding Franky's smiling eyes. "You do that sometimes, too. Gallus gallus domesticus."

"Did you know the scientific name for llamas is Lama Glama? They're part of the camel family."

"Er... nope." I white-knuckle the steering wheel, squeezing tighter the closer we come to the house where memories and reality clash, taking what *was* and making it what *is*. This house used to be a crisp white back around my senior year, but time and the scorching sun have transported it to a dull, almost-brown. The crepe myrtle I planted the year before graduation now casts a shadow over the yard, with bright pink blossoms floating on the breeze and branches that shield a grouping of sheep.

Not red. Not blue. And definitely not purple.

"Do you see that row of orange trees?" I point them out as we pass and swallow the nerves building in my throat. "I dug the holes for those. Me and a shovel, and a couple of my friends, heckling and throwing orange peels every time I cussed them out."

"How did you have orange peels if the trees hadn't grown yet?"

My lips curl higher because my baby is nothing if not a logical thinker.

"And why did they throw things at you? Did you punch them for it?"

"I did, actually." I choke out a soft laugh and bring the car to a stop about twenty feet from the foot of the porch. Then, killing the engine, I take the keys and simply... stare for a moment. I have a memory for every square inch of this place. I have a story for every day, every year, every moment. And I swear, almost every single one of them included a set of devilish twins who loved to give me a hard time. "I punched them as hard as I could. Then I swung my shovel and got in trouble with Grandma Bitsy while they laughed. She didn't believe me when I said they had it coming. As for the orange peels... well, that's why we planted the trees. We'd been in town earlier that day and came across a stall that was selling them."

"Selling oranges?"

"Mmhm. And best of all, they were already quartered and frozen. It was hot as Hades out, so we pooled all our spare change and bought as many as we could afford. Then we sat and ate most of them in the shade in town. They were so good, honey, that we just *knew* we needed our own trees. So we swung by the nursery on the way home and picked up a half dozen of them and carried them all the way back."

"How'd you buy them since you spent all your money on the oranges?"

We stole them!

"Let's go." I unsnap my seatbelt and shove my door open, then climbing out and lifting my arms to the sky, I stretch as far as my body will allow and wait a minute... then two... while Franky collects himself and makes the brave decision to open his door and follow me out.

My son doesn't much like the outside world, and he *hates* meeting new people. Even when those new people are his own flesh and blood.

"How are you feeling?" I lower my hands and, with them, my voice, so my question is just for him. Dropping into a crouch, I look up at my son and the way he hugs his Murdle book close to his chest. "What are you feeling right now?"

"Dread." He looks straight over my head at the house he's seen pictures of. The home I was born in—*literally*. "Nervous." He brings his eyes to mine, desperation glittering behind smudged lenses. "I'd prefer to go to a hotel tonight and come back here tomorrow."

"Because you're not ready to meet Grandma today?"

He shrugs, his lips pursing and his brows furrowing over bright eyes. "I guess. I don't want to talk."

"To her or to me?"

"To anyone except you." Deep dimples, just like mine, dig into his cheeks and try to convince the world he's smiling. *He's not.* He's simply holding on to so much, bottling his emotions and trying unbelievably hard to keep them in. "She'll want me to say hello. I don't want to."

"Would it be okay if I speak for you? Because you're right; she's going to want to say hello. And if you don't say anything back, she'll feel a little funny about it. But if you let me, I can tell her you'd prefer not to talk right now."

He nods, short, sharp jerks of his head. "Okay. Is it annoying when my tism does this?"

"Your *tism?*" I set my hands on his hips and gently pull him closer, chuckling under my breath as I drag him in for a hug. "Autism is not something to be ashamed of, honey. It doesn't annoy me. Not ever. It's a part of who you are."

"There are people in the world who are normal."

"And to that, I declare bull poop," I mock-grumble. "There's no such thing, and anyone who claims to be normal shouldn't be trusted. Lucky for me," I tap his trembling chin, "your diagnosis basically means I have a cheat-book, like the kind we used to have for Nintendo games."

His brows pinch tight behind the frame of his glasses. "I don't understand."

"Kind of like the Murdles." I point toward his book. "At the end, when it gives you the answers. That's like what your diagnosis is for me. Before, when you were smaller, I didn't really know what the heck I was doing. After a while, I kinda figured you out. *Then,* we got the diagnosis, which confirmed what I already knew. And now, whenever I'm not sure, it's like I can check the cheat book and know exactly how to help you."

Unconvinced, his lips drop into heavy lines. "Autism is a disability, Mom. It's not a Nintendo game."

"Do you really feel that way?" I straighten out because my thighs burn from crouching and my knees threaten to give out. But I fold at the hips and remain on his level. "I consider it a bit like a superpower. You're smarter than literally every single other person I know, including the adults. Best of all, you function on common sense and honesty. You *never* talk in circles, you *never* lie, and you refuse to partake in the annoying small talk everyone else seems to think is necessary. Do you know how many people in this world are the opposite? Constant word salad and incessant chattering for the sake of hearing their own voice? It's exhausting."

Finally, the wire door creaks open—a sound I would recognize even if I'd lost every other sense available to me—and my mother steps outside her house and onto the porch. But my eyes remain on my son.

"She's someone who'll talk just to talk. I didn't even know back then that you could make it stop simply by... not participating." I tickle his hip and earn a sweet smile. "Autism is *not* a bad word in my dictionary, and I'm not sad about your diagnosis. In fact, I'm thankful for every single thing you are. You've taught me how to be brave, which is really odd since you're the kid and I'm the mom. I never quite understood courageousness until you came along."

He peeks over my shoulder, his eyes shifting behind his glasses and his lips firming into tighter, straighter lines.

So I lower my voice. "Is she coming this way?"

"Yes."

"Does she look angry, or is she wearing a chicken for a hat?"

At that, he peels his gaze back to mine. "Are those the only two options?"

"Usually? Yeah." I stroke his jaw and flash a playful wink—signifying our last moment alone for the foreseeable future—then straightening my back, I close my eyes and draw a long, lung-filling breath. There's no true way to prepare myself for this woman, no matter the mantra I chant, the meditation I attempt, or how desperately I wish I could smooth the wounds that run deeply beneath my flesh.

Wounds created by her.

So I turn and open my eyes. *Jump in. Get it done.* But when I expect to see a woman who has always weighed in at a comfortable two-hundred and fifty pounds, I'm instead stunned to find a woman a third of that... when she's soaking wet.

"Mom?" She used to have hair black as midnight and skin like the finest china. But now, both are gray. "You look..." *Thin. Sickly. Not well at all.* "Different."

"It's my new diet." She pastes on a beaming smile and hobbles down the porch steps, draped in a dress that eats her up and leaves her a shapeless blob that would hide a lot of her weight loss if not for the way her wrist bones poke out. Her collarbones. Her cheekbones. She doesn't move nearly as quickly as she used to, but her eyes are the same, at least. Shrewd, like they can see through *anything*. "You're gonna make me walk all the way there, aren't you?" She waves us closer but steps onto the grass and quickens now that she's on level ground. She looks from Franky to me.

Back and forth as though she can't quite decide who she'd like to stare at more. "Franklin Page, you handsome little devil. Look at you!" Decision made, she makes a beeline for my baby with her arms outstretched and expectation plastered on her face. *Hug me, child.* "Oh my gosh, Grandma is happy to see you."

But of course, when she expects him to run forward and dive into her arms—*in the movies, maybe*—he steps back, shifting to the side to make me his shield.

"Oh…" Slowing, she swaps her smile for a frown. Then, her glittering eyes for something else entirely. Something I know all too well. "Uh…?"

"We're happy to see you too, Mom." I draw her in and press a kiss on her cheek in greeting. Then the other. "Franky and I have had a *long* drive, so we're a little tired."

"*We're tired…? Franky and I had a long drive…?* Did the cat take his tongue?"

"There have been no cats." I release her and stand a little taller. A little firmer. "He's simply tired. But maybe later, once he's settled in, he'd like to come say hello." I peek down and meet his wary eyes. "Can you go to the car and get your backpack, honey?"

To my mother, all she would hear is a request. But to my son, he hears freedom. His little chest—which is actually kind of broad, considering his age—deflates with relief as he spins on his heels and dashes to the back of the car, popping it open and retrieving his things. Then I bring my gaze back around. "Don't."

"Don't what?" She jabs a finger in his direction. "He doesn't even want to say hello to his own grandmother? What on earth could I have done to deserve that?"

"Why does it have to be about you? It might gall you to hear this, Mother, but his need for quiet can actually have nothing to do with you at all."

"Alana—"

"My son struggles with new people and places," I grit out. "He's allowed to establish boundaries and handle uncomfortable situations however he wants, so long as he remains respectful. Your hurt feelings are not more important than his right to peace and autonomy."

"Autonomy?" She repeats, as though the concept is foreign to her ears. "Boundaries? Oh…" And with that, her lips firm into thin lines. "I see how it is. You went and found those hip new words up in New York, and now you're bringing them back to Plainview like you think you're better than those you left behind."

Jesus. She hasn't changed a single bit since I left. The woman is impossible to please and entirely too comfortable in her victimhood, even in situations that have nothing to do with her. "They're neither hip nor new. They're basic human rights. We've just driven two days straight to get here, so instead of focusing on you for a moment, how about you consider the possibility that a nine-year-old is simply too tired to socialize right now? We're sweaty. We're overstimulated. And honestly, we'd like a shower and as little emotional manipulation as possible, please, while we settle in to this new world."

My mother has always been in the habit of looking down her nose at me. Derision and judgment—her constant companions. My father's mother treated her the same, and so that's how she acts toward me. It's a learned behavior adopted while trying to survive an unhappy marriage, and the fact I take after my father—in looks and personality—no doubt contributes to her bitterness.

"You called me, Alana." She wrinkles her nose, the action so much more severe now that she weighs less than half as usual. "You said you wanted to come home because you and Colin are... struggling. I'm doing you a favor. Let's not forget that."

"Uh-huh." Mine and Colin's marriage being over is a mere coincidence. The fact is, she called me, but letting the truth hinder a tantrum has never been something Beatrice Page stood for. "Will we be in my old bedroom?"

"You will be." She backs up and gestures toward the house as Franky wanders around the car, his arms overflowing with things; books, the teddy he's slept with every single night since he was born, a sweater he absolutely won't need in Plainview until January, at least, and a robotic hand created from Lego pieces.

"I've made the guest bedroom up for Franklin," she continues. "I think you'll both be comfortable with your accommodations."

"Come on, honey." I gently brush my fingers over his shoulder and lead him toward the house. "I'll show you my bedroom. It's the one I grew up in."

"I don't want to sleep in the guest bedroom," he whispers, drawing me down with a tug on my shirt. "I don't want to be in there alone."

"Don't worry." I wink and wait for his eyes to soften. Relax. "You can stay in my room for as long as you want. This might be Grandma's house, but I'm still your mom. I get the final say."

"I sure hope you and I get to hang out, Franklin." My mom hurries up the porch steps ahead of us, then across to hold the door open. Finally, she turns back and pastes on a friendly smile I know she saves for the people she'd like to impress. "I mean that. Plainview is a small town with lots of really cool things to do. Your mom will be busy working soon, and summer break has not long started, so there's no school yet. That means, sometimes, it'll just be me and you. I hope we can be friends."

He stops in front of the open door and glances up, meeting her eyes. The world silences, except for the scream of the cicadas and the beat of my heart pounding in my ears.

Then he nods and keeps going.

That's basically a high five, and miraculously, I think Mom realizes it. Because her false smile breaks away to something bigger. Better. Real.

"Alrighty." With a skip to her step, she follows us in and closes up to keep the bugs out. "Why don't you two head to your rooms and freshen up? Dinner will be served in an hour."

"Let's go." I take some of his stack before the Lego topples to the floor and shatters, then wrapping my hand around his, I lead him through the home that holds a million memories. The kitchen I ate in alone too many times to count, and the living room I was shunned from because my mom wanted to watch her shows, and my presence, evidently, bothered her.

I was positive I'd never come back to the house that held my torment and thousands of nights of loneliness.

But plans change. Life changes.

For my son's sake, I intend to smooth those changes out and shield him from the ugliness.

ROUND FOUR

TOMMY

"Circle around!" Chris snaps from the outside of the cage, his booming voice creating a clear distinction from the person he is outside of this gym. In the real world, Christian Watkins has no time for anybody, no inclination for small talk, and no fucking tolerance for making friends when he's already so rich with those.

It's me.

I'm his friend.

But inside Love & War, the gym we opened fresh out of high school when the world was on fire and I was on a fast track toward prison—or insanity—he's a powerhouse. A world-standard trainer who refuses to let his fighters slack off.

It's me.

I'm his fighter.

"If you don't bring that left arm up and protect your face, I'm gonna smash it with a two-by-four," he snarls. "You don't care about your head anyway, so I may as well swing."

"You're antsy today." I duck low when Oliver, my sparring partner, throws a wildly stupid haymaker and spins himself out. But while he's turning, I shoot forward on one knee, wrap my arms around his torso, and slam him to the canvas with a floor-rumbling boom. Instantly, I scramble over the top of his body and whip his arm back, throwing myself to the side and trapping his chicken wing until he barks out in pain.

And then I wait. And wait. And wait.

Until he taps. "You asshole!" He slaps my leg and grunts when I release his arm, laughter rolling on my tongue and my lungs heaving for fresh air. I simply lie on the canvas, sweating as the cage door squeaks open, and my brother's beady-eyed stare becomes all I see.

"I won."

"You're sparring with a nobody. Don't get too smug about it."

"Hey!" Ollie rolls out from beneath my legs and stops on his knees and elbows. It's the kind of position a man *doesn't* practice in prison... unless you're into that sort of stuff. "I'm not a nobody. I'm a whole human with feelings."

"You're a punching bag," Chris dismisses him coldly. "You're a heavy body with an hour to spare." Then he brings his eyes back to me. "You're not gonna win fuck all if you continue to train like this."

"Dude, it's July." I peel my grappling gloves off and swipe my sweaty brow, though the action is useless since my hands are sweaty, too. "We have loads of time. We're not getting serious until October, at the earliest."

"Get serious in July, and you won't have to train so fuckin' hard in November to be ready."

"Get serious before October, and I'll burn out by fight night." I extend my hand, waiting for him to grab on, but instead of letting him lift me to my feet, I sweep my legs out and buckle the backs of his knees, slamming him to the canvas right alongside me and shuffling away when he viciously flips to his hands and knees and pounces, all in under a second.

I know him like I know my own body, so I scramble toward the cage door, practically levitating in my haste, all to avoid his meaty fist rearranging my ribs. "You're feeling anxious because we got a date for the fight." I exit the cage and wander amongst a group of kids coming in for class, making the little punks my shields. It's my God-given right. "Having an official date means you're panicking. I understand that you're a little overwhelmed—"

"Don't talk to me like I'm a child." He prowls out of the cage, his bare chest growing with adrenaline, his lungs working hard to fill and prepare him for war. "Don't use your psycho-babble and think it makes you sound smart. Ollie's not a contender. He's a shitty fighter."

"Hey!" He flops to his back. "Stop taking it out on me 'cos you two are feeling mean."

"You never take things seriously, Tommy! Conner handed his belt back, which cleared the way for you. Now you have it, but Docik is coming for it, and he's not gonna lay down like..." He jerks a thumb over his shoulder.

Oliver grumbles.

"He's the best fuckin' fighter coming up right now, and he's hungry to claim his place at the top."

I grab one of our baby fighters—Molly—and push her giggling form toward my brother. "You really shouldn't cuss like that in front of kids. You know the moms get fussy about it."

He catches her and turns her back around. "You shouldn't use a nine-year-old as a shield." Still, he softens his touch and tickles the side of her neck. "And you're taking the kiddie class today."

"What?" I skid to a stop and glance back at the dozen almost-fifth-graders surrounding me. It's like I'm a fuckin' Wiggle, and they're my little fans. "Eliza is taking—"

"Eliza isn't in today, and you'd know that if you attended literally *any* staff meeting. Or read your emails. Or checked your texts. Or," he strides out of the room, then back again, clutching a yellow sticky note that says, 'ELIZA IS OUT!' "Ya know, paid attention to anything except your own reflection in the mirror. It was annoying in high school. It's worse now."

"You're being hurtful today."

"That's what I said," Oliver rumbles, still on his back in the cage. "Bad attitude. Hurts feelings."

"You're a little dysregulated," I *psycho-babble*, my smile growing wider with every shade Chris' eyes darken. "It's the weekend. It's summer break. Take a breath and just..." I toss another child his way. "Relax."

"You're running the kid class, then you're cooking dinner. I want steak and fries, and you better have it done before eight o'clock." He spins on his heels and stalks into the cage, scaring Ollie to his feet until they're facing each other.

Poor, poor guy. He's about to get his ass whooped.

"Can we do the frog jumps again today?" Molly grabs my arm, monkey-climbing until she reaches my shoulder, only to slide down again because her tree is sweaty. "Pllleeeeeeease?"

"You like the frog jumps?" I shake her off and spin to hide behind another kid, then another, when she tries to chase me. "What if we do round-robin sparring? But you're in the middle and get beat up by everyone else. Doesn't that sound like fun?"

"No!" She darts between her peers and punches my hip. Which, I suppose, is meant to be a *tag. I'm it.* "Plus, my dad said to tell you to stop teasing me anymore."

"Your dad doesn't scare me." I twist out of her grasp, circling behind another kid. "Your daddy and I went to school together, and he wet his pants right in front of me once."

"Ew!" A dozen kids chime in at once, laughing and holding their crotches.

"You tell your daddy to come fight me." I bend at the hips and show the girl my warrior face... ish. "You tell him the champ challenges him to a round in the octagon."

"My dad says you were always the champ," Jeremy—seven, to Molly's nine—pipes in. "But he says you're ergant about it."

Ergant? "Billy Caster said I was *arrogant*? Boy, Billy Caster ran face-first into a light pole in front of our whole grade one time! Billy Caster doesn't have the brain cells to know what that word means."

"Hey! Stupid?" Chris rattles the cage door, then he tilts his head to the side. Right where Billy Caster's beady eyes burn into mine. And beside him, Molly's dad folds his arms. In fact, a whole fuckin' platoon of eavesdropping parents who all attended the same schools I did, right around the same time I did, watch on with mean-mugging scowls on their faces. "You really think this is how to run a business?"

I wave to the group of parents, only to switch five fingers for a single, middle finger when their kids spin. Then I wink at Molly's unimpressed mom and back up to snag a shirt from the corner of the room. *Suppose I should get dressed while rolling with minors.* "Alright, fine," I announce, dragging the dry fabric over my wet skin. "Baby karatekas, line up in order of shortest to tallest. Doesn't matter if you're five-years-old, or ten, I want the tallies over here," I point to my left, "and the shorties over there." I point to my right.

Eager, they run in circles and lose all semblance of organization, exactly like I knew they would. So I clap my hands and use my commanding voice. "I said, tall to my left." I grab Molly and toss her to the right. "Shorties over there. Who remembers what you did during your last class?"

Jeremy's arm shoots high over his head. His dad is a cop; it doesn't surprise me the kid is a goodie-goodie question answerer. "We worked on our kata!"

"And takedowns!" Molly inserts.

"Which takedowns?" I grab another kid and *yeet* him to the left. Then another, directing her to the right. "Can anyone remember the name?"

"It was the one where we do, like…" Jeremy grabs a classmate and tosses that little sucker over his shoulder with a ferociousness that's gonna get my ass sued. But the kid bounces like he's made of rubber, bounding back to his feet with a megawatt grin plastered across his face.

"Right." I brush a hand over my mouth, if only to hide my smile. Then I walk down the middle of my groups to find one last kid. He lands right in the middle of short and tall. But most interesting of all is the fact I don't know him.

In this town… that's damn near impossible.

"What's your name?" I turn and take a dozen hula hoops from the wall, tossing them to the floor to create an obstacle course. But when the kid doesn't answer by the time I'm done placing them, I come back with a frown and study him again. More thoughtfully this time. I *actually* look at him, his trembling jaw and shimmering eyes hidden behind thick glasses.

He's no loud-mouth Molly or people-pleasing Jeremy. He's quiet. Shy. Terrified, even, as I crouch and search his misty stare. Lowering my voice, so it's just for me and him, I try again. "My name is Tommy. Do you wanna tell me yours?"

He merely stares, his cheeks flaming red. But I know these types. Jesus, I've lived with one my whole life, so I drop my gaze and try a new approach. "That's cool. You don't have to tell me. You're here for classes, huh?"

In my peripherals, he nods.

"But you don't really want to be here, do you?"

Again, I see the movement of his head shaking from side to side.

"It's summer, and that's usually when numbers spike for us. Moms and dads are at work, and daycare is more expensive than martial arts classes. Have you ever done a class like this before?"

He shakes his head.

"And just to clarify, do you know how to speak? Do you have a voice?"

"Yes."

Victory!

I swing my gaze up and smile, even if he gives me just one word. One raspy, shaky, barely committed syllable.

"I guess you heard all that stuff where I was being silly and loud, huh? I probably sounded like the kind of guy who doesn't know how to be quiet. But," I dip my chin toward the cage. Toward my brother pounding on our local doctor. "He's my twin, and he's probably the quietest guy I know. Except for what you just saw, he doesn't really like talkin' to people, either. So I learned a long time ago to respect a man's desire for silence."

Slowly, with every word I speak, the tremble in his jaw slows. The glow of his cheeks softens.

"You don't have to talk if you don't wanna. But I'm gonna give you instructions during class, so if you don't understand them, or don't feel safe, or if anything feels off, I'll need you to speak up then, okay? It can be as much or as little as you want it to be. But I can't know something is wrong unless you say so. Did your mom or dad sign any forms when you got here?"

He shrugs, lifting his shoulders and exhaling. "My grandma brought me. My mom is at her new job."

"Okay. Cool." I scratch my jaw. "Are you new to town?"

He nods again. "Since a few days ago."

"Is your grandma new to town?"

He shakes his head. "She always lived here. She said she knows your family and that you wouldn't mind if I came to class."

She knows my family... *Geez. I fuckin' hope not. My family is trash.*

"It's fine. I'll take care of all the grown-up stuff later. Do you have any injuries or anything we need to talk about before we start? How old are you?"

"I'm nine and a half. My birthday is in January. And I have a sore leg." He points at a yellowing bruise on his shin. "I fell over at my grandma's. She has cows, and they were looking at me kinda funny."

"The cows were looking at you funny?" A soft chuckle reverberates along my chest. "Funny, how?"

"Like they were gonna kill me." He folds his arms again, shuddering. "She has chickens, too. I think they ascended from hell and came here just to give me nightmares."

"Ascended? That's a pretty smart word for a nine-year-old, don't you think?"

He stares, firming his lips and studying me like I'm dumber than the killer cows on his grandma's property. "It's a normal word. You don't know it?"

I bark out a loud laugh and straighten out before my legs explode from swelling lactic acid. "I know it. I know all sorts of smart words, actually. But I learned them from my brother, and he's the smartest guy I ever met."

"My mom says I'm the smartest person she knows. Including the adults."

"I bet she's probably right, then. You wanna tell me your name yet?"

And just like that, he snaps his lips closed and shuts down. *Interesting.* I take a step back, then another when I'm reasonably confident he won't dart out of here and onto the road in his escape. Then I clap my hands for the rest of my class, who, while I focused on the new kid, dissolved into some kind of illegal cockfighting ring. "Molly Jenkins!" I grab the scruff of her shirt and drag her off her victim. "Control yourself, girl. You're supposed to show us dumb boys how girls have superior self-control and yada yada yada."

"Yada yada, my butt!" She turns on Jeremy with a feral glare. "He said he was better than me in jiu-jitsu."

"Yeah? Well, you sure showed him." I meet Jeremy's electric eyes. "She had you in submission, bud. She's a girl and was still whooping you. You're as embarrassing as your father."

"I can't believe we *pay* for this," Billy grumbles. "At least back in school, Tommy Watkins talked shit for *free*."

"Inflation," I chuckle, setting Molly on her feet and pushing her toward the new kid. "Go over there and make friends." But when the kid's eyes flash with panic behind his glasses, I add, "but he doesn't have to talk to you if he doesn't wanna. Be nice, but don't be bossy. Jeremy." I point him toward the first hoop. "Lead your group. Frog hop from one to the next. Go around the circle, then come back to line up again. I wanna see you all panting and sweaty before we can get started on the real stuff."

"Warm-ups are never fun," he grumbles. Though he doesn't pass up the opportunity to be first in line, either. Like father, like son. "Can we practice roundhouse kicks today?"

"Warm up first." I wander toward the cage, past Molly, whose entire demeanor softens now that she's not asserting her dominance. Then I wait for my brother's eyes to come to mine. "Anyone know whose kid that is? He said his grandma brought him in, because his mom was at work. He and mom are new to town, but grandma has lived here since always."

"Could literally be anyone." Ollie starfishes the canvas, his legs and arms spread wide while he heaves for oxygen. "Did you consider just... asking his name?"

"No, stupid. I didn't consider that." I look at Chris. "Do we have paperwork for him?"

"It's probably in the computer. Which you would know if you—"

"Read my emails." I push off the cage. "Yeah, I got it. You know his name?"

He only shrugs, as interested in that as he is in making new friends. As in, *not*. So I turn back to run my class before they create a new underground fighting ring that won't look so good with cops in the building. And though I expect the new kid to observe, at best, Molly does what Molly does well, coaxing him toward the hoops and getting him to walk over them.

The boy won't hop. But he'll go through the motions, at least.

Still, he trips on the third ring and smashes into the matted floor with a harrumph and tangled limbs.

Quiet. Shy. And *clumsy*.

Cool, cool, cool, cool, cool.

ROUND FIVE
ALANA

Not being a world-famous author means I don't have the luxury of swimming in endless royalties or six-figure advances from my publisher. And leaving my marriage without a dime of spousal maintenance or child support—*fair, really*—means getting a real job. It means venturing out into the real world and talking to actual human beings, earning a salary so I can, at the very least, afford to feed my son.

Lucky for me, there was a sign out front of a rundown bookstore on Main Street—the place is literally called *Books Books Books*—advertising a job vacancy. Mrs. Middler, the owner, who was the owner when I was a small child, too, had a stroke over the winter, and though she made it through and is mostly back to her normal eighty-something-year-old self, her grandkids felt the need to force her into semi-retirement.

They don't want to run the place themselves, and selling it in today's economy would be worse than simply having it managed.

Which makes their unwanted responsibility my desired job.

So here I am, standing amongst the chaos and walls of uncategorized novels stacked atop cookbooks, biographies towering over textbooks, romance novels mixed with dark thriller and splatterpunk horror. What are supposed to be aisles lined with beautiful bookshelves have turned into a hoarder's paradise.

And still, I can't wipe the smile from my face.

"You're trading selling books for... selling books?" Fox sneers over the phone. She doesn't even try to hide her contempt. "You could be touring and promoting your own book, but you choose to work in a pokey little store, destroy your sinuses with small-town dust, and accept the teeny-tiny salary they're paying you instead?"

"Fox—"

"You could be on talk shows! You could meet Oprah. You could meet Reese Witherspoon! You have a deal on the table and a really good story to share with the world. You could be rich! But you're running an old lady's bookstore for like, three hundred bucks a week? This is grounds to have you committed, you know that?"

I roll my eyes. "I have no expenses except groceries and whatever Franky needs, which means my salary is actually entirely reasonable. And Helen has never mentioned Reese or Oprah. You're sensationalizing."

"You're robbing the world of your art! Helen believes in it so much that she hasn't even fired you yet, despite how much of a pain in the ass you are. That means something."

"Yeah. It means she gets a cut of whatever deal I get, so of course she wants me to take it. That's hardly *believing in me.*"

"Sell your damn book and come back to New York! You don't even have to see Colin. You don't even have to tell him you're here. I'll hide you."

I exhale and lean back to study a precarious tower of... James Patterson and Tolkien. "I don't need to hide from him. Colin has been nothing but decent since the moment we met."

"He kicked you out!"

"He *suggested* we move out, expressed his growing feelings for Tasha, and explained how our marriage was affecting his relationship prospects."

"Are you even listening to yourself right now?" Her anger pulses throughout the bookstore. "Your husband is having sex with his assistant, and he *oh-so-politely* mentioned that your presence within the marital home was hampering his affair. Are you serious right now?"

"You oversimplify nuanced situations for the sake of irritating me." I leave Tolkien and Patterson to co-mingle a little longer and wander back to the desk at the front of the store. It's a counter, I suppose. With a cash register and an ancient computer collecting dust. Unopened mail—envelopes—creating a stack on the left, and unopened parcels—books—forming a tipping tower on the right. An old, already-used candle hints at what was once a store Mrs. Middler intended to be quaint. Comfortable.

Somewhere people would come for the atmosphere. And beautiful chandelier lights hang from the ceiling. Their bulbs long ago died, but her intention is clear to see. A couch sits hidden beneath books, and coffee tables, too, struggle under the weight of novels.

Mrs. Middler's plan was to run a bookstore, but not the type where you would come in, peruse the shelves, and leave again. No, she wanted to provide a space for customers to explore, selecting books according to their moods, as well as a pastry and coffee, before sitting down to enjoy their purchases for hours and hours amongst like-minded people. And fortunately for her, she had more than enough space to cater to her dreams.

Unfortunately for her, she had so much space, I imagine it all became too much as she grew older. What was once a wonderland for written adventures became an overwhelming task to keep clean. Sprawling floors to mop. Too many shelves to dust. Simply too much to keep up with.

But now I'm here, and though my reasons for returning to Plainview aren't entirely pleasant, I hope to make good of my circumstances.

For my sanity and for Franky's, too.

"Alana?" Fox's feelings about my move are complicated, from pure rage at the fact I'd leave, to encouraging me to be brave when my nerves faltered. From nagging me to stay, to demanding I get in the car and stop being a coward. She wants what's best for me, but struggles knowing *best* isn't black and white. "Come back to New York and run a bookstore here. This is where all the real readers are. It's where all the colorful, wonderful, exotic, and varied personalities congregate. Plainview is just…" She expels a noisy breath of air. "There's a reason you left."

"Yes. There was." I turn at the counter and glance out the dusty windows that overlook Main Street as old, rusting trucks putter by and little old ladies sit outside the drugstore with their purses on their laps and unkind sneers as their only expressions.

They're literally the same old ladies who sat in the same spot, doing the same thing, ten years ago.

"My reasons were valid, Fox. Even if no one besides you, Colin, and Helen know them. They were real and rational and important to me. But now my mom needs me here, and Colin needs to move on. I'm not moving into your apartment on a long-term basis, and I can't afford to live in New York on my income."

"You could if you sold your damn book!"

"Fox—"

"Your advance alone would support you and Franky *comfortably* for a year. Colin would give you anything if you asked for it. And I *want* you to move in with me. So, really, you could have no rent to pay in either place. No utilities. Just food and whatever things Franky needs. Come back," she groans. "Your life is here now."

I spy my mother and Franky wandering along the sidewalk, their steps painfully slow and Franky's sour face as loud as if he were screaming and waving his arms in the air.

But, of course, my baby would never do such a thing.

"I have to go now, Fox."

"Wait..." Stunned, she makes a sound in the back of her throat. "What? We were in the middle of an important discussion."

"No. *You* were in the middle of what you think is an important discussion. But me and Franky are already here. We already moved, and there isn't a dollar amount the richest man on the planet could offer that would convince me to climb back into my car and make the twenty-four-hour drive again so soon."

"Alana—"

"But you should come out here for a visit." I pick up my phone and take the call off speaker, then bringing it to my ear, I move to the shop door and open it, the bells above drawing Franky's forlorn eyes. "We'd love to have you, and we have an unused guest bedroom at the house, so you could stay with us."

"At your mother's house? The woman who kind of hates you because your dad cheated on her, ditched town with the mistress, and because you kind of look like him, she likes to punish you simply for existing? *That* house?"

I cough out a quiet laugh and step back to allow room for Franky to pass through. My mother, of course, is still twenty feet behind. "Yes. That house. But if you're not comfortable, there's a bed-and-breakfast not so far from my place that has pretty decent Google reviews. Consider it."

"Alana—"

"I have to go. But I'll text you later." I drag the phone from my ear and end the call without giving her a chance to argue, and for the eternity it takes my mother to hobble through, I remain patient. Impassive. "How was your day, honey?" As soon as she's in, I release the door and turn to my son. "What did you do?"

"This is a *lot* of books." Ignoring my question, he ambles the packed aisles, scouring the overflowing shelves and sliding the tip of his finger along random spines. "The fiction and non-fiction are mixed up, though." He scowls. "That's not right."

"No. It's not." I slip my phone into my back pocket and follow him. I'd prefer to be near him over my mom any day. "The lady who owns this shop is older now and a little sick, so things got messy. But that's my job now. I'll clear everything out and start again. I'm not sure Mrs. Middler even knows what stock she has anymore, so I think it could be a fun idea to write it all down and—"

"You should use a spreadsheet for that." He pauses in front of a middle-grade fantasy series, the bright purple and orange spines a beacon for his curious gaze. "Don't use a pen and paper, or else you'll lose track, too. Actually," he stares up at me through smudged glasses, "I'll make the spreadsheet for you."

"Whew." Mom moves books aside and sits on the couch with a harrumph. "This kid, Alana. Constantly leaving me speechless."

Unlikely. She's always got something snarky to say.

"He's pretty amazing." I watch as he continues browsing. "What did you get up to today?"

"We just wandered around." She picks up a cookbook penned by none other than Snoop Dogg—*though I doubt she knows who he is.* "Swung by the doctor's office because that man is obsessed with taking my blood. No better than a common thief, I swear. Then we went to the drugstore to get my pills."

"What kind of pills?"

Distracted or not, Bitsy Page is no fool. "I don't know about that fancy city you come from, but out here in Plainview, a woman's medical information is protected by law. That's a conversation for her and her doctor."

I roll my eyes and turn to follow my son. "I was just making conversation. Is that all you two did?"

"Pretty much." She flips through the pages in front of her. "Did you hear that Gus Darling recently got back from the city, too? He was visiting his daughter for a bit."

I reach the end of one aisle and move to the next, where Franky selects a book and sits on the floor to read it. "Mr. Darling went to New York?"

"No. Copeland City. It's been a minute since that girl had come back, and he was done letting her brush him off, so he hopped on a plane and went out there to see her. He only just got back a few days ago."

"Cool." Small-town living, where the old folks' favorite hobby is gossiping about all the things their kids do that annoy them. "How is she doing? *What* does she do?"

"For work?" She makes a non-committal sound in the back of her throat. "Gus says she's a doctor of some sort. But if you ask me, I reckon he's lying. Because any time Barbara—you remember Barbara, right? From bingo?"

Good lord. "Yes, Mom. I remember Barbara."

"Well, her son is an *actual* doctor. A surgeon. So when she tries to talk to Gus about it and presses for information, he doesn't really have a lot to say. And he's *never* mentioned hospitals or surgeries or anything like that. So we think he's lyin', so he can compete with Barbara's son."

"The fact they're competing boggles my mind." I stand over Franky while he reads each line, each page, with efficiency. He dives gleefully into a fictional world instead of listening to Plainview drama. A skill I developed long ago, too. He sits directly below an overhanging stack of books, a mistake that promises a headache, so I grab them and set them aside before they fall and ruin his day. "So what if she's a doctor—or not—and so what if Barbara's son is a surgeon? I bet they're not competing with each other. I doubt they even think of the other. They moved away, Mom. There's a reason they chose careers outside of Plainview."

"Oliver stayed." She sets her book down with a clatter, then stands with a noisy huff of exhaustion. "He was content to come back here after college and open his own practice."

"Good for him." I bend and brush my fingers over Franky's scuffed knees, winking when he peels his eyes from the book. Then I straighten again and head back the way I came, if only to stop my mother from interrupting the solitude he craves. "And since *you* brought it up," I stop five feet from the end of the aisle and wait for her eyes, "did the doctor say anything I should know?"

She opens her mouth to argue.

"Set aside your need for privacy. You called me. You asked me to come home. You said you were unwell and needed a little extra help around the house. So how about you stop with the vague BS and just tell me straight? What's wrong with you, and is it being managed?"

"I don't need to tell you my private business. I only need to inform you of the animals' eating routine. You're here to take care of them, not me."

"Mom!"

"You sound like Gus's daughter. Pretending to be a doctor when you're

48

not. I'm fine, Alana. Focus on feeding the chickens and collecting their eggs before they eat them."

Frustration and anger wash through my veins, a wave of emotion that sears my fraying mood and almost beats out my hard-earned ability to ignore this woman's annoying barbs.

Moving away for so long left me a little out of practice.

I paste on a smile we both know is fake, and in my mind, at least, I congratulate the doctor, who is most certainly a doctor, despite Barbara's competitive streak and tendency to pry.

"You haven't stopped doing *that*, I see." Mom gestures with an up-down flick of her wrist. "I know when you're having a whole conversation in your head, Alana. It sent me crazy when you were a teen. I doubt it'll be any less irritating now that you're an adult."

"It's how I filter through my thoughts and keep the especially unkind few to myself." I show her a real, sarcastic smirk before I stride past her frail frame and wander to the shop door. I haven't had a single customer since I got here, which kind of makes the sign redundant, but I flip it from OPEN to CLOSED anyway, only to catch a hulking shadow eating up the sidewalk in my peripherals.

A muscular chest wrapped in a tank that shows off thick arms and tattoos that *almost* tempt me to stop and stare. But in just a single beat of my heart, my eyes catalog everything my mind is not quite ready to. Short, dark hair and piercing green eyes. Thick thighs, though they're partially hidden beneath baggy basketball shorts.

Worst of all, I know there are two of them in this town, identical in every way except their personalities. And because this one walks with a grin, I spin and slam my back to the door, my heart thundering out of control and my stomach readying to hurl all over poor Mrs. Middler's merchandise.

"Problem?" My mother sashays across the shop and stops on my right to peek through the glass.

Then her eyes flicker with smug satisfaction.

Tommy friggin' Watkins.

No model wife in sight and no beautiful children in tow.

"Hmmm." She makes that sound I know too well. A subtle click in the back of her throat and an annoying flick of her tongue. It's the sound of my youth, right before she was about to destroy my self-esteem and ground me into the dirt for daring to hope for a decent day. "Thomas Watkins. Is there a reason you're making a scene right now, Alana Bette?"

EMILIA FINN

"I'm not making a scene!" And yet, I whisper-shout my words. "No one except you can even see me."

"Would you like me to head on out there and call that boy back? I'm sure he'd love to say hello after all this time."

"Absolutely not." I grab her wrist before she thinks to open the door. But I'm careful not to yank her around. Doctor-Patient confidentiality aside, it doesn't take a medical degree to know the woman is unwell.

"What's wrong?" She's devious and mean. Like a bully on the playground, aware my nerves sizzle and anxiety sprouts in my stomach, but instead of protecting me from my troubles, she'd rather treat me like an ant stuck beneath a magnifying glass in the summer heat, laughing while I suffer. "Tommy Watkins and his brother grew to be decent young men, Alana. Your judgment is showing."

"*My* judgment?" I jam the heels of my palms against my eyes. "How am I judging him? Not wanting a reunion in the middle of Main Street is not judgment. And, wait—" I drop my hands, blinking my eyes clear. "His brother?"

"Hmm?"

"Chris?" Soft contentment spreads through my belly, pushing aside the determined splinters of anxiety. "He's doing okay?"

"He sure is. Still pretty quiet, if you ask me. Tommy's the spokesperson for the two of 'em, but Chris always has a polite hello and holds doors for anyone coming by." Now that Tommy is gone and her metaphorical magnifying glass is rendered useless, she turns on her heels and ambles back to the couch. "They come out to the house a few times a week to help with whatever I need."

"T-to the house?" Panic surges once more. "Your house?"

"Not this week, though. I told them I had a guest and that I wanted them to stay away. Give you time to settle in."

"You told them I was coming to town?" Oh God. Save me. "You told Tommy Watkins I would be in Plainview and staying at the house?"

"No. I told him I had guests and to stay away for a few days to give you a chance to settle in." She meets my eyes. A smug, taunting glitter nestled in the depths of her stare. "Like I said. He didn't ask who my guests were, I didn't say, and though most would be curious enough to sneak a look out at the house, Tommy's been kind enough to honor my request."

"So they just..." *Breathe, Alana, you vapid idiot.* "They stayed in Plainview all this time? They never left?"

"Not sure they've been anywhere but here for more than a weekend in

50

all their lives. Except when they have their fights," she amends. "They head off to wherever they gotta go for those. But that's work, so I figure it hardly counts." She grabs a different book—Martha Stewart this time—licks her finger, and leafs through the pages.

Which means it's her book now, and I'll have to leave money in the till.

"You don't watch them on the television?" she asks, faking nonchalance. "It's broadcast all over the world."

"No, I..." I swipe a hand across my cheek. Though God knows why. It's not like I'm crying. "I don't really watch TV."

"Not even for the fights?" she presses. "Everyone in Plainview stops to watch when he's on. It's not often one of our own achieves that kind of fame, so when it happens, we pay attention." She looks up from her book and shows me her *I'm disappointed* look, a furrowed brow and pursed lips. "You were his girlfriend for a *long* time, Alana. You honestly expect me to believe you've never once watched, if only to tell your New York friends you used to know him?"

No, Mother. Because unlike you and Bossy Barbara, some of us are normal, non-coattail-riding jackasses.

"I guess I figured he'd move out to Vegas or something. Get away from here and join one of those famous gyms. He has the talent, and since Chris could go with him, there's no real reason to stay here."

"Not everyone abandons their roots," she sneers. "Those boys had it a million times worse than you ever did, but when push came to shove and family loyalties were on the line, you skipped town before the ink on your high school diploma was dry. Tommy and Chris knew their mother needed them."

"Their mother?" *Pamela Watkins is nothing but a neglectful, drug-addled, child-abusing whore. Screw that bitch and anything she wanted.* "Why would she need them? What happened?"

"Grady left about the same time you did. He hasn't been back in all this time, and Pamela was lonely, so her boys knew to stick close."

"They see her often?"

"No." Another page. "And she took off a few years later. Still, they did the right thing by her. A woman's child running to the other side of the country is cruel. Probably half the reason I'm sick."

Yeah, that's on me, you wretched bitch. Of course it is.

But I focus on the Watkins family. On Pamela and Grady, and though my heart thunders, Tommy and Chris, too.

"Is Grady still alive?" I swallow the dry ache in the base of my throat, pressing my palm to my stomach when nerves make me a little nauseous. "Do they hear from him at all?"

"Don't know. I don't ask. Franklin?" She shouts, startling me until I stumble and the bell on the door noisily jingles above my head. "Grandma Bitsy's ready to go home, and your mom turned the shop sign to closed. So I reckon she's ready, too."

"Don't shout at him." Crabby, I draw a long, lung-filling breath and exhale again until it feels like I might topple to the side and die. But then I push away from the door and stride through the stacks until I find my son buried deep in his story. "Honey?" I lower into a crouch and wait as he slowly emerges from his fictional world.

He blinks, reorienting himself. Then his eyes meet mine, and his lips curl into a sweet smile.

"It's time to go home. But you can bring that book if you like."

"That's stealing." He closes it up and slowly rises to his feet, holding the book between both hands and studying the colorful cover. "Actually, even reading it is stealing. I consumed something without paying for it."

"We'll pay so you can finish it and not feel bad." I straighten out and gently take it from his hands, holding it to my chest the way he so often does. Then I wrap his palm with mine and start toward the front of the store. "I have to pay for the cookbook that Grandma's reading, too."

"You're kidding, right?" Eavesdropping, my mom snaps her book closed and tosses it to the top of a precarious pile leaning dangerously to the side. "No need. I'm not even gonna cook any of those recipes."

I release Franklin and grab the book before the whole stack topples, and walking both to the counter, I ring up our purchases and hand Franky's book back with a wink. "Fun fact—" I look into his eyes, but my words are for my mother. "If you lick your finger and turn the pages, the book is no longer in sellable condition. Which means it now belongs to the finger-licker."

"Never refer to me as a finger-licker ever again," she sneers. "Disgustingly crass description, not at all fit for a lady."

Lady? Where? I see none.

"I consider this a celebratory purchase to signify the beginning of something wonderful and new. Today was day one, honey. New job. New life. New adventure."

"We moved here last week," he deadpans. "So today is actually day six. And besides, you've spent more than you've earned. That's not a good business model."

God, I love him. With everything in me and with every fiber of my soul, I love this little boy.

"That's true. But today is still a special occasion, and to make up for it, I won't buy *any* books tomorrow." I ring up the sale and tap the button to open the register drawer... tap the button to open the... open the... "I think the till is broken. But I'll fix this tomorrow, too."

I jot down an IOU and place it on the little screen at the top of the register, and then I bend and snatch up my purse and keys. "Let's go home. We still have to feed the animals before we have our own dinner."

"Do you think cows might change their mind about grass someday and become carnivores?"

Clueless to the way I warily approach the shop exit and peek at the street outside—*no Tommy Watkins in sight*—Franky chatters and pulls the door wide.

"I know, historically, they're herbivores. But there's a cow at Grandma's that looks at me kinda funny. And evolution exists. It's the literal changing of a species over time to ensure its survival. It's entirely possible that cows have realized leafy greens aren't enough, and it's just our bad luck that Grandma's cows are the start of something new."

"My cows are not meat eaters," Bitsy grumbles. "You're being ridiculous, Franklin."

Not convinced, he glances up in silence and speaks a thousand words with a single look. He doesn't believe her, but he knows voicing his thoughts comes with the risk of an hour-long lecture on why she's right and how rude she thinks he is.

It took me years, puberty, and a boyfriend who constantly and consistently built me up to figure her out.

But my son has her pegged in less than a week.

Smartest person I ever knew.

"You smell a bit sweaty today." I lock the shop door before leaning in and taking a long sniff of his neck. "Did you run around a lot in the park?"

He shrugs, then nods, then shrugs again, and starts toward the car. "Mostly did frog jumps. And made a friend."

"Really?" I yank him to a stop and swing him back to face me. "You made a friend?"

"She talks a lot and is kinda loud. *She* made a friend," he clarifies. "I met a peer."

"Oh, well..." I choke out a laugh and continue toward the car. "I mean, that's nice. Is she your age? Because that probably means you'll go to the same school after the summer. Knowing someone, even if they're a little loud, is a good thing, don't you think?"

"Easy for you to say." He reaffirms his grip on my hand, not yet at the *'don't touch me in public'* phase of childhood. "You're not the one she keeps talking at."

"She's Molly Jenkins," Mom inserts. "You remember Bart Jenkins? From the steel factory? Well, his son had a couple of kids. Molly is one of 'em."

"Molly." Franky's entire body trembles with faux exasperation. "Yeah. That's her. She's exhausting."

ROUND SIX

TOMMY

"Loading tree stumps into the bed of a truck is basically the same as training." I lift a log and toss it onto the pile with the others, swiping a hand over my brow and grinning for my sour brother. Because he'd rather be in the *actual* gym, drilling *actual* takedowns, and having an *actual* session to pen into his little diary.

Instead, I insist on finishing the job we started at Bitsy's more than a week ago. "It's a whole-body workout. No one else heading to Vegas is gonna train like this, so stop bitching." I bend and grab another log, my *whole body* flexing and straining as I lift the hundred pounds to my chest, then toss it higher to get it atop the quickly mounting pile. "We can still roll later. Then your life will be back on track, and everything will feel better again."

"You think you're a good guy." He knows he has to help, so he drags his shirt up to clean his sweaty brow, then dropping it again, he selects a log and bends in front of it. "All this '*I understand you're overwhelmed*' and '*I know you're not happy right now*' like you think you're a sensitive mother-fucker who can read my moods and cater to my needs. But all you really are is a sarcastic prick who uses my discomforts against me."

"Not true." I move to one end of a particularly large log and wait for him to toss his and come back to help me. "I read your moods because you have a tell for when you're frustrated. And I make decisions I know will make your life more comfortable. *Most of the time*." I grunt and lift when he takes his side, and shuffling back, I grit my teeth and prepare for when we have to get under it and toss it into the back of the truck. "I *am* sensitive to your needs, but I'm also aware that life really fuckin' sucks, and if I die tomorrow, I need to know you're equipped to deal with things on your own."

"You're not dying tomorrow." His chest grows with the extra blood circulation, muscles firing up, and adrenaline following right behind. Together, we toss the log, and when it rolls back this way, he places his palm on the rough bark and steadies it before it falls. "We came into this world together. I figure when shit starts going sideways, we can find a way to go out together."

"A suicide pact?" Chuckling, I stretch my arms high into the sky, the morning sun beating down on my back and the filthy heat penetrating already despite it barely being seven a.m. "Not a giant, concerning red flag at all."

"Not a suicide pact." He rolls his eyes. "Just a well-timed car accident and the end of a bloodline, the way it should be. Did you see Bitsy in town yesterday? She's looking frail as hell."

"Yeah." I drag my hat down to shield my eyes from the sun. "She's wasting away, and it's like no one even wants to talk about it. It's pissing me off, 'cos she's too fucking stubborn to admit it's happening, and Alana is just—"

"Alana?" He stops on a dime and looks me up and down with shrewd eyes. "Alana? Really? She couldn't stand her mother, *and* she busted out of this shithole forever ago. She doesn't care what happens back here."

"She deserves the truth, doesn't she? That her mom is dying. Even if there's bad blood and a lot of miles between them, it's her right to know. Same as we should have been told if Dad—"

"Fun fact."

A weak-ass yelp bounces from the depths of my chest as I spin and crash into the corner of the tail of my truck, thick steel bruising my back. Though, that biting pain isn't nearly as shocking to my nervous system as seeing that kid from class. His smudged glasses and messy hair.

"Um... Hello?"

"Lifting heavy things is dumb." He wears dinosaur pjs and clutches a book to his chest, his eyes swinging from me to Chris. Back and forth, then back and forth again.

The kid has a brain in his head, and he saw us together at the gym, but

I'm not sure he's ever seen identical twins up close before, and more importantly, I'm not sure he can tell us apart right now.

He doesn't like the handicap.

"If you create a pulley system, you'd make your work much easier. Better yet, use the stumps' weight to your advantage. Which one of you is Tommy?"

Like an idiot, I raise my hand. "Me...?"

Satisfied, he turns a fraction of an inch and smiles. "I thought so. But it was kinda hard to tell."

"Most people tell because one of us is always talking," Chris grumbles. "It's always him."

"W-why are you at Bitsy's at this hour?" I cast a panicked look back to the house, though all seems quiet over there. The curtains are closed. The doors, too. "Do you know her?"

He nods. Short, sharp, wordless. But fuck if his eyes don't swing back to Chris' in curiosity.

"Are you staying here? I don't presume to know you." I attempt a smile, but it falls flat when his eyes come back to mine. "But I guess it would surprise me to find out you regularly wander town in your pyjamas, that's all. You don't seem the type. So—"

"I live here now." He nibbles on his bottom lip and pushes his glasses up his nose. "With my grandma and my mom."

"And your... and..." *No. Fuck no.* "Your mom?"

"Ohhhh..." Chris sets his hands on his hips and drops his head. "Oh dear."

"Is Bitsy your grandma?"

He nods. He's not as animated as other kids his age, and it seems he's incapable of friendly chatter the way Molly so carelessly tosses words around. But he brings hazel eyes back to me, his stare like a fucking freight train to my stomach.

"A-and your mom? What's her name?"

"Don't make him say it," Chris rumbles. "You look stupid now."

"My mom is Alana Bette Page."

"Motherf—" I cling to the fury bursting through my veins. To the nausea and rage and the million other entirely unpleasant emotions that singe my blood.

I turn from the kid and stalk an easy twenty feet past the truck, if only so I don't pick the fucking thing up and throw it. "Alana Page is his mother. Alana Page is your mother?" Maniacal laughter takes me over, the sound entirely unhinged and not at all funny, rolling along my tongue and out to poison the air we breathe. "Alana Page is inside that house right now?" I shoot a pointed finger over his head, only to lower it again because if I don't, I worry it'll turn into a fucking fist. And that fist will hit things until I feel something, *anything*, other than the pain slicing at my heart. "She's here?"

"You knew she had a kid." Chris gives the boy his back and pins me with a look that would usually—in other circumstances—pull me up short. But his warning barely penetrates my senses this time. His approach hardly touches my consciousness, not even when he stops in front of me, so close that the tang of his sweat hits my lungs, and his formidable stance becomes an impenetrable wall. "You knew. We already had this fight, so calm the hell down before you scare him."

Nah, fuck that! I shove past my brother and stalk back toward the Page boy. Good fucking God, he's Alana's kid, all grown up and staring into my eyes. "You're Franklin Page?" I lower into a crouch and sniff so fucking violently I turn it into a huff akin to a charging bull. Which is legions better than the ache intent on turning me into a blubbering mess. "You didn't tell me your name in class."

"I didn't have to." He broadens his chest and meets my eyes without a single shred of fear in his. He's got that Page blood coursing in his veins. The bravery. The complete disregard for what's good for him. "It's polite to introduce myself. But it's not the rules."

"Completely agree." Chris glances up at the blistering sun and smirks. "Besides, who gives a shit about polite? Not me."

"You're Tommy Watkins." Franklin pushes his glasses along his nose, his little nostrils flaring with the movement. "You told me your name."

"D-do you recognize it?" I fight every single fucking urge in my body to reach forward and take his glasses off. They slide down anyway, and they're smudged as hell. They can't hardly be helping.

It's not my right. But fuck, I'd give anything to see his eyes without the barrier between us.

"Before you met me at the gym..." I lick my lips and search for her in his features. Her cheekbones. Her nose. Her lashes. Dammit, he's got her dimples. "Before we trained together, did you know my name?"

Did she speak of me? Did she miss me? Did she wish she had my *baby and not that asshole's from New York?*

"Franklin?" I rasp. "When I said my name was Tommy Watkins, did that spark recognition in your mind?"

He firms his lips into neutral lines. But he shatters my heart and pieces it back together, all in the space of a single beat when he nods. "Yes."

"Franky?" Her panicked voice, her shouted demand. It's like angels on the wind and nails on a chalkboard, all at once. "Franky?"

"Save us all." Chris presses his hands together in prayer. "Fuck me sideways and protect us all. It's gonna be messy."

"Franky!" Alana bounds out of the house and skids to a stop on the porch, her sinful legs on full view in tiny lacy shorts and a full two inches of her stomach exposed by a matching tank top of spaghetti straps and absolutely no shelf support.

She scans the yard with wild searching sweeps of her eyes, her chest pounding and her hands shaking because, *oh god, oh no, the big city girl can't find her kid out in Bumfuck Plainview.* But then she wrenches her head this way, and just like she could a decade ago, like doing so is a fucking *gift* she was born with, she destroys me in an instant.

Because for a mere second, when she locates her son alive and well and *not* being eaten by the killer cows, relief plays through her features. But that relief morphs into a primal kind of fear. And that look comes only when she looks past him and finds me.

"Brace yourself." Chris strides around me and grabs Franky's shirt, yanking him out of the line of fire and dragging him to the truck. He places one hand on the tailgate and holds on like they're at risk of being swept up in a ferocious storm. "The ground's about to shake. And if you think your mom is some kind of angel sent from heaven, I suggest you close your eyes and block your ears. Because she's about to crush that illusion."

"Shut up." I push up straight and try—*but fail*—to wipe the sneer from my crooked lips. Then I open my mouth like a fucking idiot and raise my voice so she can hear all the way over there on the porch, "He's fine, Momma." Fuck. There I go, saying it out loud. *Mom.* "He was just checking out what's happening in the yard."

"Franklin!" she snaps out his name, commanding him closer. But he's in no rush, and she's not willing to wait *alllll* the way over there, so she stomps down the porch steps in bare feet. Long, long legs like they go on for days, stretching from her tiny shorts, and because of her jerky movements, the strap of her tank slips off her shoulder and down to her arm.

Though she's quick to shove it back in place.

"She hasn't changed," Chris mock-whispers, coming to stand on my left. "Still pretty. Still ready to decapitate you on sight. It's like we're twelve again."

"I said shut up." I stalk forward, dogging the poor kid's steps, so when mother and child meet up, I'm right there with them, towering over the pair because fuckkkkk, I can't help but want to be near her. I want to smell her. Touch her.

Strangle her, maybe.

"Your kid is fine." *Your kid. You have a kid!* "I wasn't gonna toss him in the wood chipper, so you can calm your crazy down a few notches."

"*My* crazy?" Her eyes burn fifty shades of psychotic, just like I knew they would. She *hates* that word. "I'm crazy because I woke up, and my son wasn't in bed like he was supposed to be?"

"Your son." *Yes, Tommy. We know. She has a son.* "That's... different."

She wants so badly to scream and shout and kick something. I know it. She knows it. But motherhood, it seems, has afforded her the ability to bottle her shit up. Which is not a skill she possessed before New York, all the way back when we said stupid things like *I love you* and *I'll always choose you*.

"I didn't know you were back in town." I slide my tongue across the front of my teeth, if only to rearrange the way my lips curl into a nasty sneer. "Seems Bitsy ain't opposed to a little omission here and there." I drop my hands to my hips. Hell, I'm half tempted to put them on *hers*. "She mentioned someone coming to stay at the house, but she sure as shit didn't say who."

"Your memory must be faulty if you don't recall. She *only* ever tells half a story." Proud, and perhaps a little stupid, she glances up and stares into my eyes. "Why are you here, Tommy?"

"Here?" I look down at the ground we stand on. For the first time in ten years, we occupy the same land, we breathe the same air, and goddammit, we *could* touch... I just have to reach out. "In Plainview? I was born and raised here. Like you."

"Here, at my mother's house. You don't live here. You don't work here. You have no reason to be sneaking past Whacky anymore."

"Whacky is a stupid name for a rooster," Franklin grumbles. "It's creative, I suppose. And different. But it's a rooster. Who even names their roosters?"

"You haven't aged a day in ten years." I can't help the feral smile that crosses my lips. Or the way my heart thunders. My hands shake. Jesus, I can't help the way my stomach whooshes with nerves I'll never tell her about. "Motherhood has helped you fill out in all the right places. But maybe that was gonna happen anyway? Girls are still girls when their age starts with a one. Women become women when the one changes to a two."

"Tommy—"

"I kinda expected to still know you during those years, seeing as how we promised we would, and the girl I used to know had a reputation for standing behind her word. But liars are gonna lie, I guess. And Bitsy might've passed on the skill of telling half a story."

"Tommy!"

"Most of the other girls from school kinda filled out in similar ways, though, and not all of 'em had a kid. So maybe it wasn't motherhood at all. Maybe it's just what you were always gonna look like, no matter what."

She slams her lips closed and stares... stares... stares, until finally, she bites out a savage, "You done?"

"Talking about your body?" I lower my gaze and shake my head gently from side to side. "Not until the day I'm dead. Doubt either of us are surprised by that. Didn't expect you to sneak off to the big city and have a baby, though." *Fuckkkkk. Stop it, Tommy.* "Caught me by surprise, is all. Hopping on a Greyhound in the dead of night kinda left me shook."

"Tommy..."

"Hey, Franklin. You wanna come drive my truck?" Chris steps up behind the boy and places his hand on his shoulder, turning him, even if he isn't entirely committed to moving. He meets Alana's gaze and tips his chin in a silent hello, but then he's gone, walking away with her whole world.

Walking away with the giant fucking chasm that sits between us.

"Can we not do this?" She folds her arms but brings her hand up and nibbles on her pinky fingernail. "*I know*, Tommy. I know everything you want to say to me. But a whole decade has passed, and we're two entirely different people now."

"You contradict yourself." *Don't touch her. Don't grab on and beg for those ten years back. Don't embarrass yourself, dickhead.* "You claim to know what I'm thinking, but in the same breath, admit we're not the same people anymore. How can both be true?"

"Because you're still you! You're Tommy Watkins, which means you're pissed. At the world. At the life you were born into. At the family you were saddled with. And at me, most of all. You're pissed because I left." She brings glittering eyes up to mine. "But I'm not a teen anymore, dying to make you happy. I'm grown now, I'm a mom, I have a life that no longer includes you. So while I'll admit that leaving was shitty, which in turn makes me a shitty person, I no longer care for your approval."

"Such an odd thing for you to say. I don't recall you *ever* caring for my approval."

She drops her hand and turns, but I snag her wrist and yank her back again, our chests clashing and her sweet breath hitting my tongue with enough force to make me salivate for more.

"I always loved that about you, Lana." I grit my jaw and search her beautiful, hypnotic eyes. "Your wildness. Your refusal to conform. You were bred to be Bitsy 2.0, and punished every fucking day when you wouldn't fall in line. You refused to be the perfect clone everyone else in town expected of you."

"Let me go." Her nostrils flare with rage, her arm tensing as she attempts to escape. But she can't. Not until I allow it. "You don't get to touch me anymore, Tommy. We're not those kids anymore. I'm not yours anymore."

"Ya know..." I pull her closer, so her belly touches mine, and her strong thighs tremor enough for me to feel them. "I guess I just got lost somewhere back in our senior year. Because the last thing I knew, we were talking about busting out of this shithole together. Packing our bags and escaping where no one could find us. But then you just... you went ahead with our plans *without me*. No text. No phone call. Not even a goodbye. If you changed your mind and wanted that adventure on your own, then there wasn't really much I could do about it. But leaving me here to wonder what the fuck went wrong was a little cruel. Even for you."

"I'm not here to rehash the past." She tears her hand from mine. But she doesn't back up. *And fuckkkkk, she still smells like lavender and coconut soap.* "Life happened, Tommy. And we already know fairness is not something either of us get to count on. It's our responsibility to suck it up and move on."

"Seems like life treated you alright." I lick my lips and thrill in the way her eyes follow the movement of my tongue. "Went off to New York, got an agent, got a husband, and had a baby. All in the space of a year. Tell me, Lana, did it all happen so fast that you lost control? Or did your need for control have you seeking those things out, all so you could sever the ties that bound you to this crappy town?"

"The fact you know so much about me is concerning. I know nothing of your life."

"I know *everything* because I fucking loved you, even when you stopped loving me." I lean back and search her stricken face. "Plus, Bitsy has a big mouth and a tendency to tell anybody who'll listen how her daughter is gonna have her face all over Times Square soon. Everyone in Plainview has been waiting for the news about your book deal."

Two deep dimples flash in her cheeks, like a time machine hurtling me back a decade to when her happiness was easy to come by, and her belly laughter was saved for our adventures.

But she's not smiling now. She's not pleased *at all* with our proximity.

No. Dimples are for anger, too.

"It would be best for us both if we avoid each other." She swallows, her throat bobbing with the action and her eyes flickering between mine. "I know there's a lot of history here. I know there are hurt feelings."

I scoff.

"I know I'm the reason for all that history and those hurt feelings. But I'm not in a position to change the past, and I won't apologize for leaving town. I did what I had to do. I did what was right."

"What was right for *you*," I spit out. "With no concern for the lives you left on the road in your wake."

"If I see you in town, I'll walk the other way. If we end up in the same shops, I'll abandon my cart so you can go about your business. I won't cause a scene, and I won't interfere in your life." She backs up a step, taking the delicious coconut scent with her. "I'm here to care for my mom and raise my little boy. And seeing as how his very existence enrages you, it would be best if you stay away."

"Stay away from him?"

"From us both. I could apologize a million times over and it wouldn't fix a thing. So I won't. My only choice now is to leave you to live your life in peace. However, if I find out you've transferred even a sliver of the contempt you hold for me onto my son, if you so much as look at him sideways or make him feel like his existence is a bad thing," she stops moving and meets my eyes instead, deadly serious, "I'll take my father's hunting knife, and I'll slide it across your throat without a slick of remorse. I'll end your life, Tommy. To save my son, there's nothing I won't do."

"Why didn't you give him your husband's last name?"

My question surprises her. It wipes the sneer clear off her face.

"What?"

"Married or not, by the time Franklin arrived, that dude was in your life. He became your husband. Why is Franky's surname Page?"

"That's my business. And his." She backs up, then steps to the right and circles me. "Not yours. Come on, honey." She strides to the truck door and gifts my brother with a smile that she refuses me. "Chris."

"Alana…" He opens the door and climbs out, stretching tall and towering over her the way I so enjoy doing. "Good to see you again."

She's so fucking sad. She's hurting. But she extends her hand and waits for her son to latch on.

"I hope you'll forgive me someday. I know you're both angry, and I have nothing to say that'll make it better." She sets her free hand on his arm, squeezing gently. "If we run into each other around town, I hope, at the very least, you don't Hulk smash me into the pavement."

Chris chuckles, glancing down at her touch, then across to me like he *knows* he's stealing from me.

"Maybe you could leave Franklin home with his grandma one night soon. Head on down to Darlene's and have a drink. Tequila always did get you talking."

"Tequila is alcohol," Franklin butts in. "Alcohol is for alcoholics. Are you an alcoholic, Mom?"

She drops her hand and reaffirms the other around Franky's, then she turns, refusing me the opportunity to see the girl I once knew. "I'm not an alcoholic, honey. I promise. Now let's go have some breakfast."

"I'll see you in class on Monday, Franklin." *Fuck it. Fuck it all.* I'll burn this motherfucker to the ground.

Like I knew she would, Alana skids to a stop and swings back with a fiery glare. "What?"

"Three days a week. Guess Bitsy signed him up and forgot to tell you. And we have contracts down there now. It ain't no backyard tire-throwing outfit. We even had lawyers read over the paperwork before we rolled it out. If Bitsy committed him to the summer, then I guess that's that." I shift my focus and beam for the boy who is neither glaring, nor thrilled. He has the perfect poker face, which is a skill I never quite mastered. "I really enjoyed our session the other day. And Grandma Bitsy already paid for the whole season, so I hope you'll come back."

"You trained at his gym?" Panicked, Alana turns again and drags him toward the house. "Why didn't you tell me?"

"I told you about Molly. I said how she thinks she's my friend now."

"Pretty sure you're heading to prison." Chris meanders forward and stops when his shoulder brushes mine. "Lashing out at her and using her son? That's gonna send you down the river."

"I'm not lashing out at anyone." I stare at her long, toned legs and the small swell of ass her itty-bitty shorts expose. And because of how she twists to talk to her son and still walks forward, her tank top rides up, showing off a single tattoo roughly inked above the dimple on the right.

It's *us*. It's where we began. Fuck, it sets my heart on fire to realize she kept it, when she had ten years, a whole marriage, and plenty of opportunities to have it removed.

But she didn't.

No. She couldn't.

It's the ugliest fuckin' penmanship I've ever seen in my life.

I'd know. I put that ink there with my own fucking hands.

"Bitsy brought him to us. I see no reason not to respect a dying woman's wishes that her grandson learn how to fight."

"Right." He claps my shoulder and turns to pick up another log. "This is totally about Bitsy. Screwing with Alana is one thing. But messing with her kid is a line not even you would cross."

"Like I said." I watch them stride toward the porch and bicker all the way to the door, and though I know I'm going to hell for it, I wave when Alana's fiery eyes swing back to mine. "I'm crossing no lines. I just wanna hang out with him sometimes. Get to know the kid she'd kill for."

"Yeah. There's no way that could go bad." With a heaving grunt, he tosses a log into the back of the truck. "Stop staring and start helping. I wanna leave before the cops arrive."

ROUND SEVEN

ALANA

"You took my son to their gym?" I shove my mother's bedroom door open and find her standing at her window, her eyes on the yard and the twin boys she made damn sure to thrust back into my life. "Are you serious, Beatrice?"

Her fragility is extinguished by the taunting in her eyes, so when she slowly comes around and meets my stare, the sympathy I feel for the woman I *know* is hurting is gone, to be replaced with renewed anger.

"You had no right!"

"You will call me Mom," she warns on a low growl. "Or Mother, when you're feeling contemptuous. You won't call me Beatrice. Ever."

"I don't give a single shit about names right now!" I stride across her room and glare out her window, only to find the Watkins boys exactly where I left them, but their eyes are up here, and her window is open.

Because, of course, they get to listen in on this drama.

Snarling, I grab the window and slam it down until it closes with a crash, then I yank her curtains across, too, to claim even a modicum of privacy.

"You *know* you're wrong." I point in her face and fight every voice screaming in the back of my head that I'll pay for it. "You know my history with them, Mom! And you knew damn well I wouldn't approve, which is why you didn't tell me."

"It's a gym." Unfazed, she wanders to her dresser drawers and peruses her jewelry box for which pieces she'll wear today. "Franklin runs from

69

cows that hardly move, is terrified of a rooster older than Noah himself, and trips on his feet at least a dozen times a day. He needs socialization, to meet his peers, an opportunity for structured exercise, and a lesson on how to use the very limbs attached to his body."

"Mom!"

"He can't walk more than five feet without falling on his face." She chooses a heavy golden bangle and slips it over her hand. "It's not like I'm sending him out to the Watkins property, Alana. That gym is a legitimate establishment. One of its kind, actually, and caters to most of the kids Franklin will meet once the new school year begins. He's already at a disadvantage, seeing as he'll be the only new student there, and this is his final year in elementary school. Signing him up for the summer will help in more ways than one."

"And comes with the added bonus of pissing me off, right?" I throw my hand in the air. "You did this to assert your dominance and annoy me."

"What was that thing you said to me so recently?" She selects a chunky necklace, busy with dangling crystals, and reaches back to fasten it around her neck. "Oh. Have you considered that this has nothing to do with you at all?" Her thin lips curl into a devious grin. "He liked his lesson, even if he would say otherwise, and Eliza Darling runs the kid classes anyway, not Tommy. If you stopped throwing a fit and actually asked a few questions, you could be better informed and less melodramatic on the matter."

"Melodramatic?" Rage is like a living, vicious dragon breathing flames into my belly. "It is not melodramatic to not want my son spending time with a man who lacks filters or a *cool down* button and boasts a giant friggin' chip on his shoulder and a decade's worth of rage bottled up that was *caused by me*."

She rolls her eyes. "Your insinuation that he would treat Franklin badly because he's mad at you is ridiculous."

"He is Tommy Watkins!" I roar. "And he is pissed. He has every right to be pissed! Worse, he's had ten years to let his anger marinate. My son is not safe in that man's company."

"Ludicrous." She moves to her makeup case next and selects a fiery red lipstick. "If you thought he was capable of hurting a child, no matter the temper bubbling under the surface, then you would never have given him even a second of your time."

"You didn't *want* me to give him a second of my time! You were responsible for ninety percent of all the fights he and I ever had because you insisted I leave him in the trash where—your words—he belonged, and I refused to do so. You couldn't stand him being in my life, and you made that known every damn day we were together. But now you're on his side?"

"He's grown." She talks around the O she makes with her lips, coloring them a bright red. "He's matured. And believe it or not, but I'm allowed, and capable, to admit when I'm wrong."

"No, Mother. You're not capable, and this isn't a change of heart, no matter how sneaky you think you've been. This is manipulation because you thrive on chaos and get a sick thrill out of watching everyone else scramble around, cleaning up the messes you've made."

"You're entitled to your opinion." Infuriatingly calm, she sharpens the lines of red with her pinky nail. "Doesn't make them right."

"He is *not* going back to that gym." I have nothing to gain by remaining in this room and reverting to my fifteen-year-old self, bickering with my mother and turning my voice hoarse from the effort. Not when I remind myself I'm a grown woman now, and Franky is, in fact, *my* child. My rules, no matter whose house we're in.

I turn on my heels and swing her door open. "If you take him back there without my permission, we're leaving. I will put my son in that car so fucking fast, your head will spin. And I assure you, if you undermine my parenting like this a second time, I'll make sure you never see him again."

"You're being overly dramatic," she drawls. "It's a gym."

"And you're being exactly who you've always been. Underhanded, manipulative, and when called out on it, you stand atop your mountain of self-righteousness and declare yourself the worst treated mother who ever birthed an ungrateful child." I stalk through the door and fist the handle, and glancing back, I swallow the ache that bubbles in my throat. Because we're revisiting the same bullshit I grew up with, the same old drama and control tactics, but this time, I'm sparring with a sick woman.

"I would have thought, faced with your mortality, you'd learn to embrace the family you have." I look her up and down. "Your behavior is not okay."

"You know nothing of my mortality. Nor my intentions."

"Right. And there's absolutely no chance you could be wrong." Shaking my head, I close the door and start toward my room. I need a shower. Fresh clothes. A fucking bra—*how utterly apt that I faced Tommy Watkins today without one*—then I need to go to the bookstore and figure out a game plan for getting that place back into shape.

But when I blow into my room with the rage of a thousand divorced women, I come to a skidding stop and find Franky sitting cross-legged on my bed, his book nestled in his lap, but his eyes on me.

Shit.

"H-how much of that did you hear?" Anger burns in my throat, but I calm my movements, closing the door at my back and wandering across the room until I can lower into a crouch and search his green-eyed gaze. "I got kinda heated, huh?"

"You don't normally shout like that." He nibbles on the corner of his lips and studies me through constantly dirty lenses. "You were mean to Tommy and Grandma both on the same day."

It's this town! These people! This life, I want to scream.

But I lock those words away and nod instead. "I did. Lost my temper a little bit. I'm sorry if I scared you."

"I'm sorry I went outside and made you mad." His eyes glitter and turn red. "I didn't mean to upset you. I just woke up before you did and heard them outside in the yard. I wanted to see what they were doing."

"Do you... uh..." *God, I'm not ready for this.* "Um. So you met Tommy at the gym already, huh? And Chris. What was that like?"

He drops his gaze, lifting his shoulders and shrugging. "Tommy wasn't like how he was just before. He was silly at the gym." He pauses before leaning forward and whispering, "I even saw him use his middle fingers at someone's dad."

Of course he did. I choke out a laugh, hating how it verges dangerously close to hysteria. "Yeah?"

"He didn't mean for the kids to see it. But I did. And Chris was more talkative today than he was at the gym. He was trying to distract me from your argument with Tommy, so he told me how the truck's engine works and stuff. But I heard you anyway."

I take his hands in mine and release a gusty sigh. "You're too smart for your own good, you know that? People see a nine-year-old and assume you're like all the others. Kids your age are easy to divert. But *we* know better, don't we? You understand so much more than they think."

"I heard Tommy say you snuck out of town without telling him."

Aching and silent, I nod again.

"And you said to Grandma how he has a right to be angry. Because you did what he says you did."

Kill me. Please, universe, take me now.

"Yes. I did what he says I did."

"And he's mad because you didn't tell him you were leaving?" He rolls his lip between his teeth, thoughtfully processing my words. "You didn't want him to come to New York with you?"

Yes. I did. So, so, so much. "I couldn't take him with me." I hate that my eyes itch with unshed tears. That my nose stings and my throat burns. *I will not cry in front of my son for a man I knew before he even existed.* "Life can be cruel sometimes, honey. And even if we want something, we don't always get to have it. I can't even begin to explain it all to you—and I won't," I add when he opens his mouth. "It's not for you to know. That was my life *before,* and you're my life *now.* But yes, I left. And yes, I snuck out, even though Tommy was my friend back then. My very, very best friend in the whole world. We'd been friends for a long time, even when we pretended we weren't, and in all that time we had together, we'd made plans for how we wanted our lives to turn out. We had hopes and dreams and ideas, and we were so young and naïve, we were entirely incapable of anticipating a world where those dreams wouldn't come true."

"So you left..." Dimples, the same as mine, flash in his cheeks. "Will you ever leave me?"

"Oh, God. Baby, no!" I pull him in close and rest my ear over his pounding heart. Abandoning Tommy Watkins ten years ago nearly killed me. Abandoning my son, on the other hand, isn't something I'll do unless I'm already dead. And I swear to hell and back, I won't go down easy. "You and I are not the same as me and Tommy." I lean back and cup his face. "It's not even a little bit the same. He's just someone I used to know. I loved him," I admit, my voice crackling on the words, "I really did. But it's not the same kind of love a mom has for her child. Tommy was my past, but baby, you're my universe. You're my everything."

"You left Grandma Bitsy, too. And Colin." Too fucking smart. Too perceptive for his own good, he searches my eyes. "You leave people. So maybe you'll leave me, too."

"I leave situations that are no longer good for me. I left Plainview because I had to, honey. For the sake of my life and sanity, and for yours, I had no choice. I couldn't take Tommy with me. And Colin is just..." *Godddddd, how do I explain this to him? I can't.* "Colin is in love with Tasha. I don't consider that leaving. He wanted a chance at happiness with her, so we gave him the space he needed for that happiness to grow."

"What if I become a situation you don't want anymore?" His little heart pounds visibly in his throat. "I can be a lot, right? And I'm not normal like the other kids. I don't sleep in my own room, and I'm always asking questions. I can't sleep at night unless you're holding my hand, even though I'll be ten soon. Plus, I went outside just before without telling you, and I made you have an argument with Grandma and Tommy. If I didn't go outside, none of that would have happened."

"You're not a *situation*." I drag my hands away from his face, over his shoulders, and down to his lap until I can twine my fingers with his. "And you didn't *make* me argue with anyone. You have a right to be in your own yard, honey. My reaction to that is not a burden for you to carry. My temper is not your problem, and those fights were bound to happen anyway. That's not your fault."

"Tommy was being nice to me." He stares down at our hands, carefully tracing the side of my finger with his. "He wasn't mean or anything. Not at the gym, and not today before you came out." Slowly, he glances up and rewards me with smiling eyes. "He was kinda surprised, though."

"Why was he surprised?"

He shrugs. "I guess he could tell that I don't like to talk very much because he didn't get mad when I didn't tell him my name in class. He made me pair up with Molly, who is loud and a bit bossy, but he told her to be nice and stuff." Pausing, he leans closer and whispers, "I think he knows I'm autistic, Mom. Even though I didn't say so. And then when I saw him this morning, he was *really* surprised that I was here. He asked if Grandma Bitsy was *my* grandma, and when I said yes, it's like he didn't believe me at first."

He allows his smile to grow a little larger. "Chris was laughing at Tommy because Tommy was kinda too surprised to ask me proper questions." Then he adds, whispering again, "I think Chris might be autistic too. Maybe that's why Tommy wasn't mad that I didn't want to talk at the gym."

So perceptive. So smart.

I swallow the ache in my throat and nod. "Yeah, baby. I'm pretty sure Chris is autistic too. But he didn't go to the doctor like we did. He doesn't have a formal diagnosis."

He pulls back and relaxes, releasing the tension in his shoulders and loosening the hold he has on his jaw. Because we're no longer talking about things that hurt our hearts. "Why didn't he go to the doctor? I didn't even have to get needles for my diagnosis."

I breathe out a soft, barely there snicker and consider how much to share with a boy who absorbs too much. "Things were just... different when we were kids. And Chris' parents didn't treat them very nicely."

"Kinda like how Grandma Bitsy doesn't treat you nicely?"

"Well... no. Differently. Both homes were hard to live in sometimes, but Grandma Bitsy made sure I had food to eat and a bed to sleep in. She sometimes said things she probably shouldn't have, but she never hurt me. Not, like, she didn't kick me or punch me or anything like that."

"Did Chris' mom and dad kick and punch him?" His eyes grow wider because, to him, the thought of a parent beating the shit out of their child is simply impossible to accept. "That's assault, right? Even if—"

"Yes. That's assault. And abuse. Tommy and Chris' parents only sometimes parented. Sometimes there was food to eat, and sometimes there wasn't. Sometimes they weren't even home, for weeks at a time."

"Where'd they go?"

"We don't know. We never knew. They just went out of town sometimes and never said anything, and they didn't think about leaving food in the fridge or a babysitter to make sure the boys were okay. Doctors cost money," I explain. "And diagnoses cost a whole lot more. It wouldn't have mattered if Chris had two extra legs and three noses. Their parents wouldn't have done anything about it. But I think you're right..." I tap his sweet button nose. "I think Chris is autistic, too, and I agree, that's probably why Tommy was able to understand you at the gym. He's spent his entire life learning through his brother."

"Maybe that's why Tommy is extra mad at you."

"Maybe... what?" I pinch my brows and try to puzzle out his meaning. "I don't— You think he's mad at me because of autism?"

"No. He's mad because his mom and dad kept leaving him behind. And then you left him behind."

His words are like an arrow to my heart. But his arrow has a dull tip, wrapped in a rag dripping with gasoline, and set alight with the kind of fire that never extinguishes.

Ouch.

"Can I come to the shop with you today?" Completely oblivious to the damage left behind, he crawls across my unmade bed and off the other side to collect the shorts and shirt he laid out before we went to sleep last night. "I want to help you with your spreadsheet. And maybe we can go to the diner next door to get ice cream floats this afternoon when it's the hottest."

"Sure." I rock backward and drop to my butt, and though I don't consciously decide to do so, I massage my chest and hope the ache goes away sometime this decade. "I'd love for you to come with me today."

"And I still want to go to the gym." He wanders toward our shared bathroom, but before crossing the threshold and closing the door, he glances back with a sweet smile. "I never met an autistic person before. Especially not an adult kind, anyway."

I mean... I'm sure you have. You just didn't know it.

"Grandma Bitsy already paid for the entire summer. And I don't want her money to be wasted. Does it make you mad that I want to go?"

"No." I lower my gaze and allow my head to simply dangle. "It doesn't make me mad."

"You promise?"

"Mmhm." *Not mad. Just sad. And sore. And really, really scared.* "I promise."

ROUND EIGHT

TOMMY

I charge my brother and slam him to the cage wall, earning hisses and jeers from those who watch on the outside. Bringing my knee up and crushing his ribs, I scoop a hand between his legs, lift without a single thought for my back and the poor posture I exhibit when my temper burns hot, and spinning us both around, I dive toward the canvas and make sure he hits with the rage I've carried all my life.

"Jesus." Ollie clings to the outside of the cage, gritting his teeth while Chris heaves for fresh oxygen, and I, being the prick I am, use his moment of weakness to drag his arm and head between my legs, trapping him in my lock and choking him with his own damn arm.

"Dude!" Ollie rattles the cage. "This ain't the world title."

"Tap." I tighten my hold and slap my brother's forehead. "You're gonna tap, asshole."

"Fuck I am." Red in the face, he walks his feet along the cage, lifting his hips from the floor. "I don't tap."

"You will." I squeeze my knees closer together and watch him turn from a standard red to something verging on purple. "I'm not playing today, Christian. Give me this one."

Instead, he bridges his hips, bouncing them off the floor and stealing back an inch of freedom.

"As your treating physician, I suggest you idiots stop." Oliver stalks the perimeter of the octagon and shoves through the door. "It's my profes-sional opinion you need oxygen to live."

"Don't fucking touch him." My arms burn, and my legs scream, and still, Chris breaks the steely grip of my hold and inches around. Not free yet. But he's damn near close. "Get out of the fucking cage unless you're volunteering to spar, Doc."

Chris twists just enough to get his knees underneath him—and risks a broken neck in the process. But he's a fighter through and through, and we've been doing this shit since the womb. He draws his free arm back, then barrels it forward and slams an unforgiving fist against my ribs.

I swear, he relocates the fucking bones, probably piercing an organ I'll need later. And when I still don't release his head, he hits again. Then again. And a third time, until my lungs refuse the abuse and my legs fall open.

Instead of scrambling to my hands and knees and chasing after him, I simply fall flat, melting against the canvas and sweating myself dead. "I had you, asshole." I watch him from the corner of my eyes, in case he gets a sudden urge to *Watkins* and pile drive an elbow into my gut, but I don't bother rolling away. "You'd rather kill yourself than tap out." I wheeze for fresh air. "You could break your neck pulling that shit while I've got you locked up. But you'd rather squirm like an idiot than admit you were bested."

"I wasn't bested." He stands over me, grinning past his mouth guard and doing nothing about the sweat that drops from the edge of his chin and lands on my chest. "If I was bested, I'd be asleep right now."

Amused, Oliver chuckles and paces the edge of the octagon. Though I can't help but notice how he makes damn sure to stay out of reach.

"Both of you have untreated rage you need to talk to a professional about." He scratches his jaw. "One would rather kill his brother than admit he's in a bad mood, and the other would rather die than admit he lost a fight."

"I wouldn't have killed him," I grumble.

"I didn't lose the fight," Chris adds.

"How do you claim to be teaching the next generation with this family-friendly bullshit, all that *Kumbaya, don't hit, walk away from the fight*, when right here in the fucking cage, the Watkins boys have lost their damn minds?"

"You're overthinking it." I draw a long, chest-filling breath and roll lazily to the side. One arm, then the other. Then, twisting my hips, I make a damn good impersonation of a caterpillar after a big night out at the local bar. "The kids enjoy watching us whale on each other. It gives them their fix of bloodlust and keeps them from hurting someone else."

"Er... no." Eliza wanders forward, platinum blonde hair tied in a high ponytail and the ends tickling her bare shoulders. Unlike her older brother and sister, who chose the academic track after school, Eliza chose the gym, which means she can wear a tight crop top and itty bitty shorts and have the confidence to flash a perfect eight-pack and a body most of the guys in town want a piece of.

Not me. And not Chris. And especially not Oliver, since they're family and all that.

But everyone else, including the married kind, thinks the sun shines out of Eliza Darling's asshole.

"The kids constantly ask to try the '*Tommy Watkins Smasher*' move," she drawls. We're not her brothers like Oliver is, but I reckon she thinks of us the way she thinks of him. "They're also known to ask about the '*Chris Watkins Life Destroyer*' and the '*Twin Turbo Twister Upper*'." She sets her hands on her hips and burns us with a glare. "You're bad influences! Both of you. Supposed to be mature, grown-ass men. Business owners. Mentors to growing minds. Your average six-year-old student has more common sense than the both of you. Combined!"

I fall back to the canvas, my cheek smooshed against the floor and coated in, I loathe to admit, someone else's sweat. "You're being mean. Why do you insist on hurting our feelings?"

"Because—" She jabs a finger in her brother's direction. "The resident doctor is telling you to cool your shit or risk a fricken aneurysm. And word travels fast around Plainview now that Bitsy's out of the hospital. She was up at Bingo last night spouting out some real interesting tidbits of information."

Fuck. Me.

"Don't say it."

"Don't say what?" Oliver stands over me, scowling. "What's Bitsy yammering about?"

"Oh, you don't know?" Eliza taunts. "I heard from *four* different sources that Alana Page is back in town."

"What?" His voice cracks despite being thirty-two years old. "Alana's back? Since when?"

"She's back, alright. And oh, look at this coincidence." Eliza pins me with a sneer. "Tommy Watkins is out here fighting like he doesn't care if he breaks a bone before Vegas."

"Wait..." Oliver scrubs his eyes. "What the fuck is happening?"

"I don't wanna talk about it." My words muffle against the floor. Which is kind of apt, I suppose. This is how I felt after she left. It makes sense I'd repeat the fetal position thing now that she's back. "We're here to train, not to gossip."

"When Bitsy talks about it, it's gossip," Eliza growls. "When *we* talk about it, it's a Code Four, life-or-death situation. I saw Crazy Stanley on the way here. You wanna know what I heard?"

"Not really." *Die, Tommy. Just hold your breath and let it happen.* "His name is Crazy Stanley for a reason. I'd hardly consider his word reliable."

"He said you were out at Bitsy's this morning, having words with Alana while she was in the yard in her underwear."

"Fuckin' Bitsy," Chris chuckles. "She wasn't in her underwear. She was just... ya know. They were little jammies."

"Shut the fuck up." I close my eyes and groan. *Am I dying yet? Feels like it.* "Stop talking about her. I beg of you."

"And the crème de la crème?" Eliza seethes, coming in for her final blow, much like she does in the cage. Taunting, teasing, weakening her opponent, then BAM! "She brought her kid to town. She has a kid! What?"

"Technically, we already knew that," Chris inserts. "We just didn't gossip about it."

"She has a kid." I close my eyes and imagine myself on a deserted island somewhere in the middle of the Atlantic. No one else is there. No televisions. No fucking Wi-Fi. Just me and my alcohol, charging toward brain-dead and smiling the whole way. "He's a cutie, too. Quiet, but decent."

"He can't walk more than six feet without falling over," Chris laughs. "And he ain't shy about telling me to shut up. He wanted to listen to what his mom and Tommy were bickering about, and he wasn't having it when I tried to tell him the history of combustion engines."

Dead. Dying. Nearly gone. But I turn my face and stare up at my brother. "He was listening?"

"He was ready to rip the ear right off the side of his face and toss it out of the truck. He wasn't panicking or anything. He wasn't scared for her. But he was curious."

"Did I say anything I shouldn't have?" I try to remember back, but fuck, I think I had a stroke at some point during that conversation. "I didn't... did I?"

"Nah." He wanders across the cage, peeling his grappling gloves off and bending to scoop up a bottle of water. "You said some shit about how she left. But nothing inappropriate a kid probably shouldn't hear."

"Wait…" Frustrated, Oliver scratches the back of his neck. "Alana Page is back in town?"

"You're really friggin' slow." Eliza comes around the cage and saunters through the door. "For a guy with as much college debt as you have and a job that literally saves or loses lives, your processing speed is a little pathetic."

"Shut up." He parries her jab, swinging her around and tossing her toward Chris. "Cut me some slack. The last time I saw her, I was—"

"Arrested by your own father because you'd been streaking down Main Street?" Chris turns and releases Eliza, taking his mouth guard out and pinching the rubber between his fingers instead. "Had to call Tommy to pay bail. And bring you pants," he laughs. "Because your wang was embarrassingly small, despite it being summer and sweltering hot."

"Ew!" Eliza gags. "Can we not discuss my brother's dick, please?"

"Not small," Oliver grumbles. "And no, I saw her after that night. Graduation," he decides. "That's how long it's been."

"Gossip travels faster than light out here in Plainview." Wandering closer and lowering into a crouch, Chris searches my eyes. "What are you gonna do? She's here, and I doubt she's leaving anytime soon. Not until Bitsy's gone, I reckon."

Swallowing, I push up to my elbows and desperately search for Oliver.

He throws his hands up in surrender. "I'm not discussing it."

"Ollie—"

"I can't discuss it!" He charges through the cage door, stomping down the steps and onto the matted floor. "Absolutely not happening."

"Give us a hint?" Chris bargains. "Cough if she has, like, three months or less. Scratch your ear if it's three-to-six months. Do a cartwheel if it's not terminal at all."

"I'm going for a shower." He snatches up a towel and storms toward the hall. "Leave me the hell alone."

"Have a shower if it's six to twelve months," I call out. "Oliver?"

"You know he can't say." Eliza begins her warmup, lifting her legs into *check* position, then lowering them and switching sides. "He could lose his license if he did."

"Do you think she'll leave again once Bitsy dies?" Forlorn, I drag my gaze around and search for my brother. "Head back to New York once it's done?"

Of course he doesn't know. He couldn't. So he shrugs and slips the mouth guard back in. "I'll spar with you, *Darlin'*. Get my blood pumping again, but without having to sniff my own brother's ball sack."

"There's something sincerely wrong with you." Eliza begins circling the cage, bouncing and fixing her ponytail while she moves. "Guys, in general, are fucking weird."

"Not *all* guys." He jabs, knocking her off balance when she comes too close. Though his hit is barely more than a push. His smile, too fucking pure.

She's the baby sister he never knew he wanted. And now, either of us would set the town alight if she ever left.

But who am I to say? That could be residual trauma.

"There are *some* guys in the world who are decent. Not us," he volunteers, sweeping his leg out and wiping her off her feet with a fast, vicious move. But he grabs her hand while she flies, slowing her transition to the ground and standing over her when she lands. Then he grins. "Tommy and me, and Ollie, too... we're all fuckin' idiots. But I'm sure there's some kind of prince out there, just waiting for his chance to romance you."

"I'd rather fight." She yanks him off balance and scissors her leg out to buckle his knees, then she rolls to the side when his two hundred-something-thing pounds come tumbling down. "Men are exhausting. My sister has the right idea; she understands the merits of a rubber penis and avoiding men altogether."

Drained, I climb to my hands and knees, then to my feet, while my brain swims and my vision turns dark at the edges. But I start toward the cage door before they pull me into their shit. "So we *can't* talk about your brother's tiny, naked penis. But it's cool if we talk about your sister's penchant for dildos?" I shove through the gate. "That's how this is gonna go?"

"It's how it is." She stands over Chris and slams her knee into his gut. "It's how it's gonna be forever. Get up, bitch." She taps his cheek. "You're being a baby."

ROUND NINE

ALANA

"Books Books Books..." I set my elbows on the newly cleared desk and my chin in my hands, and while Franky types away at the ancient computer, I stare at the ugly, peeling stickering on the windows that face Main Street. "Was there literally no other options for them when they named this place? *Books Books Books* is the absolute best they could come up with?"

"Well... if we're talking about metadata, I suppose it was the smartest option of them all."

I tilt my head to the side and study my son's profile. "What?"

"Metadata is the data that explains other data." He stops typing and turns to me with a broad smile. "Fun fact: metadata began as an organizational system within libraries. Which makes Books Books Books not only a smart choice but historically, it's cleverly accurate, too."

"Honey..." I exhale. "You're hurting my brain."

He twists back to continue working. "If someone is driving through town and looking to buy books, so they jump to Google or even ask a random lady on the street, what do you think the first suggestion might be?"

"*Books Books Books*?" I poke my eyes and pray the new pain will distract me from the headache pounding in the back of my skull. "But it's just so bland."

"Says the writer," he quips. "Of course you'd prefer something else. Maybe ask Mrs. Middler if you could change it."

"We *are* here to breathe new life into the store." Closing my eyes, I feel around blindly for my pen and the stack of Post-Its that've had a workout since we arrived this morning. Then, opening my eyes once more, I write; *New store name?* "I'll ask. I want to mention restocking the fridges, too, and maybe updating the coffee machine to something a little less..."

"Broken?" he offers seriously. "It's being held together by rust."

"Maybe one of those automatic pod machines, so customers can help themselves. It would create an atmosphere of relaxation, and those machines are pretty cheap. Entice customers in with the free coffee, and keep them here to buy books. It would pay for itself pretty quickly."

"You need to ask about Mrs. Middler's grandson helping to move all the books, too." He taps enter on the old keyboard and moves to the next line of his spreadsheet. He creates macros and algorithms—words he taught me—and makes it so I can enter the name of a book on one page, and it'll automatically populate across a dozen more where needed. "There are too many for us to move on our own and—"

The bell above the door jingles, drawing Franklin and me around in sync, but I doubt his stomach drops the way mine does when I meet the beautiful hazel glare of a Watkins twin.

My heart seizes, and my vision darkens. But it takes only a moment for panic to make way for relief. For horror to clear out and my lungs to relax. Those boys might be identical to the rest of the world, but to me... even after all this time...

"Chris?" I press a hand over my pounding chest and lean forward to look past his broad frame, searching the sidewalk in case the other Watkins boy—*man*, now, I guess—isn't out there. "Um..."

"It's just me." He wanders in with an easy smile and a split lip—one is a surprise to me, the other isn't. Then, closing the door, he glances to Franky and lifts his chin in hello. "Franklin. How's it going?"

"You're not Tommy." He goes back to tapping on his computer. "You look the same to me. But Tommy is angrier."

"Kinda ironic," Chris chuckles. "Normally, folks say the very opposite about us." Pulling a cap off his head to reveal dark brown hair, he fusses with the bill and meanders closer. Still, he leaves an easy eight feet between us. "Alana. Heard you were taking over for Mrs. Middler." He glances along the aisle nearest him and nods his approval. "Got a hell of a job ahead of you."

"We were just saying how Mrs. Middler's grandson should come to help us move the books," Franky murmurs. "There are a lot here."

"We could help." Chris's eyes flicker with kindness, though that flicker dies away pretty quickly. "Or *I* could help. Just me."

"What are you doing here, Christian?" I angle my stance, placing myself between him and my son. "It's not a coincidence you came in here today, and we both know you're not looking for a new book to read. So say what you've gotta say, then let us get on with what we were doing."

"That's how it's gonna be, then?" His jaw clenches with the million words he doesn't speak. The countless thoughts that pass through his intelligent brain. "I didn't realize we were enemies. I didn't even realize we weren't friends. I just know that, at one point in my life, you were basically my best friend—you and Tommy both—and then, the next, you left town."

"Feels like Groundhog Day." I sigh. "I already had this discussion."

"I'm not him." He jabs a finger toward the door, his temper slipping when he so easily, under other circumstances, keeps it on a tight leash. "I'm not Tommy, and when I ask you these questions, it's not for the same reasons. But you have to forgive me for being confused, Alana. Forgive him, too. Because our world was normal, and then it wasn't. There was no warning. Not even smoke signals in the sky. You'd make this transition a hell of a lot more comfortable for everyone if you explained what the hell happened back then."

"I don't have to explain." I turn to my son and wait for his eyes. "Can you go to the storage room out back and get my purse?"

"You want me to leave so you can talk to Chris in private?"

I cough out a soft laugh. And still, I nod. "Yeah, honey. Just for a few minutes. Could you give us that privacy?"

"Fine." He snags his Murdles book and steals my pen, then circling the counter, he comes to a stop in front of Chris and looks up at the man who was once a brother to me. A part of my heart. "I'm going to be cranky at you when my mom is cranky at you. That's what loyalty means."

"Uh..." Nervous, Chris' eyes flitter momentarily to mine, then back to my son again. "Sure. You're absolutely right."

"But I'm also coming to class this afternoon. Me and my mom talked about it, and she agreed I could. So when I'm in class, I won't be cranky at you."

"Well..." He rubs his chin. "That sounds fair."

"Cranky-Me and Normal-Me aren't really very different. You probably won't notice. So I just wanted you to know I'm cranky at you right now. But later, I won't be."

"Honey..."

"I'm going to the storage room now." He lowers his chin and turns, stiff jaw and shoulders rolled back to emphasize the thickness of his chest. "I'll come back in five minutes. I'm setting a timer, Mom."

"I believe you." I watch him maneuver the overcrowded aisle, stepping around piles of books and through an archway that really should be my priority as we start the clean-up of *Books Books Books*. In the event of even the smallest tremor in the tectonic plates below Plainview, that stack will fall first. And the fact I even know the word tectonic is thanks, of course, to my son who read a book from cover to cover on the subject... *last night*.

"He's somethin'." Amused, Chris' chest vibrates with laughter he doesn't allow to become audible. "Smart cookie."

"Mmhmm." I bring my gaze back to his and lift a brow. "I don't know how else to say all this, Chris. I left. Plainview became my past, and my little boy became my future. He needs me. There is nothing else for me to focus on except those facts."

"*We* needed you. We were a team; you, me, and Tommy. And even though you and Tommy were an item, you never once made me feel like I didn't belong."

"Chris—"

"And then you left. We thought you fucking died or something, Alana. We thought something absolutely horrible must've happened because the girl we knew from before, *that* Alana, would have never left us. She would fight to the death to stay by our side. And she could fight," he growls. "She wasn't gonna lay down for nobody."

I swipe my cheek, a sizzling tear horrifyingly slipping from my eye. "Please, stop."

"You didn't fight for us. You didn't even try. It's like we didn't even fucking exist anymore. New York lights shone bright in your eyes, and that was just... it was..." He draws a rattling breath. "You started a whole new life like Plainview never happened. That's where we keep getting stuck, Alana. Not that you left. Not even that you married up and had a kid and created a whole life. You weren't the first, and you won't be the last small-town girl who ditched out after graduation in search of something more."

"Please, Chris—"

"But *why*?" He groans. "We need the why. If you wanted to go, then that's cool; he would have come with you. If you didn't want to be with him, then that's cool, too; he wouldn't have liked it, but he's not the type to tie an unwilling woman down and take what's not freely given."

A devastating sob tears along my throat and out to humiliate me.

"His heart was destined to break no matter how it shook out. And that, too, is cool. Not *great*." He scoffs. "But hearts break every damn day across this country. If that's how it was gonna go, then that's how it would go. But *why*?"

"I can't tell you." I search for the box of dusty tissues under the counter and tear a handful out to wipe my nose. "Don't make me tell you, Chris. I won't."

"Not even a text!" he booms. "Not even a letter. Not a fucking social media post. There was nothing. So, to us, it's like you died. I had to save my brother's life a hundred times because of you. I had to stop him from leaving me here all a-fucking-lone. Your absence shattered him worse than anything either of us has ever experienced—*combined*—and you were... what? Busy falling in love with someone else? What the fuck is that?"

"I can't explain my actions." I swipe my tears and pray Franky's five-minute timer malfunctions, allowing me longer to get myself under control. "I could. But I won't. Because the past is the past, and my son is the future. I will not drag him into what used-to-be, all so a couple of grown men can soothe their hurt feelings. I know I hurt you." I glance down, folding my tissues. "I know it wasn't fair. Goddddd, Chris, I know it sucks. But it happened, and there's nothing I can do to change it now."

"So that's it, then?" He sets his hands on his hips and tilts his head back to stare up at the ceiling. "You change all our lives, making those decisions for the three of us without so much as a *hey boys, we're trying something new*, and now you get to slip away from accountability with '*I said so*'?" He brings his focus back down, slamming me with haunted eyes that redden with emotion. "The discussion won't be revisited because *you say so*?"

Words fail me, replaced instead with a dizzying lump nestled in the base of my throat. So I nod. And mop the fresh tears that dribble onto my cheeks.

"Did you know Colin before you left here?" The muscles in his jaw clench and release. "Is that what happened? You met him—however, wher-ever—and realized you wanted him more than you wanted Tommy? So you hop a bus and head to the big city?"

"No, I—"

"You were married and pregnant in five seconds flat! Either you knew him already, which implies, at the very least, an emotional affair with the man you ran toward, or you met him the same fucking day you got off the bus, went to bed, and married up right after. Which," he burns me with a glare, "I gotta say, that girl *I used to know*, the one whose every fucking breath was dedicated to my brother, I wouldn't have believed she was capable of somethin' like that."

I have no words. No defense. I have nothing helpful to offer because the truths I *do* have will only hurt. So, I say nothing at all.

"Are you leaving again once Bitsy passes?"

"Passes?" My heart gives a painful thump, bruising my ribs, surely. "She hasn't said... she isn't..." I lick my dry lips and sniffle. "Is it that bad?"

He shrugs. Cold and callous. "She's not saying. But you know how that Plainview gossip vine works. Word travels fast, and I figured with how she looks, that her condition is kinda serious. You coming back to town basically confirms what I suspected."

"I don't know." My voice crackles and breaks. "She hasn't said anything. My circumstances changed in New York, and at the same time, she called and asked us to come back. She said she needed help at the house, and I..." *I needed to give Colin space, anyway.* "Circumstances changed."

I fold my arms, crossing them over my chest in a kind of defense mechanism. But the movement draws his eyes, the hazel pair latching onto the ring wrapped around my finger.

"You're married."

"Yes."

His nostrils flare, which, to a girl who studied this boy every single day of her youth, means he wants to say some things that might hurt my feelings. But instead of doing so, he clamps them down and chooses something else instead. "Do you love him?"

"It's a kind of love." I unravel my arms and link my fingers behind my back instead. "Yes. I love him."

"You going back to him when you're done with Plainview?"

"No." I spin my ring, around and around and around again. "No. He's moving on with someone else."

Intrigued, he rocks onto the backs of his heels. "You planning to come see Tommy?"

"No, I—"

"It would be the right thing to do. Might hurt—you and him—but it's a bit like a festering sore, don't you think? It's infected and weeping, and the wound keeps opening because no one is healing. But maybe if you came by and discuss a truce, things might start to scab over a little bit."

"A truce?" I lower my gaze and laugh, if only to myself, and barely audible to my own ears. "Tommy Watkins doesn't know truces. He knows war. He knows savagery and victory." Slowly, though it aches my heart to do so, I bring my eyes up again and cling to the man who looks just like the other. It's not the same, but damn, I could give convincing myself a real try. "Tommy didn't become a fighter all so he could discuss peace treaties with his opponents."

"He became a fighter because he's good at it. Because he doesn't know how to quit. But that's just a sport. It's not who he is in his heart."

No. I am who he is in his heart. Or at least, I used to be.

"I think it would be best if I kept to myself." I drop my eyes again. "He wants answers I can't give, which means his wounds won't heal. For every contact we have, the infection only grows worse."

"And knowing that..." He bites out his words as fury battles for dominance. As his temper attempts to override the tight rein he has on it. "Knowing he can't—*he won't*—heal, you're content keeping your secrets?"

Fresh tears well up and sting the backs of my eyes, but the sound of the storeroom door creaking open and, right after, Franky's sneakers on the floor gives me all the notice I need. I wipe my nose and slowly nod. "Yes. I'm content. I have to be."

Disgusted, Chris shakes his head and digs large hands into his pockets. "Not the girl I *used to know*." But he looks to his left and smiles when Franky comes into view. "Was that five minutes already? Went pretty fast."

Franky crosses no-man's-land, striding past the desk and stopping by my side, he takes my hand in his. "Felt like forever to me. Why did you make my mom cry?"

"Oh, no, honey." I sniffle and hurriedly wipe my cheeks. "He wasn't mean to me. Sometimes people cry because they're feeling big emotions. Sad or happy. It happens."

He scours my face with narrowed eyes and brows that pinch close together. Then he casts his ire toward Chris and does the same. "You made her feel big feelings."

Chris chuckles, because hell, what else can a person do in these situations? "Unintentionally, I guess. I wasn't trying to." He takes a step back and dips his chin in farewell. "I'll see you at class, alright?" But then he looks my way. "You remember Eliza Darling?"

"Little Eliza? Ollie's sister?"

"Yeah, her." He brings his hat up and sets it on his head. "She's all grown now. Twenty-two and a killer fighter that's already made a name for herself on the pro circuit."

"Seriously?" She was a child the last time I saw her. With pigtails in her hair and stars in her eyes every time she looked at the Watkins boys. "She's a fighter now? She, uh..." I clear my throat. "She spends a lot of time at the gym?"

Don't say it, Alana. Don't even fucking think it.
You lost that right a long time ago.

So I stare down at my shoes instead, shame washing through my veins. "Cool."

"She runs most of the summer program with the kids. Tommy's got his next big fight coming up at Christmas, which means we'll be busy prepping him for that. So if you're worried about coming to the gym to watch Franky train or whatever... if you think you'll run into people you don't wanna..."

"He means Tommy will be busy and not there, Mom." So helpful. So logical. Franklin twines our fingers together and smiles up at me. "You can come watch me."

"Okay..." Nerves are like ferocious wings beating in my stomach, pushing nausea up and common sense down. "Thanks." I bring my eyes back to Chris. "I appreciate you letting me know."

"And since not *everything* has changed in the last decade—" He grabs the door handle and yanks it open, sending the bells into a frantic jingle that fills the shop. "I'll have you know I saw that jealousy in your eyes, Alana Bette." Finally, his lips curl into a playful grin. "Sure is interesting to me."

"You're not even gonna put me out of my misery, are you? Tell me what I want to know?"

"Nope. Besides, you're a married woman." He steps through the door, his chuckle rolling back on the breeze. "That kind of information isn't really relevant anymore. Plus, you left me, too. And I'm not ready to forgive yet."

"Bye, Chris." Franky releases my hand and meanders toward the door. "See you at the gym."

"Bye, Franklin Page. See you when I see you."

ROUND TEN

TOMMY

"Circle and dip." I swing out with my padded hand and skim the top of Eliza's ponytail. And because she ducks—barely in the nick of time—I follow her around and drive my foot into her gut. Hard enough to steal the air from her lungs and push her back a half-dozen steps, but not so hard that either of us would consider it anything but training.

"You're gassing out." I swing again, but this time, I stop before wiping her out and knocking her head off her shoulders. "You wanna beat Chavez next month, but you're slow as fuck and puffing like a fat sixty-year-old couch warrior."

"It's a hundred degrees in here." She drops and swoops forward for the takedown, wrapping her arms around my torso and slamming her shoulder into my stomach. And because she's quick with her foot, she sweeps it behind mine and uses our momentum to drive me into the mats. Fast as a viper, she scrambles over top of me and rains fists over my face.

Though I have my training pads to block every single strike.

"Not so slow now, am I?" She sets her hands on my chest and uses me to lift herself up, then slams down again and digs her knee into my ribs. "Not gassed. You're just fresh, and I'm sparring after six hours in this oven."

"You'd win more if you talked less." I trap her hooked leg with mine and throw her to the side, crushing her to the mat and crowding her so she has nowhere to go. No escape. No fucking chance. Not even a kid who spent her life inside a fight gym will beat a guy twice her size.

Not when he's spent his life in the gym, too.

"You think Chavez is gonna gossip with you in the cage, Lizey-Lou?" I toss my pads and smack her ribs, bare-knuckle and just hard enough to elicit a grunt from the depths of her chest. "You think she won't consider it her honor to shut your mouth with her foot?" I hit her again and hold on. She's a bucking bull, trying to toss more than two hundred pounds off while frantically searching for fresh air. But we're both sweaty and every time she tries, her grip slips. "You don't turn up to that fight with your war face on, she's gonna mop the floor with your pretty hair."

"Aww. You think I'm pretty?" She twists and slams her elbow into the side of my neck, buying back a little of her defensive positioning and pulling her legs from mine. She circles my hips instead, locking her feet in and digging her heels into my back. "I just had it done at the salon." She whacks me again, stabbing me in the throat with that bony elbow. "Spent six hours in the chair to look like this."

"That doesn't look appropriate."

Stunned, I wrench my head up and lock eyes with a little boy whose smudged glasses can't hide the way his pupils grow wide and his cheeks glow red. But it gets worse. So much fucking worse when I peek to his left and find his mother, her hand clamped over her mouth and her body already half turned back the other way.

Then I look down at a smiling Eliza, her chest heaving, her tits straining her sports bra, and her legs draped around my body in ways that can't possibly look good.

"Uh..."

"So sorry." Alana grabs Franklin's hand and yanks him along with such speed, the poor kid's glasses skid along his nose. "We're leaving. We didn't—"

"Alana Page..." Entirely too pleased with herself, Eliza lies flat against the mats, dropping her arms so she becomes half a starfish. But her legs stay put. She makes fucking sure they do. And because she enjoys setting shit on fire, she twists her neck and presents a smug, beaming smile. "I heard you were back. Figured I'd see you at some point."

"Eliza..." Wary, with a side of straight-up fucking furious, Alana inches back this way and studies the scene we make. This is shit we do every day in the gym. Guys and girls. Guys with guys, and girls with girls. There's never been a part of me, not once in the history of my entire life, that has questioned being twisted up with another human like this.

Never have I stopped and thought, '*Hey, this looks bad.*' Because it's not bad. It's a sport.

But why, now, do I feel Eliza's heels pressed to my spine and her quiet laughter when I try, and fail, to dislodge those feet?

"You're uh..." Alana tries, so fucking hard, to keep her focus on Eliza's eyes and not mine. "All grown up."

"Not twelve years old anymore." To make things worse, she hooks her arm over the back of my neck and uses me to pull herself up. If I were to sit on my haunches, she'd come too and would end up sitting right on my lap.

I do not *sit back on my haunches.*

"You must be Franky?" Eliza practically hugs me, smooshing our cheeks together, and grins like the whole world is her playground. "I was told I had a new summer student coming in today. Sorry, I missed you at your first session."

He rolls his lips between his teeth and studies her a little longer. Then me. Then back to her again. "Do we have to do what you're doing in class?" He wrinkles his nose and pushes his glasses up. "I don't like to hug people like that. Except for my mom."

Alana drops her head and groans in defeat.

"Well, we were practicing takedowns," Eliza continues. "And then ground and pound. It's part of the sport."

"Don't call it pound," I snarl in her ear. "Stop it."

"Ground and pound is my *favorite*. Some people prefer stand-up combat, and others prefer takedowns. But me—" She squeezes me tighter and snuggles in as close as humanly possible. "—I like a good pounding on the ground. Jiu jitsu is where your size doesn't matter so much. Your skill does. So even when someone is twice as big as you and maybe even stronger, I still have a decent chance of getting out of a situation. Plus." She grips my neck. "The hugs are fun."

"Come on." Alana grabs Franky's hand again and jerks him around. "We didn't mean to interrupt."

"Mom—"

"That's a private training session," she hisses. "Let's go."

"You're an ass." I pinch Eliza's ribs and breathe again when she flops to the floor, her arms and legs falling wide and her taunting amusement beating like a drum in my veins. "You knew she was coming in, didn't you?" I climb to my feet and snatch up a towel to wipe my face. "You fucking knew, which is why you made damn sure we were rolling right when Alana was due here."

"I fail to see the issue." She moves to her elbows and knees and drops her head, giggling. "You're a free agent, Boss, and I'm heading to competition soon. Seeing as how it's summer, which means a lot of my training time is eaten up with kids, I thought we'd both agreed that it was important I spar with you as often as I can."

"We both agreed you're an ass." *Stellar comeback, Stupid.* "You think you're protecting me with that shit?" I snag my water bottle and start toward the door. "*Poor Tommy Watkins got his heart broken, and now the she-devil is back. Gotta make sure she knows her place?*"

"You called her the she-devil. Not me. And I reiterate; what's the problem? This is what we've always done. Why is it a big deal now?"

I stop in the doorway and peek into the hall because *fuck, what am I gonna do if I find her?*

Nothing, probably.

I glance back at the girl I would kill for. The sister I would destroy others for. The kid I would trap in a locker room for half a day if it meant annoying her and buying myself a little quiet. But when she only laughs, I turn on my heels and stride into the hall.

I mop my sweaty chest and squirt a little water into my mouth, and though one would expect to need to use eyes to find Alana Page, I'm disgusted to realize I can do it with my nose.

Ten years has done nothing to dull that fucking ability.

I follow the smell of lavender all the way through my gym, the stench of sweat and boxing gloves that never truly dry trying, but failing, to throw me off track. I walk past the regulation-sized cage and around the row of hanging bags, then past the group of kids who mill around and wait for Eliza to get her shit sorted. I hate the ball of lead that falls to the base of my stomach when I make it all the way to the sign-in desk and *don't* find Alana and her little Franklin.

I should just let her go. Allow her space and, if I'm lucky, drown myself in the dunk tank out back. But of course, I stride straight through the gym's front door and stop in the blistering sun, shading my eyes with a lifted hand and opening my mouth long before my brain has time to process.

"Alana, wait."

She attempts to coax her son into the car, fussing hands and hissed instructions. But the boy doesn't want to go, and unless she picks him up and lobs him in, I'm not sure she's gonna win this round.

"I didn't mean to interrupt." Though Franklin slams the car door, she opens it again and tries to usher him forward. *Oh, what she would give to be laying rubber on the road already.* "Franky said how he had class at three o'clock, and I was under the impression you wouldn't be here. My mother conveniently claims to be too busy to bring him today, so I had to do it. But I—"

I wipe my face with the towel and start into the parking lot, bare-chested, barefoot, and so fucking filled with rage and bloodlust, I make sure *not* to toss my water bottle.

I hate to think what would happen to Alana's pretty little neck if I suddenly had a free hand.

"Class starts in a minute, Franklin." I come to a stop a few feet from the pair and note his sneakers. His jeans. Glasses. "Go inside and ask Eliza to get you a pair of grappling shorts from the stock cupboard."

"No, thank you," Alana growls. "I'll buy him shorts myself. We'll come back once we've done that."

"I'm not offering you charity." I hook a thumb over my shoulder and wait for the boy to stumble back toward the gym door. "You'll pay for the shorts." I keep my words low, harsh, knowing they're for Alana only, though her eyes remain on his back and linger for a full minute after he's gone. "I'll have Eliza add the cost to your account. There are no handouts at this gym."

She drags her gaze from the door, but only to send them *up* to the signage that spans the entire length of the building. "Love and War." She reads each word slowly, pained with every syllable that crosses her lips. "You called it Love and War?"

"All's fair." I wipe my face again because my blood still runs hot, and the sun pelts down against my sizzling skin. "Locals mostly call it the war room, though. Ollie came up with it 'cos his daddy's a cop."

Her breathing is choppy. Staggered and shallow. But slowly, she brings her eyes to mine. "Ollie?"

"Darling. He was a couple of grades above us in school. I know it's been a minute since you were last here, but I bet if you tried, you'd remember him. He was a friend to you, even back then."

"I remember him." She keeps a tight hold on her temper. Fiery eyes and a clenched jaw. "Why'd you name it Love and War?"

"Why not?" I drink a little more water before I sweat everything out and risk dehydration. "Spent my whole life in one or the other. Sometimes, both at the same time." I take a step back. Though, fuck, I don't go far. I can't, even if I tried. "You coming in out of the heat?"

"Do I have to?" She clings to her car door like she's afraid the car will roll away without her. "Is it customary for parents to stay while their kids train?"

"Yes. In fact, it's in the rules when you join the gym. Something about liabilities and whatnot." Or *lie*-abilities. But hell, I haven't owed her a damn thing, least of all the truth, in ten long years. "Heard you're working over at *Books Books Books* now?"

She drops her gaze and exhales a huffy, chest-shrinking breath. But she closes her car door, at least. One step closer to *not* running away. "I forgot how ridiculously quick the gossip vines work around here."

"New York City is all about anonymity, I suppose. There are so many folks out there it would be impossible to be in anyone else's business except those in your immediate vicinity. Plainview's all about knowing everyone's everything. It's a hobby in a town where there's nothing else to do."

"I didn't miss it." She clasps her hands together and watches her feet. But at least she slowly starts toward the door. "You and Eliza Darling, huh? That's... cute."

I glance across and feel, for the first time in as long as I can remember, happiness beat through my chest. Humor, even. Deliria, most likely. "Eliza Darling is a child. It could be the time away makes it easier for you to see a grown woman. But I never left, which means when I look at her, I'm still looking at a twelve-year-old. Putting her in the cage against another grown-ass woman and hoping she doesn't die—well, that's different. But in all other facets of life?" I drag the gym door open and gesture for her to go first.

To be a gentleman, I wonder, or to see if her shirt rides up and shows off the ink on her back?

Definitely the second.

Unlucky for me, she's not wearing a sleep camisole anymore, and the top she chose for *Books Books Books* is entirely professional and appropriately fitted.

"Chris suggested we discuss a truce." She slows her steps and peeks back, shyly searching my eyes as I release the door and meander closer. "He came by the bookstore earlier and said some stuff."

"Yeah?" The mere talent it takes to *act* casually, even while my heart burns and my stomach turns to acid, is, in my humble opinion, better than anyone who ever received an award at the academy shows. "Chris always did find time to hang out with you, even while I was busy elsewhere. You were like siblings, so if I wasn't available, he still came to you and felt at peace. You never seemed like you minded."

"I didn't mind." She comes to a screeching stop and looks up when Oliver Darling strides out of the hall. Her cheeks pale, and her eyes shimmer.

But when he skids to a standstill and looks from her, to me, to her again, I get the distinct feeling he was coming to find me anyway. To warn me she might be near.

"Oliver..." Alana's voice cracks. But she doesn't dare step forward. Nor back. She doesn't go in for a hug, though ten years ago, she would have. Fuck, we spent our whole lives growing up in this shithole town, running around wild and getting into stupid situations our parents would've belted us for. All of us.

Me and Alana, Chris, Ollie, and his sisters. We were a group of heathens who lacked fear and possessed barely an ounce of common sense between the lot of us. But when Alana Page snuck out of town without a single word of warning, what was once a rat pack of unbreakable bonds became... broken.

Just, broken.

"Alana." He scratches the back of his neck, a nervous tic he's had since boyhood. "I, uh..." He looks at me again. *What the fuck do you want me to do, Boss?*

"You can keep going," Alana rasps, stepping to the side. "Wherever you were going or whatever you were doing. We don't have to do this awkward back and forth. I understand."

"Maybe next time." Hesitant, he shuffles past her and stops on my right, dropping his hand to my shoulder and meeting my eyes. "Was hoping to have a word with you if you had a sec?" He tries to push me back a step. "About the class schedule."

About Alana.

But even she knows he's lying, so she continues past the desk on her own, chewing on her nail and disappearing into the hall without me.

"Tommy...?"

"I'm handling myself." I shake his hand off. "Leave me alone."

"You're handling yourself?" He grabs me again, earning a fiery glare when I swing my eyes around. "Dude, you already died once. You don't get to come back from that twice. Chances are, just as soon as Bitsy no longer needs her, she'll probably leave again. It's best if you keep your distance and wait her out. She's a summer blip at best."

Funny, seeing as how we fell in love in the first place during the summer between elementary school and middle.

"I'm not gonna do anything stupid." I push his hand off and jerk my shoulder out of the way when he tries to grab on. "If she's temporary, then I'm gonna use this time to get closure. Get answers, maybe."

"Not everyone gets closure," he growls. "Sometimes, there is none. There's just a trip down the yellow brick road, and when you get to the end, you fucking die. Again."

"Leave me alone—"

"Tommy!"

"I'm not asking." I turn on my heels and move into the hall, following Alana's sweet scent and the sound of a dozen children shouting their *kiais*. But when I reach the main training room, a feral swish of panic storms through my gut. She's not here. I don't see her sitting along the wall with the other parents, nor someplace else, all alone and nervously destroying her nails.

For a single moment, I wonder if this is what may be best? Is this what the rest of them are trying to protect me from?

Blinding pain, just like when I was eighteen and couldn't find her, comes surging back. A reminder of the terror I felt back then, as fresh now as if this was our senior year all over again.

But then Eliza coughs from the front of the room and tips her chin until I turn and find Alana huddled as deeply into the corner as she can physically get.

Folded arms and frightened eyes. She's shrunken down as small as humanly possible and tugs at my heart because her vulnerability now is just as palpable as it was when we were kids, when she needed refuge with a person *not* intent on making her question every thought that passed through her mind. Every memory. Every belief.

Maybe I care for Bitsy these days, and maybe when the time comes and we have to bury her, I'll shed a tear for the old duck and send up a prayer that whatever comes next will be kind to her. But she was always, and will forever be, a master manipulator. And Alana was her target. Day in, day out. If Alana questioned anything, Bitsy rode her narrative until she was blue in the face, and her daughter, so sweet and sad, doubted her own sanity.

That's what drew us together, I think. Her need to escape a mother who twisted words with expert precision, so she came to a guy who never twisted a damn thing. And I needed her, my safe haven from the people who considered kicking the shit out of their sons a sport.

Her touch was healing. Which made us exactly what the other needed.

Until we weren't, that is.

"You wanna go to my office or something?" *Shut the fuck up, Tommy. You're angry, remember? You're furious.* "No one will stare at you in there."

Her cheeks warm, and her eyes glitter. I know she tiptoes atop a wire-line that, if she falls, will leave her destroyed.

But she clamps her lips shut and shakes her head. Then, she shifts to the right and makes a point of watching her son.

Her son.

She has a son.

Do *I* want to go to my office? Tie a rope around my neck and take care of business, maybe. Seek Oliver out and invite him into the cage? If I lay there long enough, he might beat me half to death and give me something different to hurt over.

I do neither. Instead, I back up to the wall and shield her from the curious gazes of the other parents who stick around for class.

"You don't have to do that." She speaks barely above a whisper, sniffling and hiding the sound amongst the shouted cries of training children. "Just go about your day, Tommy. This won't ever feel good, so why force it?"

I tuck my hands behind my back and enjoy the scratch of the brick wall against my bare shoulder blades.

Shirtless in front of Alana Page. *Cool, cool, cool, cool, cool.*

"I enjoy watching the kids work on their skills." *Not a complete lie.* "In a group of twelve, one or two of them might be champs someday." But when Franklin steps forward and kicks a bag, only to fall on his ass and whip his embarrassed eyes this way, I smirk and add, "*He* probably won't be one of them."

"Shut up." She gifts him with an encouraging smile, nodding to entice him to stand again. To keep trying. "Don't speak badly about my son."

"I don't consider it speaking badly. I wasn't ragging on the boy." I slide my gaze across and meet her eyes. "You had to know mixing your genes with a corporate jockstrap wasn't gonna land you with an athlete. I hope you weren't banking on him taking you all the way to the NFL or anything."

"I said shut up." Her jaw turns to granite, rock solid and unshaking.

"Don't speak about him at all. You think you know me, Tommy, the girl who fell into your arms and begged you to make the world a kinder place. But you have no clue anymore. Maybe you're pissed about it, but becoming a mother was the best thing that ever happened to me. It gave me strength I never knew I could possess. Now?" She glares straight into my eyes. "I'll slit a man's throat for looking at him wrong. So stop."

ROUND ELEVEN
ALANA

I don't bother asking Mrs. Middler's grandson for help to move books. And I sure as hell don't ask Chris—because the risk that he might bring Tommy is too much to bear. So I spend the next few days hauling dusty books from one end of the shop to the other, clearing out space and creating some semblance of organization, starting with fiction on one side and non-fiction on the other. Soon, I'll break the fiction into genres, and after that, authors and series.

But until then, I destroy my sinuses with years-old dust and work muscles I'd forgotten I owned. And all the while, I fend off all the things I don't want.

Like Helen.

"Marianne has had another discussion with acquisitions," she drones, tired of this conversation and ready, surely, to toss me on my ass.

Is that what I want?

"They're willing to increase your offer by fifteen percent, Alana. They can pencil you in for a summer release next year. But you need to come to the table, babe. You long ago sprinted past difficult-to-deal-with and dove headfirst into diva. You're making a name for yourself in the publishing world, and I have to admit, it's not a good one."

"I'm not playing hard to get." I heft a heavy box, lifting with my legs and ignoring the pain in my back as I straighten out with a huff, and then I slowly carry it toward the back of the store where my piles are growing

"I'm not trying to be a diva. I'm telling you, I'm not willing to sell the story right now."

"Why the heck not? This is literally why we're here, Alana. I'm an agent. You're a writer. We put you on submission. You even went to auction, which is a dream most others would kill for. But at the eleventh hour, you refuse the deal that shook out. They're offering *more* despite having won the auction fair and square, and now you've got cold feet?"

"It's not about cold feet, either." I waddle, much like I did in my seventh month of pregnancy when my son's head was tucked perilously low, and his little body was ready to evacuate, albeit a little too soon. "I changed my mind. I'm not ready to share my story with the world. It's as simple as that."

"Well, when *will* you be ready? Because accepting the deal today doesn't mean publication is today. Next summer is a full year away, and by then, you might wish you didn't screw around so much this year."

"I'll write you a different book." I set the box down with a grunt and press my hands to the top, leaning over it and taking a moment to catch my breath. "I can write something else entirely, and we'll submit that. Give me, like..." I draw a heaving breath and swipe my sweaty brow. "Three months."

"They do not want a different book!" She shouts and still, somehow, makes it sound classy. Sophisticated. A gift my mother possesses, too. "They want *Love and War*, Alana. They want the story you wrote about a boy whose heart was bigger than the chaos surrounding him. This isn't a game, and stories are not interchangeable in this world. Not when you're a debut and have yet to prove your worth. They're not asking for any old book penned by this unknown author. They want *that* specific story, and if you don't cut the shit soon, you're going to have their lawyers crawling up your backside."

"I've yet to accept a single dollar." Turning from the box, I head back across the shop to get more. "And even if I had, my only penalty would be to repay the advance. You won't spook me with legal threats, Helen." *I'm untouchable.* Those are the words that tickle the back of my throat. *I've already walked through hell and come out the other side.* But those are not the words I share with her. Instead, I grab another box and earn the sundae I intend to eat after dinner tonight. "I'm not playing games, and I'm not interested in arguing about it. Pull the book. I've already told you more than a few times."

"You're impossible!" She huffs and ends our call, so the music I was playing before she interrupted starts again, filling the shop with its tinny sound. And because I think of it, I make a mental note to request decent speakers from Mrs. Middler's budget. Just a modest stereo or something, so when customers wander through and end up at the very back end of the warehouse-esque building, the music they hear won't sound like it's coming from a tin can.

"Are you here alone?"

"Argh!" I throw the box and spin, ninja hands at the ready and the ghost of a memory of what were once fight lessons pulsing through my veins. But my lips peel back into a feral sneer when I find Tommy freakin' Watkins standing by the shop door, a tight shirt hugging his chest and jeans that wrap around his thick thighs, emphasizing what I suppose I'd forgotten.

He was always stocky. Solidly built, even when he was young and hungry. But now he has his own money, a training regime, dietary plans, and though it's only an assumption, I doubt he's living with a tyrannical abuser who kicks the shit out of him simply for existing.

The boy he used to be grew into a man swollen in all the right places.

"Didn't mean to scare you." And yet, he kicks one foot over the other and chews on a Silly Stix straw, his lips curling around the plastic and his perfect, white teeth glittering behind a smug smile.

Ten years ago, I'd have killed to see his eyes dance the way they do now. To see him so outwardly happy would have made my heart sing. But today, when he looks at me like that, it's like he has an inside joke, and all mocking fingers point toward me.

"Did you hurt yourself?" He gestures toward the dropped box, the sides split wide open, and books splayed on the floor between us. "That was probably too heavy for you."

"What are you doing here?" Anger courses through my veins as I crouch and try to pull the box back to its bottom. I straighten what's twisted and stack books before the covers bend. "I'm working, and you look like you've got somewhere to be. So why don't you..." I slap a heavy hardcover book to the top of the pile and wave toward the doors at his back. "Go."

"I asked you a question." His kindness slips, revealing something darker, something menacing and dangerous beneath. "Are you here alone? It's almost dark outside, and maybe we're in the asshole of nowhere, and most psychopaths linger around the cities, but times have changed since you were last in Plainview. Where's Franklin?"

"At the house with my mother." Giving up on the box, I stand tall and stare down my nose at the man who wants so desperately to challenge me. "They're making an evening of it, which means I had time to spare. Getting this place into shape is taking longer than I hoped, and lugging hundred-pound boxes is significantly less torturous when it's not as hot outside." I gesture toward the door again. "Asked. Answered. Now you can go."

"Not entirely sure why you're pissy at me." He drags the straw away from his lips. "Wasn't me who fucked us over. But here you go, swinging through town and chewing me out at every chance you get. Feels a little Bitsy-Special Gaslighty to me."

"*That's* what we're doing, huh?" I hate him. I loathe him. I want to hurt him even half as much as he hurts me. "You're *that* guy? The one who'll take my deepest, darkest secrets and lob them in my face all because you're in a bad mood? I cried about her for *years,* Tommy. But now you'll take your payback by saying I'm just like her?"

"If it quacks like a duck and waddles like a duck…"

"Get the hell out!" I will not cry. I will not scream. Most importantly, I will *not* beg for his mercy. Though, the last feels the most impossible of them all. "This store is not open for business, which means you're trespassing. Get out and stay the fuck away from me."

"I remember, back when we were young and fighting, it was more of a *knock 'em down, drag 'em out* kind of thing. We were loud and mean and often ended up in bed together, fucking away our frustrations and rewarding each other with orgasms so good they felt illegal. Honestly, I figured you picked fights with me so often *because* you were horny."

"I said leave."

"But *now,* I guess you deal with your anger by cutting a man off. Leave town. Leave the gym. Kick him out. Whatever the circumstances, you starve every argument of oxygen instead of stoking the flames."

"Yeah, it's called maturity." I sneer. "Maybe you missed class the day they taught that."

"Probably." He backs up to the door, but instead of walking *through* it, he leans against the glass pane and makes damn sure no one passes in or out. "Chances are, I was hidden away somewhere with blood in my piss and a broken rib or two. But you were always such a doll about taking notes and bringing them back to me. You didn't want me to miss out on the education we both knew I'd need. Ya know, to break cycles and escape poverty, knowledge is power and all that shit."

"Uh-huh, and seeing as how you're a successful business owner now, I guess my labors paid off. You're welcome." For the third time, I gesture toward the door. "Go."

"Chris does most of the books and stuff down at the gym." He makes no move to get the hell out of my space, folding his arms instead, which results in his shoulders growing larger and his chest swelling with what I know was a workout earlier today. "Mostly, my success comes from pro-fighting. Kinda ironic, don't you think, that I'd use the skills my parents beat into me to earn a living? Did I break a cycle, or did I dress it up and make it socially palatable?"

"Probably a discussion to have with your therapist. Which, sadly, isn't a field I specialize in. Are we done now?"

"Not even fucking close." Finally, he shoves away from the door, but he doesn't turn and leave. Instead, he charges my way and sends my heart into a thundering spasm. For a single second, I wonder if he might grab me. Kiss me. Like he used to do when we were younger, smooshing my cheeks in his hands and laying a vicious kiss on my lips.

Is that what I want?

If he tried, would I stop him?

If he touched me, would I melt into it or recoil and scream?

But long before I can rein my troubling thoughts in, he scoops up the stack of books and continues past me, his taunting scent creeping along my throat and filling my lungs as disgust becomes my newest companion.

And with it, disappointment.

Because, of course, that's how fucked in the head I am. Even after all this time, even after everything that has happened.

"I heard you wrote a book." He sets the stack atop the last box I brought down, turning back to study the horror so clearly spread across my face.

Not because of the kiss I considered nor the longing I'll forever feel. But because he knows about the book.

He knows about *the* book!

"Heard you got an agent and everything and a big fancy deal with one of the big, fancy publishing houses. Guess that probably makes you rich, huh?"

"Rich? In publishing?" I force a mocking laugh and try to calm my racing pulse. I try to play this subject off like my entire world doesn't hinge on him *not* knowing the details of the story I labored over. The pages that hold my tears, no matter how many times I read them. "I've yet to make a cent, actually. I heard you have a fight coming up in Vegas." And since he insists, I match his energy and sneer. "Guess that probably makes you rich, huh?"

"Yep." He slides his hands into his pockets and wanders back this way. "Richer than God himself and happy as a pig in the mud about it."

Touché.

"They're paying me thirty million dollars *just* to step into the cage in a few months. Fifty million if I win." He stops three feet away and rolls his bottom lip between his thumb and fingers. "Obscene amounts of money, really. Can you even imagine what we'd have done with that kinda cash back when we were younger?" He chuckles. "I don't need that many zeroes. No one does. But no way I'm handing them back."

"You could probably support a few charities. Feed some hungry kids or whatever, if you feel like those zeroes are a burden to your bank account."

"I do." His eyes, that same pair that used to look at me like I hung the moon and the stars, now study me with cold, hard derision. "I didn't forget where I came from, Alana."

Unlike you. Those are the words he doesn't speak, but the implication remains loud and clear.

"Once I got myself situated and a couple of wins under my belt, confident the rug wouldn't be pulled out from underneath me and my brother, I made damn sure every kid in this town, and the next few, would always have a meal in their belly. I won't solve world hunger," he drawls. "But it solves Plainview's hunger. And a few other counties, too."

"Oh... well..." *It's okay, Alana. Admit you're a piece of shit who never looked outside your own echo chamber of self-pity.*

Doing better starts with self-awareness.

"Why'd you leave, Alana?"

I swallow and firm my lips into straight lines. I give him silence because there's nothing else I can offer that won't make everything worse.

"*Something* happened." Snarling, he leans closer. "Someone said something, or someone did something. Or maybe I hurt your feelings. Or Chris and me, as a package deal, became too much. Or maybe your mother said some shit. Or you and that dude found each other on a fucking chat site, and things got out of hand. What, Alana?" He whips his hand forward so fast, the muscle memory I once possessed, now pathetically out of practice, can't save me from the way he wraps his hand around the side of my neck and controls my face with his thumb beneath my jaw.

He forces me to meet his eyes, refusing me any other choice. "What happened that led you to dip out of my life so fucking violently, it's like you died?"

My knees tremble. My pulse sprints. My entire body, heart and soul, spins out of control as tears slide onto my cheeks and, horrifyingly, my hand comes up.

Not to shove him away. But to wrap around his tense wrist.

"Why, Alana?" His voice shakes with desperation. "Why did you do that to us?"

"Please leave me alone." My chest and shoulders bounce with a silent sob. My vision turns blurry, tears blinding me to everything but the hulking shape of a man begging for something he is, in a fair world, entitled to. But this isn't a fair world, despite the signage he had installed above his gym. "Please just go, Tommy."

"You could save us both by sharing the things you know." He shakes me. "You ruined both of our lives, Alana. By making choices that, for whatever reason, suited only you, you changed everything." His eyes glitter with pain. With unshed tears. "You destroyed us, and you don't even have the guts to own up to it. Jesus, why is my request so fucking outlandish that you won't say what was going through your head back then?"

"Because it's *my* burden to carry!" Finally, I find a pocket of strength and take a step back, pushing his hand away when he'd rather follow and grab me again. "You're entitled to your feelings, Tommy. You want to hate me for ruining a teenage romance? Then do it. Hate me. That's fine. Because I've spent my whole life hating me, too."

"A teenage romance?" he growls. "You call that a fucking teenage romance?"

"We were teens." I broaden my shoulders and take another step back. "You romanticize memories held within a child's mind."

"You're a fuckin' liar!" He charges forward, pointing a dangerous finger in my face. "You look right into my eyes and spout that shit off like you think I haven't been calling you out on bullshit since the moment we met. We were *not* stupid kids, Alana, and I'm not a stupid man. We were *never* children, and what we had was not some fleeting bullshit. You ruined the greatest thing either of us will ever know. And maybe you have to lie to yourself to remain sane. Maybe that's how you get through. But I remember what we were. We had that once-in-a-lifetime love, the kind most never even find. I was poor and hungry and dirty, but I was rich with *us*."

"You're wrong." On this one point, at least, I don't waver. I won't. Even if the price I paid was cruel. "*We* were not the best thing that ever happened to me, Tommy. No matter how many times you scream it in my face, and no matter how good it felt back then, no matter how much it hurts now. *We* were not where everything starts and ends. My son is. He always will be. And there isn't a damn thing you can say that'll make me question that. I'm sorry I hurt your feelings when I left, but the past is the past, and there's nothing we can do about it now." The music cuts out once more, and my phone trills with an incoming call. So I stride to the counter and grab it, both thankful for the interruption and dreading the idea that something may be wrong at home.

Instead, I find Colin's name on my screen, another brutal twist of the universe's blade.

It's not enough that we hurt. That cold bitch, destiny, wants us to suffer, too.

Taking a long, shuddering breath and dropping my head back, I stare up at the ceiling and accept the call before I lose my nerve. I force a plastic-y, inauthentic cheeriness to my tone. "Hi, Colin."

Tommy's rage burns hotter. His pain, like palpable waves pulsing in the air.

"I was planning to call you in a little while," I rasp, knuckling a tear from my cheek. "It's like you read my mind."

"Fuck this." Tommy stalks toward the shop door and tears it open, the bell above screaming and the hinges on the side protesting their abuse. Then he barges through without a backward glance, slamming it again in his wake.

Small mercies, I suppose.

At least I get to be alone.

"You okay?" Colin's concern rolls through the line just as warmly as the hug he gave me the day we married. The way he cares, like nothing else I'd ever known in my life. God, he's entirely too decent to be mixed up in my messy life. "Was that Tommy?"

I lower my gaze and swallow the tears balling in my throat, and circling the desk, I yank a few more tissues from the box beneath. "Yeah. That was him."

"He sounded pissed. Did you tell him?"

"No." I blow my nose, knowing the sound must be awful from Colin's side of the line. But he's seen me at my worst. He's watched over me when I could do nothing more than lie on the bathroom floor and cry myself to sleep. "He's always pissed. That's not something new."

"Are you..." He pauses for a beat, considering his words. "Are you safe, Alana?"

My heart?

No.

My soul and sanity?

Absolutely not.

"Physically?" I blow my nose a second time and wipe above my lip. If I ignore the way they tremble, then I don't have to admit how being mere feet from Tommy Watkins destroys me. "Yeah. I'm fine. How are things in New York?"

ROUND TWELVE
ALANA

A few days after my run-in at *Books Books Books*—new name, pending—I wander through the house with a stack of clean laundry to put away and a sheen of sweat settling on my brow, despite how early in the day it still is.

"I was thinking of taking Franky over to the lake today. Do you still have—" I push through my mother's bedroom door and stop with a frown when I find her sitting on the side of her bed, her hands on her knees and her head dangling with exhaustion.

Franky and I have been in Plainview for a few weeks now, living with my mother and seeing her daily. Still, her vulnerability and frail thinness never cease to catch me by surprise.

The woman she is today, physically, is nothing like the vicious snake she was in my youth.

"Are you okay?" Changing tact, I set my laundry on the end of her bed and come around and crouch so I can look up and see her face. "You don't look so well, Mom. Are you feeling sick?"

"I didn't sleep very well." She licks her lips. The crackle of a dry tongue over dry skin is like rubbing paper together. "It was hot last night, so I kept tossing and turning. You're going to the lake?"

"Well... no." I place my hand on her forehead and search for warmth. It's the mom in me, I think. It's the first thing I do whenever Franky is feeling off. "We can stay home and have a movie day, if you like."

She pulls back, shaking her head and dragging her eyes up. Her face has aged a lot in the last ten years. What used to be smooth skin is now loose. Firm cheeks have become puffy and slack. Seductive bow lips are now flat and thin.

Worse, her skin has a gray tinge that makes my stomach do somersaults every time I look for more than a moment.

"I'm getting up now to make coffee and breakfast," she murmurs. "Then I intend to watch my shows all day. The inflatable tubes are still in the shed." She places her hands on the mattress and moves to her feet. She's slow and in pain, but if nothing else, spite spurs her on. "I'm not sure they've been moved since you last used them. So as long as you stored them well, and they didn't have holes back then..."

"Mom! Argghhhhh!" Franky's guttural scream brings me up in a flash, my legs powering me toward the window that overlooks the yard before my brain can process the fear coursing through my veins. I tear the curtains aside and shove the glass up, risking shards raining on the carpet, and then I lean my head through the window in search.

"Franklin?! Where are you?"

"It's trying to kill me!" He sprints across the lawn faster than I ever knew he could run, arms waving in the air and glasses bouncing on his nose. But before I dive under my mother's bed and find the shotgun she keeps there, Whacky II, that damn rooster, bolts in Franky's wake, hunting my baby down and—no doubt—thrilling in his place of dominance. "Mom!"

"Stop running!" I press my hand to my chest and breathe through the panic. It's like lava in my veins. Like poison coursing through my system. And then deliriousness takes over until laughter bubbles along my throat. "Honey!" I clap my hand to my mouth when Franky trips on his own feet. But damn, he rolls until he's up again. "If you stop running, he'll stop chasing."

"Save me, Mommy!" His voice breaks with genuine tears. Fear. Horror, as that friggin' chook cuts through the yard and rounds my baby up. "Mommy!"

"Whacky!" I climb through the window and onto the roof of the house's first story. It's odd how, now that I'm an adult, I'm not scared of letting my mother see the myriad ways I learned to sneak out of her prison. Striding to the corner of the house, I turn and climb down the trellis she had installed somewhere around my eleventh birthday.

"Mommy!"

"Whacky! You dumb rooster. Stop it." I descend in bare feet and shorts not at all appropriate for outsiders to see—*lucky me, there are no Watkins boys lingering in the yard today*—then dropping to the porch, I dash onto the grass to stand between my son and his villain. "Hey!" I wave my arms and jump in his way when he tries to charge. "I'm gonna cook you up and eat you for dinner if you don't cut the shit."

"Get inside, Alana!" My mother stands at her window—her need to control me renewing her strength—and pursing her lips, she looks down her nose and judges me. "You look like a fool."

"Impossible!" I back up, reaching behind me until I feel Franky's hands take mine. Then, I meet Bitsy's derision and beam. "I'm busy being my son's hero."

"You're not even afraid," Franky murmurs, plastering his cheek to my ribs, his chest to my back. "How come you're not scared?"

Because I've faced bigger, meaner, scarier monsters all my life. But when Whacky turns, bored with the hunt, and wanders away, I draw my son around and swipe the tears from beneath his eyes. "He's just a chicken, honey. He's smaller than you by a hundred."

"That's not true." He tilts to the side and studies the feathered demon. "Two or three times, maybe. Not a hundred."

"You're still bigger." *And I distracted you with data. Ha!* "If you stand your ground, I bet he won't even come near you."

"But—"

"You run, so he chases. It's a game. But I promise, if he ever caught you, he wouldn't hurt you."

"I hate him." He reaches up and drags his glasses from his face. They're fogged from his tears, so he hands them to me to clean. "I hate him so much, Mommy. I wish he never existed on this farm."

"Well..." I use my shirt and wipe the lenses. "He's so old now, honey, it would be impossible to re-home him. But if it makes you feel better, he'll probably die soon." I offer a wide smile, even if I feel like an idiot doing so. "He's already *long* past his life expectancy. So now we just wait."

"He's healthy as a horse," Bitsy declares from her window. Because, of course, she's always enjoyed terrorizing children. "And all the extra exercise he gets now only helps."

Horrified, Franky's glittering eyes swing back to mine. "Mom?"

"He'll leave you alone if you stand up to him." I hand his glasses back and pull him closer. "Do you want to go on an adventure today? I have somewhere fun to take you."

"Really?" Sniffling, he pulls back and searches my face. "Where? How far is it? How long will we be in the car? And do I have to wear shoes?"

So perfect. So sweet. *So incredibly desperate to control the world around him.*

"It's only a few minutes away. Ten minutes in the car, at most, and that includes stopping by the grocery store to buy snacks. And no." I lay a smiling kiss on his cheek. "You don't have to wear shoes if you don't want to. Come on." I straighten my legs and take his hand in mine. "You need to find shorts to swim in, though. And a hat, unless you want your nose to get a sunburn."

"Swimming?" His lips wrinkle into displeased lines. "Do I have to wear my glasses?"

"Nope. You can leave them in our room. Did you have something to eat yet?"

He nods, glancing up at Bitsy's bedroom window as we move toward the porch. We'll use the door, of course. But my baby is observant. Inquisitive. "Why did you climb off the roof, Mommy? How did you do that?"

At least it's not: *how many times did you climb off the roof when you were seventeen because you were sneaking out to see a boy?*

"Mommy magic," I explain, a concept he's scoffed at since he was old enough to think logically. It's a bit like Santa. He knows, rationally, that these things cannot exist. But behind the autism and the kid whose brain is entirely too gifted, is a little boy who *wants* to believe.

It creates a sliver of hope in a world he already knows is tough.

"Moms receive magic once they become moms, honey." I lead him up the porch steps and tug the door open. "You were scared and in danger, so I was able to use my powers and practically jump out the window to save you."

He walks ahead of me into the kitchen, glancing back with a gentle scowl. "Magic isn't real."

"It's sad you think you need to say that." I close the door and meet his disbelief with a grin. "But I *know* you believe. You know how I know?"

He folds his arms, challenging and proud.

"I know because you're scared to sleep in the dark at night. But you hold my hand, and suddenly, the dark doesn't bother you anymore. It's not like I turned on a light. I didn't open the door or change anything else. The mere act of holding your hand makes everything better." I scrunch my nose playfully. "Mommy magic."

ROUND THIRTEEN

TOMMY

"Where are we going?" Chris drags his feet, stopping at the front of the truck and scowling while I toss towels in the back. "How long is the drive?"

"Jesus Christ." I lift a cooler into the bed of the truck, my shoulder straining from the fifty pounds of ice and sodas, and fuck knows what else Eliza tossed in. "We're just going to the lake."

Suspicious, he looks straight past me. "We *are* at the lake."

"To the sandy inlet," I drawl. "Five minutes, at most."

"I'm not wearing shoes." He pouts like a child, but produces keys and slides in on the driver's side. Winding the window down, he slaps the side of his door and elicits a happy yelp as Eliza dashes out of my house and around to climb into the middle. "I'm only staying for an hour. You wanna stay longer than that, you can walk home."

"It's like you never matured beyond fourth grade." I toss the last of our things in the back and come around to the passenger door, then climbing in and crushing Eliza in the middle, I fix my seatbelt and flick her nose when she'd rather make faces than move out of the way. "You're still not forgiven after your shit at the gym."

"The ground and *pound*." Cackling, she settles back in denim shorts and a tiny bikini top, her washboard stomach already slick with sweat. "You act like we haven't been doing that for years."

"You made it look sexual!"

"I roll with my own brother." She folds her legs criss-cross style so her knee encroaches on my space. "It's not sexual when I roll with him. It's not sexual when I roll with Chris." She stops and smirks. "If you were thinking sexual things, all because your girlfriend was giving you the beady eye, then that's on you."

"You knew damn well what you were doing." I shove her knee off and drop my head back, closing my eyes as we bounce across a poorly kept driveway and onto the tar road. "You were just a kid back then, so you never truly understood the intricacies of what happened. Now you're grown, and you think it's on you to protect my heart."

"Someone's gotta do it. You seem all too happy to let her stomp you into the curb. Every time she does, I bet you even thank her and ask for more."

"Nobody curb stomped anyone." I massage my temples with my fingers. "You're making a whole big thing out of something you don't understand. It was bad." I drop my hands. "But it's not what you've made it out to be. So you can stop with your bravado bullshit and calm the hell down."

"Eh." She plasters her hand to the side of my face and shoves until I hit the window. Not hard. Just... annoying. "You *want* to hate her, Thomas. But you never stopped loving her. Which means you're not capable of making sensible choices around her."

"Never stopped loving her?" I scoff. *Yep, make the sound. Spit, even. Pretend she's wrong!* "You don't know what you're talking about. And that, right there, is the issue. You don't know." I slap her arm away. "Which means you're acting like an idiot and relying on false information."

"Not false." She studies her nails, faux casual, though I see the smirk she tries to hide. "Ollie has said his piece over the years, and he was there when it all went down. He has firsthand knowledge. And Raquel brings it up every single time she calls home."

"Your sister?" I laugh. *Ha. Ha. Act fucking casual!* "She left town the second she graduated high school. Her recollection doesn't count. And if you say Betty told Barbara, and Barbara told Glen, and Glen told Bitsy, I'm gonna drown you just as soon as we get in the water."

"You wouldn't drown me." She tilts her head back and searches my eyes. "All I'm saying is I didn't need to be there ten years ago because I'm here now. I've *been* here, inside that gym, training with you for years. *That* guy, my friend? He's not the same as the guy sitting next to me right now."

"Eliza—"

"*This* guy is hurting, and even if you've been hurting for the last decade, you could set it aside. You could run a gym and train and socialize and go out for a drink and be around us, and most of the time, you smiled."

"I'm smiling!" *Am I? Really?* I stretch my lips and paste on the fakest shit I can manage. "I'm okay, Lize. But you know what *isn't* okay? Pulling that shit you did the other day and making my life more complicated."

"More complicated, how?" She uses Chris's arm as a leaning post, which makes his gear shifts all the more difficult. But he doesn't push her off. "You're not with her, Tommy. You're a single man, and she's hitched to someone else. So explain to me how my behavior inside your gym—sexual or otherwise—complicates your life?"

"Rub yourself on him in front of Oliver," Chris volunteers. "See what happens."

She angles her head back and looks up at him with a beaming smile. "That would not be smart."

"It's all complicated." I drag my fingers through my hair and catch sight of the lake just a little further up the road. "Mine and Alana's history is complicated, but I kinda want to get to a point where we can talk for a minute without either of us screaming at each other. Just one time," I groan. "Because maybe then she'll answer my fucking questions."

"You need to consider a world where she does exactly that." Eliza wraps her arms around mine and rests her cheek on the ball of my shoulder. "Because maybe she tells you, and maybe the answers are just... not that great. Or not that helpful. Or maybe they break your heart again, or maybe they're as simple as '*I got bored and wanted to leave, and I didn't love you enough to think you deserved a goodbye*.'"

It's the last one, I think, that would hurt the most. Leaving because she was mad is one thing. Leaving because she was terrified of the intensity of our love is another. But to think I held all of her in my heart, that I would have set the whole fucking world on fire if she'd asked, only to find out she didn't care about me at all... that's the one that'll put me on the floor again.

"It's been a long time," Eliza continues, exhaling a sad sigh. "And opening all this up again might only make things worse. They say clean breaks are the best kind. They're the ones that heal most efficiently."

Alana gave me the cleanest of all breaks, really. She was here, and then she was gone.

"She doesn't exist anymore, Tommy. She made that choice, and now, it might be healthiest for you to respect and accept it."

"Ah fuck." Chris' foreboding tone brings me forward in my seat to stare at the side of his face. But then I follow his gaze straight ahead and under-

127

stand, now, why it feels like we're twelve again, and Dad is making a game of belting us with a shovel. "There will be no healing today," he sighs. "Dammit."

"Turn around." Eliza's eyes spring wide, taking in the scene ahead of us. Because Alana bends in the shade, red in the face while she blows up a floating tube. "Chris!" She slaps his arm and makes a grab for the steering wheel. "Turn around. We'll swim somewhere else."

"She already saw us." It's like a kick to the guts when Alana glances up at the sound of our approach, curious at first, then panicked when her eyes lock on to mine. Her chest caves in, her lungs expelling whatever air she has left, and despite the effort she put into blowing the tube up for her patiently waiting kid, it's all for naught when she lowers her arms and the inflatable slowly deflates.

"She looks good." Chris is just... Chris. Fuck him for his infuriatingly consistent honesty.

Because she does. She looks amazing in a short denim skirt, the front button and zipper already undone, and a blue and white striped bikini playing off her perfect olive complexion. Her hips have grown a little wider since I last saw her so dressed down, and her breasts have gone up a cup size or two.

She used to be flat all over. Now she has curves where curves should be and dips where dips are most delicious. Her stomach isn't like Eliza's. Not the washboard perfection I see daily in the gym. Instead, she's a little softer. The lines on her belly, created by folds in her skin when she bends or sits.

"Remember when she got that belly piercing?" Chris brings the truck to a stop about forty feet from her car, dust pluming because this summer has been dry as hell, and dirt is just... everywhere. He cuts the engine and scrubs a hand over his mouth. To hide his smile, no doubt. "Bitsy was screaming all over town about how she would never let her daughter get such a trashy body modification. Not for as long as she lived."

"So we drove her to Barlespy and took her to a piercing place there." I draw a heaving breath, filling my lungs and expanding my chest, and remembering that day in a town about an hour from here as clearly as if it was just yesterday, I exhale again and nod. "She wanted it so bad, and her mother wouldn't even discuss it. So we did what Watkins boys do—break the rules and celebrate after with a party... here," I realize, as sorrow washes through my veins. "At the lake."

"It's not too late to turn around," Eliza murmurs. "She saw us, but you know she's panicking, too. We'd be doing her a favor if we left."

"This is the best part of the lake for swimming," Chris inserts. Logical. Unemotional. But he taps the steering wheel and warms the side of my face with his gaze. "We can go somewhere else if you want."

"We can leave," Alana calls out.

Her voice kicks my heart into the next gear, like nitrous oxide injected straight into my blood. Tossing the half-inflated tube to the ground, she bends and grabs a plastic grocery bag and throws things inside. "Franky, honey." She looks over to find him in the shallowest section of water. She knows precisely where it's safe out here, and where it isn't, because she spent seventeen summers in this lake, just like we did. "Come out of the water, okay? The tube is broken, so let's go back to town and get some ice cream."

"Problem solved." Eliza releases a breath of relief. "She's doing the right thing."

"No." I unsnap my seatbelt and flick her hand off when she tries to grab for me, then shoving the truck door open, I move so much fucking faster than I intend. Around the back of the truck to sweep up the cooler, then over the sizzling dirt that turns to sand, which turns to patchy grass right where Alana set up camp, dappled shade from the massive tree growing above. "Don't leave."

She ignores me, filling her bag with random things and mixing soda cans with sunscreen. A hair scrunchie with the boy's shirt.

"Franky? You have to get out of the water now."

I grab her wrist and yank her to a stop, though I know she'd rather sprint straight past, scoop her kid up, and escape. I inhale her panicked exhale and hate that her eyes flare with fear.

Not nerves. Not anger. Not even confusion.

Straight-up fear.

"Stay," I repeat, licking my lips and glancing down at my fingers wrapped around her wrist. I see the outline of my grip on her pale skin. "It's a big lake, Alana, and it's hotter than Hades out here today."

"Hi, Chris!" Franky remains in the water, waving with his arm above his head so the gesture moves his whole body. He has a cute little outie belly button and ribs I can count. Though it's not the same as when I was a kid, and my ribs were visible, too.

Franklin Page isn't hungry. He's just... small.

"I don't *want* to stay." Alana gently peels her arm from my hold, swallowing so her throat bobs. She tries so hard to tamp her emotions down, but she can't stop the tears burning in her eyes. And evidently, she's forgotten the sunglasses perched atop her head. "We've already had a swim, so fair's fair. It's your turn to have the lake."

Godddddd, why is she so pretty? So tempting? So fucking perfect in all the wrong ways. "That's what they say about love and war, right? All's fair."

"Tommy—"

"You were the love, and I was the war. Anything we did in the pursuit of either was fair." I set two fingers on her trembling hip and turn her, just a few inches, until I see again the ink on her back. The date we fell in love, and with a messily drawn heart to go with it. "I had such bad handwriting back then. It's insane, actually, that you let me put something permanent on your skin."

"I don't want a trip down memory lane." She steps backward, forcing my hand to fall from her body. "I can't."

I look down at my chest instead, littered with ink. All but one of them were penned by a professional. "You drew on me, too. That's how we justified it. All's fair in love and war."

"Please stop." She brushes her knuckles beneath her eye. "Enjoy your day at the lake. Franky!"

"Chris and Eliza are gonna swim with us, Mom!" He splashes in the shallow end, waiting as Chris drags his shirt off and tosses it to the hood of the truck. Then he backs up in the water, waiting for the others to join him.

But we know—all of us—that there's a ledge in the water. A drop-off in just a few more feet. He's oblivious to what's behind him, which makes Alana's heart pound faster, and Chris' feet move quicker.

"Careful, Franky." Alana turns to go to him. She can't know that I'm thinking about his safety, too. Or that Chris and Eliza are likely thinking the same. No doubt, she probably assumes we all hate him since he's the only newb in our group, and if I concentrate too hard on the details, I might be left to wonder if he's the reason she left. "You're going to fall, baby. You have to—"

"I got it." Chris dives through the shallows, scooping Franky off his feet just inches from the edge. Spinning back this way, he tosses the boy and laughs when he lands with a splash, resurfacing with a squeal of happiness.

"You can't leave now." I set the cooler on the ground and inch forward, my chest almost touching Alana's back. "He's having fun. Take him away, and you'll have to explain why. *Mommy used to be friends with these people, but then she stopped for no apparent reason* isn't a very pleasant story to tell. He'll start asking questions, and you're not real keen on answering those."

We spent so much time together in our youth, I could touch whenever

I wanted. I could taste. I could wrap myself around her body, and never once, ever, did I fear rejection.

My heart and brain know I can't do that anymore. But fuck, my body needs reminding. Because my fingers itch to touch. My hands beg to stroke. My chest *aches* to have her resting upon it.

"I'm sorry we ruined your plans today." I drag my hat lower over my eyes to shield them from the glare of the sun. Or, at least, that's my excuse. "It wasn't intentional, I promise."

"It's fine." It's clearly *not* fine, but she's had a lifetime of saying things are okay when they're not. Her mother practically branded the words on her tongue.

Frustrated, she stalks across and grabs the tube she was working on, and moving a full ten feet away, she shakily spins, spins, spins the rubber in search of the air hole. "We'll stay for twenty minutes so Franky can play with Chris. Then we'll get out of your way."

I pick up the plastic bag she dropped and poke through its contents in silence. I pull Franky's shirt out so it doesn't get wet from the condensation of her drink, then the sunscreen tube—not closed—before it makes a mess. "I'm gonna put your drink in our cooler, okay?" I don't wait for her approval... it's not like she'd give it anyway. I kick the lid open and set her drink in with the ice, then I shut the box again and set the end of the bag beneath so it doesn't whip away in the wind.

That is, if there was any.

There isn't.

"Want me to blow that up for you?" I keep my movements slow. My hands by my sides instead of, well, on her body. Or more likely, circling her delicate neck, since that Watkins blood still sprints through my veins.

I wouldn't actually hurt her, not like my daddy used to hurt my mom and everyone else he could reach. But that doesn't stop the desire from simmering just below the surface of my thoughts.

I grab the pathetic inflatable and tug until the mouthpiece pops from her lips. "You look like you might pass out if you keep going."

It's not like I'm twelve anymore, drinking soda from her can just so I can pretend that pressing my lips to the same spot is basically as good as kissing. But I'll be damned if my heart doesn't beat a little faster when I take the mouthpiece between my lips.

"You're still as pushy as always." She folds her arms, hiding her succulent body from my gaze and cocking her hip. It's the best defense she's got while standing out here half-naked and showing off a stamp on her back that makes her mine.

Mine.

"You just do whatever you're gonna do, no matter what it is I want to do."

Sure. That's why you left town without so much as a fuckin' Dear John letter. But I'm trying to make nice, so I smile around the rubber stopper and inflate the very same tube she and I floated on back in the day.

A poor kid who never had much of anything knows a bright yellow and green inflatable toy when he sees it.

"You don't really have to blow that up," she mumbles defiantly. "We're leaving in a few minutes."

"You're not leaving." I jam my thumb against the stopper to keep the air inside, and refilling my lungs, I look to the trio in the water. Two of them are playing. The third casts daggers this way.

Eliza Darling will protect her flock to the death.

"He's having fun. And Ollie's on his way, too. He's bringing a grill so we can cook up some lunch." I look down at the wet valve and *know* I haven't changed all that much since high school. Because now her spit and mine are mixed, and my brain can't help but obsess about it. "He makes a mean margarita. Kind of a girly drink, I know. But tequila is so much fuckin' fun, and we're all secure enough in our masculinity not to care that our drinks have umbrellas in them."

"Alcohol, swimming at the lake, and ultimately, driving home. Sounds like a tragedy waiting to happen."

"Nah." I wrap my lips around the valve and empty my lungs into the tube. "We *always* have a designated driver, and it's not like we're out here getting smashed the ol' Watkins way. Two drinks. Three, maybe." I inhale as deeply as I can, then exhale into the tube, blowing until my head swims and my toes tingle. "Just enough to have fun. Dance a little. Think we can sing. No one ever drinks so much that they're falling over, and in all these years, we've never had an argument among us. Not the real kind, fueled by alcohol and bred by the asshole who came before us."

I push the stopper into the valve and seal all that love-and-war oxygen inside the tube, forcing it to co-mingle. *There will be no escape.* Then I present my achievement with a smile. "Eliza's been our sober one the last five years, since she was old enough to drive but not old enough to drink. Now she's twenty-two, so we take turns between all of us."

"She seems..." She casts her gaze toward the lake to find what I know is waiting for her. "Homicidal."

"She's a sweetheart, usually. She's the baby of the group, so it's typically us throwing shade her way 'cos she invited some dude to our party and thinks it's cool to mack on him. Ya know, like," I wrinkle my nose, "with her tongue. There's no one in Plainview stupid enough or brave enough to volunteer, so she usually finds them in the next town over or whatever. She's pissy this week, that's all. But she'll cool off soon and go back to her normal annoying self."

"Pissy... at me?" She drags her lips between her teeth, flashing two deep dimples in her cheeks. "It's not so difficult to see she has a crush on you. I figure she wants to hurt me for breaking your heart."

"A crush? Romantically?" I laugh. "No. That would be like saying you had a crush on Chris back in high school. You were close, and there was love. There was friendship, even outside of me. But it wasn't romantic like that."

A weak, rogue breeze flitters around the tree and moves through her hair, so she combs her fingers through the locks and tucks them back. Which reminds her of the sunglasses atop her head. Pleased, she tears them down and slides them onto her face, robbing me of her eyes.

Robbing me of that window into what she's truly thinking.

"Kinda looks like she has a crush from where I'm standing." She accepts the tube and hugs it to her chest, shielding her body and using the broad circle to keep me away. "And she was pretty cozy with you at the gym. Lots of hugging and all that."

"If I were a less bitter man, I'd wonder if you were jealous."

She steps around me in silence, hoity-toity and faux-unaffected, to avoid my words. So I turn and watch as she detours to the left.

I'm not saying she approaches the water a full twenty feet from where Eliza lurks. But... she approaches the water a full twenty feet from where Eliza lurks.

She's a big old alligator, just waiting to snap.

"Grab on to this, honey." Alana places the tube in the water and allows it to drift on the pathetic current. "But don't float very far. I need to see you at all times. Okay?"

Fuck staying away. While Franky waits for the tube and Alana's eyes are completely focused on him, I close the space she took and stop just half a foot behind her. "Are you?"

She startles with a gasp, spinning with a ferocious glare.

"Jealous," I clarify.

"I can be observant, and even fearful for my life, without being jealous." Committed to her act of aloofness, she moves around me again and meanders back to the shade.

So I follow.

I'm not stepping foot in the lake today unless *she* steps foot in the lake. And when she does, I'll fucking follow.

All is fair in love and war.

And right now, Alana Page, we're at war.

"You get the store sorted yet?" I wander closer, so when she sits on her towel, I do, too. *Why the fuck not?* "I heard you asked Mrs. Middler to rename it."

"You *heard*?" She doesn't lie down, though fuck, I reckon she wants to. She always used to when we were kids, sunning herself under this very tree. Rubbing lotion on her skin and untying the strings of her bikini to avoid weird tan lines. "I don't miss how much everyone talks in this town."

"I guess Mrs. Middler mentioned it to her grandson, who mentioned it to Elaine down at the news agency, who mentioned it to Pete, who mentioned it to—"

"I got it." She waves me off. "The store's coming along. Franky's been busy creating a stocking system on the computer, so with every entry into the spreadsheet, I can shelve the book. Lots of dust." She lowers her gaze and selects a leaf from the ground, pulling it into pieces and tossing each bit back to the dirt when she's done. "Lots of sweat and long days. But we've made good progress."

"Ready for a grand reopening soon?"

"It was technically never closed." She scoffs. "But in all the time I've spent there, the only people who've crossed the threshold are us, my mom, and those pesky Watkins boys."

Pesky Watkins boys. *Stop smiling! Goddammit, Thomas. Stop liking this!* "Not everything has changed, then. Franky good with computers?"

"Yeah." On this, at least, her eyes alight, visible even through her sunglasses when she looks my way. "He's very, *very* intelligent. And I don't even mean it like how any mother thinks her child is special. Franklin is..." She sighs. "He's going to change the world."

"Yeah?"

"He'll kick and scream the whole way," she adds with a smile. "He hates change and loathes attention. So when they hand him his Nobel prize, he'll probably huff about it, angry that he had to stay out late and wear pants when he could be home instead."

Chuckling, I cast my gaze toward the lake, where Franky climbs onto Chris' shoulders, and Chris walks beyond the drop-off, where the water hits his chin and the current moves just a little faster.

Seeing them together is... strange.

I wasn't sure she'd ever come back. Now she has, and her kid is drawn to my brother like a moth to a flame. Most surprising of all is that my brother tolerates it when he tolerates so few humans on this earth.

"Can I ask *some* questions?" I risk her fury, and worse, the chance she'll get up and stomp away. But I drag my gaze back and stop on the side of her face. "I won't ask *why* you left. Different questions."

Silence is like a drum in the air. Nerves, like a waterfall, pounding over the top of my head. She returns my stare, hiding most of her secrets behind her shades. But I see the racing pulse in her neck. The nervous swipe of her tongue over her lips.

"Please?"

"Okay." She sits back, using her hands to prop herself up, and stretches her legs forward. "But I promise nothing."

ROUND FOURTEEN
ALANA

"Why didn't you give him your married last name when he was born?"

Goddddddd. Straight to the friggin' crux of things.

Tommy looks out at the lake, like I need the added context to know he means Franky.

"You were married by the time he came along, right? So why is he a Page?"

"I didn't change my name when I got married." I spin my ring using my thumb. It's an old habit, a nervous tic that gives me something to do when I can't sit still. "I knew I wanted to be a writer, and I didn't want to use another man's name on the front of my books."

True. Ish.

"And Colin never insisted on having his son take his name? Even with relationships falling apart and divorce rates skyrocketing, it's not like his kid stops being his just because the wife leaves."

I stare out at my son perched atop Chris' muscular shoulders, pounding his chest and screeching his laughter because that's the sound he makes when he's being silly.

"Colin didn't insist." *Truth*. "And I didn't want a different name than my child. It wasn't a big deal to Colin, so this is where we landed."

"And now?" He matches my pose, setting his hands behind his body and stretching long, powerful legs alongside mine. "Divorce is coming, and you've already left the city. He's the one with the different name. Is he not worried about losing his child?"

"He's not worried." I flick my toes. My fingers. I spin my ring and chew on my lip. And still, I need more movement. I need to escape. "Colin is welcome to call anytime he likes. Hourly, even, if he wanted to. They video chat most days and play chess." A smile spreads across my lips long before my brain processes the pleasure rippling through my blood. "They *love* to play chess together."

"He good at it? Franky," he clarifies. "I don't give a fuck about Colin."

His words are harsh, but his eyes are kind. Amused, even. So I nod. "He's *really* good. He's extremely tactical and logical in the moves he makes. Unlike me. When I play, I'm relying on hopes and dreams and a splash of good luck."

"Like playing Chris when we were younger." He shifts his weight, accidentally brushing my hand with the side of his. But when my eyes flare wide, he moves again. "He whooped our asses before the game even began, manipulating us into making moves and cornering us in record time. He was always good at that."

"Everything I knew about chess, I learned from your brother," I admit with a smile. "Everything I know about it now, I learned from my own child. He's a patient teacher, even if it means teaching me how to beat him."

"Some people are just like that, I guess." His eyes, perfect dark green, flash in the summer sun. "Not me. I'd rather win."

Yeah. That's not a secret. I already knew.

"So you wrote a book?" He casts his eyes back out to the trio in the lake. "What's it about?"

"Small town living." *True.* "Soul searching." *Also true.* I nibble on the inside of my cheek and lean forward to hug my legs. "It's just... it's nothing, really. An idea I got a while back while I was home with my baby. My brain needed something besides diapers and sleep schedules, so I started typing and, eventually, landed at *the end*."

"Sure, but what's it about?" He leans forward, too. Maybe he mirrors my poses on purpose, or his movement is purely coincidental. But my stomach dips when he drags his knees up and wraps his arms around his legs. "Who is your main protagonist?"

No.

I shake my head, long before I even think to verbalize my thoughts.

"I don't want to answer those questions."

"Oh…" Surprised, his brows pinch in my peripherals. "Okay. Didn't realize *that* would be a boundary. Is it a love story? An adventure? A tragedy, maybe?"

All three. Sadly. And don't forget the villain.

"I don't want to talk about my book at all." The crunch of heavy wheels on dirt draws my eyes around until my next heart attack looms. Oliver pulls up beside Tommy's truck, staring back at me with his mouth wide open and eyes as large as saucers. He's not quite mastered the skill of a poker face. "You still play cards against him?"

Curious, Tommy peeks over his shoulder. "Yep. He still sucks, too, 'cos his tell isn't even a tell. It's a whole fuckin' billboard."

That's what I figured.

"Stay here," he murmurs, pushing to his feet and pressing his hand to my shoulder. He can't *know* thoughts of escape pass through my mind. But it doesn't take a genius to guess. "He's just confused, is all. I'll go talk to him for a sec, so he knows we're all getting along. Then I'm coming back. I'm not done talking."

He doesn't wait for my response. And even if he had, I'm not sure I have one to offer. Instead, I rest my chin on my arm and watch him walk away, and when he and Oliver are mid-conversation, lifting a grill from the back of the truck and otherwise busy, I scramble off my towel, shove my skirt down my legs and toss my sunglasses so they don't rust in the water.

As quick as I can, I move toward the lake and wander into the water at the same safe distance I put the tube in. Eliza Darling wants to kill me, and I haven't been gone for so long that I forget what a fighter's body looks like.

Disinterested in anything above the surface, I wade out to the drop-off and dip my head underwater. Then I swim to the very bottom and simply… stay for a little while. I search the murky depths and hold my breath, luxuriating in the cool water on my skin and the soft brush of my hair tickling my shoulders.

I haven't swum since I was last in Plainview, which, now that I think about it, is ridiculous. I haven't relaxed at a pool or a lake, not a beach or a lagoon. Not once in all the time since my son came into this world have I stepped into a body of water larger than a bathtub.

And sadly, I hadn't even realized it.

I enrolled Franky in swimming lessons, of course, and watched every single week, hunching in on myself and pouting when water splashed my shoes or got on my legs. But for ten years, I hadn't even noticed I'd given up on something that used to bring me immense joy. Such cool bliss on my skin. The freedom of weightlessness. The magic of silence. And the pleasure of floating on my back, staring up at the shady trees above.

I'm not sure my hiatus was even intentional. I just... didn't do it.

My lungs begin to ache, reminding me I don't get to be a mermaid, living under the surface and yearning for a dark-haired man I can't have. I would sigh if I could. But I can't, so I push off the lake floor, rocks and beer bottles under my feet, creating the foundations for some of my happiest memories.

I break the surface and suck in fresh air, only to turn and find Tommy's nose just inches from mine. I scream and scramble away from his fiery eyes, splashing him with water that does nothing to douse the lava in his stare.

"What the hell are you doing?" My heart hammers out of control, working that much harder because I starved it of oxygen in the first place. "Jesus! You scared me."

"You scared me." He treads water calmly, droplets settling on his lip. His nose. His shoulders. "You were under for a long fuckin' time, Alana." He keeps his words devastatingly low, each one only for me, despite the eyes that burn the side of my face. The attention we garner, simply by existing.

Probably my scream, too. That would've done it.

"Your son wasn't paying attention at first," he growls. "But after a while, he started counting."

Horrified, I swing my gaze around and find my baby, still on Chris' shoulders, a full thirty feet away.

"Chris remembers from when we were younger, when you tested how long you could stay under." Tommy's feet brush mine beneath the surface, his long, powerful legs tangling with mine.

I pull away, vowing to squeeze mine together and become a pin before I wrap myself around this man again.

"So he told Franky how you did that. To save your son from worrying, they counted together. Now you're up again, and everything is fine." His eyes flicker down to my lips. "But *I know* that wasn't a game, Alana. And if you had the choice, I think you'd disappear into the depths forever." He brings his gaze up again. "I asked you to wait on the towel for me. I was only gonna be gone for a minute."

"Just because you want something doesn't mean you get it." I tread water and add another two feet between us, since it's clear he won't. "You should go hang out with your friends. I intend to float here a little longer until Franky's done. Then we'll leave, and you can get on with your day."

"I don't want you to leave." He reclaims those two feet of space, and when I turn to take more, he only shifts, telling me without words that he plans to be wherever I go. I get no choice in the matter. "Why did you and Colin split up?"

"What?" A massive splash draws my focus to the left, to my son disappearing beneath the lake's surface, arms and legs tangling and sprawling. But then he resurfaces again, laughing when Chris scoops him up.

"You agreed to answer *some* questions." Tommy swims around, placing himself in my line of sight. "You and Colin... is that another thing you won't talk about?"

I open my mouth to speak, only for him to cut me off again.

"You don't wanna answer *why* you left, and you've drawn a line in the sand with your book. I'm respecting those. Fuck knows, I don't wanna," he grits out. "But I will. Is your relationship with Colin another boundary? Because if it is, say so. Don't run away."

"He's..." I swallow the ache tickling the base of my throat. "Colin's in love with someone else. Our relationship was always, and will always, remain cordial and kind. But he needs space to explore his relationship with Tasha, and Franky and I needed to come back here to be with my mom."

His eyes narrow to slits. Not angry. Just... pensive.

"He was having an affair?"

"In the most technical sense." I shrug. "I suppose. We were friends at the core, and respect for each other and Franky's best wishes were paramount in every decision we made. Colin and Tasha are getting serious now, and Mom asked us to come back to Plainview. I guess the stars aligned, so here we are."

"The dude is having an affair, and you're totally cool with that?" He tilts backward and floats for a moment, chuckling quietly under his breath. "Not the Alana I remember. *That* girl would tear a man's balls clear off his body for looking anywhere but at her."

"The Alana you remember was young and immature. Her emotions had not yet stabilized, her impulse control was lacking, and she suffered from crippling self-esteem due to her mother's tendency of discarding her on a whim. That Alana needed *someone* to love her, and the thought of losing that person was a special kind of torture. *That* Alana felt the need to claim ownership over another human being, all so she would never feel discarded again."

"Big words." His lips twitch with a playful smile. "Sounds to me like you've spent a great deal of time inside a therapist's office since we last hung out. Self-esteem," he repeats in a murmur. "Discard." He straightens out

141

and captures me with his all-seeing eyes. "You ran away from me and landed on a therapist's couch?" And just like that, his expression turns sour. "Colin is not a therapist, is he? Because fucking your patient is professional misconduct to the worst degree."

"Colin is not a therapist. And though I did, in fact, seek out professional help in New York, I didn't fuck them." I meet his attitude with one of my own. "But since we're discussing conquests and ownership, you'll be happy to know those fight magazines that flash your face all over the front cover, they're on New York newsstands, too. I stopped counting after the sixth or seventh *different* woman on your arm."

"Mmm. But you counted." His lips peel back into a cruel smirk. "I always wondered if you thought about me. Turned me on, thinking of you out in New York, watching me fight in secret. It would have been like sneaking porn, right? Shameful. Something to be sly about. You couldn't make it a family thing since Colin was sure to ask why you were so interested in this one guy's fights all the time. So you had to settle for the tiny screen of your phone while you sat in your closet and touched yourself."

Hatred blooms in my chest and spreads like wildfire, burning me up and leaving my heart pounding with an aching staccato. "Not only is that entirely untrue, but you're being crass and rude and ridiculously inappropriate, too. With my son in the water?"

"He can't hear us."

"And your cute little girlfriend?" *Fuck you, Eliza Darling.* If I knew back then what I know now, I might've stomped on the twelve-year-old and made sure she knew where *not* to step. "You disrespect her by speaking to me that way."

He spares a fast glance across the lake, but even I know she's moved on to annoying Oliver. She's given up on the anger directed my way—for now. Smirking, Tommy brings his blistering eyes back to me. "Nice try, Page. But only one of us is married."

"And one of us migrated from the fight magazines to the gossip rags. '*Who is Tommy Watkins dating this week?*' '*Hearts break as supermodel Catarina Dana is seen out, alone, this New Year's Eve.*' Geez," I sneer. "Forgive me for assuming your rage is a load of shit. You had no trouble crawling out of your hole of despair to make a red carpet appearance."

"And you married the first douchebag you met after arriving in New York! It's like you got off the bus with a *pin the tail* game. You didn't even care where you landed. You found your donkey and hitched your wagon without a single glance back."

"Better I marry one douchebag—who is *not* a douchebag, by the way—than fuck every blonde who fits into a size two backless gown. You act like I'm the monster here, but it looks like you easily found someone else to stroke your hair to sleep."

"You have no clue what the fuck I've been doing these last ten years." He grabs my wrist and yanks me in until our chests clash, his breath hitting my chin and his rage sizzling in the air. "Anyone with half a fucking brain knows gossip rags are no more reliable than the grapevines stretching across Plainview. Barbara to Bitsy, Betty to Paul. If I were to believe the shit that came out of their mouths, then I'd ask who you fucked the week of our high school graduation. Especially since your son told me he has a January birthday. From where I'm standing, it looks to me like you slipped and fell onto someone else's cock, and instead of telling me what you'd done, too afraid to be honest, you busted out of town and ran away from accountability."

He squeezes tighter. Tighter. And stares down into my eyes.

"The Alana I knew was loyal to a fault, and dammit, she was in love with *me*. Even if you left. Even if you won't answer my fucking questions. There isn't a guy in this town or the next that would have tempted you. So despite the math breaking my heart, I'm gonna hope with everything in me that Franky was a ridiculously premature baby, and Barbara's brother's friend's wife doesn't know what the fuck she's talking about. While I'm doing that, I suggest you reread those gossip magazines and consider giving me the same benefit of the doubt."

He releases me with a huff, pushing me back and turning over in the water, and then he swims away. Which is a blessing, really, that he left. Because fresh tears fill my eyes, and pain steals my breath. It's like I have an anvil on my chest and a bubble in my throat, disallowing even an iota of new oxygen to trickle into my lungs.

But the beauty, I realize now, of swimming in the lake when you have a broken heart is that you can fall beneath the surface once more, and no one will ever know you've been crying.

ROUND FIFTEEN
ALANA

"Oh my gosh. Alana? Is that really you?"

I spin at the sound of my name with a polite smile on standby and a gentle *'we've got to hurry home now'* at the ready, but before I have a chance to even *see* whichever new ghost is back from my past, long arms come around and wrap me in a hug so tight, they crush the breath right out of my lungs.

And Franky, being the absolute darling he is, drops my hand and darts out of the firing line.

He'd step in front of a car for me... probably. But accept a hug on my behalf? No chance.

"Oh my gosh!" A girl I once knew—a woman now—releases me from her squeezing hug but holds my arms and practically dances on the tips of her toes. "I heard you were back!"

Through the grapevine, no doubt,

"Caroline Picton. Wow."

"Caroline Davis now." She waves her left hand in my face and shows off a diamond big enough to sparkle, even in the shade. Then she grabs me again and squeals. "Oh my hell, Alana Page! I'd heard the rumors, but Pete and I have been away up in the mountains for a couple of weeks. We just drove back in last night, and I swear, the second we crossed the tracks and rolled into town, we caught a whiff of you."

"Oh..." *Kill me now.* "Good."

"And *you*!" She releases me and charges toward Franky. But before I have a chance to even *consider* saving him, he plasters his back to the brick wall of the local—and only—bank in town and burns her with eyes that would stop even the bravest of intruders.

Instead of clutching at him, she lowers into a crouch and keeps her hands to herself.

Smart woman.

"You must be Franklin Page. I heard all about you just this morning at breakfast. Your grandma thinks you're the bees-knees, and she just so happens to be friends with my momma. My momma was thrilled me and Pete and the kids were back from our little getaway, so she was on my doorstep as soon as the sun came up. And that," she oh-so-gently pokes his chest, "is how I know you're smart, and friendly, and already doing so well down at the gym. I heard you don't like to be hugged, so I won't do that. And sometimes, you don't even like to talk. That's okay, too. I'll do enough of that for the both of us." She leans in as though to tell a secret. "But since I know you *can* talk, feel free to jump in at any point."

She stops. Waits. And when he only stares, she snickers.

"Alrighty. So I heard you're heading to Plainview Elementary after the summer, and guess what? My Mikey goes to that school, too, and he's your same age."

"Really?" Surprise brings me back in, because hell, I still have small-town in my blood, and I know for a damn fact she wasn't pregnant when we graduated. Or at least, she wasn't talking about it. "You have a nine-year-old? Caroline!"

"Oh, shush." Giggling, she stands once more and pats my arm. "You knew what we were doing back then. Same thing you were doing."

"Which is not a thing we'll discuss right now." I pointedly look down at my son, then back up at her. Though laughter, the first real bout I've felt in a while, rolls along my throat. "You have a child!? I swear, my mind is blown."

"I have *three* children. Mikey, who's nine, then Daisy, she's seven. Lola is—"

"Five," Franky answers seriously. "Assuming you were consistent."

"Lord." She cups her mouth and snorts like a baby pig. "He's quick."

"Too quick, sometimes." I set my hand on his shoulder and carefully draw him in. I don't always know what he wants in social situations like these, but when he wraps his arm across my back and anchors his hand on my hip, I know I've picked right. "Three," I repeat in awe. "Geez."

"It's a lot. But once you have two, it's all the same. A mess is still a mess, and noise is noise. Pete and I are talking about trying for one more. But then we'll probably stop." Her cheeks warm with a sweet blush. "I've been working some nights at the bar to have something other than kids to keep my brain busy. If we do have one more, that'll be *it*. It's time for my boobs to belong to me again."

Boobs!

Franky drops his gaze to the ground and blushes a furious red.

Change the subject! "Which bar do you work at?"

"You remember Darlene's?" She nods before I can answer. "We bought that from her a couple of years back."

"But it's still called Darlene's?"

She giggles. "It is! Though, once I'm done making babies—oh, and we're building a house out by the drive-in movie theater, too—but when we're done with all that, I intend to sit down and have a think about the future of the bar. Might even consider a new name."

"Risky move," I tease. "I've mentioned changing *Books Books Books* to something a little less on the nose, and it's like I suggested tossing Mrs. Middler's cat into the bathtub and sitting on it till it stops moving."

She cackles. "I heard that, too! My mom had a good ole time catching me up on everything that's happened since we left. Though," again, she leans in to tell another secret, "I heard Mrs. Middler is *actually* fine with the change. She's only huffing for the sake of huffing, so press on that button one more time, and you'll probably get your way. Then make an offer on the place. Bet you a tequila shooter that you get it for a steal."

"Really?" Franky, my Mr. Businessman, swings his gaze up in interest. "How much do you consider a steal?"

Stunned, Caroline's eyes come to mine.

So I shrug and gesture down to him again. "You wanna talk business, you gotta talk to my associate. He's the brains of this outfit."

"Oh, well..." She reaches into her purse and pulls out a pen and a scrap piece of paper. "I'm gonna write a number on this page, my good sir. I say you offer her something in this vicinity." She scribbles the digits and finishes with an exclamation point, then folding the paper, she offers it. *To him, not me.* "I reckon you'll be the new owners of a little slice of the Plainview business district. Get her on a good day, and you're all set. If she says no—" She drops the pen back in her bag "—then you just ask again another day. She's ready to sell, and she wants to do it before she dies."

Franky's brows pinch—*death, as a friendly conversation piece, bothers*

147

him—but Caroline's phone trills in her purse, stealing her focus while Franky brings his hands up and plugs his ears.

She fishes for the device and huffs after reading the screen, then she silences it and meets my eyes. "You should come to Darlene's for a drink. I gotta run and get my kids now, and there ain't no way we can catch up properly with my hooligans running around."

A fresh bout of nerves settles in the base of my stomach, much the same way I imagine they do for Franky when he doesn't want to socialize. And though we don't verbalize our thoughts, we still take a step back as one. "No, I don't think I can—"

"I really want to see you, Alana." She grabs my arm and gives it a gentle squeeze. "It's been a *long* time, and hell knows, there's a whole lotta water flowing under that bridge. Don't think I didn't already hear about you and the Watkins boys spending the day together at the lake."

"Caroline—"

"It was always you and them," she murmurs seriously. "But sometimes, when I was lucky, it was you and me. So if you need a friend in this town who isn't Team Tommy, then you know where to find me." She starts around me, silencing her ringing phone a second time and grabbing the bank door.

"Wait." I turn, dragging Franky around, too. "Why aren't you Team Tommy? What'd he do to you?"

She smirks. "Nothing. He's my friend, too. He stayed, and *everyone* saw how he was after you left, so it's only natural the whole crew from back then are *his* friends. Maybe they still like you, and maybe they'll still be nice. But their loyalties are set. I never forgot you, though. Not for a single second. I reckon you must be feeling like an outsider these days, and outside is the loneliest place to be. So if you need someone to talk to, someone from back then who won't automatically jump on the '*we hate Alana Page*' train..." She gifts me a friendly smile. "Well, I can be that."

Her phone trills for a third time, so she answers with a grunt and a roll of her eyes, and then she yanks the bank door open. "You know where to find me." Bringing the phone to her ear, she bites out a sassy, "I was busy! Give me a second, Mom!"

"How long will you be out for?" Franky sits on my bed, watching me slide a hoop earring onto my ear. "What time will you get back?"

"Err..." I'm going out. God help me; I'm doing something I never actually did in my youth. Because by the time I was twenty-one and old enough to buy a drink, I was already a mom.

Jesus. Why am I nervous?

"I'll only be a few hours, honey." I finish the first earring and move to the next. "But you should try to go to sleep while I'm gone, okay? I know you don't like doing that without me, but I'll have the monitor set up to keep an eye on you, and you can use Grandma's iPad to text me if you need to."

"Can I just stay up and wait for you?"

"No. Because I want you to try to do this." I meet his eyes in the mirror. "Consider this a night of growth for us both, since I don't particularly relish the idea of going out and seeing these people from my past." *Growth is shit. I hate growth.* "It's healthy for us." *Allegedly.*

"If I go to sleep on my own, does that mean I *always* have to sleep on my own in my bedroom?"

"No. We can go back to normal tomorrow night, and the next night, and the night after that. You can sleep wherever you want from now until you've decided you want to sleep somewhere else." Dropping my hands, I brush them over my dress and along my hips, then I turn from the mirror and smile. "There are no rules about this, honey. There's just you and me and whatever you need to do to feel okay every night."

"But not tonight?" He looks me up and down, entirely neutral in his expression. *Never, ever rely on Franklin Page to make you feel good about your outfit choice.* "I don't get to feel okay tonight?"

I snort. "Nice try, but no. We're in a new town now and starting a new life. Sometimes that means we have to try new things, even if we don't want to."

"But you're a grown-up. You don't *have* to go out. We could stay here and watch TV." His little eyes beam behind his glasses. "That sounds like a good idea to me."

"And around in circles we go." I release a pent-up breath and turn toward my closet to get shoes. "That lady we saw out front of the bank? Caroline—"

"Was very loud," he shudders. "She likes it when people look at her."

"Well..." I select a pair of wedge sandals. "I don't know that she *likes* it. But she definitely doesn't know how to be any other way. Which is fine, in my opinion. We should never be someone we're not, and true friends would never try to change someone they care about." Spinning back, I move to the bed and push Franky's Murdle book backward so I can sit beside him and pull my shoes on. "Caroline was—ironically—pretty shy in school. She preferred to read in the library instead of hanging out on the playground. She didn't have a lot of friends and—"

"Did you have a lot of friends?"

"Not necessarily." Thoughtful now, I slip one foot into the leather straps of my sandal. "I was always hanging around with Tommy and Chris. And Raquel, too, and Ollie. We had our circle of friends, and we never excluded anyone else, but it's like the whole world knew it was me, Tommy, and Chris, first and foremost. Me and Tommy, connected at the hip." I sigh. "And Tommy and Chris, because they were a package deal. Caroline was a little afraid of them, I think."

"Afraid?"

"They weren't mean. They were just... they were often hurt, honey. Dirty. They lived a tough life back then, and not everyone can sit with boys who had black eyes and split lips and not feel weird about it."

"Why did they have black eyes and split lips?"

"Because their mom and dad weren't very nice." I slowly feed the leather strap through the metal buckle and picture the boys, so heartbreakingly clear in my mind, hurt and hungry. Sad and, most often, in pain. "It's easy to look mean when you're injured, and I bet it's hard to muster a smile when breathing makes your ribs ache. It wasn't their fault that they looked a little unwelcoming sometimes, and it wasn't Caroline's fault for shying away from that."

"You didn't mind sitting with them when they were hurt?" Franky's little feet don't touch the floor from up here, so he gently kicks them back and forth, tapping the frame of the bed with his heels. "They didn't scare you?"

"No." I finish the first shoe and move to the next. "I felt protective of them. I felt sad every time they were sad, and angry every time they came to school with fresh injuries. But you know what was worse than that? When they didn't come to school at all."

"Because you worried about them?"

He's so intuitive. So smart.

I nod. "Smartphones weren't invented back then, and even if they were, Tommy and Chris wouldn't have had the money to buy one. So when they didn't come to school at all, I knew they were in bad shape, and I couldn't even send a text to check in." I swallow the rage that bubbles along my throat, rearranging my face and offering my baby a soft smile. "On those days, Caroline would sit with me. She would provide space in the quiet and comfort while I worried. She never got cranky when I wasn't in the mood to chat, and she never held a grudge that, just as soon as the boys were back in school, she was alone again, and I wasn't."

"Do you wish she was brave enough to sit with them?" He studies my eyes, his perfect green stare flickering between mine. "If she were, she wouldn't have been alone."

"Yeah. But we don't try to change our friends. She did what she felt was right for her, and I did what I felt was right for me. And in the times in between, we were happy to be together, even if that togetherness was wrapped in my worry and silence."

"I guess I see why you want to go see her, then." He reaches around for his book and scoots back on the bed to rest against the headboard. "She seems nice, even if she's loud."

I breathe out a soft laugh. "Exactly."

"And I like to read in the library, too. Will you talk to me through the cameras later?"

"Maybe." Done with my shoes, I push up to stand and take a moment to find my balance, now that I'm three inches taller than usual. Finally, I stride to the dressing table and position the baby monitor I never got rid of, just in case. I point it straight toward the bed and pray that in just a couple of hours, I'll check in and find him sound asleep. "You can stay in my bed, and you can even lie right there in the middle. When I get back, I'll scoot you over and snuggle in. Oh, and Colin said that he was planning to call tonight. So you should grab your chess board and get ready."

"Okay." Uninterested now that he's reading, he rests his book on his knees and writes notes in the margins. "I think Doctor Pepper was the killer in this one. But Officer Lockemup isn't very good at his job."

"You'll solve the crime like you always do." I cross the room and press a kiss on his forehead. "I love you so much, Franky. More than anything else on the planet."

"I know." His lips curl into a sweet smile that ends with deep dimples pulling at his cheeks. "You say it all the time."

"And I mean it all the time." I brush my fingers through his hair and pull him back, forcing him to meet my eyes. "Like I mean it when I say you need to try to sleep while I'm gone. Grandma Bitsy is in her room watching her shows, but the door is open, and you can visit with her anytime. She said you could."

"Do I have to?"

I choke down a laugh and peek across at the door. Then I look back to Franky and wrinkle my nose. "No, you don't have to. You spent most of today with her. Did you like that?"

"Mmhm. I like it when we hang out, just the two of us." But then he scowls. "I don't like when she takes me to see all her friends because then it's loud and she's pushy and tries to make me hug that other old lady."

"Sadly, that's how these people are. They think they have to compete with each other, even though *real* friends are happy for each other's successes. And back when I was younger, kids were expected to do as they were told. Like, *all* the time. That included hugging people we didn't want to hug or visiting people we didn't want to visit. Grandma and her friends think I'm crazy for not following those same rules."

"You don't make me hug people. You don't even make me hug you."

"Exactly. Because kids are only kids for a short amount of time. I'd rather teach you that saying *no* is okay now and not make it a lesson you have to heal from as an adult. That's considered hokey parenting to some people. But do you know what *you've* taught me?"

"Me?"

"Mmhm." I tap his nose and earn a cute smile. "You taught me that it's okay to not care about what other people think. In fact—" I straighten and head back to the dresser drawers. "What they think is none of my business. I only care that you're happy and safe."

Behind me, he lowers his book and meets my eyes in the mirror. "If that were true, then I think I would be most happy and safe if you stayed home tonight."

I snort. "Nice try. Go get Grandma's iPad so you have it near you. Then I'm walking out the door. The sooner I leave, the sooner I can come back."

"Fine." He very carefully, very thoughtfully, places his pen between book pages and sets the book on the bed, then jumps to the floor and dashes out the door. His shoulder bounces off the doorframe as he passes, a solid thump that elicits a grunt of pain from him and a hiss of sympathy from me. "I'm okay!" He darts down the stairs. "I'm alright!"

"You'd hurt yourself less if you slowed down."

"The sooner you go, the sooner you come back!"

ROUND SIXTEEN

TOMMY

"This is Rebekah." Oliver drops a blonde in front of me, the way a cat presents a dead mouse at its owner's feet. While music pounds in the air, the jukebox inside Darlene's is rich with quarters, and the tracks are lined up for hours, he wraps his arm around a *different* blonde and beams.

Look what I did, Tommy! I caught you a juicy fish.

Rebekah and the other one look similar enough to be sisters, maybe. Cousins, perhaps. But they're definitely not from around here.

"Rebekah, that's Tommy. He's recently suffered heartbreak and could do with a little soothin'."

"Hi, Tommy." She's small in the waist and large in the chest. And when she offers her hand, taking mine and smiling up with big ol' baby blues, I know Oliver's game. He didn't go fishing for just *any* chick. He tried for a lookalike. Like blonde and blue will do—it doesn't matter whose brain or personality they're attached to. "I'm so sorry to hear about your breakup."

"He's exaggerating." I shake her hand and take mine back just as soon as she releases me. "A girl I dated in high school is back in town, and Oliver likes to create drama where there is none." I look down at the almost empty glass in her hand. "You want a new drink?"

"Oh, sure." She beams, pleased with my offer, but her smile falls into a pout when I spin away and head to the bar. Without her.

"Hey, Tommy." Caroline slaps a napkin by my arm and glances over my shoulder. "I see you and Ollie have been shopping from the kiddie section."

155

"Just him," I chuckle, nodding in thanks when she grabs a glass and begins pouring. "And she already had a drink in her hand. You card her when she ordered?"

"Yes." She burns me with a side-eye. "Of course I did."

"So that kinda implies she's not a kid. Which bodes well for me since I don't like the idea of sleeping in a cell for the night."

Finishing, she sets my beer by my elbow. "Means you're taking her home?"

"No. But I'm glad to know she's of age, simply because I was standing near her. Busy in here tonight, huh?"

She looks around with a maternal affection glowing in her eyes. This bar is her baby, just as surely as the three humans she birthed are her babies.

"Saturday night tends to do that, especially after a long, hot day in the sun. Folks get thirsty, and word gets around that the Watkins boys are spritzing on a bit of cologne."

"Jesus." I grab my beer. "The fact I know you aren't even lying is just..." I take a long sip and shake my head. "It's exhausting. People around here need to get a life."

"Why, when you provide better entertainment than whatever's on the television?"

"You're a pain in my ass."

"Mmhm. You here for a big night where I gotta call Pete to help me keep things under control? Or is mellow the new yellow, and you're gonna behave?" She grabs another glass and begins pouring someone else's beer, but before I can answer, her smile drops away, and her eyes shoot over my shoulder in panic. "You in a good mood, Tommy Watkins? If not, give me twenty seconds to make some phone calls."

"I... what?" I glance over my shoulder and feel that kick, like every other fucking time we're in the same space. Because Alana Page stops in the door-way, long blonde cascading hair tickling her shoulders and bright blue eyes burning with anxiety and scanning the crowd that stares back at her.

It shouldn't be like this, where a whole fucking bar silences just because someone walks in, where bodies stop moving, and the awkward cough of someone who can't help themselves bounces across a packed room.

But this is Plainview, where no one minds their own business, and she's Alana Page. The one who got away.

I don't even mean she's *my* one who got away.

She left us all, and her departure was, for the first few weeks, as though a serial killer had swept through town and ravaged our small community.

Questions went unanswered and understanding, to this day, remains unreachable.

She wanted to disappear and be forgotten. When really, she created the biggest fucking mystery Plainview has known since before prohibition.

I turn to go to her, but Caroline grabs my arm, setting her hand on my bicep. "Tommy..."

"I won't make a mess." I brush her off and take my beer, and since the whole fucking town needs to watch anyway, I cross the bar and hold Alana's terrified stare. She's gonna be scared no matter what. May as well face the devil she knows.

"I can leave." So quickly, she steps back and draws my focus down to her dress. Her body wrapped in white, and the tan she collected from half a summer in the middle of nowhere. "I didn't realize you'd be out, so I can—"

"Stop freakin' out every time we run into each other."

I offer my beer—not sure why, except it's the only thing I have in my hand, and I want to give her things.

Always have. Always will.

But she shakes her head, drawing her lip between her teeth and ruining the lipstick she applied before coming out.

Fuck me. Lipstick is a grown woman's decision. It's not something she even considered back when we were teens.

"You're in Plainview now, Lana. Chances are, we're gonna run into each other at least every other day. You're gonna develop an autoimmune problem if you panic every time we're within a hundred yards of each other."

"This is your space." She looks past me. Around me. Scouring those who watch us, and finding absolutely no pleasure in it. "You were here first, so I'll head out and—"

"You'll stay." I bring my beer up and take a sip. Anything to wet my desert-dry throat. "We never really got to do this when we were younger."

"Drink?" She smiles, though I'm not sure she means it in a friendly way. "That's not true. We drank plenty."

"No, I mean, in a bar. In front of the adults. In fact, I'm still consistently surprised to remember we *are* the adults now. Feels weird."

She exhales—I think it's a laugh—and looks down at her feet.

So, of course, I do the gentlemanly thing and follow her gaze along her long, trim legs and down to cute painted toenails.

"Nice shoes. Very *summery*. Franky having a sleepover with Bitsy?"

She nods, though all she allows me a view of is the top of her head and mascara'd lashes flickering down to kiss her cheeks. "He's not pleased I came out." Finally, she drags her eyes up and stops on mine. "He doesn't like changes in routine, and he's accustomed to us watching television before bed and snuggling on the couch."

Lucky kid.

"He'll be okay, though?"

"Yeah. We're considering it an exercise in growth." She sniffles and searches around me again because fuck, I know they continue to watch us. "I'm out here, uncomfortable as hell. And he's there, also uncomfortable. We'll reunite again in a few hours and lament a wasted evening spent apart."

Wasted... even though she's right here in front of me.

"Sounds like you and he make a good little team." I bring my beer up and chug half the glass—is it possible to drown my bitterness? *Here's hoping.*

Swallowing and wiping my lip with my free hand, I reach across and set the glass on a nearby table. "Must be nice having him in your life."

Her brows furrow in consideration. "How do you mean?"

"Just... relationships can be tricky: with our friends, with lovers, with siblings, even. You and me? We know not-so-great relationships with our parents. But what you and Franky have is unconditional. It's not complicated at all. It simply *is*."

"Makes you wonder what the hell our parents were thinking," she sighs. She relaxes a little, dropping her weight and a layer of defensiveness. "Back then, I figured what I have with my mom, and what you had with your parents, was just the way these things go. It wasn't pleasant, and it wasn't fair, especially for you and Chris. But I thought it was reasonably normal."

"And now?"

"Now—" Finally, she smiles, "My son is my best friend, and what we have is pure and wonderful and comes without conditions or an expiration date. He never has to worry that I don't love him or if I'll wake up one day and treat him badly for no reason at all. And I never have to wonder if he's lying or sneaking or, in his little heart, simply doesn't like me." She meets my eyes and blushes the way she used to, back when she was sixteen and already world-weary. She trusted me back then. She knew firsthand that life sucked, but she believed with her whole heart that I could—that I would—create a pocket of happiness she could climb into whenever she needed it.

Didn't matter that I was broke and broken. She merely believed.

And shit, that belief made me invincible.

"Perhaps, someday, you'll become a dad and get to feel this, too," she murmurs. "It's like nothing I've ever experienced in my life."

Maybe.

Probably not.

"Alana fucking Page!" Chris cuts through the staring crowd, louder than the rest, which is a bravery that only comes to him when tequila sizzles in his veins. Then he crashes into her side and shoves a shot glass in her hand, clear liquid spilling over and dribbling along her delicate wrist. "I know a brewin' fight when I see one." He smacks a kiss to the side of her head, strands of her blonde hair getting caught in his stubble as he pulls back. "But I'm calling it for today, 'k? We're all gonna get along. For tonight, 'cos it's my birthday, I'm declaring it so."

Confused, she leans back and scowls. "It is *not* your birthday!"

"It's my *half* birthday," he sniggers. "'Cos Tommy and me've gotta share. I got sick of always getting the second hug. The second kiss. The second *happy birthday, kiddo*. So I'm claiming the summer, and Tommy takes the winter, and finally, we get to celebrate ourselves as individuals for once in our fuckin' lives."

Surprised, she brings her eyes back to mine in question.

So I nod. "It's true. We did eighteen of them together, then he threw a fit and decided he wanted his own."

"Do you not acknowledge your actual birthday on the actual day of your birth?" She looks up at him again. "February comes and goes, and you celebrate Tommy only?"

"No, I take February, too." He giggles, already two-thirds of the way to puking in the street. "I get both. But Tommy doesn't get shit in the summer. It's his turn to sit down and shut up 'cos he gets everything else. He was born first. The ladies look at him first, even if he tells 'em to buzz off. People talk to him first 'cos they say I'm mean. And he fell in love first." Sighing, he rests his cheek on the side of her head. "Didn't work out so well. But he still got that."

"Oliver?" I drop my head back and summon someone, *anyone*, to help. "Come get him, please."

"You gotta drink that shot, Lana." He crushes her neck in his side-hug and drags her in till more tequila spills onto her wrist. "For me. For my fake-ass birthday. You owe me ten shots, really, since you've skipped the last ten birthdays."

"You want me to buy you ten shots?" She licks her wrist—*God, kill me now*—and hums with happiness when the taste hits her tongue. "I would, but you're already kinda drunk. I wouldn't feel good making the situation worse."

"Come on." Oliver comes around and pulls Chris his way. Which only ends with Alana being pulled along, too. "Time to get off her, Watkins. She ain't yours."

"I don't want you to *buy* me ten shots!" He sets his hand under her glass and pushes it up. "I want you to shoot 'em. Maybe then, you'll be a little less fuckin' stuffy and actually remember you used to like us."

"Oliver!" I peel Chris' arm from around her neck and snarl when he holds on too fucking tight. "Take him."

"Truce!" Chris declares. Not just for him or her, and not even for me. He makes a stand and speaks to everyone. "For my birthday, I'm saying y'all stop staring at her. Forget for a night that she abandoned us and pretend she's just... ya know... Alana Page. She's been hiding out in Tommy's bedroom for ten years. Since," he grins, "that's totally in character for what we thought was gonna happen anyway. Stop staring at her and stop whispering. Stop actin' like she's got the leper, and instead, buy her a drink. Once she's at the third shot, she's gonna shed that big-city sparkle and become like us again. Give it time."

"We're gonna go to the smoking area for a bit," Ollie decides, pulling Chris along and gritting his teeth when he jerks Alana off balance. "Sorry."

I grab her arm and steady her again. But also, to stop her from turning on her heels and making a dash for freedom. Since the second, of course, is way more likely than the first.

"It's okay." She tries to brush my hands off. "Let me—"

"Don't leave." I pull her closer, thankful for the jukebox that covers the sound of her exhaled breath when we crash back together. And since we're technically on a dance floor, I sway. "Swear to christ, Lana. I'm sick of seeing you leave."

Her eyes, desperate and emotional, glitter with unshed tears. "I can't be here. I can't—"

"You can." And because I'm a Watkins just as surely as Chris is, I nudge her shot glass up and hold her eyes until she drinks what's left. "Truce, remember? And everybody else has been put on notice. They don't get to stare at you anymore."

"He's drunk." She licks the tequila from her lips, and whatever sticky drops are on her wrist. Then she startles when I steal the glass and set it on a nearby table without, even for a second, releasing her or stopping our impromptu dance. "He's going to puke tonight, you watch."

I choke out a soft laugh, nodding in agreement. "You'd know. He got drunk like that a time or two back in high school."

"And then he was a total baby about it for the next forty-eight hours. Needed a cold washcloth on his forehead and soup for every meal until he felt better."

"He doesn't get soup anymore." Dancing is for touching. It's for tracing new curves and remembering old flames, so I run my hand over her hips and bury my nose behind her ear. "Since I'm not the kind of guy who's gonna make it. But he preps the washcloths before he drinks now."

Surprised, she pulls back to search my eyes. "Really?"

"Mmhm. Soaks them in water and tosses them in the freezer before we come out. By the time we're home, and he starts whining, he remembers what he prepped and goes to sleep a happy man..." I laugh. "Ish."

She doesn't find things as humorous as I do, frowning instead. "He drink himself sick often?"

She's still his mama bear, even when she thinks she isn't. Still his protector, a role she took on when she became mine. "He needs better guidance, Tommy. Drinking like that is how you end up like your parents. We know that's not what he wants, so—"

"Hasn't drunk himself sick in years." I press my hand beneath her chin and shut her up. "Seems he's working through his emotions with alcohol and bad choices tonight, because that girl he once knew is back in town, and besides, it's his half birthday. He's allowed to get loud for a night."

Her eyes glitter with anger—which is better than the heartache I catch all too often—then she brings her hand up and slaps mine away. "Don't touch my face."

"I said I'd buy you a shot." Caroline pops up on my left, brandishing a shot of tequila and a grin. Then she forces the glass into Alana's hand. "I'm under no illusions about *this*." She points between us. "This is not a reunion. This is lightning in a bottle, bound to explode soon. So, while all is contained and everyone is playing nice, I'm gonna shut my trap and pour your drinks. But the second I get so much as a *hint* of anarchy, I'm kicking you both out and putting you on the street. If you break a *single* glass, I'm dragging you out of bed first thing tomorrow morning and bringing you back here to clean my bar from top to bottom."

"What if we break a table? Respectfully," I add, teasing. "Because I might like to swing one at my brother a little later, and I need to know the terms of our agreement before I start that war."

"Start *no* wars in my bar!" She sets her hand beneath Alana's drink and nudges the glass up, emptying clear liquid into her mouth. Then she takes the glass and spins on her heels, striding back to work.

"Holy shit!" Alana's breath whistles along her throat. I know the tequila burns on its way down. "Does no one around here respect a woman's right to drink at her own pace?"

"I'm not sure she saw the first one. Probably didn't realize you'd already downed a shot."

"Under duress." She swipes her mouth with the back of her hand and closes her eyes. It's not a wistful, dancing-in-the-dark thing outsiders might assume. It's an '*I need a minute alone before I hurt someone*' thing.

So I give her that and slowly, almost imperceptibly, bring us closer to the middle of the dance floor.

"I know what you're doing."

"Yeah?" I pull her in, forcing her to straddle my leg and rest her cheek on my shoulder. "I'm dancing. I'm drinking, albeit slower than you. I'm celebrating my brother's half birthday because he needs one day a year to feel like he's not just one half of *us*. It matters to him, and what matters to him matters to me more than what matters to me."

"You're intentionally being obtuse."

"Am I?" I close my eyes, too, so I don't have to see all the assholes staring at us. Their stunned expressions remind me of everything I've already lost. They remind me she's a flight risk, plain and simple. "So what is it you think I'm doing?"

"I grew up with you." She licks her lips. I don't even have to see it to know she slides her tongue over perfect, swollen bow lips. "I grew with you, through the good days and the bad. Guys like you... trouble found you even when you weren't looking, and grudges were had, even when you weren't sure why you had them."

Fuck, she smells good.

"I was *with* you when you'd plan out your counterattack, remember? Every time someone pissed you off, you'd decide if you were gonna punch them in the face or annoy them till they lost the will to live."

And she feels so, so fucking good.

"You can't punch me in the face."

I grin, knowing she won't see it. "Says who?"

"Which means you choose psychological warfare. You'll continue to bother me till we're on speaking terms. Consistency and all that. Maybe I'll even get so used to having you around, I'll stop panicking and start thinking of you as a friend again. But someday, at some point in the future, you'll make me pay for leaving. When I least expect it, you'll swing around, armed with your sword of retribution, and you'll destroy me the way you feel I destroyed you."

"That's quite the intricate hypothesis."

"But you can't move on to the friend stage until I stop telling you to leave me alone. And you can't move on to retribution until I feel safe in your presence. So, step one is to make yourself visible to me. Being where I am, going where I go—"

"And just so we're clear: I was here first tonight. I didn't follow you."

"It's a small town," she sighs. "It won't even be difficult. One grocery store. One gas station. One elementary school. My son attends your gym for classes, and Caroline owns the only decent bar in a fifty-mile radius." She pulls back, startling my eyes open and hurting my heart with the way she stares. "I know you, Tommy. And I know payback will sting. Can't we just agree this isn't healthy? Let me go on with my life without always looking over my shoulder, worried about when that sword will meet my throat?"

She has freckles on her cheeks and golden flakes in her eyes. Then and now. Her hair is lighter now because of the summer sun, but I know from experience it darkens a little in the winter.

Not a lot. Not like mine. But still...

"I'm scared of my own shadow," she pleads, blinking her eyes clear and swallowing until her throat bobs. "Because I know you'll hurt me back. It's as certain as death. And taxes. And that, in itself, is part of the psychological warfare."

"You make out I'm some kind of evil villain in your story. Which is so interesting, considering I've done nothing but love you my whole life."

"Tommy—"

"Adored you. I fucking worshipped you." I tighten my arm around her hips and push her shoulder with my free hand, dipping her backward when the music calls for it. And because I fucking earned it, I'm rewarded with the perfect view of her swollen tits and delicate, outstretched throat. "Even when we bickered back in the day, fighting and fucking, arguing and making up again," I pull her up and inhale her explosive breath, "I've done nothing but be good to you. Yet you look over your shoulder and act like *I'm* the monster?"

"You know what I mean." Her eyes darken. "Don't act like I'm wrong."

"You want me to admit I have some long con going?" I tug her in again and thrill at how perfectly her body fits against mine. She was the exact right size for me back then, and she's exactly right for me now, too. "You're the one who left, Alana. And you're the one who came back. You're living your life, and I'm living mine, but somehow, in your mind, you've convinced yourself I've got a plan for payback?"

"I know you." Her eyes sparkle with tears she won't let fall. Anger she tries so fucking hard to bottle up. "Why don't you just say all the mean things you wanna say? Be cruel and horrible and take back the power I stole from you. Sever the ties that used to bind us, so then I might have a chance to get on with my life."

"Me, sever the ties?" I scoff. "Babe, you did that already, remember? It was right around graduation. We'd been talking about getting married, and we didn't even care what everyone else thought. We knew we were young and that people would have somethin' to say about it, and we *especially* knew the better-to-do folks would disapprove because I'm just Tommy Watkins, and you were way too good to slum with this kind of trash."

Her chest shudders, visibly rocking against mine. "Tommy—"

"We were talking about New York. You were gonna go to school, and I was gonna find a job. Didn't matter what it was, so long as it paid enough to cover rent and food since I was never gonna let you be cold or hungry."

"Tommy, stop."

"We had those plans, and you even said it was cool that Chris came, too. You were totally fucking insistent on it, swearing you didn't mind. So there I was, drunk on love and bursting with big plans, then you just... you went cold on me. We were fine, and then we weren't. Somewhere between prom and graduation, everything went to hell, but you kept saying it was okay. That's what you do, isn't it? You *say* things are fine, even when they aren't." I wrinkle my nose. "In fact, I remember you screaming it in my face. *Nothing is wrong, Tommy! Just leave me alone!*"

A single, fat tear swells over and dribbles onto her cheek.

"I didn't wanna leave you alone. That's not what I do... did," I amend, my own words like a lash across my heart. "We fight it out until we figure it out. But you didn't let us. We were fine, and then we weren't, and when I gave you the space you screamed for—just one fucking night, Alana—you weren't where I left you when I came back the next day."

She drops her head, crashing her face against my chest.

"Are those the ties you want me to sever?" I snarl. "Because I don't know if you noticed, but you snipped those motherfuckers ten years ago. Now you want to *get on with your life* but act like I'm the bad guy?"

She tries to pull away, to shake my hands off and turn and do what it is she's so fucking good at—*leave*. But I yank her back, crushing her so close she has no choice but to bend her neck and rest her chin on my chest.

"You don't get to be the victim in our story. *You* made your choices, and for whatever reasons you had, those same reasons you choose not to share with me, at least *you* got to have an opinion on the direction of your life. The rest of us fucking trash you left behind in Plainview, we were just the fallout of your storm. You were a hurricane, and I was the house I thought I was building for our futures. But you blew right through me, babe, and it was so fucking unexpected, I didn't have time to find shelter."

She tries again to pull away, grunting in the back of her throat and growling when I tug her back in.

"You don't get to stand there with tears in your eyes and act like I'm the asshole!"

"Let her go." Ollie stops on my right, surprising me with his calmness and the gentle hand he lays over mine. Then he peels my fingers back, revealing the marks I leave on her skin and the rush of blood that refills her digits now that circulation can restart. "Come on." He gently pushes us apart, freeing her from my steely grip.

Alana stumbles back, whimpering and spinning on her heels, then she strides away without a backward glance. With every step she takes, my heart aches. For every foot she places between us, my soul trembles.

"You can't do that, Tommy." Ollie comes around and searches my eyes. Because he knows me better than I know myself, he sets his hand on my chest and pushes me back since we both know I'd sooner barrel right through him and chase her.

"Either you back up, maybe go hang with the girls we came here with, or you go the fuck home." He shakes his head, the movement barely pene-trating my consciousness. Because my eyes are on Alana as she shakily climbs onto a barstool, scooping her dress under her backside and using a napkin to wipe her nose.

"She thinks *I'm* the bad guy." I want to puke. Or smash something. Or scream, even. I'll take any of the above. "She comes around, crying about how mean I am and how she's scared of her own shadow. She thinks I'm the fucking problem!"

"She can feel scared and sad, even if she was the one who left. Hey?" He claps my cheek and commands my eyes back to his. "More than one thing can be true at the same time. She left, but that doesn't mean she isn't hurting for it. Now walk."

"Where's Chris?" I back up until his hand falls from my face, then I consider knocking him on his ass and walking over his corpse if it means sitting at the bar beside Alana and continuing this conversation. But my life didn't start with her. No matter how much it feels like it did, she wasn't there from day one.

Chris was.

So I turn on my heels and stalk toward the slot machines out back. "He in the smoking area?"

ROUND SEVENTEEN
ALANA

"Here." Caroline places a shot of tequila by my shaking hand, then a second, with a lifted brow and eyes that brook no argument. "You need to take a damn breath and calm down before your heart gives out."

I don't hesitate like I did with the others. I just grab one, toss it back, then the other, and repeat. "Thanks."

"He's a lot, huh?" She ignores other waiting customers, setting her elbows on the bar and hitting me with an expression of sympathy. Which almost feels worse than anger. "He always was a whole big bunch of muscle operating on emotion. That ain't likely to change, no matter how old he gets."

"I made a mistake coming here." I push the glasses away and exhale a shuddering breath. "I should've known better."

"Coming here to Darlene's? Nah, that was just bad luck. I can count on one hand how many times he's been here in the last year." She grabs the bottle of tequila and pours me a refill. "The universe was just being especially mean, dropping you both here on the same night."

"No." I grab the first and drink again. "Coming here to Plainview. You wanna know a fun fact my kid told me? There are, like, nineteen *thousand* towns, cities, and little villages all across this damn country. Some of them are big, like New York, and some of them are small, like Plainview. I figure I should just grab a map and pick literally *any* other place except this one. Tommy deserves to move on without seeing me everywhere he goes, and I would do *anything* to not feel this... this..." I slam my shot glass down and press a hand to my stomach instead. "This! This hurt and anxiety and anger and sadness. I want to exist in a place where I'm not equally terrified and hopeful that I'll run into him, wondering if maybe this is the time it won't turn to hell."

"You *want* to see him?"

"I want to own him! Because he owns me. I want to have what I used to have, and feel how I used to feel, and be adored the way only he knew how to adore me. I want the life we planned for *us*, and I want Franky to be there, too. I wish I'd married Tommy, not Colin, and I wish he was the father of my child. I want to rock on a rocking chair and drink lemonade on the porch with Chris when the sun goes down. I want the plans *we* made. But they were stolen from me, too."

I grab the next shot and tip it back, desperate for the burn of tequila in my throat rather than the ache of a broken heart in my chest.

"I didn't give my permission for those things to happen." I set the glass down with a bang. "But they did, and now I'm the monster in everyone's stories. It's not fair, Caroline! It's *not* fair because *I* didn't do anything wrong. Not like they think I did." A horrifying sob bursts from my throat, squeezing my lungs and humiliating, because I know people can hear me. The jukebox is loud but not loud enough to drown out the sound of my tears.

"He thinks I'm the worst person in the world. And I can't even tell him different because..." Frustrated, I run my hands through my hair. "*Because.* He isn't strong enough to carry this truth. He isn't capable of processing it. Or accepting it. Or sitting with it. He would self-destruct, and I can't be the reason he does that."

"So, you hurt him... to help him?" She lowers to her elbows and studies me from under the curtain of my falling hair. "Are you protecting him, Alana?"

"Always." I choke on the tears clogging my throat. "For the rest of my life."

"What the hell happened?" She does to me what I do to Franklin, grabbing my hair and pulling me up to look into her eyes. "You can tell me, ya know? You can share the burden. I won't tell anyone."

"You'd tell Pete." Alcohol swims in my veins, happily pushing pain aside and slowing my heart. There's a reason people become alcoholics. Or drug addicts. There's a reason these things are regulated and not given to children. Because when the world hurts too much, and life is intent on crushing your soul, booze has the power to alleviate the torment. "I know you're gonna say you won't. But you'd be lying. 'Cos people in love have no secrets, and even if I promised to keep yours, I'd have told Tommy back in the day."

I look down at my empty shot glasses and lick my lips, and just like magic, despite Caroline's unhappy face, they refill anyway.

So I grab them both, one in each hand, and shoot them back to back.

Setting them down with a slam—one, two—I squint and search the mirrored wall at her back, making sure my lipstick is still cute. *It totally is.* Then I slide off my stool and turn. "I'm going out to the smoking area."

"I don't think that's a good idea! Alana!" Her voice carries over the music, announcing to the whole world my plans. But shit, who cares? The whole world is watching anyway. "Alana? Tequila and Tommy don't mix."

I merely lift my hand and wave goodbye, then I work my way through the crowd, their tightly packed bodies becoming leaning posts for me to *pretend* not to lean on.

I mean, to be completely and utterly objective, not *all* of them know who I am. And not *all* of them care what I'm doing. Some folks actually have better things to do and more important things to focus on. But damn, it feels like every pair of eyes in the place are on me.

Well, except for that one couple I pass, kissing with their tongues and grinding on each other... *is that Eliza Darling?*

"She sure grew up." A soft, silly giggle weaves through my chest and out to touch the humid air. Then I shove the back doors open, surprising the Watkins posse crowd as they mill around a picnic bench and chug their own shots.

That's what we do out here in Bumfuck Plainview. We drink, and we have sex with our high school sweethearts, and sometimes, we get the happily ever after.

It's not guaranteed, though.

"You should probably turn around and go back inside." Oliver Darling —*such a darling*—scampers my way and becomes the first line of defense, protecting his sweet Tommy Watkins. "Alana?" He grabs my arms, holding me up when my legs tremble. "Go inside, sweetheart. This ain't gonna do anyone any good tonight."

"I'm sad about you too, just so you know." I want to hug him. Punch him. Press a kiss on his cheek and ask him who he's in love with. Because Oliver Darling *is* a darling. He always was. "I know everyone is focused on Tommy right now and how horrible his bitch ex was to him. And of course,

I'm focused on him most of all, 'cos my heart hurts and my eyes cry sometimes. But you," I poke his chest, digging my finger in just a little further to drive my point home, "you were my friend. You were the reason he had to bail you out of jail. And do you remember that time Tommy's piece of shit dad beat the crap out of him? Like, I know there were lots of times—"

"Alana, stop."

"But you remember this one specific time I'm talking about. Tommy was home with a broken freakin' sternum 'cos his daddy stomped on him. He was sore and couldn't get out of bed for a few days, and there was this guy giving me trouble at school."

He's back there. I see him. Tommy Watkins, glaring at me from the corner of his eyes while he takes his shot.

"I tried to make the guy leave me be, and I definitely wasn't gonna trouble Tommy with it. He had his own stuff to worry about. But he grabbed me, you remember? Right here on my," I look down, giggle-whispering, "he grabbed my boobs. That was the *first* time some guy touched my body without my permission. You swooped in like my very own Superman and flattened that asshole. And then we promised not to tell Tommy." Smug, I lean to the side and meet Tommy's ferocious glare. "We kept a secret from you, Thomas. 'Cos we didn't want you to worry." Then back to Oliver, I try, so, so hard to stop my jaw from trembling. "We were friends, and you cared about me, and I cared about you. And you're a doctor now! Which is so freakin' cool, especially since you were the idiot arrested for streaking that time. But I can't even talk to you about any of this 'cos you're Team Tommy."

"Alana..."

"And that's fine." I sigh. "You *should* be Team Tommy because he's the best fucking human I ever met in my whole life. But I miss being part of that team, too." I push him aside and stumble around, zeroing in on Chris perched on the table, his feet on the bench seat and his elbows on his knees. "And I'm sad about *you* because there are different kinds of love in this world. There's the love I have for him." I point toward Tommy and ignore the way his eyes flash with... anger, probably. "*Had. Have.*" I shrug. "But then there's the love I had for you. It's different but still so special. I cry for you, too. Then and now. For so many nights, over so many years, I've laid in bed, begging for sleep, and wept for you. I never cried for Oliver." I turn back, snickering. "No offense."

He drops his hands into his pockets, raising his shoulders. "None taken."

I bring my eyes back to Chris and search his dark, shadowed, and a little-bit-drunk gaze. "I love you like I would've loved a brother if I ever had one. Love the same way I love my child. You're Team Tommy, too, and that's entirely okay because you were his first. But I swear to you, it feels like I lost half of my soul when I lost you."

I stumble closer and stop by his long, muscular legs. Which just so happens to be a mere three feet from Tommy. *That bastard.* "I hope you never know the pain I feel when I think of what I've lost. Because it's unbearable. For the boy I left behind and the man I never got to know. I loved you, Chris, and the world was simply too cruel, too nasty and mean and harsh for what it did to us."

Finally, I turn to Tommy and *almost* lose it all. My stomach. My nerves. My grip on stand-up-ness. But one thing I *do* lose... my ability to speak.

"That's it?" he growls. "You have sweeping declarations for them, memories, apologies, secrets, and heart fucking wrenching poetry. But you've got nothing for me?"

If I open my mouth, I'll cry.

If I even try, I'll fall to the floor, and, most terrifying of all, I probably won't get up again.

"Say something!"

I startle and drown under the torrential tears flowing over my cheeks.

"Dammit, Lana!" He snatches up their communal bottle of tequila —*not sure how they got that*—and glares into my eyes. "You're good at this, ya know? You were born with the natural fucking talent of hurting me." Turning on his heels, he stalks across the gravel yard littered with cigarette butts and slams the back gate open, then he disappears into the darkness, the bottle tipped up and the liquid glug-glug-glugging into his mouth.

I start forward.

"Alana." Oliver grabs my arm. "No."

"Don't tell me no!" I yank free of his grip and stride toward the gate. "Don't *ever* tell me not to go to him. You don't get to make that choice."

"You're gonna kill each other! And the sad reality is, I'm not even joking. This isn't safe."

"Let her go," Chris grumbles. Always my hero. Always with half of my heart. "They're fine."

I shove the gate open and step into the alleyway out back, where deliveries come during the day, not only for the bar but the bakery a few doors down and the newsagents after that. There are no streetlights out here, and the moon isn't bright enough to illuminate my path more than five feet ahead.

Fresh, cool air hits my face, almost as nice as the cold lake water, but tequila still rushes through my veins like tiny ants marching to battle. It makes my blood run hotter, and my stomach rolls nauseatingly. My heart pounds faster every minute I wander alone. Darkness is my old enemy, haunting my memories and reminding me what happens to girls when no one is around to save her.

Nerves strip away a layer of my tequila bravery, but when I come to the end of the block and consider strolling onto the road, a dangerous arm swings around, a broad, firm hand sliding into my hair and holding on.

But there's no time for panic. No room for fear.

Because I smell him, even before he pulls me into the shadows beneath the awning of the mechanic next door. I cry for him, even as he crushes me against his chest.

"*Had*, Alana? Or *have*?" He drags me to the tips of my toes and takes my lips with his, swallowing my cry of desperation and sliding his tongue over mine.

I couldn't fight him even if I wanted to. And dammit, I don't want to.

Instead, I drape my arms over his shoulders and float away on the magic of what we can pretend to be.

Alcohol means we get to pretend.

"Answer me." He bites my lip, snarling when the sound that escapes my throat is one of pleasure and not pain. "Had or have?"

"Have." I squeeze my arms and climb his broad frame, because we're in the dark, and this isn't real. It's make-believe, the way I've fantasized for years. "I don't get to turn it off."

He drops the bottle so it lands on the ground with a thud and, miraculously, *doesn't* break. Then he scoops me up and turns with fury beating in his veins, slamming me against the brick wall and stealing the oxygen from my lungs.

When that's not enough, he pulls away and slams me a second time. Because he's still so angry. So hurt and devastated and furious.

"You're wet for me." He bruises my thighs and grinds his rock-hard cock against my core. He's not asking. Not even guessing. He's making a statement, so we both know he knows. He slips his fingers beneath my panties and finds me exactly how he knew he would. Dripping wet and desperate. "You still want me, don't you, Lana? Your body still wants mine, even if your mind did some seriously stupid shit."

174

"Yes." I drop my head back and whimper when he latches on to my neck. He nibbles and laves. Bites until it stings, then soothes with his tongue until I groan.

"Alana—"

"Yes, my body still wants your body. Always. It never stopped."

"You fuck your husband and think of me?" He slides two thick fingers inside my pussy, oblivious to the fact that he's the first to do so in ten years. Unaware that pain radiates through my core and leaves me breathless. "You ever wake up in the middle of the night hurting for me? Throbbing because you remembered what we had, knowing no one else could fuck you the way I could?"

I ride his hand, whimpering as my first release washes into his palm and drips along his wrist.

"How many times did you lie in that bed in New York and wish for me?"

"So many." I cinch my legs tight and cry out when he tosses me over the ledge, once, twice, three times so easily. "So many times."

"If I can't have your heart, then I'll take your cunt and destroy us both." He pumps his fingers, effortlessly drawing me to another peak and growling when I fall apart in his arms. "I'd rather die wrapped in you than live any other way."

"Shhh." I clap my hand over his mouth to quieten his words, hissing when he bites. And though he tears his fingers free of my underwear, stealing my pleasure and risking my cry of sorrow, *I know him*. Even after all this time, I know what he needs.

He's the boy who would sleep with his hand resting between my breasts and his cock nestled inside my pussy. He chose touching me over eating, more times than I can count. Over breathing, if he thought those were his only options. He chose me, no matter what else he had to give up. So he reaches between us and unsnaps the button of his jeans, just like I knew he would, then he shoves his zipper down and frees his cock... just like I knew he would.

Like I *hoped* he would.

"Yes?" He slides the tip along my wet heat, collecting my own natural lubrication. "Alana? Yes?"

"Yes." I tug him closer and take his lips with mine, swallowing his snarl and crying when his thick head nestles at my opening. I suckle on his tongue, letting the taste of tequila spur me on, and the farce of *this is all make-believe* carry me through what I know I'll regret tomorrow. Then I choke on fresh pain when he surges forward, filling me with his cock and pinning me to the wall at my back.

Because maybe we've done this before. And obviously, I'm no longer a virgin. But he was a boy back then, and a man now, and I'm so long out of practice, it's like I'm brand new all over again.

He leaves me no room to adjust. No time to catch my breath. He pulls back and pistons forward, wrecking me with his savagery and holding me captive with his bruising hands. He kisses me with the desperation of a starving man, and because I'm just as needy as he is, I forget my pain and focus on pleasure instead. I ride him gratefully, squeezing my arms tighter and returning his biting kiss with one of my own.

I latch on to his lip, panting when he tears my thighs apart. He stretches me the way he always enjoyed, spreading my ass cheeks and playing with that opening, too.

"Still my girl, aren't you, Lana?" He slips a single digit into my ass.

"Oh, God!" I explode, heaving in search of fresh air and clinging to his powerful form. I close my eyes, though the action is hardly necessary. It's practically pitch black out here. "Tommy."

"Haven't heard you say my name like that in so long." He bites my neck and slams me backward, ensuring I'll have a bruise by tomorrow. But then he pulls out again, robbing me of completion and earning my cry of despair. He sets me on my feet and steadies me when my knees tremble. Then he grabs the back of my neck and turns me, shoving me forward and crushing my chest against the rough brick exterior.

"Heels were a good choice." He whips my dress up, exposing my panties, but only long enough to tear them clean off my body and make them disappear in one of his pockets. Then he fills me again, dragging me back with a hand around my throat that cuts off my air. "Feels good, doesn't it?" He rocks his hips with infuriatingly measured strokes. In. Out. Slowing his pace without a single care for how I desperately need more. Faster. Harder.

"I planned to have you again." He loosens his grip on my throat, allowing me to suck a long line of oxygen into my lungs. "Married or not. I wouldn't have even cared if he was in the next fuckin' room. I was gonna have you again."

"Tommy—"

He squeezes again, destroying my ability to breathe and vibrating from the power he possesses. The demand he controls. The understanding that I *won't* stop him from playing with me. It's always been like this for us.

"I didn't know our last time was our last time," he snarls. "So I waited. And planned. I didn't know when, or where, and fuck, I didn't know how I'd make it happen. The fear you'd say no left me paralyzed with indecision for so fucking long. But I knew we weren't done." He leans back and spits, the warm splash of saliva hitting my lower back. Then he slides his fingers through the moisture and draws it down to my asshole. "I was spiraling out of control, wanting and waiting. Needing, but not getting. I was readying to slide into my truck and drive all the way to you, because ten years is a long fucking time to be underwater. But then you came back. Broke my heart and mended it in one."

Tommy—"

"Lie to me, Alana." He slips his thumb into my ass and drags my face around, biting my bottom lip and sucking my soul right up through my throat. "Lie and say you love me still."

Devastating tears make his eyes glitter. But he doesn't let them fall.

He would never.

"I'm begging you." He quickens his hips. Faster. Frantic. "You have the power to make me live or die. You *are* love. So for tonight, for right now, lie. Let me live."

"I love you." The air stops in my lungs, and my heart aches, weeping for what was lost. But my body still reacts to what he can do to me. I explode around his cock, fluttering electricity pulsing in my veins that only grows more powerful when he erupts, too.

He crushes me under his powerful touch, bruising my flesh and branding me on the inside. And when that's not enough, he pulls back and slams forward again, claiming my body with the brutality of a man deranged.

"Say it again. Lie again."

"I love you."

ROUND EIGHTEEN
ALANA

Whoever said nothing bad ever happened when tequila was involved is a liar. A thief. A regular scoundrel intent on making a woman's stomach ache and her eyes feel as though they roll around in sand.

Nausea pulses with every beat of my heart, my constant companion I neither invited into my home nor do I wish for it to stay. But I am at home; of that, I'm sure. In my own bed. My face, mercifully crushed against my own pillow.

Which is good, I guess.

Life could be so much worse.

Whacky II *cock-a-doodle-doos* on the front fence. His scream, more of a sickly yelp. His announcement that a new day has begun, as welcome as my nausea. I carefully peel my eyes open, a soft whimper disappearing into my pillow as I turn my face and search desperately for... anything. Water and Advil, hopefully. A hammer, if the first is too difficult to come by.

But I find neither.

Instead, I'm met with the ferocious glare of the morning sun pelting through my bedroom window. My phone and lipstick are dropped haphazardly on the bedside table, and beside those, Franky's Murdle book with a pen stuck in the middle to act as a bookmark.

I draw a long breath and groan when it smells of liquor and barf, then I swallow the taste of bad choices, wetting my throat and praying I don't puke.

Because I don't want to revisit that flavor ever again.

"Franky?" I try to turn over. I swear, I do. But my body doesn't move. So I use my arm instead, blindly patting the mattress in search of my son.

He's not here.

And though I'm pretty sure I'm ninety-eight percent deceased, I find some of that *Mommy Magic* I drone on about and push up to my elbows so I can look. Because being dead won't stop me from seeking my baby out. Violent illness won't keep me from being his mom.

I blink once. Twice. Again and again and again until my blurry vision makes way for something a little less... *looking through muddy water*. But when I find his side of the bed empty, but hear his sweet laughter from somewhere downstairs, I flop back to the mattress in relief, only to regret my actions because my stomach swirls and bile tickles the base of my throat.

I've gotta get up. Get dressed. Pack the car and run back to New York where everything is safe and Tommy Watkins can't destroy my heart every single day.

Unfortunately for me, though tequila seems to have deleted the sections of my memory that include how the hell I got home and whether I puked in an alleyway last night, it wasn't so thoughtful as to erase *what* we did together.

Nor the bits about love.

Worst of all, it left the part where he begged me to lie and, with his whole heart and soul, showed me his pain.

No, tequila wouldn't be that kind.

"You're not still in bed, are you?"

I startle at my mother's droning judgment and turn my face just far enough to spy her too-thin body at my door. Her shrewd stare and sneering expression. I think she wakes up each day with a plan to be a decent human being, but just as soon as she looks at me, her real self springs to the surface, and her top lip curls back in disdain.

"You're wasting your day lying about. If I thought inviting you to stay here meant you'd abandon your child to party all night and sleep all day, then I might've reconsidered my generosity."

"Ugh." I drop my face back into the pillow and wish for death. Because it's better than listening to Beatrice Page's self-righteous lectures. "I was out till... like... ten." *I think. I seem to recall checking the time when I set my phone down. Maybe.* "And now it's barely seven."

"You were out till ten-thirty," she counters. "And it's nearly eight. The animals still need to be fed, eggs need to be collected, there's poop on the lawn, and your son hasn't had breakfast yet."

Shut up, shut up, shut up, shut up!

"My son can pour his own cereal, Mother. He does it, literally, every other day. And I can hear him laughing, so clearly, he's okay and happy." But I toss my blankets off, knowing I won't get a single moment of rest now until *Bitsy* deems me worthy.

I look down at my body and find pyjamas... not my dress from last night. "How'd I get home?" I cover my mouth and contain the bubbles of air strolling leisurely along my throat. "And how'd I get changed?"

Please don't say, Tommy. Please don't say, Tommy. Please don't say, Tommy.

When she says nothing at all, I push off the bed and stand on shaking legs. "Mom?"

"Caroline brought you in. I suggested you sleep on the couch downstairs instead of interrupting Franky's rest, but she insisted on bringing you up and changing your clothes." She turns her nose up at me. "You were a mess, Alana. Humiliating yourself, just like you did when you were a child."

Yeah, but we both know that's not true.

Before last night, I'd never once stumbled home drunk in my entire life. When I was younger, it seemed ironically safer to wander to Tommy's home. To sleep in the house of horrors and cuddle into my boyfriend's arms, hoping the cockroaches wouldn't scare me awake and that his father would fall asleep in his own drunken stupor instead of being awake enough to pick a fight with the boys.

It was always a gamble, and it didn't always pay off.

"I don't feel humiliated." I mean, I do. But only an idiot would admit such a thing in front of this woman, so I step around my bed on aching feet and knees that consider going on strike, and grabbing a short, silky robe to wrap myself up just long enough to pour cereal for my son, I walk straight past my mother and into the bathroom.

I need to pee, and I intend to ignore what is surely a ghastly reflection in the mirror. Messy hair. Red eyes and swollen bags take up residence beneath.

I squeeze toothpaste onto my brush and shove it in my mouth, then I wander to the toilet and drop my shorts, pouting because I know, *I know,* I'm probably destined for a UTI.

Unsafe sex, and you didn't pee before bed? Rookie move, Alana Page. You know better.

I allow my eyes to close, since I have the time, and my brain to shut off. And for just a moment, I luxuriate in a micro nap.

But it's short-lived.

"Oh, for God's sake!" My mother startles me awake. "You're an embarrassment. This is *not* what I was expecting when you said you would come back to Plainview, Alana."

"You act like I go out every single night." I finish on the toilet and fix my clothes, fastening my robe and the sash that sits annoyingly on my stomach, then I go to the mirror and brush my teeth properly, scraping away last night's poor decisions and buying back even a modicum of dignity.

Though I'm not sure if I can go into town again. Like, ever. I certainly can't look Ollie or Chris or Tommy in the eyes for the rest of my life. Or Caroline. Or really, any person who lives in this godforsaken town.

"You infuriate me, Alana. Motherhood has done nothing to mature you." Folding her arms, Bitsy leans against the doorframe and huffs. "Always sneaking around. Drinking. Going out till God knows what time. You think I didn't already get a call from Barbara this morning? She said that Bill said you were arguing with Tommy Watkins at Darlene's last night. Have you no shame?"

Arguing with Tommy Watkins? Ha! My shame is too busy worrying about other, worse things.

"You are not a teenager anymore! You're a grown woman who should be able to—"

"Oh, shut up, Mother." I spit into the sink and run water right after it to wash the white foam down, then I cup a little more and drink straight from my palms, chugging the clear liquid like I haven't had any in days. Weeks, even.

"Excuse you!" My mother bursts, exactly how I knew she would. "You do not speak to me like that in my own—"

"You insist on hating me." I flip the tap off and wipe my face on the towel hung on the wall. "For reasons I'll never relate to, you seem to enjoy building yourself up by tearing me down. And you know what?" I don't even care if she cares. I simply push past her and into the hall. "I'm not who I was ten years ago, Mom. I was a child back then, constantly squished beneath the weight of your impossible demands, begging for your approval and lashing out when I couldn't get it. It's apparent you believe you've birthed the worst daughter in the history of the world."

I move onto the stairs and make my way down. Though I hold the banister because I'm not sure I won't tumble to my death if I rely on my legs to do all the work. "Maybe I really am the worst. Maybe you got *really* unlucky. Or maybe you're a miserable cow who can't see how much I truly wanted to please you back then."

I reach the bottom stair and glance back to find her still at the top, holding the rail and glowing an ugly, angry red.

"I tried so hard, Mom. Every single day of my childhood, I tried to make you happy. But there are only so many times you can tell me how horrible I am before I stop giving a shit."

"Watch your potty mouth in my home!"

"So maybe you got the worst daughter in the world. Or maybe I got the worst mother in the world. Or *maybe* we just weren't a good fit for each other. But either way, I no longer care. Because I see now, as a mother myself, that a child should *never* beg for love. It's not a privilege. It's not something that should be given with conditions or taken away because they didn't act how you wanted them to act. Love is forever, and it's unconditional. It's tragic you never learned that. But that's on you. Not me. Because my son knows he's safe with me, he knows my feelings will never go away."

I turn and wave her off so I don't have to listen to her argue back, and then I push through the kitchen door with the best smile I can muster on a hungover Sunday morning, only to skid to a stop.

Because Tommy *fuckin'* Watkins sits at the table across from my son, a chessboard set up between the pair, but both sets of eyes silently stuck on me.

My face.

My horror.

"You have *got* to be kidding me?!"

Tommy's lips curl into devious lines, his eyes dancing with a taunting playfulness. But he has the good sense to drop his gaze and swallow the laughter bubbling along his throat.

"Hey, Mom." Franky extends his arm, summoning me while he studies the half-complete game. But when I don't move—*I can't*—he flicks his wrist in demand. "This one is Tommy, Mom. He almost tricked me, because the first time I met him, he was smiley. Then the second time, he was cranky. He's smiling again today, so I wasn't sure..."

"Mmm. I can see how that might be confusing." *God, kill me now. Smite me down and make sure it's permanent!* I wander forward, folding my gown tighter across my chest and retying the sash in the time it takes to reach the table. And though I would normally breathe a little better simply because my son wraps his arm over my back and pulls me in for a side hug, my eyes remain firmly on Tommy's barely hidden smirk. His dancing eyes. "So you're, uh... playing chess, honey?"

Tommy lifts his head, opening his mouth to speak.

But I stop-sign him, shaking my head when his brows pinch closer together. "I was talking to my son." I look down at the board—*Franky is winning*—and draw a long breath. "I guess I'm a little confused, baby. You don't usually play chess in the mornings." Or with people other than me or Colin. *You especially don't play a fucking Watkins!* "And it's still really early."

"He was fixing something or..." He moves his knight and shrugs. "Something. I forget. You were still asleep, and I said how I like chess."

"And Tommy suggested a game, of course." My lips peel back into a snarl when the man grins. "Interesting. Are you nearly done? Because Tommy needs to go back to his house, and we have jobs to do here."

"I'm usually treated to a cooked breakfast on Sundays when I help around the house." Tommy moves his pawn—I'm not sure if he's bad at the game or brilliantly suicidal—then he links his fingers together and tilts his head to the side. "Bitsy needed some work done in the shed, and as payment, she typically cooks for me."

"Such a shame." I press a kiss to the top of Franky's head before circling away and moving to the fridge. "Since she's not down here cooking for you, I guess she's not feeling up to it today."

"You could cook for me." He sits back, leisurely stretching his legs under the table and burning the side of my face with his smug stare. "Bacon and eggs sound good. And it's hardly rocket science. Bet you could figure the stove out if you wanted to."

"But that's just it." I grab a bottle of juice and slam the fridge door, jars audibly rattling inside, before I move to the cupboard to my left and pull down two glasses. One for me. One for my child. "I *don't* want to. In fact, I have absolutely no desire to figure it out at all. What I would like to do is hang out with my son, watch some Sunday morning cartoons on the television, and ignore literally every other person who exists in this world."

I pour the juice and ignore the liquid that rolls along the side of the glass, cruel flashbacks of tequila spilling over a shot glass playing in my mind. But I can't go there. I won't. I refuse.

I set the bottle down and take one juice in each hand, and placing Franky's by his elbow, I bring the other up and take a small sip. "Sorry. Not enough for three."

Tommy's eyes slide back to the half-full bottle, my lie flickering through the room like it's wrapped in neon lights and sparkling glitter. But then he chuckles and goes back to studying the board.

"I see."

"I heard you arguing with Grandma, Mom." Since it's not his turn, Franky folds his neck back and searches my eyes. "I don't think you're the worst daughter in the world."

My heart splats, dead inside my chest. I scratch my fingers through his hair and pull him in to rest his cheek against my belly. "Thank you, honey. I'm sorry you had to hear us arguing again. That must get pretty annoying, huh?"

"It's interesting, mostly." He straightens and swallows up Tommy's poorly placed knight. "You never used to shout at all in New York. Now you shout all the time here."

"A study in human beings," Tommy mutters. "Something about how we revert to who we used to be when placed in an environment we used to exist within."

"Also known as stupidity and shortsightedness." I drink my juice and pray it washes down the frustration intent on clawing along my throat. "The girl I was when I last lived in Plainview was young and naïve. Silly and rarely considered the consequences of her actions."

On this, at least, Tommy seems to agree. He coughs out a scoff that verges on a *yep*.

"She was also a child of trauma," I continue. "Someone who didn't know how to love herself. And that's not to say her trauma was, like, the worst in the world. It wasn't. But its insidiousness made for complicated internal monologue and codependency on outside voices to make her feel worthy of love at all."

You, Tommy Watkins. You were who I relied on for love.

"But that girl no longer exists. Because that's what happens when we grow up. The person we used to be is gone, making room for the person we're meant to become."

"But that doesn't make sense." Franky, too friggin' logical for his own good, glances up again. "Because maybe the person you used to be went away, and the person you became existed in New York. But then we moved to Plainview, and you're different again. So did the first person go away, or was she on pause, waiting here in Plainview?"

"She wasn't here, kiddo. We thought she died." Tommy charges forward with his queen, knocking pieces off the board and earning a panicked gasp from the depths of my son's soul. "Checkmate."

"That's not how you play the game!" Frantic, Franky tries to put the pieces back where they should be. "Tommy! That's wrong."

"It's the queen. She can do whatever she wants."

"No!" Franky shoves to his feet and puts his fallen king back on the board. "That's not the rules!"

"Queen makes the rules." Standing, too, Tommy comes around the table and takes my juice before I think to stop him. "Can we talk on the porch for a moment?"

"Mom! He messed up the pieces!"

Chuckling, Tommy sets the glass down and meets my son's eyes. "Sorry. You won. I was just being silly."

"I didn't win! You didn't play it right."

"But I forfeit, which means I lose. You won."

"That's not winning!" My poor baby spins out of control, his mind racing and his hands flying across the board. "You have to play it properly."

"Porch?" Tommy's eyes come back to mine, burning with a quiet mix of rage and hurt. Wonder and, dare I say, hope. "I just need a moment of your time."

"You're not allowed to play chess anymore!" Franky growls. "You don't play it right."

"Alana..."

Tell him to leave and cut him off completely?

Or give him his two minutes on the porch and explain why *this* isn't happening?

The first, I did ten years ago. The second, my penance, I suppose, for the hurt I've caused.

So I nod. "Alright. Two minutes. Then I'm coming inside." I meet my son's eyes. "He was never a very good chess player, honey. You should ask Chris. He's way better and *always* follows the rules."

Unhappy, Franky screws his nose up and glares at a smiling Tommy.

"Reset the board for us." I bend and kiss the top of his head. "I'll play you just as soon as I get back. Come on." I step around them both and move through the door and onto the porch, and though I might wonder if

Tommy will leave me waiting, he follows on fast feet, snatching my hand and crushing it in his steely grip.

He drags me down the steps and around the side of my house.

"Tommy!" I try to pull free, hissing when I step on rocks in bare feet and yelping when I almost stumble. But he yanks me around and slams my back to the side of the house exactly how he used to when we were younger.

In fact, right *where* he used to do it.

"You need to stop!"

"I wanted to make sure you woke up okay." He pins me to the wall, his legs pressed to mine and his eyes searching my face. My lips. My flushing cheeks. "You drank a lot last night."

"We can't do this." I won't participate in the game he's set on playing. I refuse to re-ignite the relationship I ran from a decade ago. "I'm not doing it."

"Doing what?"

"*This*! Us." I set my hands on his infuriatingly firm chest and push back... or at least, I try. "No."

"You did it last night." He tilts his head and peels a lock of loose hair off my shoulder. "Worked out fine."

"It didn't work out fine! We were drunk and angry. We were toxic and mean. You can dress it up however you want and call it whatever you think sounds nice, but it doesn't change the facts. We are no longer who we used to be, and we cannot recapture what we used to have."

"We could." So gently, so sweetly, he traces his thumb over my bottom lip. "We still want each other, Lana. We're still *it* for each other. Sure, we have some shit to overcome, but that's what couple's therapy is for. We're not done for as long as that spark is still between us."

"You're fooling yourself," I groan. "And you'd rather destroy yourself to prove a point, than admit we no longer exist."

"We *do* exist." He licks his lips, stealing my focus as my eyes drop to the movement. "We're standing right here, Lana. You're still love, and I'm still war. And even though it feels like you're trying to flip that, like you think it's a badge of honor and a way to break us, I'm still saying it'll work out. You be war if you need to. I'll be love. The pieces are still there. They still fit."

"Tommy—"

"Was it a lie?" His eyes flicker between mine, searching and sorrowful. His hands slide down to caress my hips. "I know what I said. I know what I asked for. But was it a lie, Alana, or do you still love me?"

I still love you! I never stopped loving you.

New York Alana never existed, because one cannot live without their heart inside their own body.

But those are words for me. They're selfish and mean, and they serve no purpose except to extend the time a man is expected to suffer.

Tommy deserves to heal. To move on. He deserves to find love with someone better.

So I look straight into his eyes and tell the worst lie I've ever muttered. "I don't love you." *God, it hurts. It hurts so bad.* And when his eyes shutter with pain, I almost lose my nerve. My willpower. My resolve. "Not the way you mean, and not the way you deserve."

"Alana—"

"I have love for you. For the boy who saved a girl. For the friend you were, and the safe haven you created when I needed it. Those kids existed, and they needed each other more than they needed anything else in the world."

"Stop—"

"I sincerely think we saved each other in a time we might not have survived if things had been different. And we're so blessed, Tommy." I loathe the tears that sit on my lashes. The ache in my throat. "Because those kids still live within us. Memories of what was once really, really beautiful. Those are our gifts, and no one can take those away."

"Kids?" His jaw clicks with tempered rage. His hands squeeze my hips, perhaps tighter than he even realizes. "Memories. That's it?"

"I have love for you. And Chris. And Oliver. And even Eliza, though she wants to kill me."

"But you don't love me anymore?" He barrels straight past my attempt at a joke and searches my eyes with a devastating intensity instead. His heart pounds visibly in my peripherals, and his Adam's apple bobs with the nerves in his throat. "You'll stand right there, my hands on your body, and yours on mine... You'll look into my eyes and tell me, without so much as a fuckin' stutter, that you're not *in love* with me?"

"No." I swallow the tears that desperately try to drown me. "I don't love you. Not the way you mean. Not the way you deserve."

He drops his hands, their absence as devastating as if he'd just slapped me. He places them on his own hips and stares down at the ground, his nostrils flaring as he takes a single step back. Then a second. He nods in the silence, then looks up again.

"How did we end up here, Lana?" He drags his lips between his teeth, swinging his head from side to side. "How were we those kids, so fucking in love, and now we—"

"Can't we just stop?" I plead. "Stop trying so hard to pick through it."

"I'm not trying to argue with you." He brings aching eyes back up to mine. "I swear, I'm not gonna shout or cuss or imagine throttling your pretty little neck—which is something I do *a lot*. I just don't understand how this happened."

"It just..." *God, it just did. The choice was taken out of our hands.* "I don't have better answers than the ones I've already given, and it breaks my heart that we keep going around and around and around on the same thing."

"It breaks *your* heart?" He growls. "Yours? Really?"

"Your pain is my pain," I rasp. "My heart breaks because yours is breaking. I can't be what you want me to be, and I can't change how we ended up here. All I can do is move forward, *not* with the life you wish we could go back to, but with the life I now have. With my son. He's my future, Tommy. He needs me."

"I never stopped needing you." He drops his gaze again, kicking rocks. "I never got to a point where I could thrive without you holding my hand, Lana. And I know we're not supposed to rely on other people like that. I know I'm supposed to be strong and able to stand up on my own, but—"

"You are strong. You've been standing on your own this whole time." I knuckle a fresh tear that rolls onto my cheek. "I know it hurt at first, and I know you were mad, but at some point in the last ten years, you were able to move on. You created a gym and a family and a career. You feed hungry children and teach clumsy little boys how to kick above their heads. You're literally the world champion in your weight division and going back in a few months to defend your title. You *are* standing. You're strong. And I'm so proud of you for doing that."

"I came looking for you." He brings a hand up and scratches his stubbled jaw. "In New York."

Stunned surprise floors me. It sends my heart skittering and my knees weak. "What?"

"You left me here all alone." His voice crackles with an ache I feel in my soul. "Without saying goodbye. Without taking much more than a backpack full of clothes. You said nothing to your mom, or if you did, she wouldn't tell me. You said nothing to Chris or Oliver or Caroline. You just left. And at first, I tore the town apart trying to get to you." He searches my eyes. "I'm not proud to admit I broke Ollie's arm and Chris's nose. It took both of them to pin me to Plainview. But eventually, they had to go back to living their lives, too. The second they turned their backs, and I scraped enough money together for a flight, I went to New York and tracked you down at your school."

My breath comes out in an aching shudder. "Tommy..."

"I was gonna grab you," he groans. "Literally toss you over my fucking shoulder and steal you back. But when you turned around, not even realizing I was right there, all I could see was your... your..." He touches his stomach, lowering his gaze. "You were carrying someone else's baby and had a shiny rock on your finger."

I look down at the ring I wear now. Still. Though I can't be entirely sure why. I should send it back to Colin. It was his mother's, and even if he's not quite ready to give it to Tasha yet, the ring still belongs to his family.

I'll send it back. I have to.

"I'd spent all those months back here, Lana, wondering what the fuck happened and what I did to deserve that kind of pain. I was so scared I'd said something or done something that broke us, and the fact I was too stupid to figure out what it was made it all so much worse. I was in hell. Meanwhile, you were in New York, falling in love and starting a new life with this other guy. I couldn't throw you over my shoulder. I couldn't even say hello, because you'd already moved on."

"I'm sorry." I lose my battle against tears, droplets falling to my cheeks and tracking toward my jaw. "Truly. I'm so, so sorry, Tommy."

"I *still* don't know if I broke us. Was it my fault?" He drags his hand up and clutches at his heart. "Was I not enough? Was I mean and didn't even realize it? Insensitive to your needs and too self-absorbed to notice?"

I shake my head, frantically answering these questions at least. This, I can give him, even if words fail me.

"Was it because of where I came from? Was it *who* I came from? Was it the cockroaches in my house or the moths that ate my clothes or the fact I didn't have enough food for me and Chris, so you knew in your heart you could never rely on me to feed you, too?"

"Tommy..."

"I wouldn't have let you go hungry," he groans. "I swear to you, there's nothing I wouldn't have done to keep you safe and warm and fed."

"It wasn't you, Tommy." I should walk away. Turn and run before I make things worse. But his pain is my pain. His heartache is because of me. So I push off the wall and crash against his pounding heart instead, wrapping my arms around his body and whimpering when he does the same. "It wasn't you. I'm so sorry you've spent ten years not knowing this wasn't your fault."

"Tell me what happened." He rubs my back, long strokes of his broad hands. "It's not too late to fix this."

"I can't." I squeeze as tight as my aching arms allow and bury my face against his chest, inhaling his perfect scent and trapping it in the base of my lungs. Maybe later, when I'm all alone, I can call upon the memories that smell brings me, revisiting the only person I've ever known—besides my son—who loves without reservation. "I can't, Tommy. And I'm so sorry for that, too."

"It's not too late—"

"It is." I pull back and swipe my cheeks, wiping the tears away and inhaling a shuddering breath. "It *is* too late. But I'm setting you free. I want you to find happiness. *Please.*"

"The girl I used to know would never have wanted that for me." He grabs my wrists and pulls me closer. "*That* Alana would laugh at the thought of me being with someone else. Then she would have mopped the floor with whichever idiot stepped forward to take her spot."

He's right. He's absolutely, completely, heartachingly accurate.

"I'm not her anymore. I can't be her. That Alana died ten years ago, and no matter how many times you ask for a different outcome, death is death, and there's no coming back from that. Move on." I take a step back and twist my wrists out of his grasp, swallowing the sob that tries so fervently to break free. Then I look anywhere but into his eyes. I can't. It hurts too much. "You're love," I murmur, rolling my bottom lip between my teeth. "I'm war. The two were never supposed to coexist."

"Alana—"

"I'm sorry." I spin and stride away, leaving him behind again—*again and again and again.* Stalking up my mom's porch steps, I wipe my face clean and yank the door open. Then I grab Franky's hand, startling him when I continue walking. Through the kitchen, then the living room. I keep going to the laundry at the other end of the house until we emerge on the porch again, but far and away from where Tommy lingers.

"Mom?" Franky stumbles on the steps, grabbing onto the porch railing so he doesn't fall. "What's wrong?"

"Nothing's wrong, honey." *Cool. Lie to him, too.* "Grandma wants us to collect the eggs and feed the animals. Once we're done, we can go inside and relax."

"The eggs?" His eyes flare in panic, his shoulders coming up as he searches the yard for his arch-nemesis. "Whacky always hangs out around the coop, Mom. If he knows we're coming, he's gonna—"

"I'll protect you." I wipe my face and ignore the rumble of Tommy's truck engine. The crunch and scrape of his wheels on our gravel driveway, and then the roar that echoes back when he hits the tar and gains speed. "Whacky won't bother you, okay? I'll come outside with you every single day to make sure of it."

Unconvinced, but trusting—barely—he tiptoes toward the coop and casts a wary eye back to the front fence, right where the damn rooster sits, choking out his morning song. When he's sure the coast is clear, he flips the catch on the coop and opens the door, releasing the dozen hens that escape into the yard to spend their day pecking at the worms that live in the grass.

"Are there any eggs, honey?" *Stop crying. Stop crying. Stop crying.* "Do you see any?"

"Yeah." He pulls the front of his shirt forward, creating a pouch, and lays each collected egg inside to take into the house. "We should cook some up for breakfast, don't you think?"

"Sure." I wipe my face and yearn for a shower. Time alone. Privacy to cry and clean the mess I made last night. Tommy's dried cum on my thighs. His handprints on my legs. "We can make eggs."

ROUND NINETEEN

TOMMY

"Hands up, buddy." I stand on my knees and hold the kick pads for a ridiculously clumsy Franklin Page.

It's cruel, in a way, that Alana would devastate me with her words and still allow her son to come to the gym. It's a vicious taunting, allowing me to spend time with him one-on-one, learning his quirks even when he hardly speaks, and looking into his eyes, even when he struggles to make eye contact.

The fact he's still here, taking part in the classes I insist on coaching, and partnering with me when we run drills is, in a sick, warped way, probably a compliment.

Instead of tearing him out of my life and hiding away at her mother's home—*out of sight, out of mind*—she trusts me not to hurt him, despite the pain she and I share and in spite of the shitty father figure I had growing up.

It's not like I'm working with much here.

Still, it's been two weeks since she destroyed my heart—*again*—but she plays nice at the end of each class, neither rushing her son out the door nor does she linger once he's done. She doesn't scowl or sneer or say a damn word other than *hello* and *goodbye*. She doesn't growl when I walk a little closer than I probably need to. And when I stare, she doesn't even seem to get pissy about it.

She's perfectly neutral.

And I fuckin' hate it.

"You need your left foot forward," I coach, tapping Franky's left knee and dragging it my way when he attempts to move the right.

I meet his eyes and smile. Because his cheeks warm and the thought that such a smart little boy would mistake left for right probably makes him feel silly.

He's not silly. He's just not athletically gifted.

"Then you put your left fist here." I grab his wrist and place it where I want it. "That's for hitting. Use your shoulder for blocking. Bring your right fist up, too, but it'll go second."

"Why do you always pick me when we need a partner?" He ruins my placements, dropping his guard and pushing his glasses up his nose. "Every single time."

"Because we have an odd number of students. Here." I draw his fists up again. "You need a left jab, then a right hook. Can you show me that?"

"Chris is partnering with Molly." He neither jabs nor hooks. "If you don't partner with me, and he doesn't partner with Molly, then we have an even number again."

"Well... do you *want* to partner with Molly?"

Together, we peer across and watch the little shit dive over my brother and trap his neck in a choke. She's too small to do any damage. But fuck, she's got the right enthusiasm. She'll get him someday.

Franky's lips flatten into straight lines. "No, but—"

"Exactly. So put your hands up and show me the combo I asked for."

"Did you ever meet Mas Oyama?"

"Did I..." Stunned, I lower my hands. "What?"

"Mas Oyama. He was the founder of Kyokushin Karate." He looks me up and down with an unimpressed sweep of his eyes. "It's a full-contact style of karate. As a full-contact fighter, I would expect you to know that."

"I know who Mas Oyama is! How do *you* know who that is?"

"I read a book about it." He strikes out with a left jab, grazing my jaw and grinning. I've been bamboozled. *My hands weren't up.* "Did you meet him?"

"No. Did you?"

He straightens his legs and searches my eyes. *Like fuck, Tom. Are you really that stupid?* "He died before I was born. Of course I didn't meet him."

"Oh, well..." I grab his wrists and reset him again. "Just checking. Left-left-right, let's go."

"In Japanese, did you know Kyokushin means the ultimate truth?"

"Mmhm." I pull his hand forward and *make* him perform the movements before I'm forced to admit I might be a shit teacher. "Read that in your book, too?"

"Uh-huh. You do MMA when you compete for money, but Chris told me you learned Kyokushin Karate. That it's your favorite style."

"Sure is." *Left-left-right.* "It's the *best* style. Mas Oyama was a legend." *Left-left-right.* "Can you try a left, right upper hook, right middle hook?"

"Do you know what ironic means?"

I sit back on my haunches and try, so fucking hard, to understand. "What?"

"According to Merriam-Webster, ironic means—"

"I know what ironic means!" *Jesus.* The kid thinks I have meatballs for brains. Which, now that I think about it, is probably why his mother dumped me and married a dude who went to college. "Are you gonna quiz me every single day we're in here? Or can I have a day off soon where I don't feel like an idiot?"

"Oh. So you *do* know." *Damn, Tom, I underestimated you. My bad.* "So, since we both know what irony means, I guess I want to know why Kyokushin means the ultimate truth, but you and my mom keep lying to me every time I ask a question."

"What?" I cast my eyes to the right, to the rest of our class who work independently of us, then to the left, where Alana sits by the wall with a paperback novel folded over at the spine, her eyes glued to the page and not on us. Then I bring my focus back to Franklin. "What do you mean?"

"When my mom cries, and I ask her what's wrong, but she says *nothing.* That's a lie."

She cries?

"When I ask about you partnering up with me in class, and you say we have odd numbers when we don't. That's a lie."

"Well—"

"When I ask Grandma Bitsy if she's sick, but she says she's not and that I don't have to worry, that's a lie. And when I ask Chris why my mom is so mad at you, and he says he doesn't know and that I shouldn't worry about it, that's a lie, too."

Fuck.

"When I ask Eliza why she's mad at my mom, and she says she's not— but she totally is—that's a lie."

"Franky..."

"When everyone in Plainview says how proud they are of your gym since you're famous and all that, but your gym is founded on Kyokushin—which is the ultimate truth—it's ironic. Because everyone is always talking about someone else, and most of the time, the things they say aren't even the truth. They think I'm not listening because I'm a kid. But I am. Everything here is a lie. Plainview is a lie."

Can't argue there, buddy. This place is a fuckin' shithole.

"Anyway..." He throws his combo, smacking me in the jaw and following it with an awkward hook to my ribs. "Mrs. Middler says she doesn't want to sell the bookstore, but then Caroline says she does. And Grandma Bitsy says Oliver and Eliza's sister isn't a real doctor, but I looked her up on the internet, and she totally is. Not all doctors work in a hospital."

"No." I draw a deep breath, filling my lungs. "Not all doctors work in the hospital."

"And I heard that Oliver ran down the street with no pants one time. But when I asked Caroline, she laughed and said she didn't think that was true. That was a lie."

"Yeah." I choke out a bubbling laugh. "He really did that. And Caroline was there, so she definitely knows it's true. She was probably just trying to retain Ollie's modesty or something."

"Everyone in this town lies," he grits out. "Every single person. And since *I* don't lie, I thought maybe Chris wouldn't because we're kinda the same sometimes."

"The same?"

"Yeah, like, we're both autistic. Though Mom says he isn't diagnosed, so I shouldn't say so out loud."

Curious, I cast my eyes around and stop on my brother.

"Chris doesn't like to wear shoes, and I don't like to wear shoes. He likes to read, and I like to read. He has fun facts, and I have fun facts. He likes math, and I like math. And my mom says he's a really good chess player, too. I'm the best chess player I know. Mom says I remind her of Chris a lot, and we even have the same color hair. And we both like olives, but we hate cheese. Neither of us has ACHOO Syndrome."

My heart thunders with a deep, dark ache as I slowly bring my eyes back around. "I'm sorry... ACHOO Syndrome?"

"Yeah. We don't sneeze when we look at the sun."

"You don't?"

"Nope! And neither does Chris. I asked him, and then we tested it the other day."

"Oh, well..." *Can't say I've ever noticed.* "Alright."

"Sometimes, I feel like I'm weird, and no one will want to be my friend when I start at my new school after the summer. And it's not like I even want to hang out with other people. Kids my age climb trees or ride skateboards or whatever. I don't enjoy doing those things. My mom said I'm not weird at all, that my personality is my personality, and my real friends will come along eventually, and until then, she'll be my friend."

She was that for me and Chris, too. Our friend, even when we had no others. Our safety, when no one else wanted to be near us.

"Moms are *supposed* to say those things," he insists. "That's her job. And I know she gets sad when I'm sad, so I stopped talking about all of this ages ago. But then I met Chris, and I thought maybe that's what my life would be like when I'm a grown-up. He has friends, and he likes his job, but he's also quiet and still reads and doesn't wear shoes if he doesn't have to. I thought it was nice to meet a grown-up autistic person, even if I didn't tell him he's autistic."

"Er... right."

"But then he told a lie. Which means he's not like me at all." He exhales a long sigh. "He's just like everyone else here. *A liar.* So now I think I'm weird again. And even if I don't like people, it makes me sad that I'll be the only kid at my new school with no friends. Sitting alone is no fun when it wasn't your choice in the first place."

"No..." Which is probably why he wants to be paired with Molly again. Or someone else. *Anyone* else. For the love of God, the boy just wants to make a friend before summer is over.

I push up to my knees again, but I twist and wait for my brother to tap under Molly's assault. "Chris." I lift my chin in summons when his eyes come up. But before he arrives, I bring my focus back to Franky. "I'm sorry I lied to you. And Chris will be, too. If he told a lie, it was because he was trying to do the right thing. And since we're on the topic, I bet your mom is the same. He," I point Chris's way, "and her," I point to Alana, "they were my best friends for a really long time. They're still the *best* people I know. Sometimes adults feel like they have to tell a lie because it's our job to protect kids from grown-up truths. And I know that's frustrating to you because you're only nine, but your brain makes you feel a hell of a lot older."

"Hey." Chris stops on my right, towering over us until he moves into a crouch. "What's up?"

"We're gonna pair Franky and Molly together. And then Franky and Sean. Then Franky and Mike, since Mike is nine, too." I meet my brother's eyes. "The summer will be over soon, and he needs to know who his peers are so he's not so lonely when school starts. Molly?" I wave her across. "I'll keep close," I whisper for Franky, "in case she tries to kill you."

His eyes widen in terror.

"She'll be on her best behavior, I promise. If you make Molly Jenkins tap before the school year begins, you'll be the king of the cage."

"King of the *school*." Chris chuckles. "We don't call it a cage anymore. Principal Fowler specifically asked us to stop because it was creating a *negative connotation in students' minds*." He shuffles aside and gives Molly room to plop into our space. "You got this, Page. You inherited some of the toughest DNA known to man."

"You're gonna roll with him," I tell Molly. But then I point two fingers at my eyes, then I do the same in her direction. "I'm watching you, girly pop. And I'm ready to throw down if you try to turn this into WWE."

"You're being silly." She moves to her knees, knowing already what Franky doesn't. That that's where we initiate a round on the mats. Then she offers her hand and waits for him to tap it to get them started. "Fun fact," she teases, taunting him with a grin. "I'm probably going to get you in an arm bar. So keep your chicken wings tight, and don't give me your back. Follow those rules, and you're gonna be just fine."

"I changed my mind." Franky's panicked eyes swing back to me. "I'd rather sit alone."

"Too late." But I set my hand on his shoulder and gently coax him down to his knees. "I'm gonna be right here helping you. Molly's ego is already too big, so I'm gonna tell you exactly what to do and how to humble her. We'll tap this little turd out soon. I promise."

"Little turd?" She dives on the poor boy and slams him to his back, taking mount and hooking her feet around his. She *could* whale on his face. Fists. Elbows. She *could* grab his arm and throw herself to the side, trapping him in an arm bar in less time than he takes to blink.

But she doesn't.

Because damn, she's a good kid. "You need to bridge now." Softly, oddly sweet, she reaches back and pokes his hip. "I'm sitting up here, queen of my castle, where I could mess you up. So put your feet on the mats and shove up to knock me forward."

Worried, Franklin's gaze swings my way. So I nod. *She's right, buddy.*

"If I'm sitting up here, balanced, then my hands are free to hit you. But if you buck me forward and I have to use my arms to balance..."

"Then you have no weapons to hit me with."

Franklin Page may not be a natural-born fighter. But he's a thinker. A planner. He understands theory, and it's clear Molly already knows that about him.

She flops forward, despite his lack of bucking, and places one hand on the mat beside his face. Then she grabs his wrist and shows him how to loop her arm. "Now you can lock me in. If you trap my arms and keep me off balance, I'm completely stuck. Then you're in charge and can flip us over."

ROUND TWENTY
TOMMY

I wander through Bitsy's shed and turn out the lights, one by one, now that I'm done working on her tractor. It's acting up, and I know enough about the diesel engine to keep it semi-functional, at least until the storm season ends.

If she loses another tree, she's gonna need it to clear away the debris

I've been sneaking in during the hottest parts of the day, which is, in theory, the most likely time for Alana and Frankie to either be inside in the air conditioning or in town, at *Books Books Books* as they prepare for the reopening.

In the evenings, I've been sneaking out around dinnertime, when delicious scents play on the cooling breeze, and I'm almost guaranteed to escape without eyes on the back of my head.

It's a system that's been working for a few days, anyway.

So far, so good.

Sweat and dust cling to my skin, tempting me to go home and dive straight into the lake to clear off the sticky layer. But the lake is for friends. For fun and silliness, for floating in the cool water and staring up at the trees.

Showers, on the other hand, are for washing off a hard day's work and crawling into bed.

Alone.

'*Who is Tommy Watkins dating now?*' my ass. '*Supermodel with a broken heart?*' Jesus. How little they know of the boy who took no one to bed, *except* Alana Page.

The fact I was never even tempted, no matter who strut through the clubs nor who entered my locker rooms pre and post-fights, would make headlines. They called me a playboy in the magazines, known for having a new woman on my arm at every event.

In reality, those I dated were nothing more than business decisions.

Aspiring model wants to be seen? Tommy Watkins could do with a plus-one. Friend of a friend who has had a rough life and could really benefit from a night out? Tommy Watkins has a seat to fill. Not-A-Doctor from the city needs a fun excuse to dress up and catch up with an old pal? Tommy's gotcha.

I roll my eyes and walk the length of the shed, forced to flip each individual light switch off, leaning around messy machinery and pulling my shirt free when sharp edges grab onto the fabric.

If only the gossip magazines knew the truth about me.

Though, really, I'm glad they don't.

Fuck them.

"No, Helen! I'm not coming to New York for a press tour." Alana shoves the shed door open, oblivious to my presence as I freeze in the shadows, and then she closes the door and claims what she thinks is privacy.

She leans against the door, dropping her head backward until the two connect with a *thunk*, running her free hand through her hair. "I *am* thinking clearly, and now I'm stating a hard, firm boundary. It's not happening. My son starts school in a week, and my mother isn't doing so great."

Cough, Tommy! Clear your throat. Do a fucking spinning heel kick. Anything!

But before I make a choice, Alana's body stiffens. Her caller—Helen—chatters, but she brings her head forward and searches the darkness.

She knows I'm here. *She knows.* So I step out from between machinery and stop under a beam of light sneaking in through the high windows above.

"I'm sorry." I lift my hands in surrender, inching closer. Though I need her to move so I can leave. "I was working on the tractor. But I'll go now."

"I'm gonna call you back, Helen." Alana ends their call and lowers her hand, and though her eyes scour my face, a warm embrace in a world gone cold, she remains pressed against the door. Unmoving.

Her chest lifts and falls in delicious temptation, her small tank top hugging perfect curves. And because I'm a hungry man, even when I know I shouldn't, I allow my eyes to fall to the gap of belly her top exposes, then the flowy, spotted skirt she wears beneath.

Girl. Teen. Or a woman. She's never not been perfect.

"I'm sorry for interrupting your private call." I set my thumbs in my front pockets and wait... watch... *not* make things worse. "I wasn't trying to scare you or anything."

"I wasn't scared." Her nose twitches, even as her lashes come down and kiss her cheeks. "I could smell you. That's how I knew."

I lift one arm and take a whiff. "Sweaty, sorry. I've been working in the heat all day."

"I didn't mean you smelled bad. I just..." She stops and exhales. "You have a smell. It's a mix of your cologne. But your gym, too. And... I dunno. Something. But it's all you."

"Kinda like how you smell of lavender. And coconuts. And you." I need to get past her. To escape, I need that door. "I was heading out now, so if you could..." *Put a bullet in my brain and a stake through my heart. That'd be swell.* "Move."

"In a sec." She drops her head back again, setting her phone on the wheel well of Bitsy's tractor before sliding her hands through her hair. She tugs just hard enough to make herself groan, stress rolling through her frame almost as visibly as fumes coming off a hot engine. "I need a moment before I lose my damn mind, and if I do that outside of this shed, I'm afraid my son will see and ask questions." She draws a long breath, filling her lungs and pushing her chest up with the movement. Then she exhales again and drops her hands. "He knows when I'm lying to him, but it's not right that I place adult stresses on his shoulders, either. To save him from himself, I have to melt down where he can't see me."

"What's got you worried?" I meander a little closer and dig my hands into my pockets. Keep them to myself before I make things *much* worse. "You could hand them to me, maybe. I'm not a kid anymore."

She smiles up at the dark ceiling, allowing her head to loll side to side. "Business stuff. It's not important, really. Just annoying."

"You could tell me." Another step closer, because I really want the scent of coconuts in my lungs. "Even annoying things can weigh on us. If you share it, you might feel better. Then you can go inside and have dessert with your kid, and he won't have to worry that you're upset."

She flattens herself against the door and studies me with long sweeps of her perfect blue eyes. To confide in me or not? To remember that, before we were lovers, we were friends.

"I think I made a mistake submitting my book to my agent. Or, by letting my agent submit my book to the publishing houses," she amends with a slight lift of her shoulder. "Whichever. I was wrong for sharing it."

"Why?" I close the space between us, but only so I can turn and press my back to the door, too. So I don't have to see her.

Fuck knows, I want to. But I'm man enough to know it's not good for either of us. "Isn't that what writers do? They share it so readers can read?"

"I shouldn't have shared *this* book." She turns, resting her ear against the rough wooden door. "The things I wrote are exceptionally personal to me, and though I like the story, and I stand behind the things written, ever since receiving an offer from Elyte, I've realized I'm not ready for the rest of the world to read it."

"Elyte is a publishing house?"

"Mm." She brings her hand up and nibbles on her pinky nail. "They keep pushing their contracts my way, and they've increased their offer twice. I guess they think I'm playing hard to get, which, in a sick way, has made them want it more. I've told Helen to pull the manuscript and make all this go away."

"She won't?"

"She thinks she's protecting me. She assumed with the move, and Colin, and..." She hesitates before adding, "everything that's happening, that I'm not thinking clearly. So, instead of pulling it when I tell her to, she's nagging me to reconsider. She's convinced I'll regret pulling out."

"Do you?" Fuck it, I turn my head, too, and look down into her beautiful eyes. "Do you think you'll regret it?"

"No. I can change my mind later, if that's what I want. I can self-publish, even if Elyte goes on a rampage and shit-talk me to every other editor in the industry. Nothing bad will happen if I pull the manuscript, but some pretty awful things could happen if I don't."

I want to slide the hair off her cheek and tuck it behind her ear. But I don't. I won't. "So I guess you should pull it. Reevaluate when you've had time to settle in, and things with your mom are easier. Just say the words, and your agent *has* to listen. She works for you."

"I know. And I've done all that."

"But she keeps calling you," I surmise. "Hounding you to go through with the sale."

"Hounding me to go on a talk show." Scoffing, she drags her bottom lip between her teeth, suckling on the sweet, plump swell. "My book isn't some fun summer beach read. It's more serious than that. It's..." She searches my eyes. "Not something to be discussed over breakfast. That she and Elyte insist on a press tour that includes gossipy morning shows proves they're the wrong people for the book, and honestly, it makes me wonder if Helen is the right agent for me."

"So I suppose it's decided then." My hands fucking itch to touch. My palms actively tingle in anticipation. So I lock them deep in my pockets and save us both from *additional* heartache. "Fire her and take back your book. If she's not listening to you, then she's not the right fit for you."

She breathes out a soft laugh, her sweet breath tickling my chin and feathering over my tongue.

In response, my lips curl higher. "What's so funny?"

"You." She twists and rests on her shoulder, her cheek on the door, and her succulent body entirely too close to mine for safety. "You literally never listen to me. Even before. You were always too bossy for your own good."

"I only didn't listen when I knew you were wrong." *God, save me.* I drag my hands from my pockets and turn to face her. "You'd say you didn't need a coat because it wasn't gonna be cold out. But I'd force you to carry one anyway. Nine times out of ten, it was cold enough."

In the darkness, but for the sliver of light coming down from the windows in the rafters, I catch sight of her dancing eyes.

"You'd say you weren't hungry," I tease, "or that you didn't need to pack something that day. I knew your body better than you knew it yourself. You were *always* hungry."

"And you always had something for me, even though you had such little to spare."

That's love, Lana. It was my honor.

"You didn't think you needed sunblock, but then—"

"Yeah, yeah." She waves me off, the tips of her fingers brushing over my chest. Her touch sends my heart into a skittering mess. "I got it. You were bossy, but every now and then, you were possibly right."

"Every now and then," I snort. Fuck, the loose fabric of her skirt tickles my fingers. I don't know how. I don't know why. I just know that I pinch the material between my digits and hope she doesn't notice. "Almost always," I tease. "Sometimes, I felt like you intentionally made bad choices so I'd be forced to pick up the slack. Like you enjoyed when I took care of you."

Which, when her eyes flicker with acknowledgment, I realize how right

I am. She came from a home where her mother did nothing except make her feel like shit.

She was just a girl who wanted to be cared for.

Psychologically, it's as simple as that.

And, plainly put, I wanted the same in return.

"We were exactly who we needed, huh?" Her voice comes out with a wistful sigh. Breathy and sweet. "It seems impossible that we could come from such different homes and wildly different worlds, but beneath all the noise, we were just two souls that needed what only the other could give. I often wonder... Would we have survived adolescence if we never met?"

"I would have survived. For Chris." I roll the soft fabric of her skirt between my fingers and wish for a way to ask to take it home and it *not* be weird. "Not sure I'd have stayed out of prison, though, if not for you."

Her plump lips curl into a seductive bow. "Yeah. You often lacked control over your temper back then."

"Back then?" I brush the side of my finger over her silky thigh. Good fucking lord, I swear I don't mean for it to happen. But she doesn't run away, and I'm not sure I could stop, even if the whole place caught on fire. "Pretty sure some would say my temper *still* runs a little hot. You don't agree?"

"I wasn't gonna say anything." Her heart creates a heavy, steady beat in the air between us. Not racing. Not slow. Simply constant. Comforting. "I wouldn't have survived without you. At the risk of sounding ridiculously dramatic, I don't think I could have gotten through those years if *her* voice was the only one I heard. How embarrassing I was. How flighty and dumb. I never dressed right, never walked right. My grades were never good enough."

"You had A's across the board. Always."

She searches my eyes, the truth of my words floating gently between us.

"So much damage." She sighs. "And for what? Did she think I would be better if she criticized me more? Did she think I could try harder than I already was?" She drops her gaze, tilting her head from side to side. "She was mean. Like she fed off my misery, and even to this day, she won't acknowledge it. She sees no fault in her actions. I doubt she ever will. But then there was you..." She brings her eyes up again, a wrinkle in her nose and a sweet curl of her lips. "Your kindness was the antidote to her poison. Your love, and the way it never wavered, saved my life."

"Lana..."

"If not for you, I would've assumed my mother's example of love was normal. And if by some cruel twist of fate, I *did* survive it, then Jesus, maybe that's the kind of love I would've shown my child. Could you imagine a world where I spoke to Franklin the way my mother speaks to me? The viciousness. The spitefulness."

Bravely—or stupidly, maybe—she rests her hand on my chest and strokes right where, beneath my shirt, she penned ink into my skin back before we knew how foolish and permanent such a thing would be. "You came from an awful home. From parents who wouldn't know love if it smacked them in the face. But for reasons I'll never truly comprehend, you loved me. You saved my life."

My heart skips, but it's not like they speak of in the movies. It's not a pleasant feeling.

"If not for that light in the dark, I wouldn't be who I am today."

"Have you been drinking today?" I slide my fingers over the side of her thigh—proving to us both it's no accident—and cup her cheek with my other hand. "Tequila for dinner?"

She snickers. "No. Though I'm beginning to wish I had. Just a little to help me be less afraid."

"Afraid of what?" I rest my forehead on hers. Too close. Way too fucking close. "Me?"

Her single, fast nod shatters my heart. *She's afraid of me?* When, in my soul and with my actions, I thought I'd proven I would trade my life for hers.

I would've taken a bullet for her when I was seventeen. I would have stopped a speeding car. Derailed a fucking train. I would destroy any man with no hesitation, spending the rest of my life behind bars, if that's what I needed to do to keep her safe. And even now, though I'm not sure it's healthy for me to admit, I would do the same.

There is no point in my existence if she's not safe and happy.

That's why all this hurts so fucking bad.

"I'm afraid of making things worse," she whispers, stepping just a little closer so *I* know it was no accident. "Afraid of hurting you more. It breaks my heart that ten years have passed, and you're *still* so angry, because it terrifies me to consider a world where you haven't found love again. A world where the greatest soul, the greatest man who ever existed, escaped the parents he was burdened with and the life he was tossed into, only to be broken by a silly girl not nearly worthy enough to have hoarded the best years of love he would give."

Fresh tears settle on her lashes while her eyes glitter in the shadows.

"It's not fair that you fought through so much pain and such cruel beginnings, and now, because of *my* horrible choices, you can't feel the happiness you deserve."

"You seem to think you get to dictate who I deserve." I slide the pad of my thumb over her plump bottom lip, stroking until I'm rewarded with a brush of her tongue. "You're trying to jam a square peg through a round hole, Lana. Constantly fighting against what's right, what fits—"

"We don't—"

"When all along, I've only ever wanted *you*." I pull her to the tips of her toes and gently press my lips to hers.

She sighs, her breath sprinting to the base of my lungs, and then she kisses me back, ensuring I'll never again retrieve my soul, suckling on my tongue and wrapping her arms over my shoulders to keep me close.

It's not like last time when tequila, loud music, and the safety found within the shadows ruled our hormones. This is sweeter. Softer. Her tears mingle on our tongues, and her breath is choppy because of how she cries.

I slide my hands around her thighs, tugging her closer in my quest to eliminate even a sliver of space between our bodies. But she wants more, jumping into my arms instead and trusting me to hold all of her.

I would normally turn and slam her to the door. It's as natural to us as breathing. As arguing. Living. But I bend my knees instead and earn her whimper of approval as I lower to the floor.

The rough wood catches on my shirt, tugging threads and crackling in the evening silence, but the fabric saves me from splinters, and her lips on mine make me not give a shit anyway. I wouldn't care if the skin was torn from my bones. If my bones were fed to a fucking wood-chipper. I wouldn't care if the entire world was burning. Not when I place her over my lap and her fingers go to the snap of my jeans.

Alana Page and I are good at fucking.

We might have been young ten years ago—*probably too young to have practiced as much as we did*—but fuck, we know exactly how to make the other fall apart.

But this isn't fucking. This will be lovemaking.

And hell, I like that, too.

"Say the words." I drag the strap of her tank off her shoulder, trailing my fingers over her delicate skin until she breaks out in goosebumps.

She draws my cock out of my jeans, humming with pleasure and carefully lining it up at her fiery opening. Then she slides down, swallowing me up and dropping her head back with a whimper.

Her breath turns choppy.

Desperate.

But fuck, she's so beautiful sitting atop her throne.

"Hey?" I wrap my palm around her throat and force her eyes back to mine. So blue, even in the waning light. So bright despite the hurt circling between us. "Lie to me, Lana. Say the words."

"I love you." She rides my cock with slow, languid strokes that stoke an inferno in my blood, and when I free her tits from her top and take her pebbled nipple between my lips, she mewls. "God, Tommy. I love you."

ROUND TWENTY-ONE
ALANA

"You slept with him?" Fox's voice hits me like an assault, her words slamming through my headphones rather than out into the shop for my son to overhear.

"Alana! You slept with your ex?"

"Yes." *Am I mad? Sad? Happy?* Jesus, I don't know. But a warm blush fills my cheeks. "More than a few times."

"Alana!" She walks amongst New York foot traffic, laughing and stepping around others as she makes her way closer to work. "This is the guy you swore you wouldn't go near."

"Yes."

"The one you said has a temper hotter than Hades, and, I quote, '*he will probably want to kill me for what I did to him*.' That guy?"

I stack books on a shelf and play with positioning so the brighter, more alluring covers face outward. "Mmhm. I did."

"More than a few times?" She chokes out. "You hoe! You knew you wouldn't stay away."

"I tried." I lower to my knees to save my back and arrange books on the lower shelves. "I swear, Fox. I tried so hard. But this is a small town, and he's just... he's..."

"Got a giant donkey dick? Eyes that burn into your soul. Lips that even I kinda want to kiss, ya know, just to try them out."

A low, warning snarl rolls along my chest.

"You're *so* possessive," she teases. "You act like I didn't see the magazines, too. He's sex on legs and has that dark, dangerous allure about him. His job is to smash other dudes for money, which in today's society is kinda savage, but also, it's got those Neanderthal hormones twitching, ya know? He stayed in that tiny ass town and waited for you. There are some seriously slick fighters in Brazil, so he could have gone there. Or Thailand. Or even Vegas, since that's where he goes for his title fights, anyway."

"You're not helping me."

"He could have gone anywhere! And you know he's rich enough to do it. His family is trash—you already said that—so it's not like anything was holding him to that town. But he stayed anyway." She releases a wistful sigh. "He's the man who couldn't be moved."

"His brother is here. And his friends."

"Oh, please. Don't act like I haven't read your book. His brother is his best friend and would follow him anywhere. Half of your high school friends have already left for the city, and those who haven't, could. Did you tell him yet?"

My stomach drops, just like it does every other time someone asks me that question. But my answer remains the same. Eighteen or twenty-eight, my decision remains firm. "No."

"And you won't?"

"No."

"Because you think if you do, he'll beat the absolute shit out of the guy and end up in prison?"

"Yes." I sit back on my haunches and study my work so far. The rows and rows and rows of shelves I've rearranged. The books I've stacked. The dust I've cleared out and the couches I've deep cleaned. We're almost ready for the public to come in, make a coffee, and settle in with a book. "I can't tell him, Fox. He wouldn't cope."

"So you'd rather lie to him. But also, sleep with him sometimes."

"I'm not lying to him!" I push to my feet and brush the dust off my legs. "I've established a boundary of not telling him. He's not happy with it, but I think he's coming to accept it."

"Clearly, since you moved from '*he's going to kill me*' to '*he makes me come three to five days a week.*'"

I roll my eyes and head back to the front of the shop to collect my next stack of books. "You're crass and rude, and it's only been four times, total. Not even all in the same week."

Franky looks up from the computer. "What is four times?"

Fox cackles. "Oopsie! Explain yourself out of that one, hooker."

"Four times Fox has called this week and annoyed me." I lean across the counter and kiss the top of his head, sneaking a look at his spreadsheet and the cells filled with numbers. Barcodes. Descriptions. Author names. Publishing houses. So much information, and all because of a nine-year-old who likes organization. "Fox says hello, honey. She misses us."

"Miss you too, Aunty Fox." He speaks in monotone, barely interested in the woman on the other side of the line. But she gets the words, at least. Which is a gift in itself. "You can take all those books now—" He points to a trolley filled with romance novels. "They go on shelf eleven. Make sure they stay in alphabetical order."

"Yeah, Mom." Fox taunts. "Don't screw with his system."

"Shut up."

When Franky's brows shoot high on his forehead, I point back at my ears to let him know that was for her, not him. Then I turn and take my next load toward shelf eleven. "You're a pain in my ass, Fox. You almost got me in trouble with my own kid."

"How does it feel to raise a forty-year-old man? Shoot." She gasps and jumps, the jingling bell from a messenger bike echoing through the line. "Ride on the road like everyone else, jackass! Get out of my damn way!"

"You should come to Plainview." I find shelf eleven and scour the books my son has already stacked in the order he wants them. "It doesn't take more than ten minutes to drive *anywhere*."

"And risk chicken poo on my shoes?" She scoffs. "No, thanks. I'm a city girl, Alana Bette. You know this about me."

"New York stresses you out. It's busy and crowded and smelly."

"And always has somewhere open to eat," she counters. "Never gets quiet. Never gets dark. Multiculturalism is beautiful. I bet Plainview folks all have the exact same skin color."

"I mean—"

"Exactly. Which means they probably have just one boring ass flavor of food and no inclination to try anything else. New York is a boiling pot of music and scent and color and life. Everyone is friendly. Which, I know, sounds weird since small towns are *supposed* to be friendlier."

"They romanticize places like this," I confess. "Like everyone knows everyone, which means they're all friends. But in reality, no one likes *anyone,* and everyone likes to gossip."

"Exactly! So why in the world would I come there? There's nothing there for me."

Ouch.

My heart thuds with a deep ache, sorrow stealing my smile and forcing me back to my childhood. *Not good enough. Not important enough. Not worthy enough.*

Not even for my best friend.

"Franky's starting school in a few days, and I made an offer on the shop." Dejected, I grab the books at the top of the pile and begin shelving. "My mom's health is declining, and I just... This is where our lives are now, Fox. We can't leave. And maybe it's a shitty town right now, but that's because the same old people live here. The same families. The same elders. The businesses are run by the same people, the town council has all the same faces, and traditions have been in place for the last hundred years. Nothing can change unless something changes."

"That's why they call those places backwards. As in, nothing ever progresses forward."

"Right. But the older folks will eventually die off."

She chokes out a laugh. "Savage!"

"They had kids, who had kids, who are having kids. And I know, in my experience, anyway, a lot of the people I went to school with are less tolerant of the same old shit. Some are moving away to escape it. Others stayed and are opening their own businesses. The local pediatrician isn't eighty-seven years old anymore, and he doesn't subscribe to the idea that rubbing dirt on a staph infection will fix it."

She snorts. "Sounds like a good way to speed up Plainview's evolution."

"People like my mom would have the rest of the world believe this town is scandal-free and entirely too *proper*. But the new pediatrician—who is also oncology, and orthopedics, and immunizations, and every other specialty too, because he's the only doctor in this town—well, I went to school with him, and on the night of our prom, he was arrested by his own father for running along Main Street in the nude."

She laughs. "He sounds fun."

"Yeah..." Memories wash over me like water lapping at a sandy beach. Coming closer. Closer. Closer. "You know about him, Fox. You've read the book, remember?"

Her laughter cuts off with a gurgle. Her breath stuttering. "Him? The one Tommy had to bail out?"

"Mmhm." I move to my knees and carefully place books on the lower shelves. "I'm just saying, yes, Plainview sucks. But there's a chance it won't *always* suck. And if you visit, you can stay at a house that has no chicken poo. Maybe." I snicker. "I'd have to ask around. But I'm sure I'll find somewhere."

"I'll consider it." The tick-tick-tick of a pedestrian crossing plays through my headphones, though people rarely pay attention to those in New York City. "So you're casually banging your old flame. You *haven't* told him your massive secret. Annnnnd, Helen?"

"Is still trying to mother me. She insists I'm making rash business decisions that I'll someday regret. But I told her to pull the book. Officially." I move away from sweet romance and come to the darker, grittier stories with covers that convey exactly the content written within the pages. "I've formally declined Elyte's offer and told Helen to tell them the book is no longer available for sale. It would kill Tommy if the story got out. It would destroy him and Chris, and I'm not willing to be the reason they're hurt." *More.* "I'm especially not ready for it to be read and picked apart by the masses."

"So that's it? You're putting your dreams of being published in the trash?"

"Not in the trash. Just on hold. My life here will be busy for the next few years, getting Franky from elementary to middle, and then middle to high school. I intend to buy the store and turn it into something kind of special. Things between me and Tommy are..."

"Hot?"

I roll my eyes. "Salvageable, maybe. Not romantically."

She scoffs.

"I mean, it is. For now. But ultimately, the best thing I can do is let him heal. Let him find someone else. What we're doing is fun, but it's not end-game for him. It can't be."

"Have you told him that?"

"Every single time." A blush makes my cheeks hot and my stomach tingle. So I drop my gaze despite being here all alone. Well, except for Franky. "We do that... thing. And then I tell him no more. He laughs and says until next time."

"And then there's a next time," she teases. "And another. And another. And another, until eventually, you look up and realize you've been together for months. Or years. And maybe you're already living together. That's when you look back and realize you're already a couple, Alana."

"I won't let it happen." I silence when the shop bell rings above the door, then swallow when I hear *his* voice. I feel his presence. I press my hands to the floor, almost as though expecting to feel the vibration of his footsteps. "He won't want me when he understands the whole truth," I whisper. "And I won't trick him, nor will I tell him. It would be cruel."

"So, you say nothing and let him go the rest of his life not knowing?"

"Yep." I slowly push to my feet and peek through the gaps in the shelves, finding him leaning on the desk by Franky, his elbows on the counter and a broad, playful smile transforming his face.

"I've gotta go, Fox. But I'll talk to you later." I wander away from my shelf, only to stop in my tracks when Tommy's heated eyes swing my way. His hungry stare. His taunting gaze. He has this way of undressing me with just a look, of seeing inside my soul and uncovering my secrets with just a glance.

That's why he's so frustrated, I suppose. Because he can't ferret out my last secret.

"Talk to you later, Fox." I tap the side of my ear and end our call, then I pull my headphones out and hold them in my palm. Dammit, my eyes fall to his muscular legs and a girlish grin spreads across my lips. It's like I'm a teenager again, and he's the big, bad Tommy Watkins, challenging me in the lunchroom.

"Hey." He sets his hands in his pockets and looks me up and down. "You look like you've been working hard."

"We have," Franky answers. "We're relaunching the shop in a few days. Mom's putting an ad in the paper after we've finished stacking all the books, and we're gonna have a sale and fill the fridge with cupcakes and stuff."

"Sounds like you've planned for success." He tilts his head to the side. "Franky agreed to another game of chess later, out at your place, if you're up for visitors."

"Um—"

"I could bring steaks. You could make a salad. Chris could come, too, and we could see who the better chess player is."

"It's me," Franky inserts dryly. "I'm the best. I already beat Chris the other day."

With a smirk, Tommy hooks a thumb back at my son. "Arrogance in fighting means he'll sweep the floor, or he'll end up on it. Either way, you know I can't back down from that kind of challenge."

"Why do I feel like I'm sixteen again, and you're asking me to host a party at my house?" Shaking my head, I wander a little closer. "I can already hear my mom screeching in my ears. Something about how I'm trashy and cheap and how it's not her job to feed everyone else's kids."

"You could come to my place." His smile grows wider. "That was always the backup, wasn't it? Except now I'm an adult, and I don't have to worry about what my dad will do when he gets home drunk."

"I'm gonna live with my mom forever," Franky declares. "Even when I'm a grown-up. She said I could, so long as I'm at school or working towards something for my future."

"No bums allowed," Tommy smirks. "I can get behind that."

"You want us to come to your house?" *Why am I so nervous? So anxious? So scared!* "Where do you live?"

"You've been in Plainview for *how long,* and you haven't figured it out?" He tsks. "It's like you're not even trying, Lana."

I purse my lips.

"I bought the Sanderson house a couple of years back."

"Edwin? The one on the lake?"

"Mm." He knows—*he knows*—my mind spins back a decade to the fence we forever snuck through because Edwin Sanderson's private property was the gateway to some of the best parts of the lake.

"Did he cuss you out the day you exchanged contracts?" I snicker. "Bet he tacked more onto his asking price once he realized you were interested, purely to recoup the money he spent repairing the fence you cut through every other weekend."

He snorts. "He didn't say so with his words, but he *for sure* failed to mention the rotting bathroom floor while we were inspecting. Put my foot through it within three months of moving in."

"Fair's fair."

His eyes flash with heat. Knowing.

God, why do I continue to say the words that hurt us? *All's fair in love and war.*

"What do ya say?" He rolls his lips and studies me through long, beautiful lashes. "We could grill some steaks on the patio and pretend we're not being terrorized by the mosquitoes. Chris has been wanting to see Franky, but without the stench of a sweaty gym, and he's too shy to say he's missed you." He pauses. Then swallows, lowering his smile. "Remember how you used to be his friend, too?"

"Tommy—"

"Totally chill evening. Early start so Franky can get home at a decent hour and not feel like we've ruined his night."

Franky nods his approval. "I like to be alone with my mom by eight."

"See?" Again, with the hooked thumb. "Gotta be home by eight. So why don't you get to mine by five? Gives us plenty of time to hang out."

This is not allowing him to move on.

This is not healing his heart or setting him free.

This is playing happy families while ignoring a giant, hulking, horrifying elephant that sits happily at the table beside us.

"Please?" Tommy presses his hands together. "It's just steak, Lana. And chess. And my brother, who would really, really like to see his old friend again."

"Fine." I exhale a heavy sigh and drop my gaze. For this round, at least, he wins. "We'll close the shop at five and head home to make a salad. We'll come over after that."

"Close the shop and come over right away," he counters. "I'll take care of the salad, so you don't have to waste your time."

"So I'll bring the steak?"

He shakes his head. "I'll provide it all. I'll always feed you, Lana."

ROUND TWENTY-TWO

TOMMY

"Got the steak. Made potato salad and regular salad. Got soda for Franky. And wine for Alana." I stride from my kitchen sink to the table. Then back. Then around again as nervous energy sends me into a meltdown. "I don't even know if she likes wine. But it's classy, right? It's what people have with dinner. Tequila is for bad choices."

"You look like an idiot, just so you know." Chris sits on the counter, his feet crossed at his ankles and a cold beer nestled between his hands. "Remind me again; are you playing nice so she'll spill her secrets and you'll get your revenge, or are you in love and completely incapable of surviving if she walks again?"

"Shut up." I stop in the middle of my dining room and push my hands through my hair. Scratching my scalp and tugging the locks. Anything so I can feel something other than nerves. "Don't mention any of those things while she's here."

"What things? Revenge?" He sips his beer. "Love? Complete and utter devotion to someone other than yourself?"

"Yes. Those things." The sound of tires on my driveway sends my heart into a galloping frenzy. The reality that she's here, in the house I bought for her, on the lake we fell in love in, makes my pulse skitter and my hands sweat.

My hands are sweating!

"Fuck." I grab paper towels and wipe my palms like a fucking idiot striding to the trash can and stomping my foot on the pedal that pops the lid open. "You wanna see her. You like Franky. *I* wanna see her. *I* like Franky. It's gonna be like how it used to be, except now we have Franky, too."

"And he's kind of the coolest little dude I've met since... ever."

"Exactly! He's cool. He's smart. He's protective as fuck; I can get behind that. He's his mother's son, for sure, with her sass and ability to put me on my ass with just a look."

"And the fact she has a husband?"

"We don't talk about that." I release the trash lid and stride to my back door. Which works out, since the front door is all the way on the opposite side of the house, away from the driveway, the porch we sit on at the end of a long day, the view I bought, and the memories I like to keep bottled up, right here where a large portion of them were created.

"We don't talk about the husband?" Taunting, like he enjoys seeing me sweat through my shirt, Chris drops to his feet and follows me across the kitchen to hover near my shoulder. "Pretty sure, here in the Plainview, the fact she's married to someone else, but banging my brother, is actually illegal. You want Ollie's dad to come over here and lock her up for her adulterous actions?"

"It's not adultery." I shove him back and watch through the glass panes of my door as Alana and Franky climb out of their car. "They're separated, so shut the fuck up."

"She's married." He taunts, whistling under his breath. "Do you ever feel like there was a glitch in time? Like, we saw Ollie get older. And Eliza. You and me. We saw it all, so it's fine. But she bolted at eighteen and came back at twenty-eight. It's like the ten years between didn't exist."

"Shush. They're coming up the stairs."

"And of course, they did exist. Since that's when she grew up and got hitched and all that. My logical brain knows it. But sometimes, when I'm not concentrating, I forget. So then I'm surprised when I see her again."

"Yep. Now shut up." I rearrange my expression and paste on a friendly smile, then I open the door before they get a chance to knock, looking to Franky first and the little chessboard he carries tucked under his arm. "Hey." I set my hands on my hips and wait for his hazel eyes.

If he was a toddler, I'd get down on his level, crouching so I'm not towering over him. But he's not a toddler. He's not fully grown, either. He's in this weird in-between age, and I figure, if I try to crouch, or God forbid, bend at the hips and fold myself in half, he might pop me in the face with the same jab I've been teaching him down at the gym. "You brought your own chessboard? We have one if you wanna try ours."

"I like mine." He studies me through dirty lenses. "Mine's magnetized, so the pieces don't accidentally fall over."

"Smart. Thanks for coming."

"It's okay. Did you start cooking yet?"

"Franklin," Alana warns in a murmur. "Don't be rude."

"I've got the grill already warming," I tell him. "Just as soon as we're ready, we can toss the steaks on. Then, ten minutes after that, it's time to eat. You hungry?"

He merely shrugs, peeking past me and smiling at my brother.

I mean, it's not like I think he hates me or anything. But damn, he for sure prefers Chris' company.

"We had a snack at three," Alana fills in when Franky wanders through the open door. She links unadorned fingers in front of her sundress and anxiously fidgets. "We're not starving. But we're ready to eat when you are."

"You look pretty." I step forward instead of back, and surprise her when I pull the door closed behind me. Then I take her hand in mine and bring it up.

She's made a change, a *massive* change, and my obsessed brain can't help but notice. "You took your ring off."

"Oh..." Nervous, she nibbles on her lip. "Yeah. I've mailed it back to Colin."

"He asked for it back?" That cheapskate motherfucker. Now he's gonna nickel and dime her all the way through divorce. "Aren't rings a gift? They don't have to be returned."

"I wanted to." She draws a breath, filling her lungs and expanding her chest. Then, exhaling again, she brings her eyes up and rewards me with a sweet smile. "I suppose you're probably intent on hating Colin. He's the villain in your story."

"Obviously." I draw her closer and slide my hand around to rest on the small of her back. *Mine. Mine. All mine.* "He kinda swooped in and married the girl I was gonna marry. Gonna be honest; felt a little unfair to me."

I lean in, intending to take her lips with mine, but she backs away and gives me her cheek instead.

Ouch.

"Colin isn't the bad guy, Tommy." She reaches around and grabs my wrist, peeling my hand away from her body. I could stop her. I'm stronger. But there hasn't been a single moment in our lives when she couldn't control me, body and soul. "He's actually a really decent guy. He's very kind. Generous. Sweet."

"Forgive me for not giving a shit about the guy who stole the woman I loved. If he was so generous, he'd understand the tradition of wedding rings. As in, they're intended to be a safety net for women in the event of separation. You're supposed to sell the ring and use that money to support yourself."

"I don't need that money to support myself, and the ring belonged to his mother and grandmother. It's only right that I send it back." She attempts to step around me. "Should we go in?"

"Thirty more seconds." I yank her back and bury my nose in her hair, right where I smell lavender most. "I can't touch you in front of Franky, so I just need—"

"You shouldn't touch me at all." She slips out of my reach again, robbing me of what I want so desperately to have. Smell. Taste. But she takes my hand, at least, twining her fingers between mine and looking up into my eyes. "We can't keep doing this."

"You said that last time." I press a kiss to her wrist and grin when her thundering pulse pounds against my lips. "You say no, but then you say *yes*. Then you try to backtrack to how we should just be friends and—"

"And how it would be best for you to see me as a friend." Gently, she peels her hand free of mine and destroys me with pity in her eyes.

Anger, I can deal with. Rage is even better. I can handle her tears—most of the time—and fuck knows, I can be what she wants when she's wet and needy.

But pity... pity is where men go to die.

"I think we could use the next little while to learn to get along," she murmurs. "To be in the same space and be friends."

"We are in the same space. We're even getting along."

"You're trying to wear me down." She lays her hand on my chest, predicting my next move. "We need to learn how to coexist, but not be together."

"I disagree."

"For the sake of your happiness," she groans. "We both know it's the right thing to do. And of course, it's not going to be fun at first. No one likes change."

Oh, you mean like how you left ten years ago, sneaking out of town without a word of warning and no chance to change your mind?

"I think you'll eventually realize I was right. Once the hard part is done and hearts are mended, and you meet someone else... Someone better." Her voice crackles with the lies she speaks. The fucking atrocities she attempts to will into existence. "If you really tried, we could be doing dinner like this again in two or three years. I'll still be here. And Franky, too. But you'll have healed, and whoever you choose, whoever is lucky enough to capture your heart, maybe she'll be here, too."

"You're lying to us both," I growl. "You're gonna come to a fuckin' barbecue while I have this hypothetical lover on my arm? She'll be pretty. Maybe even blonde. She'll have amazing tits and legs for days."

Her eyes flash with bitter hatred.

"She'll be sitting on my lap since you know I like that." *Remember, Alana! Remember back to what it was like before.* "When I'm no longer fighting for my life and trying to stop a woman from running away all the damn time, you know I like to pull up a chair and keep her close. A beer in one hand and her leg in the other."

"Exactly." It's like she's sucking on a lemon. Her lips, twisting in anger and her voice breaking on the word. "You see it, too. The future you could have, if only you'd try."

"I see you smashing some blonde bitch's head open with a baseball bat." I slide a long lock of hair off her shoulder and thrill in the goosebumps spreading beneath her skin. "The Alana I knew would run a hoe down for even looking at me. You were the least demanding person I knew." I lean in and inhale the scent of her shampoo. "You didn't care what we ate. Where we hung out. Who we were with or what we were doing. But dammit, Alana, you demanded *me*."

"And now I'm demanding something different."

"You were so sweet. So placid. So fucking *easy*. Because you never expected anything materialistic, ever. But babe, you demanded that lap to sit on. My hand on your leg. You settled for nothing short of absolute fucking devotion."

"You're confused," she groans. "You *gave* absolute devotion. That was you."

"And you grew accustomed to it. So if I slipped, even for a day, and forgot to tell you I loved you, you were so far up my ass, calling me out on it, it almost became a fun game to see how wound up I could get you."

"Makes you an asshole."

My lips curl into a devious grin. "Remember when Kayla Reddington asked me to ask her to prom?"

She breathes out a dangerous snarl. "Stupid, suicidal bitch. What'd she think was gonna happen? Do I look like I share?"

I laugh, my chest and shoulders bouncing because of it. "Sure, Lana. I'll invite this other hypothetical whore to our future barbecues. Since, according to you, you're a different person now. Matured or something."

Frustrated, she pulls back, tucking her own hair behind her ears and exhaling a tired sigh. Then she meets my eyes and shrugs. "I'll learn. And when the time comes, you'll be thankful you listened to me. Now let's go inside before my son thinks I've run off without him."

"Can we still have sex while we're waiting for my future hoe to arrive?"

"No." She smacks my stomach and pushes through the door, ignoring my wheeze and the way I rub my belly. Then she changes, like night and day, from the Alana I knew once upon a time to the Alana she is now, a mom, a caretaker. Matured, allegedly. "You guys have started a game already?" She leaves me behind and crosses to the table, stopping beside her son and sliding her fingers through the hair at the nape of his neck. "Sheesh. You're already a whole bunch of moves in."

"Makes my brain happy watching him play." Chris sits back, quiet contemplation as he sips his beer and looks *my* Alana up and down. "How's it going?"

"Can we stop feeling awkward yet?"

She doesn't notice me as I wander through my kitchen. As I move to my counter and position myself perfectly to witness his stony stare and her nervous worry.

She wrings her fingers together again, fidgeting while he appears as nothing more than completely fucking cool and unbothered.

"You feel awkward?" He sets his right foot on the opposite knee, bouncing it. Which, really, is proof he's nervous, too. "I don't feel awkward."

"Yes, you do!" Ten years apart did nothing to stunt her ability to read him as easily as she reads me. She points down at his bouncing foot. "We never used to be like this, Chris. We used to be friends. *Good* friends."

"Lot of time has passed since then." He's an ass, playing with her emotions as payback for her screwing with mine. "I'm not even sure you'd like the guy I became. Maybe I drink from the carton and put empty bottles back in the fridge."

"*I* drink from the carton," Franky snickers. "Sends my mom crazy."

"And it would send you crazy if literally anyone else came into our home and did that," she scolds. Then back to Chris, "Be my friend."

His eyes dance with affection. "Excuse me?"

"You heard me. Be my friend."

"And you just..." He casts a glance around the room. "You think you can demand it and make it so?"

"Yes." She sets her hands on her hips. "My son and I are here in Plainview to stay. I wasn't planning to force my company on anyone since I know the mess I left behind and the pain I caused. But now I'm tired of that. I don't have leprosy, Tommy and I are..." She hesitates before settling on, "Friends. And you know damn well we have a history worth fighting for. It wasn't always me, you, and Tommy. And it wasn't always me and Tommy. There was a me and Chris, too. Independent of him. So stop with the shit and just be my friend already."

"Chris' move," Franky declares, oblivious to the double meaning in his words. And because Chris has never been a guy to rush for anyone, he gently brushes Alana aside, sets his foot on the floor, and leans forward to study the board.

His lips curl up on the side, a taunting smirk he doesn't allow Alana to see, and after a moment of consideration, he moves his queen and goes on the hunt. "Gonna get you, kid. Watch your back."

"Don't make me take your games away until you acknowledge me, Christian Watkins." Alana grabs his face, clutching his jaw between her thumb and fingers, and drags his focus back to her. "Be my friend. Or I'll hit you with a baseball bat."

"Mom." Hardly alarmed, Franky pulls his knight around the front and reinforces his king's guard. "That's coercion."

"Yeah, Mom." Chris snickers. "Coercion is bad."

"Don't make me beg." Demand turns to vulnerability, and confidence makes way for the constant doubt her mother hammered into her heart. "Please."

"Jesus." He brushes her hands away and pushes to his feet, wrapping her in a tight hug and crushing her face to his chest. He holds her when a sob crawls along her throat, and presses a kiss to the side of her head, closing his eyes for a long, cathartic hug I'm not sure either of them realized they needed until now. "Don't cry on me. You know I can't take it." He squeezes her extra tight and sighs when she circles his torso with her arms, holding on for as long as she needs it. But his eyes come to mine in the silence, apology in his gaze like he thinks he owes me something. "We can be friends," he murmurs. "Never actually stopped, just so you know."

ROUND TWENTY-THREE

ALANA

Tommy serves dinner on the patio, mosquito zappers adding a kind of musical harmony to our meal, and though I try to regain a little distance, my boundaries are a mere joke as far as he's concerned, because he sets my plate beside his and places the best steak of the bunch on top of it.

Because he always wanted to feed me.

"Dig in." He selects a smaller, more easily managed steak for Franky, then offers a choice of the last two to his brother. Like I knew he would, Tommy takes the leftovers. Always the last to receive. And yet, he sits on my right with a smile that would swear pure contentedness.

He pours me a glass of wine without asking and scoots his chair as close to mine as he can physically manage. Then he sets his hand on my thigh beneath the table.

I brush it off and cross my legs.

He smirks. "What are your favorite subjects at school, Franky? Your mom used to be really good at math. Like, genius level with some of that stuff. Her and Chris always did their homework together like it was a race, and then when they were done, they'd kinda turn around and look at me like I was a stray mutt in the street. Like, *alright, now we help the stupid one*."

"That's not true." I brush his hand off when he tries again. "We never thought you were stupid."

"We definitely didn't say it out loud," Chris teases. He holds his fork in his right hand, though being right-handed would imply doing things the other way around. Cutting through his steak, he peeks across at Franky and finds him doing the same thing.

Same quirk and all.

Anxious, I risk a side glance to see if Tommy notices, too.

"You like math, don't you, honey?" I cut through my steak and push Tommy's hand off my leg. I'm not angry every time I have to, and he's not sad every time I do. He's turned it into a game, and I'm terrified that if he doesn't have that to focus on, he might notice the similarities between his brother and my son. "And you're especially good with algebra."

"Algebra?" Tommy sips his beer. "Geez. I *still* can't do algebra."

"Means you didn't pay attention in school," Franky counters dryly.

He doesn't mean harm, and neither Watkins boy takes offense. But in my heart and mind, I know Tommy wasn't given a fair chance. He lost half his education to broken bones and too little energy due to too little food. And the other half, he was treated poorly by the teachers and so often punished for being behind instead of congratulated for overcoming horrible circumstances in the first damn place.

My baby can't know that.

But I do. And Tommy does, too.

He looks my way, massaging my tense thigh, and winks. It's an '*it's cool*' wink.

"Do you play any instruments?" He fixes his face and looks back at my son. "Guitar, maybe? Piano? Or maybe you're gonna try out for theater?"

In response, Franky pokes a finger into his mouth and mock-gags.

"Theater is literal, legal child abuse," Chris inserts playfully. "It's fine for those kids who like it and all, but for the ones who don't..." He shakes his head. "No one should be forced onto a damn stage just because the state made it part of the curriculum."

"Remember when Mrs. Tower made you try out for Hamlet?" I grab my wine and snicker at the memory. "There was no reason for her to do that except to make you feel like crap."

"She was mad because I might've said something about her sweater the week before." He looks at Franky. "It was a pea-green color. Super ugly and frumpy and loose. But the color—"

"Like vomit?"

"Yes! Exactly. And I wasn't even trying to be mean. I see what I see, and I say what I think. She mentioned the stain on my hoodie, 'cos I don't know if your mom told you, but me and Tommy came from a pretty poor family. I had this one favorite hoodie that I liked to wear a lot, but it got a stain on it at lunch that day. We had Mrs. Tower's class after, and she made a whole big deal about it until everyone stopped to stare."

Franky's eyes narrow with disdain. "That's bullying."

"Well..." Chris shrugs. "Where we come from, the adults were allowed to do whatever they wanted, and it was called *authority figures*, and *do as I say, not as I do*. She was flapping on about my hoodie and making me feel like shit. Your mom stepped up for me, actually. She tried to get the teacher to shut the hell up. But your mom had to be careful, too, because if *her* mom found out she was being sassy, she'd get in big trouble."

Searching for confirmation, Franky looks at me.

So I nod. *It's true.*

"Anyway. Tower was yapping, yapping, yapping. And I just happened to mention the color of her sweater."

"And next thing we know," Tommy adds happily, "Chris is the worst Hamlet who ever stepped on a stage. She's still teaching to this day." He strokes my thigh under the table, flicking my fingers when I try to brush him off. "But don't worry. If she's still around when you get to high school, me, Chris, and your mom will head on in and let her know what's up."

"You make it sound like we're going to shake her down," I laugh. I meet Franky's eyes. "If she's still teaching when you get to high school, Mommy will talk to her. *Without* her muscled entourage. I'll make sure she knows you have no desire to play Hamlet, or any other character, on stage."

"What if she tries to make me?" His eyes glisten with emotion. "What if she talks about my clothes in front of the whole class and says I have to be in the play, even after you talk to her?"

"Baseball bat," Chris and Tommy speak as one. Then Tommy adds, "You don't ask questions, buddy. Then she won't have to lie. You just trust that the situation has been taken care of."

"Good lord." I shove his hand off and glare. "Can you stop? You'll have my son thinking I work for the mob, and that old lady is gonna lose her kneecaps if she keeps up with her shit."

"It's who you are, Alana Page." He flashes a teasing grin, chipping away at the armor I try so hard to place between us. "You take care of the people you love. It doesn't matter who the enemy is, and it doesn't matter how scary they are. You protect."

I protect.

It's what I do.

"Besides," he quips. "You learned a long time ago how to take care of business quietly and cleanly. It was a defense mechanism, knowing that if *I* had to step in, it would be loud, messy, and likely end with me in cuffs."

Exactly.

Which is why I left all those years ago without saying goodbye. Because telling the truth would end in cuffs.

That's the damn problem.

Seven forty-five approaches, and the sun settles amongst the trees surrounding Tommy's property. Rays bounce off the water, creating a kind of diamond sparkle that covers the grass and turns dusk into magic.

It takes a young girl's memories, where love was allowed, grown, and celebrated, and mixes it with what's left now.

That same love exists. Within me and, sadly, within him, too. But it really shouldn't. It can't.

Coveting Tommy Watkins' heart is the wrong thing for me to do.

"We have five minutes." The moment the door closes, and Franky and Chris move through the kitchen to sort dirty dessert dishes, Tommy snatches my hand and tugs me from my seat.

A yelp of surprise bursts from my throat, echoing on the night air and lingering back where we began. But he pulls me along, catching me when I stumble and dragging me down the porch steps until we're on the grass.

"Tommy!"

He slingshots me forward, tearing me around the side of his house, then pins me to the wall, crushing my chest beneath his and stealing my breath when he selfishly sucks it into his lungs.

"Tommy—"

"I need my five minutes, Lana." His hands roam my body. My thighs. My hips. He nibbles on my lips and crumbles the willpower I've been building all night. "Fuck, is this how drug addicts feel? When you just want something so bad, your mouth waters, and your hands shake. When you can't think about anything else. Can't focus on what everyone else is doing or saying.

"We need to stop."

"Four minutes," he groans, "and your kid is taking you away from me. He set a timer. An actual fucking timer, like he knows I'd take a mile if he gave even an inch."

I drop my head back, exposing my neck and frantically working to refill my lungs.

"You're a really good mom, Lana." He shatters me with his words, so simply put, and pulls back just far enough to search my eyes. *Addiction?* He fights it easily and smiles when my vision turns blurry. "I know it's a whole thing, and I know his existence is…" He hesitates. "Messy. I understand."

"Tommy—"

"I want you to know that just because I wish you never left doesn't mean I wish he didn't exist." Gently, so very carefully, he brushes the hair off my cheek and tucks it behind my ear. "He's an amazing little boy. He's special, Lana, and he's half of you. So, if going back and keeping you means he doesn't get to be here anymore, then I'll stop wishing for that. I'll stop being mad that you left. I'll stop holding anger. Because I wouldn't trade him."

My heart pounds, a painful staccato bruising my chest and leaving tears in my eyes. "You wouldn't?"

"He doesn't *have* your heart, Lana. He *is* your heart." He leans in and nibbles on my bottom lip. "And I think we can both agree I've been in love with your heart since the start."

My jaw trembles as ten years of pain threatens to spill over.

"I'm not sure he'll love me back." Chuckling, he slides a thumb beneath my eye and collects a fallen tear. "I'm not even sure he likes me. But I'm not gonna live in the past anymore. I'm not gonna demand answers or hold that anger or wish I could wrap you up ten years ago and change your plans."

"Tommy—"

"Because things *had* to go the way they did. For you to be as whole and beautiful and perfect as you are today, those things had to happen. But please, Lana," he cups my cheeks and drags me to the tips of my toes, *"please* let me be a part of your future."

I lose my battle against pain and choke out a sob I wish desperately I could keep inside.

"I'm not asking to take Colin's place. I won't talk shit about him, even if I think he's a cocksucker who probably can't fight."

I laugh and cry, tears streaming onto my cheeks and pooling where his hands touch my skin.

"Can he fight?"

"No." I step forward, pressing my face to his chest and wrapping my arms around his back. "And I forbid you from even *thinking* about what you're thinking about."

He chuckles. "You can't read my mind."

"Yes." I lean back and search his eyes. "I can."

"We were always supposed to be together. Don't you get it? Love and War. *We* are love and war, and you know damn well we'd fight to the death to save those we love. L and W. Lana and Watkins. You didn't change your name when you married because you knew if you weren't a Page, you were a Watkins. You left, Alana, but you came back to me."

I take his wrists in my hands, my breath coming out on a shuddering exhale. Because even if he *says* he accepts the past, it doesn't mean he actually does.

He couldn't.

I know him better than he knows himself.

"We've already lost ten years," he groans. "And I can still see the no in your eyes. But why won't you just try?" He crushes a demanding kiss against my lips. "Why can't we just try?"

"Mom?" Franky steps onto the porch with the bleating alarm of my phone playing in the air. "It's time to go."

I startle back and hit the wall, fresh tears spilling onto my cheeks. I reach up and swipe my face clear. *Again.* So damn often when it comes to this man.

"Lana—"

"I have to go." I smooth his shirt down, flattening the wrinkle that sits over his heart. Then I wipe my eyes again and take a step away. Then another. "Thank you for dinner. And for dessert."

He grabs my wrist, but his grip is gentle. It's a request, not a demand. And when I shake my arm free, he releases me again.

"Thank you for a lovely night. And for playing a *proper* game of chess, so my son isn't forced to hate you. He wants to beat you fairly. Not because you messed up the board."

"Mom?"

"I'm coming, honey." I wipe my nose and tidy my hair, and stealing one last glance back at the man whose eyes turn just a little darker, a little less free every time I walk away, I try to offer him a small smile. A shitty consolation prize, really. "I promise not to hurt your future hoe."

He lays his broad hand over his pounding heart.

It aches, I know.

"I promise to pretend to be happy for you. And maybe, eventually, I'll actually mean it. By then, you'll be happier, too, and that's all I ever wanted for you."

"Say the words." His lips tremble. "Lie to me."

I stop, my knees shaking and my heart stalling. Then, drawing a long breath until it fills my chest and leaves my lungs in pain, I destroy all the progress I've made and charge back in his direction, crashing against his powerful body and squeezing him in a hug like he's just a boy again, and I'm just a girl. He needs confirmation that he matters. That he's worthy. He needs to be told he's loved. *And dammit, I do.* "I love you, Tommy. I will *always* love you."

He crushes me in his arms, kissing my hair and breathing me in until I know he's hoarding what he can. Like he knows this is goodbye.

I'll still be around tomorrow, and so will he. We won't have changed, really. But we need to try.

I need to try.

"I've loved you since the moment I first laid eyes on you." I kiss his chest, right where he has my ink embedded in his skin. The date we met, way back in elementary school. It was chaotic back then, too. Loud and messy. We argued more than we talked, and we made hating each other an art form.

But there was no one I would have protected more. And there wasn't a single moment in history I doubted his devotion to me.

"This will take time." I sniffle. "We have to learn how to walk again. To exist. We have to learn how to *be*, but without being in love."

"Not sure I'm gonna be able to do it." Swallowing, he leans back and slides his hands to my cheeks. "You keep putting these rules between us, expecting me to abide by them. But I don't wanna."

"A kid would eat chocolate cake for every meal if they could. Sometimes, rules are in place for a reason."

"You're gonna mother me now?" He attempts a smile, ignoring the fact that it shudders. "Can't say I've ever had a mommy kink, but if that's the game you wanna play, then I suppose I could let you pour my milk and tuck me into bed each night."

"You're a freak." I tap his stomach and laugh when his breath comes out in a sweet chuckle. "If mothering you is what has to happen to ensure your best future, then that's what I'll do."

"Mom?! The timer went off!"

"Oh, my gosh. I'm coming, honey." I swipe my cheeks and search Tommy's beautiful hazel eyes in the waning light. *Has he even noticed yet that my son's are the same?* "Maybe I'll see you at the bookstore's grand reopening in a few days."

He scoffs. "I'll come find you tomorrow. You forget, I *want* chocolate cake."

"Such a pain." I wave him off and walk around the side of the house, drawing Franky's gaze when I step into view. He waits by the door, scowling his displeasure. "Sorry, honey. I was talking to Tommy, and he wouldn't stop yammering."

Tommy snickers, the soft sound tickling the back of my neck. Because, of course, he's nearby. *How could I expect any different?*

"Have you got everything you need? Got your chessboard?"

"Yep. Let's go." Franky charges down the porch steps and grabs my hand. "It's nearly eight."

I try not to notice Tommy's playful eyes as my son marches me to the car, and I say nothing of Chris' smug observation from the door, his arms folded and one foot kicked over the other.

I don't even acknowledge Tommy's wink when I climb into the driver's seat, and I sure as hell say nothing when he takes out his phone and taps away at the screen, only for mine to bleat with a text message a moment later.

I try not to read it; I swear.

But it's right there on my lock screen.

> Chocolate cake for my birthday? Special occasions deserve cake. Fair's fair, right?

"Mom..." Franky settles in the back and fixes his seatbelt. "It's getting late."

"Yep." I place my phone face down on the passenger seat, then I turn the key in the ignition and start my car.

It doesn't seem to matter how desperately I try to create boundaries between me and Tommy. It doesn't matter that I want to set him free.

He never had much sense of self-preservation, even when we were young, and the fact I spent ten years on the other side of the country, cutting all contact and raising a baby with another man, still ended with us here.

We haven't moved on. We didn't fall out of love.

He deserves so much better.

"Let's go home, honey."

I pull into my mom's driveway, passing Whacky II, that bastard rooster who chases our tires and risks being run straight over, and coming to a stop by the shed amongst a plume of dry dust, I cut the engine and simply sit.

Wait.

Cicadas scream from the trees, and the click-click-click of my car's warm motor plays through the almost-darkness. But it's Franky's clearing throat, I notice most of all.

It's not a regular throat clearing that most people do when they have a tickle to get rid of. It's a nervous tic. A slight squeak that tells me my baby is anxious.

"We made it home right on time, honey." I check my phone screen and the 8:01 plastered over my son's beautiful face. A memory. A laugh.

Well... Almost right on time.

"Want to watch The Simpsons after we brush our teeth?" I turn in my seat, leaning on my shoulder and resting my chin on the top of my chair. "Did you eat enough at Tommy's, or are you still hungry?"

He rubs his chess board, sliding the pad of his thumb over the corner with a rhythmic consistency.

"There's been a lot of change lately, huh?" I reach around and place my hand on the seat beside his leg. I don't touch. I don't take. But I breathe a sigh of relief when he sets his palm on top. "Moving. Meeting all these new people. Exploring a new town. You're even going to the gym. That's a lot."

"Are you going to marry Tommy?"

My breath comes out on a nervous shudder that leaves my stomach empty just in time for the dread to take its place.

"Um... No, honey. I'm not."

"But you want to?"

God... how do you explain these things to a child without making everything so much worse?

"It's really complicated."

"Explain it to me." He brings his eyes up, pinning me with such maturity, such grown-up intensity, I know I could never have achieved the same at his age. "Before we came to Plainview, you never used to lie to me at all. But now you do." He drags his glasses off, clearing every smudged barrier that sits between us. "It hurts my feelings. You said coming to Plainview was the right thing to do, but it doesn't feel right when in New York, you

241

always told the truth, and you never shouted. Here, you lie, and you cry a lot."

Shit.

Fuck.

Goddammit.

Save me, please.

"Explain it to me," he presses. "And don't lie."

"Tommy was someone who used to be very special to me." I lay my cheek against my chair and nibble on my lips. The way my pulse thunders in my throat and ears, I swear, must be audible to my son and every farm animal within a hundred-mile radius. "For my whole life, before I left, Tommy was the person I thought I would marry. He was my whole world back then when I thought love wasn't complicated and everything would work out just because we said it would."

"But it didn't work out? And then you moved to New York and had me?"

"Yes."

"And you married Colin instead. Even though he's not my dad."

I swallow the ache in my throat. "That's right."

"Now that we're back, do you want to marry Tommy?"

"I can't." The backs of my eyes itch, tempting me to reach up and crush them with the heels of my palms to relieve the annoyance. "Returning to Plainview was about Grandma Bitsy wanting us around more." And since he asked for honesty, I give it all. "I think she's dying, honey, and I don't even know how long we have left with her. Which makes this all feel worse because every time we talk, we argue, but when we're not in the same space, I miss her again." I slide the pad of my thumb along his narrow wrist, stroking his silky skin. It brings us both comfort. "I *want* to make up and be better for her, but Plainview brings a lot of emotions back to the surface for me. That's why I cry here more than I did in New York. It's why I argue with people. We have ten years of feelings to work through, and sadly," I breathe out a quiet laugh, "none of us learned how to express our emotions in a healthy way."

"Will you marry Chris?"

My heart jumps with surprise. Sweet delight. Humor. But I shake my head. "No. I won't marry him, either. Though, I hope he finds someone nice soon. He deserves a special lady who knows how to bring him peace in a crazy world."

"He told me that you used to do that for him." He looks down at our joined hands in consideration, rolling his lips between his teeth. "He told me how you used to make the world quieter for him because he doesn't like when it gets too loud. And you used to scratch his hair, 'cos he said it felt nice. He said how Tommy got to hug you most of the time, but sometimes, when he was lucky, you would hug him, too."

I bring my free hand up and swipe beneath my eye. "He told you all this?"

He nods. "When we were playing chess, and you were talking to Tommy on the patio. He said how you were his best friend and when you left, he was really sad. He missed you."

God. Why did our lives have to go the way they did?

Why did I have to trade such pure, good souls, all so I could have my son?

"I missed him, too. I *still* miss him. Though it was nice that we got to become friends again tonight, don't you think?"

"If you marry Tommy, do you think you would cry less?" He drags his hand from mine, but only so he can trail the tip of his finger along my wrist. "I want you to cry less, Mom. And if you marry Tommy, we get to hang out with Chris, too. Which would make him happy."

"But what would make *you* happy?" I turn my hand over and trap his wrist between my fingers. And when I don't release, I wait for his beautiful eyes to come to mine. "I made a choice ten years ago, honey. It was a big, scary, grown-up decision I knew would come with consequences. I knew it would hurt some very special, good people. I knew it would destroy some parts of my life but that it would save others."

"You decided to have me." His long, dark lashes come down to kiss plump cheeks. "You got pregnant with me, and you knew Tommy would be mad. You picked me."

"And I don't regret it." I unsnap my seatbelt and lean around to be nearer him. To take his hand between both of mine and pull him forward. "I can be sad for hurting people I love, and I can mourn for the future I didn't get to live. I'm going to miss the boys I left behind because I loved them *almost* as much as I love you. We *should* feel our emotions, baby. It's how we heal. But I need you to know there isn't a single part of me that regrets choosing you. I'm not sure what's going to happen in a year. In five years. I don't know what that future will look like, or if Tommy or Chris, or even Grandma, will be in it. But I do know that you and I will be together."

He stares into my eyes. Searching. Probing. Processing.

"How's that for explaining?" I choke out a soft laugh. "I'm not sure I helped since I don't have answers for what's coming. I just know what came and the choices I made that got us here. Most of all, I know I love you, very, *very* much."

"I think..." He draws a long breath, then exhales, so I feel it on our joined hands. "I think that Tommy is a bad chess player."

I burst out with the kind of laughter that feels cathartic on my soul. Bubbling giggles I haven't experienced in too long.

"I think Chris is way better," he continues. "And I like that he told me the truth when I asked about you and him. I think Chris is a lot like me, and Tommy is a bit more like you."

"Like me? Really?" Surprise is like a warm caress in the dark. A soft blanket laid across my chest. "I guess I considered us opposites most of the time."

"You take care of me the way Tommy takes care of Chris."

"You think?"

His lips wrinkle into sweet lines. "He said after you left, Tommy took care of him most of all. He said the world was really loud, and everything felt hard, and he said Tommy was the loudest of them all. But when Chris needed help, Tommy was able to find the quiet again. Then they opened the gym and got to beat people up without going to jail."

I snort, even as fresh tears slide onto my cheeks. "That tracks. Trust them Watkins boys to find a way to legalize Tommy's temper."

"I think..." He inhales, filling his chest and expanding his stomach. Then he exhales again and holds my eyes. "I think... I'm glad you picked me, even though it was scary. And I still feel sad that you couldn't pick Tommy."

"Honey—"

"I can feel both. And you said I *should* feel my feelings. It makes me sad when you're sad. But I'm also glad you picked me." His sweet jaw quivers. "I wouldn't want someone else to be my mom."

"Thank you, baby." I lean closer and press a kiss on his wrist. "I wouldn't give you up for anything." *Evidently. Not even Tommy Watkins.* "We should go inside, don't you think? It's, like, eight-oh-nine now."

He snickers and drags his hand from mine, collecting his things and scooting along the seat to open his door. So I turn and climb out my side, that familiar ache, my constant companion, plaguing the base of my stomach, but as my son comes around to stand on my left and drapes his arm across my back, I find the peace he brings simply by existing.

He does for me what I do for him.

We find quiet in the chaos, and comfort in the uncomfortable.

"Do you want extra dessert?" I close the door and comb my fingers through his hair, hip-bumping him to the side and grinning when he glances up. "We could be a bit sneaky and take ice cream up to bed. Grandma Bitsy doesn't have to know."

He giggles as we cross the lawn and traverse the porch steps, shaking his head when I pull the wire door open. "She would know. She knows *every-thing* that happens inside her house."

"Not *everything*." I slide a key into the wooden door, twisting until the locks tumble open and the lights from inside spill out onto the porch. "I used to do all sorts of crazy stuff when I was only a little bit older than you are now. She had no clue."

His eyes glitter with mischief. "What kind of stuff?"

"The kind that I'm absolutely not telling you about until you're already twenty-one." I push the door open and step inside, only to catch sight of my mom's too-thin body splayed on the floor.

My breath explodes, and my heart squeezes. "Mom!?"

I dash across the kitchen and skid to my knees, grabbing her shoulder and pulling her my way. "Mom?" A line of blood trickles from her brow. "Hey! Wake up."

"Mommy?"

"Call an ambulance, honey." I toss my phone and place two fingers against my mom's neck, right where they taught us in school. She's too cold. Too gray. Too sick. "Mom? Wake up."

ROUND TWENTY-FOUR

TOMMY

I tap my knuckles on Bitsy's hospital room door while nurses wander by at my back, and the Plainview Gossip Vines continue to do that thing they do.

Phones ring, old people pass messages from one set of ears to the next, and my heart aches knowing that news of Bitsy's hospital stint reaches me via the grapevines rather than the one person I'd rather hear from.

Carefully nudging the door open, I poke my head into the shadowed room and find Bitsy's too-small, too-frail body dwarfed by a bed larger than her by double. She's barely sixty, but I swear she looks eighty. They have her hooked up to wires and machines, an IV hanging above her bed, and plastic tubes that trail down to feed liquid into her veins.

Seeing her weak and dying, compared to the strong and vicious I spent nearly thirty years knowing, makes my throat burn. It makes my heart stutter and my lips dry, so I lick them and cast my eyes further toward a silent Franky, sitting in a visitor's chair with an old-school Gameboy held between his hands and his feet comfortably tucked on the chair, his knees pointing toward the ceiling.

Then I look at Alana. The bags under her eyes and the pale coloring on her cheeks. Hair tied in a messy ponytail, and fatigue etched into her every feature.

She's exhausted, and instead of calling me last night and asking for support, she decided to handle the ambulance and EMT on her own. She escorted her mother here, alone. And spent the night sitting beside her bed, alone.

"Hey." She attempts to smile. That's who she is, isn't it? Pretending everything is okay when it's really not. But when I stay put, she dips her chin. "You can come in. It's alright."

Swallowing, I drag my hat off and step into the room, then I move to the side and wait for Chris to follow.

"Both of you?" Alana's eyes flicker with faux happiness, but the fakery makes way for real when Franky flips around in his chair, setting his game aside and grinning for my brother.

He doesn't really give a shit that I'm here. But Chris...

"Must be a special occasion," Alana murmurs. "Both Watkins at the same time, even though it's the middle of the day."

"You wanna come for a walk with me, Franky?" Chris wanders across and stops in front of the boy. "I don't know about you, but hospitals give me the heebie-jeebies, and last I heard, you've been here since last night. Wanna get a snack?"

He swings back around to search Alana's eyes.

"Of course, baby." Listlessly, she releases her mom's hand and leans to the side of her chair. "Let me get you some cash so you can—"

"We're not broke anymore." Quietly chuckling, Chris presses his hand to the back of Franky's hair and guides him through the door. "Not gonna nickel and dime you for the price of a pack of gum, Page. Come on. Let's see if we can find some wheelchairs. We'll race 'em in the halls."

Once they're gone, Alana rights herself in her chair, lifting her feet to the cushion and folding her arms. She's hiding from me, which is something only this adult after-New-York version of her does. Before, when we were younger, she would have come to me *first*.

And I figure she's thinking the same thing, because she nibbles on her pinky nail and looks anywhere but into my eyes.

"You could have called me, Lana." I want to walk around the bed and scoop her into my arms. Force her to love me. Beg her to rely on me. But I go to Franky's abandoned chair instead, dragging it a little closer to Bitsy and setting the game by her leg.

Sitting, I rest my elbows on the bed, too, and my chin in my hands. But I don't even look at the old woman who lies between us.

She doesn't need me the way her child does.

"You didn't want me to know?"

"I didn't have time to think," she rasps. "I didn't want to bother you."

"Bother me," I bite out. I sit back, open my legs wide, and search her eyes. The tears that glisten in her lashes and the sadness that envelops her every thought. Every feeling. Then I pat my thigh and breathe easier when she drops her feet and dashes around the bed. Her breath catches. Her shoulders and back bouncing with emotions she won't verbalize. She sits on my lap for the first time in ten long years, curling into my chest and tucking her head under my chin.

And when I wrap her in my arms and squeeze, she releases the sob she's been holding on to since last night.

"You must be so tired." I press a kiss to the top of her head. "Did you sleep at all?"

"No." She slides her hand beneath my shirt and rests her fingertips over my heart. It's the *old* her from before life tore us apart, when she knew she could come to me and I'd make everything better. "Franky slept for a while."

"How's he coping?"

"Okay." She sighs when I stroke her thigh, breathing perhaps for the first time since she discovered her mother unresponsive on the kitchen floor. *Yeah, I got that from the gossip vines, too.* "As long as I'm calm, he's calm. As long as it's quiet, he's okay."

"Which is good for him. But it means you've locked everything up since last night." I draw patterns against her thigh. Pictures. Words. *Love.* "You can let it all go while he's gone, Lana. Let it out, so when he's back, you can be strong again." I lay a kiss on her forehead. "What's happening with Bitsy?"

"They're not expecting her to wake up." She chokes on her tears, bouncing against my chest and whimpering when I simply pull her closer. Tighter. "Ollie came by about an hour ago. He said she's already signed directives that meant, in the event she ended up here, like this, he could tell me everything."

"And?"

"It started in her lungs and traveled to..." she moans. "All over. Everywhere. He gave her six months to live... six months ago."

"Fuck." I bring my hand up and cup her face, crushing her against my chest so maybe she'll hear my heart. Maybe she'll feel it. "I'm so sorry. I know things are complicated between you two, but that doesn't make the pain go away."

"He said she refused treatment around the start of the year. That she wanted to spend her time with her friends instead and with me and Franky." Tears burst free of her soul, drenching her face and rocking her chest. "She asked us to come home, Tommy, and it was easy to see she wasn't well. But I didn't know it was so bad, and the whole time, we argued."

"*She* knew." I drag her face up and search her eyes. "She knew, Lana, and she still did things the way she did. Maybe she wanted the *real* you and not a fake everyone-has-to-be-nice-to-the-dying-lady show."

"I don't think we had a single kind conversation since I got to town." Her voice breaks. "Every time we talked, we bickered."

"If she wanted something different, she would have asked." I slide my thumb beneath her eye and clean away the tears. Useless, really, when more follow. "She asked you to come, and you did. That's what matters."

"I called her a self-absorbed jerk before we left the house last night." She strokes my chest, thoughtlessly massaging the muscle where our ink sits. "She said I was selfish and stupid for bringing Franky to your home for dinner since it was clear I would only pack up and leave again eventually."

My worst fears. The very thoughts that keep me awake at night.

"I told her to mind her own damn business. Then we went out anyway when we could have stayed home and eaten with her."

"You didn't know." I tilt her head back and force her to look into my eyes. "Baby, you didn't know."

"It's like she brought us home just to torment me one last time," she whimpers. "We're not here because she wanted to spend time with us. She did it so she could hurt me again."

"Did she treat Franky badly? Did she hurt him?"

"No, she—"

"Maybe she realized her mistakes as a mom. She knows where she went wrong, and she wishes she could change it. So she called you back and gave Franky what she couldn't give you."

"She hated me because I reminded her of the man who left. Because he got to travel and do whatever he wanted, while she was stuck here in Plainview with an ungrateful daughter and no way to escape."

"Lana..."

"I hate her." She crushes her eyes closed and weeps. "Because it wasn't my fault he left. It wasn't my fault he didn't want us. And most of all, I hate her because she couldn't find it in her heart to forgive me for the things that were never my fault."

I rest my lips on her forehead. Kissing. Feeling. Comforting, maybe. And when her cries grow louder, I rock us back and forth. "You deserved better, Lana. You always did."

ROUND TWENTY-FIVE

TOMMY

Beatrice 'Bitsy' Page woke only once more after she landed in the hospital. She slept for seventy-two hours straight, clinging to life and drawing Alana to the very ends of her sanity.

It was a long, drawn-out torture for the girl who only ever wanted her mother's approval. Three days of vigil. Watching. Waiting. Chris came and went, dedicating his time to Franky. And Caroline came, too, to sit with her friend and lend a little strength in the quiet. Ollie visited. Eliza visited. Half the town came by to say their piece and ensure they caught the latest gossip.

And then, in the early hours of Wednesday morning, while Franky slept on a cot the hospital provided, and Chris sat on the floor beside it, while Alana curled into my chest, and I did what I do... I held her while she needed me... Bitsy woke.

She looked across in the shadows and observed her daughter's trance-like state. Saying nothing while Alana was oblivious. Smiling when she knew I wasn't.

Gray in the face and too sick to do anything else, she moved her hand and drew Alana's attention. Then she shed a tear for the baby she had birthed and gave Alana the only gift she could.

She told her she loved her.

Which sounds nice and all. But fuck, the bitch could've shared those words a million times over the last twenty-eight years. She could have told her daughter that she was perfect the way she was. She could have smiled more and criticized less. Accepted more and judged less.

But those are my thoughts. My unhealed, child-of-trauma, abusive daddy to the nth degree, feelings, all of which I intend to take to the grave rather than risk the serenity Alana has walked around with since.

"It's almost time to go, Franky." In a beautiful black dress with sleeves that go to her elbows and a skirt that drapes elegantly around her knees, Alana crosses her mother's kitchen in bare feet and crouches by the dining chair her son perches on.

She pastes on a sweet smile—I get a perfect view from my place by the counter—and when Franky's Gameboy makes that dun-dun-dun sound that declares his game is over, she carefully takes the device and places it on the table. "It's time, baby."

"To go to the funeral..."

I don't think he's asking a question. Or even inviting a response.

He's just processing as best an almost-ten-year-old can. Kind of how I've been silently processing my thoughts on Franky's parentage.

I've found dissociation works best, especially when he and my brother are in the same room, and their glaring similarities threaten to shatter my heart.

But that's a trauma for another day.

"To Grandma's funeral," Alana confirms. "I'm going to put my shoes on, okay? So I'd like for you to go to the bathroom while I do, then we can leave."

"Who else will be there?" He pushes to his feet, slowly circling the chair and sliding it into place under the table. "Chris?"

Amused—and entirely oblivious to how her easy affections for my brother make my heart ache—she pats his shirt down and carefully fixes the tie he insisted on wearing. "Yeah, I think Chris will be there. Probably most of the town, actually. Grandma never left Plainview, and she met everyone at least once. I think it's going to be busy."

He holds her wrists in his hands, searching her eyes as worry flitters through his. "What if everyone tries to talk to me?"

"They might." She licks her glistening lips and draws a deep breath. "But you don't have to talk back if you don't want to. It's polite to say thank you when they tell you they're sorry for your loss. But if you run out of *thank yous* or you just don't want to—"

"Me and Chris will be your bodyguards." I smile when two sets of eyes come across, then moving away from the counter, I wander closer and stop beside the pair. "The people who matter will know your heart. And those who don't matter," I shrug. "Don't matter."

"That's right," Alana confirms. "Those who don't matter aren't worth worrying about. Now, go to the bathroom, please." She straightens out, then she tilts her chin toward the doorway. "We can't go until you do."

He sighs, turning on his heels and stalking away. "Fine."

"Now, you lean on me." I wrap my hand around the back of her neck and pull her in until her cheek rests on my heart. I hold her close, squeezing her shoulder and sliding my palm along her arm. "You need to take five minutes to breathe. You've been green all morning, Lana. Don't think I didn't notice. And you're being brave for Franky, but eventually, you're gonna fall if you don't rest."

"Thank you."

I exhale a quiet snicker. "Is that a polite *thank you*, the kind you toss out the day you bury your mom? Or a regular *thank you* because you like the way I hug you?"

"The second." She slides her arms around my back, linking her hands together. "I know you have other stuff going on. You've hardly even begun training for Vegas, and Chris is getting itchy about it. You—"

"Have absolutely nowhere else I'd rather be." I kiss the top of her head. "And don't worry about *us*," I tease. "In a few days, once things have calmed down and life goes back to a new normal, you'll remember your vow to keep me away. Something about me falling in love with someone else or some such thing."

She sniffles and giggles. Humor and devastation in the same breath.

"Maybe my new hoe will come to the funeral today. You could introduce us, since that's what nice, selfless women do."

"You're annoying me." And yet, she squeezes tighter and buries her face against my chest. "And speaking of hoes, my best friend will be there."

"I know." I lean back and swipe her cheeks clear. "I'm your best friend. I'm literally riding with you. Though calling me a hoe is a little hurtful."

She rolls her eyes. "My *other* best friend. My New York best friend, who freaks at the idea of chicken poo and a lack of high-end department stores."

"She sounds perfect." I cup her face and set a chaste, dry kiss on her swollen lips. "Make the introductions, and I'll see how things go from there. Maybe it'll be love at first sight, and since she's already your best friend, you could probably be the maid of honor at our hoe wedding."

"You've set yourself a mission to irritate me as much as possible today, huh?" The toilet flushes, and the tap switches on in the bathroom, so she looks up at me with glittering eyes and a sweet smile. "It's helping. Thank you."

"You're welcome."

"When we're done with all this, I kinda want to talk to you about something."

Curious, I pull back and search her eyes.

"Something important," she sighs. "Something private."

"You wanna tell me now?"

She shakes her head, but even if she wanted to, Franky wanders back into the room and Alana steps out of my embrace. So I move to the door and grab her shoes.

"Are we going to Darlene's after?" Franky stops with damp handprints on the thighs of his pants and a shirt twisted from redressing.

Realizing this, Alana quickly steps into her shoes, then she turns to her son and straightens him out. "Caroline's putting on a lunch thing at the bar, and some others said they'd help cater it. So anyone who wants to go will be there."

"Are we going there?"

She finishes with his shirt, sets her hands on his shoulders, and looks down into his eyes. Then she sighs. "I'm not sure. Is it just me, or are we all freakin' exhausted already? It's barely after ten in the morning, and I'm ready for a nap."

That's called trauma, I think. Grief. Healing, perhaps. Fuck knows.

"I guess we'll see how we feel after the cemetery. There will be a lot of people there, and they'll all want to talk to me. I might need quiet afterward."

"We could watch The Simpsons," Franky volunteers. He moves around his mom and sneaks the Gameboy off the table. But when their eyes meet, and she shakes her head in answer, he puts it down again. "We could take some of the food from Darlene's and bring it back here. But we should lock the doors, or Aunty Fox will come in and try to make us *dance it out*." He flattens unimpressed lips. "I *hate* when she does that."

Alana wipes her face and takes his hand in hers, and when I open the door, she rewards me with a gentle smile and leads the boy onto the porch outside, then down the steps and across to her car.

Nice clothes and a dusty old truck don't really suit.

"Fox's gonna stay with us for a few days." She unlocks the car and opens the back door, allowing Franky to climb in. She waits for him to fasten his seat belt before she closes it again. Then she turns and startles when I step in her way.

Her nerves are shot. Her emotions, dangerously close to the surface.

She looks up at me, doe eyes brimming with sorrow. But when I extend my hand and wait, she figures me out quickly enough, placing her keys in my palm and moving around to the passenger side so I can drive.

"I'm gonna be with you guys the whole time, okay?" Which, as I search Franky's eyes in the rearview mirror, I know isn't a comfort to the boy who wants only his mother. "I'll be quiet, and I won't get in your way. But I'll drive you where you've gotta go and stand nearby to get you anything you need. I want to help you guys through this."

"Did you know you can hire caskets?" Franky reaches for the book he keeps in the back seat, pulling the pen from the middle and resting the book on his knees. "Because sometimes people choose cremation, but the family still wants to have a viewing and stuff."

"I *did* know that." And I'm not pleased about it. At all. "It would be a lot of money to waste on nothing if you don't need the casket after the funeral."

"Did you know one million seconds is eleven days, and one billion seconds is thirty one point seven years?"

"Uh..."

"That means the average human life is around two and a half billion seconds long."

Stunned, I glance across at Alana and find her eyes glassy with tears and humor.

"That's one way to simplify things," I decide. Because *fuck, what else do I say*? "Chris memorizes these sorts of things, too. I don't know where you keep it all in your brain, but it hurts mine every time one of you throws numerical *did you knows* at me."

"Did you know three hundred million cells die in the human body every minute?"

"Alright," Alana twists in her seat and looks over at her son. We bounce our way out of the driveway and onto the tar road, and in just a few minutes, we're both brutally aware we'll be entering the cemetery. "Can we talk about something else? Like, did you know a crocodile cannot stick its own tongue out?"

He smiles. "Did you know the average person eats around seventy insects over their lifetime while they're sleeping?"

My stomach jumps with disgust. Dread. Remembering the fucking bugs that openly crawled on me as a child, I loathe to accept the fact my brother and I are probably '*above average*' on this one.

And, like Alana can read my mind, she places her hand on my stomach and offers quiet kindness when our eyes meet. Comfort, even when she's the one who needs comforting. Protection, though it's really not her job.

"Give us fun facts, honey. *Fun*. Not gross or scary or morbid."

"Did you know Los Angeles' full name is actually *El Pueblo de Nuestra Señora la Reina de los Ángeles de Porciúncula*? And you can remember which Disney is at which location because Disney World has the OR, for Orlando, and Disneyland has the LA for Los Angeles."

Bugs are done. I bring the car to a stop at an intersection and glance back to search Franky's eyes. "Really?"

He closes his book and sets his hands on top, grinning. "Yep. Did you know Maine is the only US state that has a one-syllable name?"

"You just soak all this stuff up and bring it out like a party trick when you have an audience?" Shaking my head, I drive through the intersection when both sides are clear. "I could barely keep up with my actual school curriculum, and most of that is gone, too, but you're out here speaking a whole new language with *El Pueblo Nuestra something something*."

"You know a bunch of words in Japanese," he counters. "And how to fight someone, but in a safe way. Some people just swing their arms around and hit things, but you know how to do it for a sport. That's smart."

"This is true," Alana murmurs. "You claimed I was smarter than you, but I can't speak Japanese, and I don't remember ninety-nine percent of the names of all the moves you teach in the gym."

"You forget the names, but you know the actions." And since her hand is still on my stomach, I place mine over the top. "And you wrote a book."

"Did you know only three percent of people who start a book actually finish it?" Franky inserts. "And of the three percent, less than one percent of those actually publish it."

"Well, I haven't published." She gently peels her hand from beneath mine and drags down the mirrored visor so she can check her face and hair. "I probably won't publish it. But maybe I'll write a different one."

The cemetery overflows with mourners as I turn off the main road and into the narrow driveway. A sea of black, howling men and women who wish desperately to benefit from the attention of someone else's loss. *Yeah, I know. I'm a prick.* Chris and Ollie are already here, hanging out on the fringes, watching, waiting for our arrival. Eliza, too, and their sister, Raquel.

I pull up in the first available parking slip I can find, but before I open the doors and let the rest of the world in, I cut the engine and turn to Alana first. "Do you feel like you have a different story to tell now?"

"Maybe." She pushes the visor back up. "Or maybe I can take the old story and rework the ending. The original grates on me."

"Is that why you never agreed to the deal?"

"My mom's story is about you, Tommy."

My heart simply fucking stops. Dead in my chest, and yet, impossibly, butterfly wings bat around in my stomach. "What?"

Alana tries to lean between our seats to do that thing moms do—the *shut the hell up* eyes that never fail to silence a child—but I press my hand to her chest and move her out of the way so I can be the one to look at him. "Your mom wrote a book about me?"

"Tommy—"

Franky shrugs. "She didn't name the guy your name. And she didn't name the girl her name. But she wrote about a fighter who had a twin brother. And how they were her best friends and how the girl moved to New York and had a baby and—"

"Enough." Alana fists my hair and yanks me back. Then she meets her son's eyes and silences him with a single look. Unsnapping her seatbelt and pushing out of her door, she comes around and opens his, nervously fixing his collar while mourners watch every move we make. Every breath. Every shift of her hands. "This probably won't be fun, okay? But you don't have to leave my side, not even for a single second. If someone tries to talk to you or tries to ask you to come to them, and you don't want to, you can say no."

"Can I stand with Chris sometimes?" He scoots across the seat and dangles his legs out the door, and even with an aching heart, I come around and become their guard, shielding them from the masses while they get themselves organized. "But I want to be with you, too."

"Sure, honey. We'll bring Chris wherever we go. And Tommy, too. Because I need you, and you need Chris, and Chris needs Tommy, and Tommy..."

Needs Alana.

What thing do you want to tell me?

Will it hurt more than not knowing?

She clears her throat, tense as she helps him from the car and takes his hand in hers. Then she comes around, warmth filling her cheeks and emotion glittering in her eyes.

"It's gonna be okay." I set my hand on the small of her back and escort her forward. I'd rather drape my arm over her shoulders and tuck her against my side, but I know it's not what she'd prefer. And today, and for the rest of my life, everything I do will be based on what she wants.

"Hey." Chris wanders closer first. The bravest one, which is odd since social gatherings are his least favorite thing to participate in. He leans in and presses a kiss to Alana's cheek—*I will not smash his face. I will not smash his face. I love my brother, so I will **not** smash his face*—then he offers a fist for Franky and grins when the boy taps it. "You look pretty good, kiddo. Clean up nicely."

He pushes the glasses up his nose and tilts his head back to meet Chris' stare. "You do, too. Did my mom pick out your pants also?"

He snorts, rubbing his mouth as though to hide his humor. Because God forbid anyone laughs at a funeral in front of hundreds of fuddy-duddies.

"I picked these out myself. But thanks for noticing."

"Hi, Ollie." Alana accepts his kiss when he leans in and brushes one over her cheek. Then Eliza steps forward, tension turning Alana's body into stone.

It's a rivalry we've not yet put to bed.

"Sorry your mom died." She was always our youngest. Silliest. Last to mature and quickest to explode. She doesn't offer a kiss or a hug. But she flashes a bright smile and taps Alana's arm. *Good game.* "I'll stop picking on you now. If Tommy's happy, I'm happy."

"And if he's not?" She clutches Franky's hand in both of hers. "What if I'm mean to him again next week?"

"Then I'll hunt you down and teach you a rear naked choke. But you probably won't be awake long enough to remember the steps."

"That's enough." Oliver wraps his arm around his sister's neck and pulls her out of the way. "There's something wrong with you, Lize. I swear you *like* causing trouble."

"It's been a minute." The final Darling sibling steps forward next. Platinum blonde hair and bright blue eyes; Raquel is my type exactly, *in theory*. But we never went there. We didn't even consider it.

Her lips glitter a perfect red, but when she leans in to hug Alana and kisses her cheek, none of the color transfers. "You look good, Lana."

"You, too. How's the city and life as not-a-doctor?"

She snorts, shedding the awkwardness ever present at funerals. "You heard that, too? Ya know, my boss is gonna be *pissed* when she finds out I've been faking my qualifications all this time."

"Knowing you?" I question. "I'd bet your boss is pissed always, simply because she has to work with you every day. You coming back to Plainview anytime soon?"

"I'm here right now, aren't I?" She scoops her purse onto her arm, resting the straps at her elbow, and peeks over her shoulder. "Anyone else feel like taking a decontamination shower after this? I swear, the only people who actually give a shit are standing right here. All the rest of 'em just hate the idea of missing out on the most exciting thing to happen in Plainview this month."

"I'm here! Oh my *god*!" A woman tip-toe-runs across the cemetery lawn, drawing eyes and snide lip-upturns from scandalized mourners. "Jesus, Alana! I'm here. I made it. I'm not late."

It's funny how our group tightens just a little more. How Chris and Oliver, and even Eliza, step closer and protect those they considered the enemy not so long ago, because now, as a woman in heels and a skirt suit, long tan legs, and flowing brown hair, noisily dashes this way, they create a wall of safety.

The woman walk-runs on uneven grass. Big, brown eyes zeroing in on those we shield behind us. She has expressive eyebrows and, *evidently*, zero spatial awareness, because she bowls straight through us, dragging Alana into a hug and tugging Franky in, too, so his poor face is crushed against the woman's ribs.

"It took me half an hour to get here when the GPS said it would only be three minutes." She leans back, cupping Alana's cheek. "Someone's a filthy rotten liar, or the GPS lady doesn't know what the hell she's talking about."

"It couldn't be that you didn't listen to the instructions, right?" Alana's eyes glitter with unshed tears. Her jaw trembles. And then she yanks her friend in again and squeezes extra tight. "Holy shit, it's good to see you, Fox."

"Aw, hey." She swipes the tears from Alana's cheeks. "Don't cry for me, pretty girl. I told you I'd come."

"Uh, excuse me, hi?" Eliza muscles her way in. "It might be normal in New York for folks to conduct a conversation and rudely exclude others, but here in Plainview—"

"Here, people are rude to your face," Alana finishes with a soft chuckle. She wipes her face and gestures. "That's Eliza Darling. She's mean."

Protective, Fox sneers at Eliza's offered hand. "I've heard about you. I sharpened the heel of my Louboutins especially for this visit."

EMILIA FINN

"And that's Oliver." Alana marches right over the girl drama. "He's Eliza's brother. Raquel," she adds, as Fox moves from one person to the next. "They're siblings. Tommy—"

She burns me to a damn crisp. Her stare vengeful and unkind. "I know of you. I'll reserve my judgment for now." Then she turns on her own to the only other person here who looks just like me. "Makes you Christian." She takes his hand and studies him with long sweeps of her eyes. "Heard about you, too. I'm assured you're mostly decent to my friend."

"Mostly." He looks her up and down, too. Appreciating, maybe. Then smirking. "Most of the time."

"And last but not least—" She tosses his hand and meets Franky's eyes. "My boy! Holy heckin' chicken poo! I've missed you."

She pulls him in and...

Well, he doesn't shove her away. Which surprises me until I remember she's been in his life since infancy. She's allowed to be eccentric and loud. She's allowed to hug because she's basically family to him. She's known him longer than any of the rest of us combined.

"I think you got more handsome, Franklin." She allows him to step back, but cups his cheeks and earns a goofy smile. "Grew a whole foot since we last broke bread together. I'm not pleased, little boy."

"Pop quiz," he beams. "What's the fastest land animal ever?"

"Er... the bunny."

"The largest?"

"The mouse."

"And what's the seventh digit in Pi?"

"Apple."

His eyes dance with amusement, soft laughter rolling along his chest. "Wrong, wrong, wrong. You were supposed to study, Aunty Fox."

"I did study! You're just too smart for me."

"Hang on." I frown, earning twin stares from the pair. "*She's* allowed to claim the largest animal on Earth is a mouse, but I mess up a chess board one time, and I become the antichrist?" I set my hands on my hips. "I smell favoritism, and I already have to tolerate so much with your clear preference for Chris."

"You prefer Chris?" Fox wrinkles her nose, smiling. "Why am I not surprised?"

"We should go." Alana kills that line of discussion and draws a deep breath as she glances out at the crowd waiting in the mid-morning sun. She

262

nervously nibbles on her bottom lip, then takes Franky's hand in hers. "We've made them wait a pretty long time."

"We don't like 'em anyway," Raquel teases. "Bunch of gossips."

"Come on." I take Alana's free hand and lead her toward the casket already set in place. The flowers Caroline organized. The music Oliver oversaw. The funeral director Raquel connected us with.

For the girl they declared their enemy ten years ago, they step forward and circle the wagons. Because we protect those we love.

ROUND TWENTY-SIX
ALANA

Funerals suck.

There are no words available to change the narrative. No long, sweeping descriptions of the flowers that make the landscape pretty, or the birds singing in the trees. Not the rolling green lawns, or the cool breeze that keeps us comfortable under the warm sun.

Funerals do, in fact, suck.

Even the funeral for the woman who made my life a living hell, tormenting my every inner thought, squashing each moment of hope I was foolish enough to conjure, criticizing what I thought were achievements and highlighting my poorer choices, not so I would learn from them, but so I could be shamed for them.

My mother seemed to take great joy in holding me down when all I ever wanted was to rise up.

Perhaps worse, she knew what happened to me ten years ago. I confided in her the moment I stumbled home. Begged for her help. I pleaded for her understanding and asked for guidance on what I should do next. But in the end, I was met with a sneer and cold derision.

Statements like, '*This is what happens when nice girls dress like sluts,*' and '*We knew this day would come when you insisted on spending time with the Watkins trash.*'

The Watkins boys weren't trash. Not then, and not now.

And I wasn't dressed like a slut. I was wearing my prom dress.

Though, as an adult, I know now my clothing choices never mattered at all.

Instead of helping me, my mother shamed me. And instead of explaining the options I had, she focused only on how stupid I was to drink underage.

God, how her words play on repeat in my mind. How she had a chance to change my life for the better, but chose to stand on my throat instead.

But she's gone now, and though my stomach turns with sorrow and my heart aches with contradiction, tears flow from my eyes. Because a girl wants her mom. She wants the reassurance most others receive freely. She wants the comfort of a mother's bosom to rest on and sweet words of love whispered in the dark. Those are the same words I offer my son when he's afraid. Or lonely. Or merely bored.

"She wasn't perfect." I read the eulogy I prepared, sniffling and wiping the moisture from beneath my nose. "I'm not sure she knew how to be the mom I needed, and I think that's because she didn't love herself the way she needed. But today, and into the future, I choose *not* to focus on what I didn't have and, instead, focus on what I did. I had a mom who was present every single day of my first eighteen years of life. I had a mom who helped in the school cafeteria and a mom who bought craft supplies so I could complete every assignment asked of me. I had the mom who made sure my clothes were clean and pressed, shoes that shone, and schoolbooks I could always rely on."

I pause and search the crowd for familiar faces.

"She struggled after my dad left, and I know, sometimes, I romanticized the memories I had of him. I imagined him riding his motorcycle along the California coast, enjoying his life of freedom and excitement. I know I hurt my mom when I whined about how she was lacking, and yet placed him on a pedestal like he was a kind of celebrity worthy of praise. The impact of my views—of him and of her—was not something I could comprehend back then, when all I could focus on was bubbling teen resentment and a yearning for things I never had. But I know one thing for sure." I lower my page and glance up at the hundreds of mourners who spread across the cemetery. Wet eyes and noisy sniffles. Too many faces; I can't even place them all.

Drawing a deep breath and folding my paper, I allow forgiveness to slide into my heart.

Acceptance.

"She stayed," I declare.

Franky's sweet little hand wraps around mine. He stands in front of a sea of eyes, his actual worst nightmare, but he does it for me.

Inspired by his bravery, I wipe my nose and paste on my best smile. "My mom deserved more credit than I ever gave her. Because while he was traveling the world, ignoring his responsibilities and garnering some illogical, immature benefit of the doubt in a teen's mind, she stayed and did the actual work. So, Mom," I drag my gaze to her casket. "Thank you. You did your best, even though you didn't have to."

With a shuddering breath and a newfound resolve bolstered by Franky's hand, I take a step back and signal for the funeral director to continue his work: he reads a passage from the bible. Or maybe two or three. He plays a song. Reads some more.

I pay little attention to most of it. But I take comfort in my son on my right and Tommy *freakin'* Watkins on my left.

He proves, once again, how pure and unconditional his love remains.

I broke his heart and destroyed our future, and even now, with nothing promised besides *'in a few days, I'll tell you to move on again'*, his support remains absolute. His adoration, pure. His strength, unwavering.

He leans closer while the funeral director lowers my mother into the ground, his aftershave settling in the base of my lungs, providing a nice distraction from the rich perfume of flowers. Freshly cut grass. Pollen in the air. All of which make my sensitive stomach tumble with nausea. "You holding up okay?"

I'm not sure I have words, so I chew on my trembling lips and nod.

"You need to sit down?"

I shake my head.

He drapes his arm over my back anyway, not to hug, though it may appear that way to those who watch on. He takes my weight and makes it so I'm barely standing of my own accord at all.

"You ready for the long line of *I'm sorrys*?" he murmurs. "They're about to begin."

I choke out what I think is half sob, half smile. And because I can, because I feel safe enough in his arms, I lean against his chest and find comfort in the constant beat of his heart. The rhythmic bass. The gentle thrum that remains consistent as the line starts and mourners say the things expected at a funeral.

I'm sorry.

Thank you.

So sorry for your loss.

Thank you.

She'll be missed.

She will. Thank you.

Touching eulogy.

Thank you.

She would be proud of you.

Not sure she was capable. But thank you for saying nice things.

For a hundred or more faces, the tone remains the same. Muttered words, soft appreciation, and then they move along to make room for the next. It's a production even the least experienced know how to fulfill. Expectations are put upon those who live, on behalf of the one who died.

In my case, I doubt the one who died even likes half of the people here, and I'm certain half of those here feel the same for her in return.

I allow myself to slide into a comfortable, meditation-like state. Nodding. Cheek kisses. Hugs, when I must. Fake platitudes and promises to *catch up soon*, though everyone knows we lie. But when Tommy's pulse scatters, I wake again. When his heart pounds and his hold turns to iron, adrenaline spikes in my blood and brings me charging back to reality.

Tommy's hands bruise my skin, holding me close and allowing me no space for freedom, but it's not until Chris shoves nearer, his broad form shielding Franky's and his shoulder almost touching mine, that I realize what I so stupidly allowed to approach.

If I was paying better attention, I could have prevented it.

Maybe.

I don't know.

Nausea spears through my stomach and up to touch the base of my throat when Grady Watkins steps forward. With dancing eyes and lips curled into a disgusting smile, he stops in front of me just as everyone did before him, but unlike those who know to pretend to be sad, he practically does a jig.

Tommy's father. Returned from what I was so hopeful was the seventh circle of Hell.

His grin is rotten, his teeth chipped. His lips are thin, crooked, and taunting as he leans forward and attempts to take my hand. But before Tommy has a chance to smack the prick away, that strength I discovered when I became a mother comes rocketing back into my blood. I have a son to protect now, and before him, I was a child, tending to broken boys and the wounds this piece of shit inflicted upon them.

Franky will witness my ferocious wrath *long* before he becomes a victim to Grady Watkins' existence.

"You shouldn't be here," Tommy snarls, mistaking my trembling hands for fear instead of anger. My racing breath for nerves and not rage. He steps in front of me, almost shoulder-to-shoulder with his brother, but a foot of space remains for me to see the vermin and his date through.

The woman on his arm is not even Pamela, Chris and Tommy's mother. Just some other toothless mole. Sickly thin, jittery, and too far gone to the perils of a hard life and poor choices.

Whether she knows this family's history, or even cares, remains unknown, but when she stupidly reaches through the gap to touch my son, I slap her hand away with a sharp crack that reverberates through the cemetery.

"Don't touch him." I yank Franky around and place him behind my back for safekeeping. But when I feel him being pulled away, panic lances through my blood until I spin and find Fox's hand holding his.

Panic makes way for relief. But relief only lasts until I meet her eyes and remember she knows *everything*. She knows my childhood. My teen years. She knows all there is to know about Plainview and the Watkins family and the reason I left this town ten years ago.

She knows it *all*, including the role Grady Watkins played in the most important years of my life. And I think, most importantly, she knows I'm not that child anymore, defenseless and scared. She knows the murder I've prevented for a decade already, the one I was terrified Tommy would commit, may eventuate today.

But I'll be the one who faces a jury of twelve when it's all done.

"Come on." She gently tugs Franky backward. "We're leaving."

"Mom!" Franky fights against her hold, reaching out and grabbing my wrist. "Come with us, Mommy."

For a single moment, just a blip in the enormity of my life, Grady's hand stops on my hip. I feel him in the way my blood cools. In the way my pulse skitters, and my stomach rebels.

But Tommy wrenches the parasite away, grabbing him by the collar and lifting him an inch off the grass. "The fuck are you doing here? You had no right to intrude."

"Mom!" Franky demands, his eyes glittering with terror and, worse, knowledge. Because New York-me never lied to him. "You need to come with us! Now."

"I suggest you take your hands off me, boy." Grady's voice has visited me in my nightmares for a decade. The lisp his dental hygiene creates, an added detail to join those I've obsessed on for three decades. "You forget respect since I was last in town?"

"Respect?" Tommy laughs. But the sound is anything but kind. "Motherfucker, the only thing you deserve is my boot down your throat."

"Mom!"

Decided, I loop my left hand around Tommy's belt, so when Fox tugs Franky, and Franky tugs me, I pull Tommy until he releases his father. Then I turn and walk, sucking fresh oxygen into my lungs and swallowing the nausea clawing mercilessly along my throat.

Chris follows without hesitation, leaving his father behind and creating a long line of *no fucking chance are we dealing with this shit today.* And because Eliza is a good girl beneath the fire, she steps in the way, closing ranks beside Ollie and Raquel, and stopping Grady and his taunting laugh from following us.

"Wait, don't leave!" He calls out. "Tommy! Don't you want to spend time with your dear old dad?"

Tommy changes our grip and speeds his steps, walking *with* me instead of forcing me to drag him along, and whether it's a newfound maturity or a desire to protect me from an inevitable explosion, he controls his temper in a way that leaves me breathless.

"Okay, so we'll just see you at Darlene's, then?" Grady waves in my peripherals. Is he truly so delusional? Is it the drugs? Entitlement? Has he forgotten?

"God." Disgust spreads throughout my stomach the way oil spreads on a smooth surface. Difficult to contain and all but impossible to clean up. Sweat beads on my brow as a million memories come sprinting back to the forefront of my mind, and with them, stars dance in my vision. The darkness wants to take me. To flatten me. To put me face-first on the grass and leave me vulnerable the way I have been in the past.

But when my knees shake, and my steps falter, Tommy catches me, dragging me close until I'm not sure I'm walking at all. Gliding, perhaps. Flying, but with my feet barely skimming the ground.

"We're *definitely* not going to Darlene's." Eliza leaves Grady behind and jogs to my car, yanking the back door open and nodding when Chris climbs in first, and Franky follows right after.

Fox folds in third while Tommy walks me all the way to my door.

But he doesn't open it yet. He doesn't shove me inside.

"Hey?" He grabs my jaw, pulling my face around and forcing me to look into his eyes. "Take a breath, Lana. You look like you're about to fall on your ass."

"Why is he here?" I try to turn. To search for the filth in the sea of faces. Was it only moments ago I held disdain for the false pretense and faked kindness? Did I seriously judge them so harshly when the likes of Grady Watkins exists? "I thought he moved away. My mom said—"

"He did." He strokes the underside of my jaw. "Haven't seen him in years. Are you..." He frowns. "Are you okay?"

"I don't want to go to Darlene's." I step out of his steely grip and search for my son. His hand isn't in mine. His little arm isn't draped across my back. "Franky?"

"He's with Chris and Fox. Hey?" He jerks me back around. "You need to take a fuckin' breath. Why are you freaking out?"

Fox climbs out of my car and glares across the top. "Get in."

"Alana—"

"Let's go!" She slaps the roof. "Now."

ROUND TWENTY-SEVEN

TOMMY

"Why are you green?" I drive one-handed, the other in her lap, and with one eye on the rearview mirror as we speed away from the cemetery and onto the road toward home. But fuck! My father knows where she grew up, too. Should I take her to my house? Will he follow us? "Alana? Hey?"

"Take us home." Her eyes are glassy and fearful. Jittery as she avoids my gaze. "I want to go home."

"That's him, huh?" Franky scrunches his little body tight like he's trying to avoid touching Fox and Chris on either side. "Mom?"

"Don't, honey." She presses a hand to her mouth and stares out the window, her cheeks deathly pale and a sheen of sweat on her brow. "Please, not right now."

"For years," Chris snarls, "that prick has been gone. He wanted nothing to do with this town and nothing to do with us. He didn't even bother us when Tommy took the title, which is prime fuckin' time for a leech to come searching for blood. But he left us alone. Not a single word. Now Bitsy's in the ground, and he thinks *this* is when he should cause a scene? The fuck is that?"

Alana's chest heaves, her lungs spasming in search of fresh air. Her pulse thunders and tears glisten in her eyes, but she doesn't let them fall. Steely, she clamps her lips shut and waits us out. Clenching her jaw and gritting her teeth, she only shakes her head.

So I say nothing, and I ignore the panic desperately clawing at my stomach. I ask no questions and demand no answers. I merely drive, speeding just a little too fast and cutting corners when corners are empty and cuttable.

I take a five-minute drive and turn it into two, and when I sling the car into Bitsy's driveway and slam on the brakes, I meet my brother's eyes in the rearview mirror, thankful to find his arm over Franky's chest and the boy safely held all the way home.

"I need to use the bathroom." Alana pushes her door open before any of the rest of us make a move, then, climbing out, she goes to Chris' door and peeks in past his hulking frame. "Can you hang out with Aunty Fox for a few minutes, honey? I need to wash my face and take a second. Funerals are always icky."

"Go." Fox gently unsnaps Franky's seat belt, sliding out of her side and taking his hand to bring him with her.

She doesn't give him the chance to choose Chris's door, which is interesting since he was leaning that way in the first place.

I meet my brother's eyes in the mirror—if Fox is Alana's representative, then he's mine—so when he nods, knowing what I need, I snatch the car keys and storm around to follow Alana into the house.

Already, she's through the kitchen, her shoes left abandoned and toppled to the side on the tile flooring, and though her perfume lingers in the air, the woman is nowhere to be seen.

"Alana?" I stalk into the living room, the TV still on from this morning, but no one here to watch it. Then I continue through when the creak of the stairs gives me the only hint I need. "Alana! Babe, come down here and—"

"I just need a minute!" She tries for fake cheeriness. False pleasantries. Exactly how her mother raised her to be. "I need privacy for a moment, then I'll come down and make lunch."

"No." I jog up the stairs and emerge on the carpeted landing, glancing left, then right. I need no invitation and have no use for a map. I've snuck through this house more times than I can count, and even if I'd forgotten the way, I need only to follow my nose.

Lavender will *always* call me home.

I push through Alana's closed bedroom door and keep going until I reach the attached bathroom, only to find her on her knees, her head hung over the toilet bowl and her back heaving with the sounds of her sickness.

"Hey?" Sorrow slides through my veins, shoving aside the anger I came in here with, compliments of my piece of shit sperm donor. "Lana." I grab a light blue hand towel and soak it under the tap, then I cross the room and crouch behind her heaving body, dragging her hair back and placing the cold towel on her cheek. "Jesus, Lana. I thought you were stomping up here to get your baseball bat so you could sneak out again to knock his head off. I didn't expect you to be puking. Are you alright?"

"Go away." She vomits again, her body caught in the clutches of a spasming stomach. "This is so gross."

"Smells kinda gross, too." Teasing, I try for humor when all I *really* want to do is get in my truck and pay a visit to the prick who made an already bad day worse.

If I could repay eighteen years of torment and physical abuse without landing in prison, I would. For Chris. And for the boy I used to be.

But I know my limits. I know the rage bubbling in my blood is as fiery today as it was in my youth. So, I focus on Alana instead. On brushing her hair back and rubbing her shoulder. "That ugly motherfucker's face is enough to make *anyone* sick to their stomach. But I'm actually starting to freak out a little bit. So maybe you could do me a favor and take a breath? I need you to feel better."

"Can you call Ollie?"

Surprise brings my brows together. "Ollie?"

"His dad," she groans. "The cops. Anyone. I need Grady out of Plainview. Now."

"I mean... so do I. But you don't have to worry about him, okay? He's drug fucked and too stupid to do much more than act a fool in front of a crowd. He won't step foot on your property, I promise."

"I need him gone." She heaves again, but there's nothing left in her stomach. Her chest clenches, and her breath catches. Taking the cloth from my hand, she tumbles back and sits on her butt, resting her head on my chest while she wipes her face.

"Alana!" Fox booms from downstairs, pounding her fists on the wall. "Alana Page! Ass down here, now!"

"God..." Alana pushes dizzily to her feet, swaying dangerously to the side until I stand and hold her arm, but she brushes me off and stumbles to the sink, turning on the tap and folding at the hips to drink from her cupped hands.

She chugs enough water to give her something to bring back up again in ten minutes, then she washes her face and rubs her eyes.

"Alana!"

"I'm coming!" She slaps the tap off and dries her face with a different towel, then she stalks out the door, slamming her shoulder to the frame on the way past.

Frustrated, I hurry behind and scoop her arm with mine before she tumbles down the damn stairs. "You should've had breakfast, Lana. Attending a funeral and dealing with all those people on an empty stomach was never gonna be a good idea."

"I wasn't hungry." She wipes her cheeks with the heels of her palms, drawing a long, shuddering breath into her hitching chest and swallowing to wet her dry throat. Then she frees her arm from mine—adding just another lash to my heart—before striding into the living room and skidding to a violent stop when her name flashes on the television screen.

A talk show. A stack of books placed between the hosts. And a woman sitting on the end, gushing about the novel titled '*Love and War*' and its summer release date.

"No." Alana's cheeks drain whiter than they've been all day, her eyes glued to the screen and unflinching, even as Ollie and Eliza stride into the room.

"Alana is so sorry she can't be here today." Helen—her name slides across the bottom of the screen—is a woman sitting somewhere on the other side of fifty-five, with midnight black hair and bright red lipstick slathered over thin lips. She lovingly hugs a copy of the novel, stroking the cover the way she might an infant's cheeks. "Her mother passed recently, and today was the funeral."

"Oh, that's so sad." The female host—Tanya—long ago perfected her television eyes and the way they glitter with emotion. She brings a hand over her heart as though to drive home how falsely sympathetic she is. "That's devastating news. We're so thankful you could make it, considering the circumstances. As her agent, it's your duty to step in during these diffi-cult moments, right?"

"As her agent," Helen agrees. "And as her friend. I think you'll find, once you read this book, you'll understand a young woman's journey and the amazing strength she holds within her heart. You'll grieve for her, just as I do. And celebrate her, the way those of us who love her do. Alana proves, with her writing and in how she lives, just how far inner peace and persever-ance can carry you."

"No, please." Alana stumbles toward the back of the couch, setting her hands on the frame and searching the room, almost in a daze. Oliver and Eliza. Chris and Fox. "W-where's Franky?"

"He's outside with Caroline." Chris folds his arms and glances back to the television. "She drove in after us and said he could stay out there with her and her kids for a bit."

"Of course, we wish Alana could be here herself," the male host murmurs. "But we understand this is a difficult day and should absolutely be spent with her loved ones. In the meantime, Helen, we'd love to hear your take on the story so special that Elyte would not only go to auction to secure the rights, but that they would increase their offers *twice* more. That's unheard of, isn't it?"

Whimpering, Alana drops into a crouch and rests her elbows on the back of the sofa. "Please don't do it."

"Of course!" Helen sets the book on her lap. "Love and War is a story written in the first person point of view, from the female lead's perspective only. It's a coming-of-age tale, spanning the protagonist's early years and the love she shared with her male best friend all through their school years. There was an inciting incident during the time surrounding graduation which changed the trajectory of what she thought her life would look like, and soon after that, we're taken on a tour of sorrow and loneliness. Marrying another man and giving birth to a beautiful baby boy. Alana has, in my humble opinion, encapsulated the raw and honest reality of a life plan changed by someone else's villainous actions."

"Make it stop." Alana trembles. Her hands shake, and her jaw quivers. Her entire being vibrates with a desperate devastation that propels me forward. I pull her to her feet and draw her around, pressing her cheek to my chest in the hopes I could give her a moment of reprieve. But she bounces back again, bucking free of my embrace and slamming into the back of the couch.

"Lana—"

"No. You can't... We...." She knuckles the tears from her eyes and brushes my hand away. "Tommy..."

"What do you need?" I snag her wrists and force her to stay put. "Alana? What do you want from me?"

"I want you to leave." She exhales a shuddering breath and swings her gaze to Chris. "Both of you. I need you to go. Turn the TV off and don't—"

"You speak of tragedy," Tanya continues. "But when I consider books and tragedy, I think of Romeo and Juliet. Cleopatra and Mark Antony. Death, perhaps, for one of the main leads. Is this what you mean?"

"Tommy?" Alana grabs my face, forcing my eyes down to hers. "I'll give you *anything*. I'll be with you forever. I'll marry you if you want or leave you alone if that's what you'd prefer. I'll be anything you want me to be. But you need to go now. Please," she chokes out. "Don't watch this."

"In the case of *this* story," Helen pushes on, "the tragedy is in a young woman's stolen innocence. It's in the loss of her autonomy and, ultimately, not having a voice when she needed it most."

"Tommy, please," she weeps. "Please stop."

"Without giving too much away, I could say that, on the night of their prom, these minors had made a poor choice and consumed alcohol. Which," she adds happily, "despite the law, we know is apt to happen. The female lead's home life wasn't wonderful, and turning up with alcohol on her breath was not something she felt comfortable doing. So she and the main male lead went to his not-so-great home instead. *He* had been responsible, choosing not to drink so he could keep his friends safe, but after arriving home and falling into bed to rest, he received word of a friend in need. A hero is not a hero unless his protective instincts spread far and wide."

The heavy slick of nausea coats my stomach as I cast my eyes to a horrified Oliver. And beside him, Eliza and the tears in her eyes.

"While the hero was away, having left our heroine safely asleep in his bed—or at least, safety was reasonably assumed—she awoke to the hero's father... well..."

Helen hesitates, as though her marketing schtick makes her almost as sick as it makes me to hear. "He did things to her that the heroine spends the rest of the book running from. This is how she ended up with a son: flowers growing after a rainstorm, so to speak."

"Oh my goodness," Tanya presses a hand to her lips. "And this story is based on real events? I-it's a true story?"

"Tommy?"

Rage is like a drug slicing through my veins and sharpening my vision. It's like waves in my ears, and still, I hear every scrape of a grasshopper's legs outside. It's slowing time but speeding my actions. It's like an elastic band, *pulling, pulling, pulling* at my sanity as I bring my eyes back to Alana's and the tears that trickle onto her cheeks.

And then it snaps.

"Stay here."

"Tommy! No!" She grabs my arm, only to cry out when I shake her free and stalk across to the door. "Tommy!"

I stop in front of Ollie. "You keep her here. No matter fucking what, you don't let her leave."

"Tommy!" She sprints across the living room, slamming through the door after me and grabbing my belt just like she did at the cemetery. But there is no walking away anymore. There will be no discussion.

There's just me and my father. And soon, there will be one less Watkins in the world.

"Tommy!"

I exit the kitchen and stomp onto the front porch, but when I'm met with curious stares and startled surprise from the kids on the lawn, I work on fixing my expression so I don't scare the shit out of them.

"Don't go," Alana sobs, pulling me around and cupping my face in her palms. "Please. *This* is why I didn't tell you. This is what I was afraid of happening."

"He. Raped. You." Voice low, heart pounding, I wrap my hands around her wrists and feel her pulse under my fingertips. "He's the reason for all of this? He's why I've wondered—*shamefully*—for weeks—but never had the guts to ask if you slept with my brother?"

Fat, fresh tears dribble onto her cheeks.

"They're practically the same person, Lana. Their quirks. Their personalities. The way they eat and think and act. I'm so sorry." I groan, my breath pushing her hair back. "I thought the most horrible things about you, but I was always too much of a coward to ask. I was terrified of the answers, and still, I wanted to be with you so fucking badly I vowed I'd never press. Better to live in oblivion than face the reality that you might have loved him more than you loved me."

"Tommy—"

"I was so focused on me and my pain when, all along, it should have been about you. I should have been supporting *you*. Protecting *you*." Tears burn my eyes, stinging until the ache travels to my throat. "I blamed you for ruining my life, when all you've *ever* done is comfort me when I hurt. You shielded me from the very fucking monster that violated you."

"Tommy, please—"

"I blamed you for ruining my life! How dare I, Alana? How could I?"

"You didn't know," she whimpers. "I didn't tell you. I didn't *want* to tell you."

"You left to protect me. To heal and to raise your son away from the town that only ever caused you pain. You stood right in front of me, Lana, toe-to-toe, staring into my eyes while I was absolutely fucking cruel, and no matter how horrible I was, you wished only for my healing and happiness.

You sacrificed yourself to save me." I swallow the aching lump in my throat. "I failed you."

"No, I—"

"I won't kill him." I draw her to her toes and press my lips against hers. It's something I've been doing all my life, gleefully, without remorse, and so often, without consent. But I do it gentler now. Slower.

Because Watkins blood courses through my veins, and the risk that she may put me and him in the same basket is enough to make me sick to my stomach.

"I won't. Because that's the outcome you sacrificed yourself for." Carefully, I lower her back to flat feet and peel my fingers from her fiery skin. I look her up and down to make sure she's steady, then I take a concentrated step back, forcing my lips into a smile and trying, so fucking hard, to bring her comfort in a shitty world. "I won't go to prison, Lana. Not for him. I won't make your sacrifice for nothing."

Chris stalks through the door at her back, stomping onto the porch in silence. His eyes burn with a rage I feel in my blood. His jaw clenches with the same tight grip I feel in mine.

He doesn't stop to talk. He doesn't even slow to look into Alana's drenched eyes.

He merely nods and keeps going, down the porch steps and onto the grass. Toward my truck because he's riding with me today.

"Tommy, please..." Alana cries.

I cup her cheek and press my thumb to her deep dimple. "I'm coming home to you, and then we're gonna discuss the marriage thing you were talking about."

"Don't go," she whimpers. "Please."

"I know the *I'll be with you forever* thing was said in panic. But maybe we could try it out when I get back."

"Tommy..."

"Lie to me, Lana." I lean in and feather a kiss to her cheek. "Say the words."

"I *don't* love you." Her eyes glisten with fat, unshed tears. "That's my lie. I *don't* want to spend the rest of my life with you, and I'm *not* carrying your baby right now."

My heart gives a heavy knock, bruising my chest and stealing my breath as my eyes drop to her hand gently laid over her flat belly.

"That's what I wanted to talk to you about this afternoon," she chokes out. "Now, I'm terrified that if you go, I'll only ever get to see you through three-inch plexiglass. Is that what you want for us?"

"M-my baby?" My pulse skitters faster and faster, dizzying enough to make me reconsider everything. "You're pregnant?"

"I wasn't sure." She swipes falling tears. "I've been sick and stressed and tired. I thought it was just..." She shakes her head. "The funeral and the store and all that other stuff."

"Lana—"

"I tested this morning."

"My baby?"

"Tommy!" Chris slams his palm to the roof of my truck. "Let's go!"

Alana's eyes widen with fear. "Please stay."

"I have control over myself." I pull her to her toes and kiss her plump lips. "I learned that from the strongest person I've ever known." Finally, I release her and take a single step back. "I promise, I'm not going to prison for this. Wait here for me." I turn on my heels and head toward my truck, dragging the keys from my pocket as Chris slides in on his side. But when a pair of hazel eyes, just like mine and my brother's, follow me across the lawn, I make a quiet detour and stop in front of a watchful Franky.

Not just her son. Not Chris', either.

My father's son.

Jesus fucking Christ, he's one of us.

"Go to your mom, okay?" I set my hand on his shoulder and exhale a shuddering, aching breath. "She needs a hug right now. A really big, really squishy, Franky hug, alright?"

He nods in the silence, glancing his mother's way. So I look at Caroline next. "You left Darlene's closed and came here instead?"

"What's going on?" Her eyes flicker from me. To Alana. To Franky. To the house. To my truck. "What happened?"

"Answer the question. Is Darlene's closed?"

"Yes, it's—"

"Excellent." I spin and yank the truck door open, sliding in and slamming it shut again as I stab the key into the ignition. "I'm sorry for thinking shitty things about you." I start the engine and drive forward, circling the chicken coop rather than reversing and risking a kid—Alana's or Caroline's —unintentionally being hurt. Then I peek at my brother, shame washing through my veins as we bounce and roll from grass to dirt. "I didn't say a damn thing out loud, because I *knew* you and Lana were too fucking loyal and decent to stoop so low. The mental hoops I've been jumping through this week have been insane."

Unhinged laughter sprints along my throat as I pull out of Bitsy's driveway and onto the road. "I lost my grip on reality at least half the time. Because the similarities between you and Franky were too much. He talks like you. He walks like you. Eats like you. Argues like you. Trying to understand it hurt my heart so much, I wasn't sure I'd survive with my sanity intact. But having her back was more important than protecting my feelings, so I was gonna put on my fuckin' blinders and convince myself there was a valid reason for all this."

"I didn't sleep with your girlfriend." He presses his hand to the dash, holding on as I speed around a tight corner and the wheels screech against the tar. "I would never. And she would never."

"I know." I swallow. "She was raped."

"So, what's the game plan?" He opens the glove compartment and takes out a fishing knife I've kept in there since forever.

I should make him put it back. Fuck knows I should push him out of the truck and do this myself. But rage is my only companion now, and revenge is best served ten fucking years after the fact.

"Tommy?"

"I'm gonna show him how it feels to be violated." Minutes after leaving the house, I skid into the cheapest hotel Plainview offers, with the *vacancy* sign hanging limp and the building's façade faded from decades of brutal summers. Cutting the engine, I look across to my brother. "He took something from her, so I'm gonna take something from him. She protected me, when all along, she was the one who needed protection. She wished for healing for me, when all I did—"

"If you accept this as your fault, then I take it on as mine, too."

"Chris—"

"She wasn't my girlfriend, but she was the best person I knew, second only to you. So either we go in there, knowing exactly where to lay the blame, or we sit out here and wallow because *we* failed her. Personally," he shakes his head, "I'm not interested in watching you hate yourself for the next seventy years, ruining the life you *could* have with her."

"She's pregnant."

He startles, his eyes flipping to mine. Questions flash through his mind, and then gentle, easy acceptance. Finally, his lips curl into a smug grin, and his fist comes up in offer. "Congratulations. So now we celebrate by putting this where it belongs."

"Fine." I slam my fist to his and smile when rage turns to giddy anticipation. "For Alana."

"Fuckin' A." He shoves his door open and circles to the bed of my truck, snatching out a tire iron and looking it up and down before tossing it my way. "He liked to hit us with those, remember?"

A curtain shifts in my peripherals—*Room Five*—followed by the click of a lock echoing throughout the dirty, dusty parking lot, empty but for our truck and one rundown station wagon worth more for its scrap metal than it is as a drivable vehicle.

Lucky for us, Grady Watkins will *always* choose a cheap hotel, not because he's dead broke—though he's that, too—but because he won't risk CCTV footage capturing the deals he makes with cash and little baggies of white powder he slips into his pockets.

"We aren't going to prison for this. I promised Alana."

"Can't." Chris beams, menacing and feral. "You still have to fight in Vegas. I put a lot of work into your schedule for that, and I'm gonna be pissed if you mess it up."

Snorting, I stalk along the uneven ground, my hand flexing around the heavy steel, and my brain focused on just one thing.

Just one, satisfying outcome.

Stopping in front of room number five, I don't bother knocking. It's not like they'll let us in anyway. Instead, I lift my leg, chamber my shot, and slam my foot down over the crappy lock until the metal handle pings free of its frame. Splintered wood scratches my skin, but the pain only spurs me on. The excitement I have for revenge is fuel in my veins. I stride through the door and grin, bigger than I have in way too fucking long, at Grady's stunned shock.

Fear.

Pants-pissing horror that turns to a squeal as I grab him by the throat and throw him to the ground, driving my fist into his face. Once. Twice. Three times. Maybe more. And because Chris is such a good guy, he closes the door behind us and stands guard over the bitch whose lips snap closed.

You sleep with dogs, you're gonna catch fleas.

"We're gonna discuss consent, Grady." I shatter his cheekbone and grab his jaw, yanking it back until the whole fucking thing dislocates and tendons snap. Then I pick up the tire iron and hold it lengthways across his throat, pressing down and cutting off his air. "You overplayed your hand, motherfucker. You could've stayed away. You could've hidden." I crush his larynx and thrill in the blood filling his eyeballs. "I would've come looking either way. Once that chick put Alana's book on national television, it was already all over for you. But coming to Bitsy's funeral like we were all friends?"

I pull back, then push down harder until something cracks in his neck. *Oops. Bet that was important.* "You made the hunt all too easy. Now we're bigger than you, and you're gonna pay for what you did to us. What you did to my brother. But most importantly, what you did to Alana."

I loosen my grip on his throat and allow him a moment to breathe. To suck air into his lungs and try to get up and scramble away. But when his body fails to move at all, I thrill at the terror in his eyes.

"Sucks losing control, don't it?" I swing my arm back and hold the tire iron like a baseball bat. "Sleep now, bitch."

FINAL ROUND

ALANA

Las Vegas

"It's so noisy, Mom!" Franklin crushes the cups of his noise-canceling headphones to his ears, wrinkling his nose in displeasure when the crowd roars and the referee thrusts Tommy's hand in the air.

His chest is sweaty, pounding with adrenaline and scrambling for air, while behind him, a semi-conscious Henrik Docik lies flat on the canvas, medics crouching over his prone form to make sure he's okay.

Docik came to Vegas tonight hoping to take the title belt. In the end, all he took was a beating.

The moment officials let them, Eliza and Ollie shove through the cage door and wrap themselves around Tommy. And right behind them, far calmer, Chris follows.

"He's wearing earplugs, Mom!" Franky tugs on my sleeve, pointing toward his favorite Watkins and beaming because his aversion to noise is, once again, normalized.

When Chris is around, Franky no longer feels *weird*. "He said he would!"

"He always says what he means, honey." I drag him closer, hugging him to my hip and riding a swell of emotion when he drapes his arm across my back. My baby is happy. My world hurts far, far less these days. And when Tommy's eyes scan the crowd, his dark, dangerous stare skims over the top of those who jump and scream for his attention.

Finally, he stops on me and exhales, his glare turning to pleased amusement.

"Well, that was…" Colin releases a cautious breath, tilting closer and tapping his shoulder against mine. "Brutal. Are you seriously telling me *this* is the guy you left behind? You let us get married and didn't even warn me my life was in danger for ten long years?"

"Oh, stop it!" Laughing, I lean forward and find Tasha on his other side. "He's being a baby! Tommy made sure he'd have front-row seats to this, and the best he's got are complaints?"

"I think he gave us front-row seats so I'd know what was coming for me!" Colin drapes his arm over Tasha's shoulders, dragging her closer and kissing her temple. "This wasn't a gift, Alana. It was a warning."

"You're being dramatic." I focus on the cage and watch Chris wrap the shiny new belt around Tommy's hips. He claps his brother on the shoulder and yanks him in for a hug, pride swelling between them both.

But when they part and Tommy crosses the canvas, poking just one finger through the cage and beckoning me closer, my heart spins out of control.

Adrenaline and anticipation mingle. Love and pride, too. The fear of being splashed all over live television—*again*—a remembered trauma I hardly wish to relive. But to stay away when he's calling me closer is… impossible.

Helen's stunt in the summer ended with her not only losing me as a client, but her agency letting her go, too. And because her actions were so publicly visible, last I heard, she's yet to find a job at *any* agency since.

That's what happens when you can't take no for an answer.

My *new* agent has, so far, respected my wishes and remained entirely professional, eagerly awaiting my new book to arrive in her email—*I'm nearly done.*

"Alana!" Tommy's shout travels above the din, his playful eyes a dancing torment. He knows I don't want attention, but *I* know he will forever be *the* most protective person in my world.

"I'm gonna go to the front for a second, okay, honey?" Nervous fear runs rampant through my veins, sprinting through my stomach until our daughter kicks against my ribs in retaliation. I look down and wait for

Franky's eyes. "I want to tell Tommy congratulations. Do you want to stay here with Colin and Tasha? You'll still be able to see me."

He shakes his head, grabbing my hand and holding on tight. Then, he surprises me with a beaming smile. "I want to come, too."

"Really? It'll be louder over there. And everyone will see you."

"Chris is over there." He turns and takes the lead, gently pulling me along the row of seats, glancing back to make sure he's careful with me. To make sure he isn't the reason I stumble or fall. "He said I could come to the cage, too, if I wanna. And that I can look at the guy on the ground."

"He said that?" I laugh. "He predicted there would be a guy on the ground?"

"He *promised* it." He has to shout over the cheers of ravenous fight fans, and brims with approval when a guard even larger than Tommy himself meets us at the end of the row and envelopes us in a cocoon of safety.

He keeps the hordes away, protecting us from those who want to come closer. Shielding us because we know Tommy, and fans will do anything to be near him. He moves people out of the way, like Moses parting the sea, and leads us where we need to go.

"Are you tired, Mom?" Franky twines his fingers with mine, matching my pace instead of rushing toward the cage. "Are you alright?"

"You don't need to worry about me, you know?" I drag him in and run my fingers through the hair at the back of his head. "It is *not* your job to take care of me."

"I know." He pushes his glasses up his nose. "Did you know there are about eighty-two million moms in our country? Two billion worldwide. And it's so weird, because you're the best one."

Godddddd. My heart thrums, and tears prickle the backs of my eyes. I stop in place and turn to face my baby, setting my hands on his shoulders and sliding my thumbs over his cheeks. "How long have you saved that one up to drop on me?"

"Since last night. Did you know an average mom has changed about seven-thousand diapers before her baby is two years old?"

"I mean..." I snicker. "I didn't know the data. But it sure felt like seven thousand by the time I was done. How are *you* feeling about all this?" I set one hand on my rounding stomach. "Are you okay with it?"

He grins, nodding eagerly. "I wonder if she'll be like me or like you?" He looks past me, which means I *don't* jump when Tommy sets his sweaty arm on my shoulder and a gentle kiss on my temple. "If she's like me, I'll finally have someone decent to play chess with. But if she's like you," teasing, he looks to Tommy instead, "I'll teach her how to count one plus one and hope she can keep up."

"Oh, you think you're clever, huh?" He reaches out and musses Franky's hair. "I win either way, buddy. If she's like your mom, I'm gonna be obsessed. And if she's like you and Chris, then—"

"You'll teach her how to fight and annoy her when you ruin a perfectly good game of chess?"

"If she's like you, then I'll consider myself the luckiest guy on the planet."

Franky's eyes glisten with happiness. With emotion. And below that, approval, which I know is what Tommy wants most of all.

He turns into me and rests his forehead against my temple. "I love you, Lana. Did you see me win?"

He's just a boy in a man's body. A child of trauma wrapped in a whole lot of muscle and hidden behind a handsome face.

"Next time I'm here, we'll bring our baby girl, too."

"Next time we're here, I'll have a new last name, seven thousand diapers to change, and if I'm lucky, I'll stop thinking this is all a dream, and I'm bound to wake up in New York soon."

"Not a dream." He closes his eyes, circling me in his arms and holding me close despite the hungry crowd attempting to intrude on our moment. "I only ever had nightmares until you came back. The kind that made a man never want to go to sleep."

Franky pokes a finger into his mouth, gagging as cameras flash and the media eat up his theatrics.

"The good stuff only started when you walked back into my life." He lays a kiss right over top of my dimple. "You ready to go home?"

Continue the Love & War series with Chris' deliciously sizzling, enemies-to-lovers sparring match with none other than best-friend Fox Tatum in Crazy In Love

What happens when the world champ is desperate to spend time with a

woman who is unavailable, complicated, and far too shy for her own good? He trains her how to fight, and enjoys every sweaty second they have inside his gym. Go back to the beginning of Emilia's world and read the story where it all began.
Get your copy of Finding Home and dive in.

*Looking for a **free** fake-dating laugh-out-loud romcom where our heroine is forced to attend her cheating ex's wedding—not only attend, but be in the freakin' wedding party!—so she hires a date for the week?*
Grab your copy of If The Suit Fits today.

ALSO BY EMILIA FINN

Reshuffle

Game of Hearts

Full House

No Limits

Bluff

Seven Card Stud

Crazy Eights

Eleusis

Dynamite

Busted

Gilded Knights (Rosa Brothers)

Redeeming The Rose

Chasing Fire

Animal Instincts

Pure Chemistry

Battle Scars

Safe Haven

Inamorata

The Fiera Princess

The Fiera Ruins

The Fiera Reign

Mayet Justice

Sinful Justice

Sinful Deed

Sinful Truth

Sinful Desire

Sinful Deceit

Sinful Chaos

Sinful Promise

Sinful Surrender

Sinful Fantasy

Sinful Memory

Sinful Obsession

Sinful Summer

Sinful Sorrow

Sinful Corruption

Turkey Trouble

Sinful Deception

Sinful Reality

Hell In A Hand Basket

Lost Boys

MISTAKE

REGRET

Crash & Burn

JUMP

JINXED

Underbelly Enchanted

The Tallest Tower

Diamond In The Rough

Lost Kingdom

Luc and Kari

Tulips and Lost Time

Nick and Mel

If The Suit Fits

Love & War

Tell Me You Love Me

Crazy In Love

Rollin On Novellas

(Do not read before the Rollin On Series)

Begin Again – A Short Story

ACKNOWLEDGMENTS

Eeeek!! It's another fighter series. Another obsessed hero.
Another slice of my heart!

Thank you so much for following me on this crazy ride and reading my —*hold up while I count*—73rd book! Maybe you've read all 73! Maybe Alana and Tommy were your first foray into my world.

No matter how you got here, I sincerely hope you enjoyed the ride.

More than that, I hope you enjoyed it enough to stick around and join us for CRAZY IN LOVE, which is Chris and Fox's explosive enemies-to-lovers spice fest where opposites attract and love is, often, hard!

As always, I want to thank my team for consistently having my back. For caring about me, as a person, before the books, even though the books are what brought us together.

My editor, Britt... from strangers to sisters. Thank you for all you do for me. I smile every time I think of you.

My proofreader, Lindsi, for helping make my books perfect.

My cover designer, Amy, for covering my babies and making them so, so beautiful. And in this case, holy shit, girl! These boys are delicious!

Thank you, my model photographer, Katie Cadwallader, for photographing Jordyn so exquisitely. He's perfect!

To my kids for always keeping me grounded and humble. Thank you for existing. Because without you, I wouldn't, either. Thank you for always being my biggest, bravest, loudest cheerleaders. And thank you for so graciously sharing me, so I can have both families: fictional and real.

Thank you to my readers for supporting my work, reading my stories, and allowing me to write for a living. I'm living my dreams (even if those dreams stress me out and impact my sleep, haha!).

Thank you for being here.

I appreciate every single book picked up. Every single page read. Every single message sent, comment posted, and review written.

From the bottom of my heart.
    Thank you

Printed in Dunstable, United Kingdom

68434424R00180